SINGULARITY

SINGULARITY

BILL DeSMEDT

per Aspera

SEATTLE, WASHINGTON

"The Aleph," from COLLECTED FICTIONS by Jorge Luis Borges, translated by Andrew Hurley, © 1998 by Maria Kodama; translation © 1998 by Penguin Putnam Inc. Used by permission of Viking Penguin, a division of Penguin Group (USA) Inc.

"Coasting," from THE MOON AND OTHER FAILURES by F.D. Reeve, © 1999 by F.D. Reeve. Used by permission of Michigan State University Press.

Designed by Karawynn Long
Edited by Jak Koke
Printed in the U.S.A. by Phoenix Color Corporation

Published by Per Aspera Press, a division of Viridian City Media, Seattle. Visit us online at www.perasperapress.com.

Library of Congress Cataloging-in-Publication Data
DeSmedt, Bill.
   SINGULARITY / Bill DeSmedt. — 1st ed.
      p. cm.
   ISBN 0-9745734-4-2 (hardcover)
      1. Tunguska meteorite–Fiction. 2. Siberia (Russia)–Fiction. 3. Meteorites–Fiction. I. Title.
PS3604.E759S56 2004
813'.6–DC22

                                                      2004018210

FIRST EDITION: NOVEMBER 2004
10 9 8 7 6 5 4 3 2 1

For Ted DeSmedt
friend, father, ancient mariner

—'Tis not too late to seek a newer world

Introduction
The Tunguska Event

*Suddenly the sky split in two, and high and wide above the
forest the whole north of the sky was covered with fire.*
— S.B. SEMYONOV, EYEWITNESS

THE REMNANT HAD sailed the empty spaces between the stars since
time began. Had journeyed far, far in space and time from its birth
at the beginning of all things, far from its forging in the primal
fires of Creation.

There was no destination on this voyage, though there were occasional ports of call. Here and there throughout the void tiny orbs circled their parent primaries, huddled close against the cold and the dark.
Most such solar systems were bypassed without incident. Still, every
once in an eternity, some unlucky world would chance to swim out into
the remnant's path.

As one is doing now.

In this, the summer of 1908, there is no science or technology anywhere on earth that might avert the impending catastrophe. Heavier-
than-air flying machines have only just begun their conquest of the
skies, and space flight remains but a distant dream, the exclusive prov-
ince of visionaries like Jules Verne and Herbert George Wells. The con-
troversial theory that the entire physical world might be made up of

tiny particles called "atoms" is still waging an uphill battle for scientific acceptance, against the strenuous opposition of influential physicist-philosopher Ernst Mach. It will be another fifteen months before a young Albert Einstein will leave his safe berth at the Bern patent office and devote himself fulltime to generalizing the theory of relativity he first broached a mere three years earlier. For all the secrets that nature has yielded up in the two centuries since Newton, the scientists of Earth still stand helpless before the threat posed by the remnant.

But they can, just barely, detect its approach.

In the main physics lab at Germany's Kiel University of Applied Science, beginning at six in the evening on June 27th and continuing over the following two nights, Professor Ludwig Weber has been observing faint but regular disturbances in his magnetometer readings. After ruling out streetcar vibrations and Northern Lights, he concludes that a powerful magnetic point-source must be nearing the Earth from somewhere out in space. But when Weber points the observatory telescope at the likely region of night sky, he sees — nothing.

What could be close enough and charged enough to interfere with the magnetic field of the Earth itself, yet remain invisible to the most sensitive instruments early twentieth-century optical technology can muster? This is the question that confounds Weber throughout the evening of June 29th as he watches the magnetic disturbances grow in strength. He is still wrestling with the riddle when, at 1:14 on the morning of June 30, 1908, the frenetic jitter of his magnetometer needle comes to a sudden dead stop.

Six time zones to the east of Kiel, far out on the Central Siberian plateau, there yawns that vast, silent emptiness known as the Stony Tunguska basin — three hundred thousand square miles of watershed, peopled, even in this eighth year of the new century, by fewer than thirty thousand souls. Here, in this land of expatriate Russian frontiersmen and nomadic Evenki tribes, there are no telescopes, no magnetometers, precious little technology of any kind. Here in Tunguska, nothing but a dying shaman's vision has foretold the remnant's coming, and nothing more than the naked eye will be needed to witness its arrival.

Here in Tunguska, the morning of June 30th has dawned bright and clear, scarcely a wisp of cloud in the sky. By seven, the sun has been up for hours, banishing the chill of the brief subarctic summer night, promising another sweltering noontide. Herds of domesticated reindeer, lifeblood of the Evenki nomads, are already grazing on new shoots in the thickly-forested taiga. Dense veils of mosquitoes swarm the pestilential bogs of the Great Southern Swamp. The living world goes on unchanged, just as it has for centuries. Despite the shaman's warning.

Perhaps no one finds more comfort in the very ordinariness of this fine summer morning than a young Evenki herdsman by the name of Vasiliy Jenkoul. For today Jenkoul must tend to his father's southern herds. And that will mean riding down the long Silgami ridge, directly into the Tunguska heartlands.

Into the lands where—to believe the shaman's deathbed prophecy —on this morning, the great god Ogdy, Old Man of the Storms, will send forth his thunderwinged minions to visit death and destruction upon the clans of the Stony Tunguska.

7:14 A.M. The forest falls silent. Even the ceaseless susurration of the Great Swamp's insect life fades. Far off in the southeastern skies, clearly visible in broad daylight, a bright blue star appears.

The remnant is close now. Four hundred miles out and a hundred miles up, just beginning to brush the lower edges of the ionosphere. The resulting shockwave fluoresces in the ultraviolet. Thickening atmosphere absorbs the radiation and re-emits it at longer wavelengths. Trailing a plasma column of cerulean blue, it descends.

Scattered outposts throughout the sparsely-inhabited Tunguska region awaken to a cannonade of sonic booms echoing down from the cloudless sky. Villagers pour into the streets to watch in amazement as a blindingly bright blue "pipe" bisects the heavens. Old women burst into tears, crying that the end of the world has come.

Fifty-seven miles southwest of ground zero, on the outskirts of a ramshackle of sod-roofed wooden huts that styles itself the Vanavara Trading Station, Semyon Borisovich Semyonov is sitting on his porch, trying to tamp a new hoop onto a cask of flour using nothing more serviceable than an axe. Nothing to be done for it; out here on the taiga one learns to make do with what is to hand. "If you have no plow, you must furrow with a stick," as the Siberians say.

He fumbles the hoop into position. There. He is just raising the axe for a final blow, when the sky brightens directly overhead.

Semyon arrests the axe in mid-swing and looks up. The sky—the sky splits in two! A broad streak of impossibly brilliant blue cleaves it from south to north. Semyon clambers to his feet. As he watches, the blue line touches the horizon.

The closest human being to the event this summer morning is not Semyon, but a young Evenki herdsman. Yet, with his view of the heavens obscured by dense forest canopy, Jenkoul is the last to see it coming. Nor, even in this eerie silence, will he hear the rumble of its approach, for the remnant's speed far exceeds that of sound. No warning will have a chance to reach his senses, before—

Impact!

A patch of sky framed by the empty arms of a blighted birch suddenly flares blue-white. Jenkoul reins to a halt, begins to dismount, and is nearly thrown from the saddle as the first in a series of thunderous concussions hits him.

Ogdy! The Old Man of the Thunder has unleashed his terrible winged minions against the clans. Peal after peal deafens Jenkoul, as all around him ancient stands of larch and pine crash to the ground, uprooted and smashed flat by the hurricane-force blast wave. Beyond toppling trees, a mountains-high tongue of flame reaches up.

Ogdy is kindling his lodge-fire in the heartlands of the Stony Tunguska.

Only the lore of the Evenki saves Jenkoul now. It is said a hunter caught in the open by a blizzard can survive by hunkering down alongside his mount, using its body as a shield against gale-force winds. Perhaps this will work for fire as well as ice. Jenkoul yanks his steed to the ground and cramps into the lee of its torso. The thunder is one continuous roar. Jenkoul exhales and holds his breath, lest his lungs be seared by the superheated air now washing over him.

Fifty-seven miles away, at Vanavara Station, Semyon's axe clatters to the floor. His eyes squeeze shut against a flash too bright to look at. The northern half of the sky erupts in flame. The sky has split open, and, in opening, has disclosed not the heavens, but the fires of hell.

Semyon opens his mouth to call out. A monster wind stirs the trees. Suddenly he is running off the porch, tearing at his clothes. His shirt is smoking, so hot it burns his skin. As Semyon clears the stoop, the blast wave hits. It picks him up and flings him like a rag doll all the way across the yard. Fissures open in the ground around him. Flat on his back now, it is all he can do to throw an arm across his face and block out the sight of the hideous sky.

Directly above ground zero a pillar of fire punches a path twelve miles up into the stratosphere, creating a partial vacuum at the blast site that sucks thousands of tons of earth and ash skyward. A churning black pyroclastic column ascends fifty miles into the sky, pumping tons of particulate matter into the upper atmosphere, to an altitude where the mesospheric air currents can sweep it up and circulate it around the world.

Sunlight scattering off the high-altitude debris will paint the night skies with noctilucent clouds. In London on the night of June 30th the air-glow illuminates the northern quadrant of the heavens so brightly that the *Times* can be read at midnight. In Antwerp the glare of what looks like a huge bonfire rises twenty degrees above the northern horizon, and the sweep second hands of stopwatches are clearly visible at one a.m. In Stockholm, photographers find they can take pictures out of doors without need of cumbersome flash apparatus at any time of night from June 30th to July 3rd. These strange "white nights" will continue, gradually fading in intensity, throughout the month of July 1908. Scientists across Western Europe, unaware of events thirty-five hundred miles to the east, are at a loss to explain the phenomenon.

But here in Tunguska, where the cause is clear, the sky is far from bright. Darkness descends at mid-morning, as the heaviest clumps of dirt and ash precipitate out in a black rain.

The force of the blast continues to propagate outward, though it must traverse hundreds of miles of taiga before coming into contact with the first outposts of twentieth-century science. At the Irkutsk Magnetic and Meteorological Observatory, the free-swinging weights of hermetically-sealed Repsold balances chart the onset of a massive earthquake five hundred and fifty miles to the north. Instrumentation as far west as the eastern seaboard of North America will soon follow suit.

But it doesn't take a seismograph to detect these seismic effects: close in, the isolated encampments of the Stony Tunguska clans are smashed flat, their birchbark *choums* sent flying as the subterranean pulses slam into them. Further out, houses sway and windowpanes craze throughout a circle two hundred fifty miles in radius, centered on ground zero. On the newly-completed Trans-Siberian railway line three hundred seventy five miles southwest of The Epicenter, a locomotive screeches to a halt lest it be thrown from the tracks by the tremors; the terrified engineer tells the conductor to get out and check for signs of a boiler explosion.

Magnetometers at Irkutsk Observatory, five hundred fifty miles due south of ground zero, record the raging of an unprecedented geomagnetic "storm," beginning at 7:23 A.M. local time and lasting nearly five hours. Echoes of the storm are picked up at the observatory at Pavlovsk, on the outskirts of St. Petersburg two thousand five hundred miles away. Even as far west as London, the *Times* will report "a slight, but plainly marked, disturbance of the magnets on Tuesday night." The next time the world will witness disruptions of the Earth's magnetic field on such a scale will be in 1958, following the detonation of an H-bomb at Bikini Atoll.

Moving at the speed of sound, a massive airborne shockwave thrums the coda to the event. Thirty minutes after and two hundred miles downrange of the impact, the barometers at a backwoods meteorological station in Kirensk record its passage. It will reach Irkutsk Observatory a quarter of an hour later. Attenuating with every mile, the concussion still retains enough energy to be heard as distant thunder a thousand miles away.

And even after dropping below the threshold of audibility, the pressure wave travels on. When it finally dies out twenty-five hours later, it will have circled *twice* around the globe, and left traces of its passage on barographs in Potsdam, London, Washington D.C., and Djakarta.

Miraculously, the event has expended its fury on one of the most desolate regions on the face of the globe. Had the impact occurred five hours later, the Earth's rotation would have shifted the impact zone to the outskirts of populous St. Petersburg, and the death toll would have risen into the hundreds of thousands.

But, here in Tunguska, the only human casualties are from secondary effects: heart attacks and strokes suffered by a few of the Evenki tribesmen closest in. No one has died as a direct result of the catastrophe's hellish violence.

Jenkoul uncrouches from behind the steaming carcass that had been his mount. The young Evenki braces himself and—slowly, so as not to inflict further torment on his parboiled flesh—rises to his feet. In so doing, he attains what is now the highest vantage on the ruined Silgami ridge. The old-growth forest that had soared above his head has been leveled to the ground. He can see the whole of the sky.

And, in that sky, a towering black column shot all through with lightning—the lodge-pole of Ogdy—rises up and up forever.

In years to come, a multitude of explanations would be advanced for what became known as the "Tunguska Event."

Most scientists initially assumed a giant meteorite had crashed that summer morning in the forests northwest of Vanavara Station. That hypothesis stood unchallenged for the nearly two decades that separated the event itself from the first on-site investigation of it—two decades during which scientific inquiry languished in Russia, preempted by war, revolution, and socio-economic upheaval. The few expeditions that did set forth in the intervening years were forced to turn back when their Evenki guides refused to enter the blast zone, fearing to trespass on the abode of the storm-god Ogdy.

Finally, in 1927, a team of researchers headed by mineralogist Leonid Kulik reached the site of the impact, where surrounding hills cupped the sloughs of the Great Swamp to form a landscape Kulik dubbed "The Cauldron." The Epicenter itself was easy enough to identify: for hundreds of square miles all around the Cauldron, across an area half the size of the state of Rhode Island, the ancient forests of the taiga had been scorched and flattened by the blast. Hundreds of thousands of trees had been toppled like matchsticks in all directions, forming a radial "throw-down" pattern in the shape of a gigantic target, with the impact site at the bulls-eye.

But, in reaching ground zero at last, Kulik had dealt a death blow to the meteorite hypothesis he himself espoused. For there was no crater.

With a yield of forty megatons—thousands of times more powerful than the atomic bomb dropped decades later on Hiroshima—the explosion should have gouged a hole in the Earth's crust to dwarf the mile-wide, 500-foot-deep Great Barringer Crater in Arizona. Instead, what Kulik found at the very center of the blast pattern was a peat marsh contorted into a nightmare landscape. "The solid ground," he wrote, "heaved outward from the spot in giant waves, like waves in water," as if stressed by some unimaginable force.

With on-site observations all but ruling out the meteorite-impact hypothesis, the Tunguska Event became fair game for ever more bizarre conjectures: the collision of the Earth with fragments of a comet? a solar plasmoid ejected by the sun? the crash of a nuclear-powered alien spacecraft? a chunk of infalling antimatter?

Not to mention, of course, the Evenki nomads' steadfast conviction that Ogdy had vented his wrath on the clans of the Stony Tunguska.

But perhaps most outlandish of all was the explanation concocted some six and a half decades after the event, by two young astrophysicists at the University of Texas in Austin. Writing in the September 14, 1973 issue of *Nature*, Albert A. Jackson IV and Michael P. Ryan Jr. had the audacity to theorize that what had struck the Earth in June 1908 was a remnant of the Big Bang. That the bizarre circumstances of the impact all pointed to a cause that could only have been engendered in the unimaginable heat and pressure attending the birth of the universe itself.

That the Tunguska Event was nothing less than a collision between the Earth and a submicroscopic black hole.

—BILL DESMEDT
JULY 2004

Part One
CROM

*My own suspicion is that the universe is not only stranger
than we suppose, but stranger than we can suppose.*
—J.B.S. HALDANE

1 | Proliferation Threat

MARIANNA BONAVENTURE EASED through the access door and out onto the roof of 17 State Street. She paused a moment for breath and visuals. To one side, the mirrored façade of a setback penthouse held only her own reflection — a slender figure in black body armor with helmet to match. Straight ahead, nothing but an arc of deserted skyterrace and, beyond it, the forty-one story dropoff down to Battery Park. No one, and nothing, in sight.

They'd gotten past her somehow.

Or not. Audio was picking up what sounded like the prole and the extractor, talking in low tones somewhere past the curve of the penthouse curtain wall.

Marianna smiled behind the helmet's silvered plexiglas visor: *Gotcha!* Then she frowned. This was going to be almost *too* easy. From the top of this gleaming column at the southernmost tip of Manhattan, there was simply no place left to go. Her quarry had already run out of island, and now they'd just run out of sky.

What kind of an extractor paints himself into a corner like that?

She'd find out soon enough. Marianna darted across twenty feet of rooftop garden and into the cover of the penthouse. She hugged the glass wall, began inching along its length.

One of the voices had started yelling. Still couldn't make out words. They'd be in Russian anyway.

Marianna risked a look, then ducked behind an art-deco heat-ex-changer hood, out of the wind and line of sight.

Because there, silhouetted against a wedge of Lower Manhattan skyline, stood her wayward prole — the proliferation threat she'd chased through downtown's dog-day streets.

Seen by the flat, filmy light of a late July afternoon, the prole looked deceptively nonthreatening. Looked like what she was: a fright-ened, middle-aged woman.

Looked hardly at all like a renegade WMD researcher out to sell her expertise in weapons of mass destruction to the highest terrorist bidder. Which was also what she was.

The extractor, the big guy hired to snatch the prole out from under CROM's bodywatch, stood beside her. He was the one doing all the shouting, most of it directed at an unwieldy contraption of fabric and aluminum tubing propped against the guardrail.

That explained some of it.

"Compliance?" Marianna whispered into her helmet mike. "Got the prole up here."

There was a barely perceptible pause, then the man from the New York Compliance office came back. "On the damn roof?"

"The extractor's got a hang glider, looks like."

"You're shitting me. How'd he get it up there?"

"Don't know. Maybe —" Marianna glanced around, spotted a dou-ble door further down the penthouse wall. "There's a rooftop elevator. He could have broken the thing down, bagged it, brought it up that way. It's just…"

"Just what?"

"Just I don't get where he thinks he's going with it. The park's staked out, and there's nothing but river beyond that." Even with a twenty-to-one glide ratio and the weak westerlies of a summer after-noon, that rig would never make Jersey. Unless —

Now she could hear it: the sputter of a ten-horsepower motor firing up. "It's not a glider, it's an ultralight! They're good to go."

"Let them. They can't hide from the spystars."

"Guess again." Marianna was looking at more bad news on her wristtop display. "Alpha set ninety seconds ago."

"Damn! How long till Beta's overhead?"

"Seven minutes." Too long. Whoever'd planned this extraction knew exactly where the holes were in CROM's piggybacked satellite surveillance.

"Okay, sit tight—I'm on my way."

But Compliance was down at street level. By the time he could get here, her quarry would be long gone. And, with them, her last hope of making the Grishin case stick.

It was going to be up to her.

Compliance was still talking. "Don't go trying anything stupid now, Bonaventure. Not when all you're packing is that damned toy. I'll be—"

She cut the connection then. But he was right: she'd been going by the book, and for urban engagements the book mandated non-lethal armament only.

Hence, her Squirt gun—a second-generation handheld version of the antipersonnel web-cannons in use since the mid-'90s. When it worked, which wasn't always, it shot out fifty square feet of ruggedized microfilament coated with fast-drying binary adhesive. Ensnared in the stickyweb, a perp would be down for the count and gift-wrapped to boot. It had all sounded good on paper.

Out here in the field, she'd have given a month's per diem for a twin to Compliance's unauthorized Glock. Book or no book.

Oh hell, here goes. She stepped away from the wall and brought the flared muzzle of her "toy" to bear. "Hold it right there!"

The perpetrators froze. She edged toward them through rippling ninety-degree heat. Sweat trickled down along her ribcage under the stifling Vectran body armor. Her forehead was bathed in perspiration. A droplet felt poised to run into her eye, but she'd have to lift the visor to wipe at it.

Just a little further.

The prole raised her hands. Behind her, Marianna could see the extractor fiddling with some sort of handheld. He looked up. Marianna glimpsed a raw-boned, dark-complected face. Through wraparound goggles, cold black eyes stared back at her.

Unnerving, that lifeless gaze, like looking into the eyes of a predator. Marianna felt the gun tremble in her hands. As if scenting her fear, the man grinned at her—a feral grin, widening to reveal two steel-crowned upper canines.

It was like looking death in the face.

Marianna shrank back. Her stomach knotted. Adrenaline coursed through her veins, priming her whole body for flight.

No! She was *not* going to panic. She planted her feet, steadied the non-leth, and squeezed the trigger.

The Squirt gun emitted a hollow click.

No canister chambered.

The damn thing had malfed *again*. She slammed a small fist against the side of the barrel, pulled the trigger a second time. Nothing.

Still grinning, the man punched a button on his handheld. The elevator doors at her back slid open. Marianna whirled at the sudden hiss, but there was nothing there—not even an elevator. The penthouse express that her fugitives had commandeered was gone. She could hear it hurtling down to street level, leaving behind forty stories of empty air.

She turned back just in time to see the extractor raise a gun and fire.

A sledge hammer slammed into the pit of her stomach. Another, driving all the breath from her body. But—no worse, thank God! Her Vectran body armor, the same stuff they made the Mars rovers' hard-landing airbags out of, was living up to its advertising, absorbing the brunt of the bullets' impact. Too bad it couldn't dissipate their momentum as well. A series of body-blows pummeled her, propelling her backward, back toward the waiting maw of the empty elevator shaft.

For an instant that stretched to an eternity she teetered on the edge, fighting to regain her balance. Fighting and losing. Gravity seized her in its unrelenting grip.

Fetid air swirled around her as she fell, the square of light from the open door above her receding fast, faster.

Oh, God! Only one chance! Marianna gripped the Squirt gun in both hands and fired it at a passing stanchion. Please, *please*—work this time!

The gun kicked in her hands. Compressed gas exploded from the canister and propelled a spray of microfilament out through the expansion chamber at forty-five meters per second.

The stickyweb snagged the stanchion, the binaries fused, and—it held.

And—she held. Her hands tightened on the weapon's grip as deceleration shock tried to wrench her arms from their sockets. She slammed into the near wall hard enough to rattle her teeth. Still she held on, still alive. For the moment.

Numbers stenciled on the opposite wall told her she'd halted her descent at the thirty-seventh floor. The Squirt gun and holster ensemble were interlocked with her body armor, helping bear some of her weight. Still, both hands clutched the butt of the weapon in a death grip. Scarcely daring to breathe, Marianna dangled above the abyss, a pendulum on borrowed time.

Her helmet headset had been knocked askew, but not so far that its mike couldn't pick up her voice.

"Compliance... need help! Come... get me!"

She told him where, between gulps of machine-oil flavored air. "But... call Building Services first. Tell them... lock down... the penthouse elevator." She couldn't see the elevator car where it had come to rest more than five hundred feet below her. The extractor might have deactivated it to prevent reinforcements arriving, but no sense taking chances.

A hiss from above her. Four stories up, the elevator doors were closing again. Through them she could hear the engine's drone rise to an angry buzz. The ultralight was taking off for the wilds of New Jersey. Taking her prole with it.

Guess they hadn't run out of sky after all.

One more thing, then. "Compliance? See if you can raise HQ. ...Tell Pete, tell him got to... go with the Archon option."

✳

Like the two before it, the third email incident of the day found Archon consultant Jonathan Knox in a very strange place — his own office.

Strange, because Knox's clients usually demanded his full-time physical presence on *their* premises, consistent with their belief that they owned his ass. A not altogether unreasonable assumption, given the breathtakingly exorbitant rates Archon Consulting Group charged for the services of its most senior analyst. But it did mean that in an average year Knox saw the inside of his office about as often as the guys who came in to shampoo the wall-to-walls. And, like the carpet cleaners, he saw it mostly at night.

No one, least of all Knox himself, would have expected him to be sitting there midway through a midsummer Tuesday afternoon.

If he hadn't been, there's no way he could have found out that somebody was stealing his identity.

As it was, though —

"You've got mail," the desktop announced.

Knox's gray eyes, strangely old-looking for what was otherwise an almost boyish face, flicked from the five-hundred-page document in his lap to the little email icon now blinking in the upper righthand corner of the twenty-four-inch display.

Definitely weird. No one ever sent him email here at Archon, there wasn't any point to it. Knox had been on assignment at Broadband Utilities Unlimited longer than most of BUU's employees. Anyone who needed to reach him emailed him there.

Probably just a system glitch, like the first two.

Knox stretched his lanky six-foot-plus frame, tipped the contoured chrome-and-leather armchair back even more precariously, and returned his attention to the Functional Requirements spec.

That five-pound cinderblock of a document was his sole reason for being here. It would take total, Zen-like concentration to review it by the Friday drop-dead date, and BUU's North Jersey headquarters was hardly conducive to that. The place was even more of a madhouse than usual this week, caught up in a paradigm shift of tectonic proportions as the latest management methodology-du-jour kicked in.

No, better the relative peace and quiet of his commodious corner suite at Archon's New York headquarters, with its expanse of burgundy broadloom and its floor-to-ceiling view of the East River twenty stories below.

And its periodic announcements of email that wasn't there.

If Knox had been engaged in anything more absorbing, he'd have ignored the interruptions. But whoever said "reads like a novel" wasn't talking about this Functional Requirements specification. He looked up, cleared his throat, and said "Mack, open my mailbox, please."

A brief pause while Mack, Knox's desktop computer, processed this utterance. Then: "Your mailbox is empty."

Huh! And yet the incoming-mail icon was still blinking merrily away in the corner of the screen. For the third time since he'd arrived this morning, his system couldn't seem to decide if he had email or not. Knox ran his fingers through his already unruly brown hair, thought a moment, then said, "Mack, see if Bob is in."

In response, a videoconference window popped open on Knox's screen, complete with the dreadlocked talking head of Bob Stevens, Archon's system administrator.

"Hey, Jon," Stevens's grin was dazzling white in his dark face. "You coming to the bash?"

"Huh? No, I was just calling in a couple rogue emails. Why, what's up?"

"Boss man's taking the gang down to Radio Mexico for quesadillas and Dos Equis."

"That's our Richard." In the fifteen years Knox had known him, Archon CEO Richard Moses had never passed up an excuse to throw a party.

But, still and all, Tuesday afternoon? "Any particular reason?"

"We just won us a slice of the Psyche project. Word came in an hour ago, now it's raining beer and nachos. You coming?"

"Sounds fun. But duty calls. Got to get through this thing—" Knox thumped the Functional Requirements for emphasis, "—before I leave for London next month. Now, about my email…"

"First thing in the morning, okay?" Stevens was already glancing off screen, toward his office door.

Knox grinned. "Sure. Enjoy."

The window closed, leaving Knox alone with the BUU document.

He re-read the page he'd stopped on without any noticeable increase in comprehension. Something was nagging at him. He'd learned to trust that feeling.

What was the old saying? "Twice is coincidence, third time is..." Knox snapped his fingers. "Third time is enemy action!"

Despite, or perhaps because of, having perpetrated more than a few email spoofs in his time, Jonathan Knox found he did not enjoy being made the butt of one himself. But that's what it looked to be: someone—one of the backroom code jocks, most likely—had hijacked his account and was carrying on an electronic correspondence pretending to be Knox.

Those bozos! All's fair in love, war, and the pissing contest that had raged unchecked between Archon's programming and consulting staffs since day one, but this crossed the line. Knox grinned unkindly as he contemplated various retaliatory options. Perhaps a Trojan horse?

Just then, his speakerphone beeped.

"Jon," said the voice on the other end, "bag what you're doing and come on down, boy!" The slightly slurred baritone belonged to Richard Moses. Calling, no doubt from the Radio Mexico fête. Yes, in the background Knox could hear voices raised in off-key song, counting down "A Hundred Bottles of Beer on the Wall" in hexadecimal notation. Programmers!

Which reminded him. "I can't right now, Richard. I'm hung up on something here."

He said goodbye and hit the *off* button. Best not to be too specific. For all Knox knew, Richard himself could be behind this—he was no less an arrested adolescent than the rest of the Archonites.

Knox could see them now, swilling brew, carousing, having a good laugh at his expense, while he—

Wait a minute. The Archon offices must be all but deserted, emptied at quarter of five on a Tuesday afternoon by Richard's impromptu celebration. So, *who was running the scam?*

The few stragglers in sales and accounting didn't count: none of them had the skill-set for a world-class goof like this. Even if the thing itself could run unsupervised, the fact remained that the culprit hadn't hung around to see Knox's reaction to the prank.

And that was just plain unthinkable. Knox had never aspired to membership in the coder fraternity himself, but he was an astute observer of its folkways. And not showing up to gloat once a trap had been sprung was, he knew, an unpardonable breach of alpha-nerd etiquette.

Can't have been anybody here, then. What did that leave? It *must* be just a mail-server glitch.

But that old feeling—that sense of a larger pattern lurching around in the darkness behind the veil of immediate sense experience—wasn't going away. On a hunch, Knox reconfigured his desktop to pull mail the instant it received notification. Then he waited.

Not for long. On the next "you've got mail" announcement, he found himself staring at a system error: MAILBOX IS LOCKED BY AN-OTHER POP3 PROCESS.

He tried retrieving the message manually. Now the mailbox was unlocked again. And empty again.

Enemy action! Somebody had installed a daemon in the server, an autonomous process that was intercepting his email. If it was a prank, it was a damned elaborate one. But it was looking more and more like identity theft pure and simple—the misappropriation of Knox's cyber-space persona for purposes of illicit correspondence.

That correspondence, at least, was easy enough to trace.

"Mack, show me the IPM log for *jknox@thearchongroup.com.*"

Archon's central server came equipped with state-of-the-art Internet Policy Management software. Among other things, the IPM tracked all the emails moving into and out of the organization and could list them on demand. Not the message-bodies themselves, just subject-lines, senders, and addressees.

But that was enough. Considering Knox almost never used this account himself, the log should have come up empty. Instead it held eight or nine entries, the oldest of them—entitled "Long time no see"—dating from this Sunday. That message, and about half the others, had been forwarded through the *jknox* account to someone called *kosmo@gei.ru,* and had originated from...

Knox frowned as he read the sender's address: *reack2@crom.doe.gov.*

Doe-dot-gov? That was the federal government—the, um, Department of Energy. A quick websearch brought up the DOE home page, but there was no "CROM" listed among its agencies. An undercover op, maybe, and of some hitherto uncatalogued subspecies.

What had he gotten himself into here? Knox had pissed off a lot of people in his time, but that was just *una cosa di biznes.* And, anyway, he couldn't recall any feds among them.

Why were the spooks messing with his email?

Damned if he knew, but he did know the quickest way to find out.

"Mack," Knox addressed his computer again, "link in Weathertop, secure circuit. I need to talk to Mycroft."

Spooks or no spooks, *some*body's gonads were going to wind up stapled to his office wall tonight!

✳

What was keeping the Compliance guy?

Marianna hung in near-total darkness, trying not to gag on the oily reek filling the elevator shaft. Trying not to think about how long the stickyweb would hold. The adhesive wasn't designed to support a one-hundred-thirty-two pound load, was it? Not swinging back and forth?

Think about something else. Like what? Like how bad she'd wanted this first field assignment? And how bad she'd gone and screwed it up?

But it was *her* case, dammit. Her analysis that had tied the last two disappearances back to the shadowy Grishin Enterprises conglomerate, her late nights and weekends that had put CROM out ahead of the curve on this one.

She should have left it at that. She couldn't. Call it a chance to settle an old score, call it a misplaced search for some sort of redemption, but she'd had to get out from behind her desk and into the field. She'd cashed in favors and half-forgotten promises, lobbied Pete mercilessly, all so she could be in on the bust. And now—

Where in *hell* was Compliance?

Look on the bright side. At least the email spoof was still running —going on two days now without a hitch. One thing that hadn't gone wrong yet. And with any luck the mark wouldn't catch wise till too late. By Thursday night, she should—

Wait one. What was that?

If she strained, she could almost hear—yes, a rumble coming from below, faint at first, but growing with every second.

Oh, *shit!*

The power must've come back on before Compliance could find the cutoff. The penthouse elevator was beginning its ascent, building speed. It would be here in less than half a minute, moving fast as an express train—and she had no way to get out of its path!

2 | Resource Recovery

"**C**OMPLIANCE?"

Marianna hung in the lightless shaft straining her ears for an answer. None came. The onrushing elevator car was very close now. She could make out the low-watt service lights set into the frame of its roof. Only seconds left.

She couldn't die like this. *Do* something!

"Compliance?" What was the guy's name again? "Whitehead? Talk to me. I—I've got a situation here."

"Keep your pantyhose on, Bonaventure," a voice crackled over her headset, "We're coming to get you."

Daring another glance down, Marianna could see the elevator slowing, slowing, easing to a stop inches below her feet. A muffled clang and a hatch opened in its roof.

Light poured up out of the hatch, catching Compliance's angular features from below and twisting them into something vaguely Mephistophelean. He reached up for her.

"Thought it'd be quicker this way," he said, helping her down into the car. "No telling how long till the stickyweb broke. Then—*splat!*"

He wasn't bothering to hide his smirk. She wouldn't put it past him to have arranged that business with the elevator just now deliberately. A field agent's way of showing the desk jockey with the fancy job title her real place in the order of things.

Assistant Director, CROM Reacquisition. What a crock!

She was silent the whole ride down to ground level, afraid that if she spoke her voice might tremble. She couldn't bring herself to look at the man from Compliance, just kept her eyes straight ahead. From the burnished surfaces of the elevator doors a woman in black body armor peered back at her — tall, slim, dark-haired, young.

Above all, young. Too young, maybe, to hack it, out here in the field.

The doors slid open. She followed Compliance out into a double-height lobby newly festooned with Day-Glo *Police Line — Do Not Cross* tape. They walked through the exit doors and out into the late afternoon heat.

Marianna jerked a thumb back at the growing police presence. "Have you talked to NYPD?"

"We can't bring the cops in on an extraction. You know that."

"Dammit, I'm not talking about need-to-know! The cops run a river patrol, don't they? If not them, the Coast Guard. *Some*body's got to've seen which way they went."

Compliance paused beside the car. "Face it, Bonaventure — that prole is long gone."

She got in and waited till he'd joined her. "You're calling it a hand-off, then?"

"Yeah, might as well make it official. But —" His hand hovered over the STU-IV keypad. "You sure we don't want to get our story straight first?"

She shook her head. "We'll play spin control some other time. Just log the handoff so I can get started fixing this." If it was even fixable. If the black hats hadn't already won, like they had eleven years ago.

With a shrug, Compliance punched in the code and nodded to her to jack in. Handshake tones fluted in Marianna's headset as the Secure Terminal Unit negotiated a one-time encryption, then: "Critical Resources Oversight Mandate. How may I direct your call?"

"Uh, this is Whitehead, New York Compliance office. I need to make a field deposition."

A momentary pause, then: "Recording."

"Right. As of—" He glanced at the dashboard clock. "—5:23 P.M. Eastern Daylight Time, July 27th, Compliance Directorate is transferring anti-proliferation action 04-057, Galina Postrel'nikova, to Reacquisition. Hardcopy follows."

If it hadn't been her case before, it sure as shit was now.

"Line's still up," Compliance was saying. "Want to talk to your boss?"

"In a minute." Marianna tabbed down the passenger-side window and stuck her head out. Her dark brown eyes made a futile scan of the empty sky.

Where in hell could her prole be *going?*

✳

Natalya Petrovna Zolotova clutched frantically at the harness straps as the ultralight looped high out over waterfront towers and atriums toward the broad sweep of the river hundreds of meters below. She shrieked as the flimsy craft lurched sickeningly in the updraft from a rooftop airconditioning unit, stifled another scream when it dipped unexpectedly on entering the regime of cooler air over the water.

The rushing airstream bore her small cries away, rendered her terror inaudible even to herself.

Certainly the pilot gave no sign of having heard her. Natalya risked a glance over to where he hung suspended alongside her, so close she could have reached out and touched him. Not that she would have dared. If possible, she feared this grim-visaged man, this Yuri Vissarionovich Geladze, more than she feared falling into the river below.

And with good reason. He had killed that woman back there on the roof. Shot her as casually as one might shoot a stray dog.

Surely it had been a woman. The visor had concealed her face, but the body, stance, and voice were unmistakably female. The woman's shouted English had gone by too quickly to register, but her brandished weapon had made the meaning only too clear: Natalya was being arrested. But for what?

All she had done—all!—was to leave *Rusalka* that morning and, on her way through customs, show the counterfeit passport she had been given. The passport with the photograph of Natalya's own face above that other woman's name: Galina something.

Yes, it had been wrong. But it had been her only chance to disembark and explore the great city rising into the sky beyond the 39th Street pier.

And besides, what choice had she had? A lowly clerk-typist dared not disobey the orders of Vadim Vasiliyevich Merkulov, head of security for all of Grishin Enterprises International, and the third most powerful man on *Rusalka*.

Rusalka. Natalya squinted against the wind and turned her gaze upriver, up to where *Rusalka's* shimmering white form towered over the ferries and dayliners, a visiting queen holding court amid the plebian denizens of the waterfront.

Any moment now, the glider would swing north toward the great ocean-going yacht. And once Natalya was back onboard, things would be all right again. It could all be fixed. Forged passports, a broken corpse at the bottom of an elevator shaft—no matter: GEI, the all-powerful Grishin Enterprises International, could fix anything.

Pray God, let it be so! Natalya willed her right hand to release its deathgrip on the strap. Just long enough to make sure that Mama's locket was still securely nestled beneath her blouse. She clasped it to her heart for a moment, feeling its surprising weight again. Yes, thank God, it was still there—still safe.

A foolish indulgence. The simple silvery locket hanging in the window of the Eighth Avenue pawnshop had been priced at an unthinkable hundred and twenty-five dollars. And, bargain as she might in her halting English, the aged proprietor had refused to part with it for less than ninety.

"Pure silver," he had claimed. But it didn't have the feel of the silver tableware aboard *Rusalka*—too heavy. Could it be silver-plated lead? Fearful of being swindled in this strange city, Natalya had hesitated. But when the locket had opened to reveal, of all things, a little Orthodox cross engraved on the inside of the lid, she knew she was lost.

It would make a perfect gift for Mama—a gift to commemorate her youngest daughter's day in New York.

A day that was ending. Natalya would be home soon. She braved a look down to see if they'd begun their descent. She saw huge tankers and container vessels plying the river below, each attended by a retinue of tugs. Saw the wakes of small, swift powerboats tracing their obscure calligraphies across the placid surface. Watched the pastel green of the Statue of Liberty, luminous in clear afternoon light, pass below immediately on her right.

Surely that was wrong. They must have missed their northward turn, continued out over the river and angled south. The expensive apartment buildings crowding the far shore, almost directly ahead of them when the flight began, had slid off northwards. In their place, the shoreline ahead now held what seemed to be an old, unreconstructed industrial quarter.

They were already much lower. The little motor was laboring to clear the roofs of the abandoned wharves lining this stretch of riverbank. They could not be going very much farther, but where—?

They spiraled downward into a wasteland of rusted storage tanks, junk-strewn empty lots, the burnt-out hulks of factories and warehouses—a no man's land transected by truck-filled highways. Here and there, last-gasp urban renewal strove to stem the tide of post-industrial blight, manifesting in compact corridors of incongruously bright and cheery buildings cordoned off from the pervasive decay.

The ultralight was vectoring toward one of those islands of order amid the chaos.

Very close, almost directly below them now, she could see a wide, flat roof with a name painted on it in large white letters. In the Latin alphabet, of course, as everything here was, but Natalya could read it well enough: RESOURCE RECOVERY SYSTEMS, Inc.

And beneath that, somewhat smaller: BAYONNE NJ ENTERPRISE ZONE.

And beneath that? A logo of some sort. She couldn't make it out from this angle, but its shape and color looked right. Her heart lifted in hope.

The ultralight overshot the roof and looped back toward it, lower and slower now, heading into the wind.

She started at a sudden sound. Her companion—silent ever since they had taken off from the tower—was shouting something at her.

"Lower your legs and push back on the control bar," he bellowed over the howl of the wind. "No, like me. Watch, do as I do."

Natalya tried to copy his movements, letting her legs hang down as she straightened her arms against the control bar. The craft's nose rose into the air. Their airspeed dropped to a stall as they skimmed the rooftop, its tarred blackness very close now, mere centimeters from the soles of their shoes. Closer, closer. Contact!

She nearly stumbled as her feet skidded on the bumpy surface, but the pilot compensated, taking the brunt of the landing with knees flexed and feet spread wide. He stood there a moment, then held the wingframe aloft with one arm as he shrugged out of his harness, motioning her to do the same.

Natalya looked around for the logo she'd glimpsed from the air a moment ago.

The mottled, uneven texture of the tarred roof made for a poor canvas. Even so, the bold, stylized lines were instantly recognizable: the great blue globe crosshatched with white striations of latitude and longitude, the continents of Europe and Africa outlined in a verdant green. And embracing the whole, completely obscuring the equator, an image out of myth—the emerald coils of a world-encircling serpent, its fangs sinking into its own tail. The crimson letters GEI arced over the north pole like an aurora.

At that moment, the corporate icon looked so radiantly beautiful she could have knelt down and kissed it. She slipped a hand beneath her blouse to pat the little locket once more in thanks.

Natalya had made it back safe after all.

✳

"You rang, Jonathan?"

Knox looked over at his display and saw Finley "Mycroft" Laurence peering at him from a conferencing window. Half an hour. Most callers wouldn't have rated so quick a callback. Wouldn't have rated real-time at all, just a GIF of an old TV test-pattern and instructions where to send an email. Mycroft didn't waste bandwidth on nonessentials, a category that, for him, included most social interactions. Knox was one of the few he deigned to favor with his full telepresence.

And what a telepresence! Weathertop's image enhancer had gone all-out today, painting Mycroft in straw hat, candy-striped jacket, and white ducks, and then bluescreening him into a scene of punting on the Thames.

But the dark, solemn face made an odd contrast with the whimsical Jerome K. Jerome virtuality: in the eighteen months since Knox had last seen him (it doesn't pay to abuse some privileges), Mycroft had aged. The lines of the lean, regular features seemed incised a little deeper, the grizzled hair peeking out from under the boater had gone grayer, playing catch-up with his scraggly salt-and-pepper beard, and the piercing brown eyes behind the granny glasses were rimmed with circles darker than the mahogany of his cheeks.

They were working him too hard.

It was hard not to. Mycroft was too damned useful. Not to mention lucrative: if Knox's billing rate was exorbitant, Mycroft's was astronomical. You could buy a Bentley for what two weeks' worth of Finley Laurence's time would cost you. A well-accessorized Bentley.

Mycroft's official title—vestige of a time when Richard Moses had foolhardily let his top people make up their own job descriptions—was Senior Vice President for Intractables. Unofficially, he was Archon's one-man Research Department. Best in the business, if you could get his attention. Knox knew the magic words.

"Hi, Mycroft. I've got a puzzle for you."

Mycroft couldn't conceal the gleam in his eye, but all he said was "Timeframe?"

"ASAP. Yesterday, if possible."

"Time travel?" Mycroft shipped his computer-generated oars and cocked an eyebrow, "I believe you want Mr. Wells—Mr. *H. G.* Wells. Given my current workload, I'm not sure I could help you with future deliverables, much less past ones."

"This is just a quick hack-and-slash. You'll be done in less time than it would take you to convince me you haven't got time to do it."

Mycroft sighed. "Perhaps a quick look. Search parameters?"

"I haven't got much, just an email address. But I have faith in you." Not only was Mycroft a world-class net warrior, he came equipped with an eidetic—what used to be called a photographic—memory to boot. If an elusive factoid couldn't be found on the web, it was probably catalogued and cross-referenced in the capacious vaults of Mycroft's cerebral cortex. His quirky brilliance, coupled with his self-imposed exile to a hilltop in rural North Carolina, had earned him his office nickname: the original Mycroft was Sherlock Holmes's smarter, reclusive brother.

"And the address is?"

"Oh, sorry: reack2@crom.doe.gov."

"DOE—as in Department of Energy?"

"The very same," Knox said. "CROM looks to be one of their subagencies, but there's no hotlink for them on the DOE homepage, and all my searches come up empty."

"And your interest in this *crom* is, if I might ask?"

"They hijacked my email. I want to know why. I want them researched with extreme prejudice."

"You can't imagine any reason the Energy Department might be after you?"

"Not offhand. I'm all paid up on my utility bills. Oh, and—Mycroft? There's one other search criterion."

"All grist for the mill, Jonathan."

"Right. I'm particularly interested in any connection between this CROM crowd and an outfit goes by the name of Grishin Enterprises International. Them, I could find. They've got a corporate website at *www.gei.ru.*"

The "dubbya-dubbya-dubbya" keyphrase inadvertently triggered the desktop's speech recognizer. A browser-window popped up to display the GEI homepage. Knox left it open. He'd already paid the site a cursory visit, but a re-look couldn't hurt.

"*Ru* for Russia?" Mycroft was saying, "Mightn't this have to do with your former life?"

Knox didn't answer immediately. He was looking at the home page logo now filling the browser window: the stylized image of an Ouro-bouros, crushing the world in its great green coils.

✳

Boris Petrovich Volin watched instant replay of the ultralight land-ing on the rooftop of his plant. Nicely done, that. He spoke the words that switched his large-screen monitor back to real-time display. Now it showed a uniformed guard escorting pilot and passenger down the ac-cess stairs toward the headquarters suite. Volin leaned forward, taking the opportunity to study his guests.

The woman was nondescript, hardly worth a second glance. A dumpy dishwater blonde waging her lonely battle with middle age, and losing.

Her companion was another story altogether.

Perhaps it was just the contrast with the pallid skin and hair of the woman, perhaps some trick of the stairwell lighting or the closed-circuit video, but the man seemed…dark. A darkness somehow more than physical, though it started with physical attributes, with the black leather flight jacket hugging the hulking frame, with the swarthy com-plexion of the grim, heavy-boned face, the straight, sable hair and black slashes of eyebrows and mustache, the empty black eyes.

Darkness personified. Volin repressed a shudder.

He swiveled in his chair and called up the instructions he had been emailed regarding this visit. What was the man's name again? Ah, yes, Geladze, Yuri Vissarionovich Geladze. A Georgian—that explained it. Explained both the dusky Transcaucasian cast of his features and the aura of a ferocity barely held in check.

Volin had keyed his monitor off and was striding out from behind his rosewood desk by the time the visitors were shown into his suite. His Armani suit rustled silkily as he extended a hand.

"Welcome to Resource Recovery Systems. Boris Petrovich Volin, General Manager, at your service. We have been expecting you."

"Very pleased. Zolotova, Natalya Petrovna." The woman all but curtseyed. Her dark companion merely grunted.

The woman looked simultaneously shaken and relieved. Good. More manageable that way. Merkulov had chosen well: she seemed only too willing to be led by the nose, like a lamb to slaughter. Only too willing to take everything around her at face value.

Including Volin himself. Not that he did not look the part of a chief executive for a major GEI subsidiary: tall and slim and polished, his angular features framed by wavy brown hair just going gray at the temples. Certainly neither he nor his operation bore any resemblance to the low-tech competition in the greater metropolitan area's thriving waste-disposal business. Still, if pressed, he might have acknowledged more than a little kinship with his rivals of Sicilian extraction, under the skin.

"Your driver just phoned in," Volin said. "He has encountered congestion at the Lincoln Tunnel." He smiled an apology. "Unfortunate, but only to be expected during peak traffic hours on a weekday. We now estimate your vehicle will not arrive for another forty-five minutes."

The dark man shrugged and nodded, the barest minimum required to keep up his side of the charade. The woman, predictably, acquiesced.

"Since you must wait in any case, please permit me to show you our facility." Volin grasped the woman's arm and motioned her companion to follow.

The flooring underfoot changed from noise-absorbent parquet to ringing steel grating as they walked out into the main bay of the plant and up onto a narrow catwalk. Ten meters below them, the floor was crisscrossed by a maze of color-coded piping, most of it leading into a mammoth stainless-steel cylinder standing on end in the middle of the hall. At evenly-spaced intervals along the catwalk, eight enclosed tubes angled down like opaque water-slides to intersect the top of the cylinder. Every surface in the room sparkled and shone in the overhead fluorescent lighting, lending the facility an air of obsessive cleanliness.

"Just a skeleton crew on duty this afternoon." Volin leaned on the catwalk's rail and indicated three workers in Day-Glo orange envirohazard bunnysuits tending widely-scattered control stations down on the plant floor. "All reliable men. In view of the sensitivity of your presence here, the rest of the day shift has been sent home early."

"Night shift?" the dark man said in Georgian-accented Russian. He could speak after all.

"Instructed not to arrive until eight P.M. I trust that is satisfactory?" Would a hired killer appreciate the economics of the situation? "We here at RRS are, of course, eager to support the goals of the parent organization in any way we can. But that does not relieve us of responsibility for our own contribution to the GEI bottom line. And canceling tonight's shift altogether would have had an unacceptable impact on quarterly earnings."

Volin trailed off. The man was staring at him now.

He swallowed. "It—it would have meant shutting down the catalytic reactor, you see." He pointed at the huge cylinder. "And we would then have lost a good ten hours, and many kilowatts, cold-starting it back up to operating temperature."

The dark man made no reply, simply continued to fix him with that baleful glare.

A palpable silence descended, stretched out uncomfortably.

"You must understand," Volin began again, "how essential it is to keep a plant like ours running continuously. Our EPA-approved recycling process involves immersing hazardous waste in a "bath," as it were, of molten iron. As has long been observed in steel mills, red-hot iron possesses solvent and catalytic properties able to break down organic waste products into their component elements. In a triumph of Russian metallurgy, our Resource Recovery business unit has harnessed this effect in the service of environmentally-friendly conversion of toxins into useful raw materials.

"This means, however, that it is far more energy efficient, far more *profitable*, to maintain the bath at constant temperature on a twenty-four-by-seven duty cycle. It becomes prohibitively expensive to allow the reactor to cool down overnight, only to reheat it next morning to the melting point of iron, or higher."

"Higher?" Did the gravelly voice betray a hint of interest for once?

"Well, yes. Normal operating range is around fifteen hundred fifty degrees Celsius, but we can bring the bath all the way up to seventeen hundred for special decontaminations—chemical demilitarization of VX nerve gas, for instance."

The woman paled.

"No, no, nothing like that going on right now," Volin said, all reassurance. "Today's run is quite routine: carcinogenic byproducts from local pesticide and chemical plants. Never a dearth of dioxins and PCBs here, you know. Here in New Jersey we are sitting on a gold mine of toxic waste."

The dark man spoke again: "This waste goes in how?"

"You see these eight chutes?" Volin pointed to the tubes angling down to the giant cylinder. "They empty out over the molten metal pool at the core of the reactor vessel. We simply load them with hazardous material, solid or liquid, and let gravity do the rest."

"Show me."

"Of course. If you will just step this way." Any moment now. Why was the man waiting? Surely he intended to do it before—

Volin led them to where the catwalk flared out into a rectangular balcony. To their right, thick red piping ran up vertically from the floor below, then elbowed toward a chamber occupying the center of the platform.

Volin strode over to the chamber's solid steel door. "Behold: the Vestibule to Hell!"

He chuckled at his small joke, then sobered when no one joined him. "Nothing so dramatic, actually. Merely an airlock. The hazmat is loaded through this outer portal into the holding chamber." Volin entered a code into a keypad set into the jamb, and the door swung open soundlessly to reveal a cubical interior two meters on a side. "Then, when the run is ready, the chamber is sealed, the floor retracts, and the material slides down the chute into the bath. Any questions?"

"No," said the dark man.

And with that, he seized the woman by the nape of her neck and hurled her bodily into the chamber. He swung the heavy door closed on the beginnings of her scream.

He turned to Volin. "How long?"

"To, um, ah, cycle through, you mean?" Volin was having trouble getting the words out. "As, as soon as an airtight seal is reestablished. Twenty seconds, no more. Y-you can watch the countdown on the display over here."

He led the dark man around to a control console built into the right side of the chamber. Away from the incoherent sobs and frantic pounding now issuing from the other side of the door.

Alive! She was going into the bath *alive!* Volin's stomach heaved. He fought to keep his rising gorge down, fearful of losing control in the other's presence.

Calm, calm. Nothing too unusual here. After all, total, traceless obliteration of inconvenient bodies was RRS's most lucrative sideline, a premiere service offered to a select East Coast clientele.

But up until now the bodies had always been *dead* first!

Oh, Volin understood the logic of not simply putting a bullet through her brain: Someone at the top, perhaps Arkady Grigoriyevich himself, had required there be no evidence of this woman's passing, not even so much as a spent cartridge casing. But surely she could have been stabbed or strangled or—anything but this!

The futile pounding ceased; in its place, an equally futile pleading began. The woman had evidently understood enough of Volin's orientation lecture to guess what would happen once the airlock's cycle completed, and its second door—the entire floor of the loading chamber—swung open to dump her down the steeply-sloping shaft.

Then she had no need to guess. The countdown stood at zero.

✳

Yuri watched status lights flashing red, indicating the load chamber's second, inner door was swinging open. Above the blaring of the klaxon he could hear a series of clangs as the floor retracted, then a dull thump as the woman dropped into the lance.

The engineers who designed the Resource Recovery plant had seen no need to soundproof the walls of the chute feeding into the molten metal bath. Until today all of the bulk solids slated for destruction had gone mute and unprotesting down its throat to the inferno. So it was perhaps understandable if the heat insulation lining the chute could not contain the echoing wail that accompanied Natalya Petrovna Zolotova's scrabbling slide toward the red glow of the bath below. A wail that rose freakishly in pitch as the cascaded ventilation system pumped hydrogen into the tube in place of oxygen.

Out on the plant floor, two of the orange-suited workers raised their heads at the surreal scream. Yuri glared down at them. They quickly bent to their instruments again.

Yuri turned back to the RRS manager. The man's face was ashen. With all his fine talk of quarterly earnings and EPA approvals, the administrator here had forgotten what business he was in. No matter. The squeamishness of others was what ensured there would always be a market for Yuri Geladze's services.

He looked the man in the eye. "I must see."

"S-see?"

"See her die," Yuri said. Arkady Grigoriyevich Grishin, CEO of Grishin Enterprises and their mutual employer, had ordered Yuri to confirm personally that the Galina stand-in was gone without trace. Now *there* was a man who did not flinch from what must be done.

"We, we cannot really see into the reactor vessel, as such," the manager stammered. "It is much too hot inside for conventional optics."

Yuri frowned. The man added hastily, "There *is* a monitoring capability employing high-resolution ultrasound. It can image both above and below the surface. Will that be satisfactory?"

"Show me."

In response to the manager's keystrokes, the console's main display came to life. Grayscale images depicted the interior of the cylinder below them in ghostly relief.

"I-I think we should see—yes, there!" The manager pointed to where a writhing shape, rendered in halftones, plummeted from a dark aperture near the top of the screen into the molten metal occupying its lower half.

The liquefied iron was far denser than water, its surface tension much higher. That made for an unexpectedly small splash, followed by a slow but inexorable engulfment of the thrashing victim—the briefly thrashing victim. Like a worker caught in a steel-mill spill, she might last a second or two but the outcome was never in doubt.

The woman's mouth was locked open impossibly wide, as if for one last scream. Nothing came out—her lungs and diaphragm, together with the rest of her soft thoracic and abdominal organs, had already burst and dissolved in the metallic flux. Bodily fluids vaporized into gouts of superheated steam. Sudden gaseous ventings animated what was left of the limbs in a grisly parody of life. Finally, the spinal column collapsed, scattering vertebrae like poker chips and plunging the skull itself into the incandescent broth.

Yuri watched the skeleton dissociate into individual bones. They bobbed a while on the red-hot surface before they too dissolved. He shrugged. He had seen worse. Had done worse.

"No burning?" he asked idly.

"No, no, of course not." The manager removed his spectacles and wiped the sweat from his brow with the sleeve of his expensive-looking suit jacket, "The whole decomposition process takes place in a reducing atmosphere. Burning is impermissible: there can be no oxidation whatsoever, or we would lose our EPA certification as a nonincinerative waste-disposal technology."

Yuri turned back to the display.

"The bones are the last to go," the manager was saying quietly. "Those, and the teeth, of course. Almost pure apatite: the same material rocks are made of." Color had returned to his cheeks. He no longer looked as though he were going to faint or vomit. *This* part he would have seen many times before.

"What is that?" Yuri pointed to a small blob on the screen. It was sinking slowly through the melt, jostled from side to side by convection currents.

The manager put his spectacles back on. "I — hmm, I don't know. Most metal objects lose their integrity in the bath. But there are tapping nozzles installed in the base of the reactor unit for just such eventualities. If you will wait a moment, we shall see."

The manager dispatched one of the orange-clad workers to retrieve the curious object from where it had settled at the bottom of the reactor tank. Yuri continued to watch the now-unchanging display.

"Yes, here it is." The manager took a silvery lump from the worker's gloved hand. Its true shape was hard to make out, so much iron had congealed around it in its trip through the molten bath.

"What is it?"

"It appears to be a, ah, pendant of some kind." The manager handed it to Yuri. "The woman must have been wearing it beneath her clothes."

Yuri lifted it to the light. It was still warm to the touch. "Silver?" he asked.

"What? No, no, silver would have dissolved. No, my friend, from its weight, its color, and especially its high melting point, I would say this is made of purest platinum.

"Keep it, if you like." The manager smiled wanly. A souvenir of your visit to Resource Recovery Systems. It is worth more than gold."

3 | Schwarzschild Radius

WHERE IN *HELL* could her prole have been going?

For maybe the fifth time that night, Marianna Bonaventure sat up in bed and turned on the nightstand lamp. Not that her cramped government-rate hotel room was much to look at, but the light helped push back the thoughts that kept crowding in on her in the dark. Thoughts that began prosaically enough, on a sidewalk in lower Manhattan — not so many hours ago, not so many city blocks away from where she now lay, sleepless at three in the morning — thoughts that then mutated into a nightmare montage of breathless cross-town pursuits, rooftop confrontations, elevator shafts —

Shit! Even the light wasn't helping. She switched it off and flopped back against the pillow again. Think about something else, Marianna, think *good* thoughts. Good thoughts like...

Ghostly scrawls inscribed the darkness: S-curves and tridents, angle-brackets and lissome, leaf-like glyphs. Puzzle-pieces from a primeval alphabet known as Linear A, whose still-undeciphered secrets, and those of the Bronze Age Minoan civilization that devised it, had held a lifelong fascination for her father, Jeremy.

Her eyelids fluttered closed. Behind them formed another vision — a cratered crescent rising out of the sea. Marianna's lips shaped a word, though no sound came out: *Thira*.

The isle of Thira, where everything was to begin, was where everything had once come to an end. In the year 1450 BCE, it had been the locus of a volcanic eruption, one so great it not only vaporized the core of the island itself, but spawned the earthquakes and tidal waves that brought the Aegean Golden Age to a cataclysmic close, and gave rise to legends of lost Atlantis.

What little remained of Thira might have gone on slumbering in the Mediterranean sun forever, save that in 1967 the ruins of the ancient Minoan seaport of Akrotiri had been discovered there, entombed like Pompeii beneath tons of lava and ash. With new inscriptions being unearthed almost daily in the ongoing excavation, Thira became a magnet for Linear A scholars from around the world. Including, in the mid-seventies...

Jeremy Bonaventure, ink still drying on his doctorate in classical civilizations, was eager to try his luck in the hunt for the Minoan equivalent of a Rosetta Stone. Crete was only to be a brief stopover en route, until he met the guide the Cretan Antiquities Administration had assigned him.

Ariadni Kalimanakis was a raven-haired beauty almost thirteen years Jeremy's junior. A first-year archaeology major interning that summer at the museum in Iraklion, she had, thanks to her excellent English, been stuck with the job of babysitting a shy, bookish American.

Marianna smiled in her half-sleep at the unlikely pair, the scion of San Francisco society and the Greek fisherman's daughter, touring the palaces at Knossos, the dig at Taras — anywhere and everywhere the tablets, door lintels, and other artifacts bearing traces of Linear A were to be found. It was mid-July before they finally boarded a packet-boat for the day-long trip to Thira.

Ariadni remained lost in thought all through that long afternoon, but by the time they docked she had made her choice. She knew full well it could spell ruin, not only for her own reputation, but for the honor of her family. Yet over the past weeks she had grown to love

Jeremy for his gentleness, his breadth of mind, his depth of spirit. And she was not one to deny her deepest feelings, no matter the cost.

At sunset they left their pension and wandered up into the gentle, grassy hills above the village of Emborion. There, on that warm July night, with the full moon a shield of beaten silver rising out of Homer's wine-dark sea, she gave herself to him.

It was a love story Marianna had heard again and again, told in less and less sanitized versions as she grew from childhood to adolescence. Told in exotic accents by a mother young enough almost to be an elder sister. In Marianna's youthful imagination, this mythos, set at the fountainhead of a romance that still quietly infused her parents' lives, came to take on the dimensions of an ancient archetype, of mysteries already old when the first Aegean civilization was fresh and new. Once she grew old enough to have the biological details more or less sorted out, she used to fantasize that she had been conceived on that first moon-drenched midsummer night.

Against all expectations, for all their differences of age and origin and temperament, Jeremy and Ariadni had made a life together. A life together filled with joy and learning, twin legacies they had bequeathed to their daughter, their only child. A life together tragically cut short on April 17th 1993, when they chanced to be on Hellenic flight 803 from New York to Athens.

Marianna rolled over and checked the clock on the nightstand again. Half-past three, and she had to be up by six. Up and back on the job, back trying to salvage what she could from the wreckage of her investigation, from the wreckage of her life...

The crash investigators were never able to determine if it had been a suicide mission or just a run-of-the-mill hijacking gone terribly awry. All they had to go on were the screams and curses—and the echoing gunshots—on the cockpit voice recorder. That, and the physical evidence strewn across a mountainside in Switzerland: 613,786 twisted pieces of Boeing 747, ranging in size from a tabletop down to a matchbook.

The two people Marianna had loved most in all the world. Who had loved each other more and better than anyone she'd ever known. And all of a sudden they were just—gone.

A hard lesson for someone only eighteen years old—for anyone, at any age: don't even try holding on to those you love. You can't.

Love dies.

In the waters off the island of Thira, where everything had once begun, everything came to an end. Marianna stood alone at the stern of her grandfather's fishing boat and scattered the ashes of her mother and father wide across their beloved wine-dark Aegean. No ceremony. No prayers. Nothing.

Nothing but a single truth.

Love dies.

✳

Yuri Vissarionovich Geladze had no eye for understated elegance, else he could not have failed to discern it in *Rusalka*'s spacious, high-ceilinged headquarters suite with its varnished, quarter-sawn anigre paneling and matching leather-topped desk. Or in the graying, ruddy-faced man seated behind that desk, draped in a caramel Lanvin blazer, its golden highlights complementing his cream-colored shirt and matching silken cravat. In the whole room, the only item that looked out of place was a distorted metal cylinder, no longer than a pencil and perhaps twice as thick, resting in the man's manicured hands.

"You sent for me," Yuri said. Not a question, merely a statement of fact.

Arkady Grigoriyevich Grishin, CEO and Chairman of the Board of Grishin Enterprises International, seemed not to hear. His fingers continued stroking the engraved surface of his talisman. For long moments still his gaze was held by the scene out the panoramic window to his left: a flotilla of small boats, their sails aglow in early morning light, wending their way upriver toward the gray towers of a suspension bridge. It was with seeming reluctance at relinquishing the view that Grishin sighed, pushed his chair back, and looked up.

"Ah, yes, Yuri. Thank you for coming so quickly." The voice was quiet, cultured, pitched just above a whisper.

Yuri nodded impassively.

"To begin…" Grishin leaned back in his chair, and favored Yuri with one of his dazzling smiles. "Permit me to congratulate you on yesterday's twofold success: a false trail for CROM and their lead investigator dead, all at once."

Yuri permitted himself a tight smile. "Two flies with one slap," he said.

"Yes, exactly. Ah, of course, Postrel'nikova herself is to learn nothing of this action on her behalf. Not even Sasha can be told."

That didn't merit a response. It wasn't as if Yuri had, or sought, any social contact with the Project's chief scientist or its head planner.

"In any case," Grishin went on, "that is not why I asked you here. It seems another matter has arisen. Merkulov's people have been tracking it for some time. I had been waiting for them to make some show of initiative on their own, but then…" Grishin's handsome, regular features rearranged themselves to hint at a frown. A jewel-encrusted ring sparkled as his tanned hands pantomimed an indulgent helplessness. "Well, you know Vadim."

"Yes." Yuri shrugged. One might as well wait for some show of initiative from a stone as from Vadim Vasiliyevich Merkulov. The GEI security chief's energies were directed, first and foremost, at protecting his own fat ass. It was, in fact, Merkulov's continual reluctance to do the necessary that had led to Yuri's engagement in the first place.

"Then *this* arrived." Grishin looked down at the warped metal object resting in his hands. "Apparently the matter is more critical than we had thought. I fear you must miss tomorrow night's gala in consequence." He sighed as if breaking this sad news to an honored guest. "Vakhtang will coordinate security in your stead. Please brief him on the status of in-transit and on-site arrangements. But do so quickly. You must leave within the hour; there is a long way to go, in little time."

Grishin nodded at the travel documents on Yuri's side of the desk. Yuri took them and glanced over the itinerary: New York to Moscow to Krasnoyarsk to someplace called—Tunguska?

"And here," Grishin handed him a sheet of thick, creamy paper, folded over twice, "is your subject." In situations such as these, Grishin exhibited a certain delicacy: he would not speak the name of the victim in the presence of the assassin.

Yuri unfolded the sheet. Clipped to it were several color images —full, three-quarter, and profile shots of a thin, middle-aged man wearing a t-shirt, jeans jacket, and an American cowboy hat. The paper itself contained a single line of type. Unfamiliar English words, transliterated into a Cyrillic approximation.

Yuri sounded it out slowly: "Professor Dzhek Adler. University of Teksas."

✳

As the old Mikoyan-3 helicopter rattled its way into the heartlands of the Stony Tunguska, Professor Jack Adler's faded blue eyes drank in the vista he'd come so far to see.

When he really got fired up, Jack's forty-something, borderline-ugly face—a little too narrow in the jaw, too thin in the lips, too broad at the forehead—radiated an intensity that made him seem almost young and good-looking. And right now he was wholly transfigured by the scene passing before his eyes. For, through gaps in the successor-growth canopy, he could see all the way down to the forest floor. Down to where the old forest lay strewn at the young one's feet, its rotting trunks all aligned radially inward, pointing like thousands of directional arrows toward the epicenter.

Toward the secret heart of the cosmic mystery of the millennium.

They would not be following the path pointed by those arrows today. Instead, the copter was skirting the Great Swamp's southwestern perimeter headed for Kulik's Landing. By craning his neck, Jack could just make it out up ahead.

From the air, the landing on the banks of the sluggish Khushmo River hardly looked like the base camp for this year's high-tech Tunguska expedition. More like a pioneer outpost, and a deserted one at that. Its scattering of rude log structures stood baking in the ninety-five-degree heat of a Siberian midsummer afternoon, silent and seemingly as forsaken as they had been throughout most of the seventy-odd years since the explorer Leonid Kulik had first built them. Only a pall of woodsmoke gave any evidence of human habitation.

The pilot set the Mi-3 down gingerly, as if the ground might buckle beneath its runners. Not an unreasonable concern: the permafrost that started just a meter below the surface had suffered incalculable stresses in the 1908 impact. That was almost a century ago, but who could say if the oddly fragile stuff was fully healed even now? Better safe than sorry, especially when burdening the treacherous substrate with the weight of a helicopter under load.

One major component of that load was strapped down right beside Jack. He directed a look of mixed affection and chagrin over at his inseparable traveling companion: a bulky black hardshell equipment case marked *Fragile* and *Property of U. Texas, Austin*. It was resting innocuously on the floorboards for now, but, soon as the rotors spun to a stop, the fun of moving it would begin all over again. Not a prospect Jack relished: the thing had to be half the size of his desk back at the Austin physics lab, with a mass nearly the equal of his own hundred eighty-five pounds.

Hauling this monster across thirteen time zones to the remotest spot on earth had taxed Jack's strength and endurance near the limit. And he hadn't had all that much to start with. Tall and stringy and slightly stooped, he was not what you'd call an imposing physical specimen. That shouldn't have mattered much: theoretical physics was supposed to be one of those inside jobs with no heavy lifting. Not this time.

With a grudging assist from the pilot, Jack manhandled the unwieldy case out of the hatch and eased it down to the ground alongside the rest of his luggage. He clamped his trademark ten-gallon hat tight down on his head against the downdraft as the chopper lifted off for the return trip to Vanavara.

And left Jack all alone. He looked around, then down at the case. Was he supposed to lug the thing into camp by himself, in this heat? He couldn't leave it sitting here, that's for sure. Without the SQUID, the half-million-dollar instrument nestled safe inside the hardshell, there'd be no hope whatsoever of proving the far-out theories of one Dr. John C. Adler, mad cosmologist. With itwell, let the Doubting Thomases beware!

Speaking of Doubting Thomases, Jack's heart sank as he spied the one-man reception committee now emerging from the main lodge and lumbering toward him through clouds of gnats. Jack recognized that burly giant from the snapshots plastered all over the Tomsk University website: the organizer of this year's expedition, the man who'd done his level best to block Jack's participation in it: Academician Medvedev himself.

The man's name, Jack recalled, came from *medved*—Russian for "bear." It sure fit. Professor of Planetology and Member of the Russian Academy of Sciences Dmitri Pavlovich Medvedev bulked tall and broad, barrel-chested and big-bellied in a way that bespoke muscle rather than flab. An unruly black mane threaded with gray reached almost to his shoulders, a match for the scraggly beard, mustache, and brows that framed his sneering mouth, bulbous nose, and glittering black eyes.

"Academician Medvedev." Jack held out his hand and launched into standard Russian first-contact protocol: "*Ochen' priyatno.* Very pleased to meet you. I am—"

"I know who you are, Adler." Medvedev brushed aside the niceties, along with the handshake. "And I wish I could say *I* were pleased to meet *you*. But, frankly, the only thing that would please me would be for you to return where you came from. Better yet, for you never to have come here at all."

"I can understand your reservations about my research program, Professor, but I—"

"Research program?" Medvedev's face reddened alarmingly. "What research program? You…you eat our food, drink our water, consume our fuel, occupy space that might instead have gone to a scientist,"—he did not quite say a *real* scientist, though that was what his tone implied—"a scientist with at least some prospect of advancing our knowledge of the Tunguska phenomenon. Instead, what have your American dollars bought you? The privilege of wasting our expedition's time and resources on your…" The Russian waved his outsized hands in the air, momentarily at a loss for words to describe the enormity of it all, then exploded: "…your discredited fantasies!"

"Black holes aren't fantasies, Professor. If theory alone doesn't convince you they exist, the evidence from the Hubble galactic survey certainly should." Ever since the late nineties, the Earth-orbiting Hubble telescope had been beaming back images of gargantuan black holes infesting the hearts of nearby galaxies and slowly swallowing them whole.

"Bah!" Medvedev's arm slashed the air so ferociously Jack could feel the wind of it on his face. "No one doubts such monstrosities are real. But how could one of these have impacted the Earth without utterly destroying it, and the rest of the solar system, too?"

Jack sighed. "Black holes can come in all sizes, Professor."

"Yes, yes," Medvedev broke in again, "you will have an entire week in which to recount these fever dreams to any who will listen. I, for one, will not stand here being eaten alive by these infernal insects while you prattle on!"

And with that, he turned on his heel and stomped off in the direction of the camp, leaving Jack alone with the SQUID once more.

✸

"Déjà vu all over again." Yogi Berra's immortal one-liner drifted through Marianna Bonaventure's head as Compliance chauffeured her down John Street in the direction of the South Street Seaport. The same street where, less than eighteen hours ago, her quarry had... No, she'd promised herself she wasn't going to get into that.

The cafés and storefronts lining the narrow street seemed subtly different today: sharper, realer, more fully dimensional somehow. Was that a trick of the clear mid-morning light, or just the way things always looked when you weren't focused on the chase to the exclusion of all else? Not that this present operation wasn't a pursuit, too, of sorts.

The Secure Terminal Unit beeped twice. Marianna was already reaching to jack in her headset when she remembered she wasn't wearing one. Whole different look for this op: body armor, adieu. Business casuals were lots more comfortable.

"Bonaventure," she said into the handset.

"Marianna? Pete. Listen, I've been thinking..." Uh-oh! She could feel her boss beaming his heavy-jowled frown at her all the way from Chantilly, Virginia. Pete was having second thoughts.

"Relax," she told him, "we're good to go. I'm moving to acquire as we speak."

"It's too tight on time, is what worries me. We don't even know if Bondarenko will take the bait."

"Already covered. As far as Sasha knows, he's been in contact with the Archon resource for the past three days."

"He's *what?* You know damn well you can't involve a civilian without authorization!"

"Take it easy, Pete. It's done, okay? And it worked."

"Marianna—"

"Look, we wouldn't have had time to set up the email spoof if we'd waited till we'd lost Galina first." Slow down, inhale. "We've only got the one shot at this, what with the gala being tomorrow night. We had to have all our ducks in a row before *Rusalka* sailed. You get that, don't you, Pete?"

Pete wasn't saying anything. Not a good sign.

"I knew you wouldn't buy into it," she went on, "so I just went ahead and did it. You'll see; this is all going to pan out."

The silence on the other end of the secure line was growing uncomfortably long. Pete could still pull the plug, and she couldn't buck a direct order. C'mon, Pete, think it through. It's not like you wouldn't have green-lighted the Hail Mary eventually—you'd have just been too late.

"Okay," he said at last. "Make it work."

"Pete, you won't regret it."

She hoped.

✳

"*Dio mio*, Jack, my arm hurts still!" *Dottore* Luciano Carbone slumped down by the campfire and rubbed his shoulder demonstratively. "That box of yours must weigh a ton. Why in God's name did Medvedev make us drag it all the way out to *choum* seventeen?"

"Why do you think, Luciano?" Jack Adler grinned at the tubby, balding University of Bologna geologist—the only friend he'd made in his first half-day on site. A friend in need, too. If the little Italian hadn't lent a hand, it would have taken all night to get up and running. Even so, it was well past the dinner-hour before they tramped back in, sweaty and exhausted, from what had to be the remotest *choum*, or birchbark tepee, in the camp.

The Italian stroked the black curls of his goatee. "That man does not like you so much, is what I think, to put you so far away."

Jack chuckled. "I'm not exactly his favorite guest researcher, am

I? But there's a simpler explanation for sticking me out in the boonies. Hear it?"

He cupped a hand to his ear. Sure enough, the faint *chuff-chuff-chuff* of his diesel-powered compressor was audible even at this distance.

"That unit's going to be cycling on and off day and night just keeping the SQUID cold enough to operate," Jack said. "And getting a good night's sleep out here isn't all that easy as it is, what with the skeeters and such. No sense my adding noise pollution to the problem."

Luciano opened his mouth to respond. A cough came out instead. Understandable, since he was directly downwind of the smoky fire. At first Jack had wondered why they were sitting around the campfire at all. It sure wasn't for warmth; Siberian summers might be short but they made up for it with extra helpings of heat and humidity. Turned out, though, that the woodsmoke kept the ravenous Siberian mosquitoes—"flying alligators," the Russians called them—at bay. It was the one deterrent that worked. Conventional bug-spray only served to encourage the insects.

"Sorry, Jack, sorry,"—cough, cough—"what I wanted to say: perhaps the real reason our esteemed Academician has isolated you from the rest of the party is for fear of infection."

"Quarantining my contagious ideas, eh?" Jack smiled again. He liked this rotund, genial little man with his cherubic face and sly Machiavellian wit. "Don't worry, Luciano; from what I can tell, my 'discredited fantasies' aren't catching."

"Because you do not trouble to explain them." Luciano stifled another cough. "Your theories, I mean, not your fantasies. I have read the abstract of your research proposal twice, but I confess this business about the very little black holes still remains a mystery to me."

"Didn't seem much point going into detail, seeing how our friends from Tomsk were going to take the money and run, regardless." As the premier center for studies of the Tunguska phenomenon and the host institution for the expedition, Tomsk University had final say on what research might be conducted at the site.

Jack swiped at the air with his Stetson, beating back another insectile assault wave. "And close their ears to what I had to say in the process," he added.

"Not all of them, perhaps." Luciano flicked his eyes off to Jack's left.

Jack turned to see a young blond Russian standing five feet away, listening to them. And looking at the Stetson. What was the real attraction here: Jack's theories or his cowboy hat?

Caught eavesdropping, the young man blushed and pushed thick bifocals back up his nose. "Excuse, please … Zaleskii, Igor Andreyevich, aspirant in molecular biology at Tomsk University. I could not help but to overhear…"

"No harm done." Jack said. "Sit down, Igor, pull up a stump and join the party."

The newcomer gave a grateful nod and joined them at the fire. He squatted down, looked both ways, then reached into his hip pocket and pulled out a metal flask. "Russian mosquito repellent," he said, handing it to Jack with a grin. "For internal use only."

Jack unscrewed the lid and took a sniff. Vodka—what a surprise. He glanced at his watch: if he'd managed to keep pace with all the time-zone changes, it was past ten in the evening. At any reasonable latitude, the sun would've been over the yardarm hours ago. Even here the sky was beginning to stain with sunset. Close enough.

"Thanks." He took a swig and passed the flask back to Igor. "So, what's a biology grad student doing on this junket?"

"I assist Professor Nakoryakova with her studies of trace radioactive isotopes in local soils and flora." Igor sipped at the flask and handed it to Luciano. "Other than the physical evidence of treefall and the like, residual radiation is the most persistent signature of the Tunguska Event. But please, I did not wish to interrupt. I, too, am interested in what you say about your little black holes. Are they very different from the big ones?"

Jack shrugged. "Depends. What do you know about the big ones?"

It was Luciano who finally replied. "They are said to form when a star grows so heavy that it collapses under its own weight."

"That's good, but it's not the whole story. Maybe it's better if we back up a bit, begin at the beginning. And, for a black hole, the beginning is gravity."

Jack downed another slug from the passing flask. The vodka did seem to be keeping the mosquitoes at bay. Or maybe he was just noticing them less.

"The thing of it is," he went on, "gravity's just not very powerful, as forces of nature go. Compared to the strong nuclear force, it's the next best thing to nonexistent. Even plain old electromagnetism's got it beat hands down. You ever pick up a three-penny nail with a toy magnet? Then you know how even a teensy bit of electromagnetic force can overcome the gravitational pull of the whole Earth."

Jack shook his head. "When you get right down to it, the only thing gravity's got going for it is, it just keeps on adding up."

"But is this not true of the other forces as well?" Luciano asked.

"Not really. The nuclear forces are too short-range to amount to much over the long run. Electromagnetism's got the reach, all right, but it comes in opposing flavors: positive and negative charges, north and south poles. That puts a natural upper limit on how strong an electromagnetic field can get before it attracts enough opposite charges to neutralize itself."

"And gravity, you are saying, only works one way?"

"Uh-huh. Never lets go, never cancels out. That's unique for a long-range force, and ultimately it's decisive. Pack enough mass into one place—like in a planet ten times the size of Jupiter—and the field-strength at the core exceeds anything electromagnetism can stand up to. The electron shells that give things their structural strength, why, they just up and buckle. What started out as nice, solid matter—like this," Jack rapped his knuckles on the log he was sitting on, "dissolves into a soup of dissociated electrons and free nuclei."

"And so this is how you make black holes?" Igor said.

"Not quite. No, what I just described—" Jack pointed up through the branches to where the first faint pinpricks of light were just beginning to appear in the darkening sky, "—is how you make *stars*."

✳

Knox had been at his desk and sitting on his hands half the morning, waiting for normal business hours—or Mycroft's peculiar definition of them—to begin.

The country of the night is the coder's true homeland, and Mycroft, a loyal native son. In the fresh, clean hours after midnight, with the petty interruptions and annoyances of the day fading like dreams at dawn, he essayed prodigies of system design, assembling soaring fairytale architectures of logic, elegance, and power from the dry dust of global variables and reserved keywords. But it did make him a devout late sleeper.

Knox flicked his gaze to the timestamp in the corner of his widescreen: 10:25. Give it another five minutes.

His speakerphone emitted a muted chirp.

"Mycroft?" Calling in early? That would be a first.

"Front desk," the voice of Archon Office Manager Suzanne Ledbetter corrected. "Were you expecting a visitor, Jon?"

"Unh-uh. My calendar's clear far as I know."

"Well, you've got one. Take a look."

A small conferencing window popped up on Knox's screen, offering a real-time view of a young woman in casual dress. She was standing at the reception desk, communing with her wristtop. Knox zoomed the window to full-screen mode. Did he know her? She didn't look like someone he would soon forget. She looked … striking, the way that dark hair complemented her ivory complexion.

"I don't know her," he said finally. "Not that I wouldn't like to. Did she say what she wants?"

"What who wants, Jonathan?" A second voice broke in, issuing from the new conferencing window now staking out its own piece of screen real estate.

"Oh, good morning, Mycroft."

Knox didn't need to ask how the night's researches had gone. If Mycroft's sly grin weren't enough, his computer-enhanced imagery—the black eyepatch and rakish red bandana, the Jolly Roger fluttering against a backdrop of sky and sea—all betokened a successful hack.

"Jon?" Suzanne again. "What should I tell her?"

Oh, right—his unscheduled visitor. "Uh, I could be tied up with this for a while. See if she wants to hang out, or maybe come back after lunch, okay?"

"Okay." The reception window irised shut.

Knox turned back to Mycroft. "Took you long enough."

"I trust you will find it well worth the wait, Jonathan."

"The wait got old an hour ago."

"Yes, well, I'm afraid it must get a little older. There are a few pre-liminaries to cover first."

"Can 'em." Knox pulled his chair in and leaned forward. "Get to the good stuff."

✶

Half a world away, Jack Adler was getting to some good stuff of his own. He peered through the smoke of the campfire at the expectant faces of his listeners, thinking how best to put it across.

"Stars are really just controlled gravitational implosions," he began. "Take that super-Jupiter we were talking about. Once gravity overcomes its structural integrity, it starts to shrink. It'd go right on shrinking, too, except compression generates heat, and enough compression'll heat the planet's core to upwards of ten million degrees Kelvin. That's the flashpoint: at that temperature, the free atomic nuclei are moving fast enough to start slamming into each other. The strong nuclear force takes over and thermonuclear fusion kicks in."

No matter how many times Jack told this story, he was always struck anew by the wonder of it. "Fusing hydrogen into helium releases energy. Colossal amounts of energy. Enough energy to push back against the pull of gravity. Enough to light the heavens. Enough to warm the worlds and spark the chemical processes that lead to life, to us.

"Enough to make stars," he breathed. He paused again, looking up. This sense of awe was as close as he got to what, he supposed, other people felt in the presence of the sacred.

A hush fell over the little group. No sound stirred the still, warm evening air, save for an occasional pop from the fire.

Jack shook himself. "Of course, things can't go on like that forever. It takes fuel to keep those fires burning — hydrogen, in particular. The average star holds enough to chug along for billions of years, converting hydrogen to helium. But sooner or later it's got to run out. And, when it does, the squeeze starts all over again."

Once it resumed, gravitational contraction would raise the core temperature back up to where the fire rekindled. Only now the helium "ash" itself became the fuel, fusing into heavier and heavier elements: carbon, lithium, oxygen, neon, silicon, finally bottoming out with iron. Then, nucleosynthesis having reached the point of diminishing returns, the stage was set for the final act.

"At the very end there, gravity can grip hard enough that the core of the star just…collapses." Jack stared into the campfire, seeing instead the cataclysmic last moments of a dying sun. "Collapses so fast it rebounds. You get a gigantic explosion, a nova or supernova. The star puts out more energy in that single instant than it did in a lifetime of steady shining. The shockwave is powerful enough to transmute elements wholesale." In its spectacular death throes the star would seed the universe with the building blocks of new worlds, new life.

"In the aftermath," he went on, "the key thing is how much of the star's original mass the explosion leaves behind. If it's only around a sun's worth, no problem: atomic nuclei have got more than enough structural strength to hold up under that much weight. You wind up with a brown dwarf star the size of the Earth.

"But go upwards of that, and things start to get interesting."

Jack looked up. Three more expedition members, two middle-aged men and a younger woman, had come trooping in from the twilight forest and were walking purposefully toward the firepit. They gave Jack a perfunctory nod but continued talking quietly among themselves. Not here for the soapbox seminar, then—just more refugees from the gnats.

"Please go on, Jack," Luciano said. "You were saying?"

"Oh, right. Well, if the leftovers weigh much more than the sun, things start to happen. The pressure in the interior of the "cinder" is enough to mash electrons and protons together, so you get neutrons. That triggers another collapse, into a neutron star only a few miles across. Bizarre enough in its own way, I suppose. But the point where us relativity theorists really sit up and take notice is when the supernova remnant is more than three times the mass of the sun. Not even neutrons can hold back that much gravity; they just up and cave. And neutrons are the last line of defense. Once they go, the whole mass collapses to what we call a singularity—a dimensionless point of infinite density, infinite space-time curvature, infinite you-name-it."

"Now you go too far, Adler," a rumbling bass broke in.

Jack turned and saw Medvedev's great bulk looming just beyond the circle of firelight. "Oh, good evening, Academician," he said. "I didn't see you standing there. I'm sorry, what did you mean, 'go too far'?"

Medvedev sighed in seeming exasperation. "As everyone knows, the infinite is purely a mathematical construct. It can exist nowhere in nature."

"Maybe not for material objects and such. But gravity's different. When you get right down to it, gravity *is* mathematics — geometry to be exact."

Medvedev said nothing, just stood there glaring at him.

"Look," Jack went on, "imagine that our three-dimensional space is a two-dimensional sheet of rubber. Then gravity'd just be a measure of how much that rubber sheet stretches when you drop a mass on it — a little for a marble, a lot more for a bowling ball. Drop a planet-sized mass onto that rubber sheet and the nearby surface'll dip down to form a gravity well, one so steep it can curve the path of a moon into orbit around it. Drop in a sun, and you've got a deformation deep enough to trap a whole family of planets."

"This much I grant you," Medvedev said. "Still, I hear in it nothing of your supposed infinities."

Jack held up a hand. "Hang on, I'm getting there. Turns out when a really massive star dies, it can form a sink-hole so deep that the well-walls wrap around and pinch shut, sealing off its remains from the rest of space-time. Remember *Alice in Wonderland,* where the Cheshire Cat vanishes, leaving only its smile behind? Well, here, all the matter disappears, collapses to a point, and only the mass is left. Enormous mass, taking up zero room. I don't know about you, but that sure sounds like infinite density to me."

Jack glanced at Medvedev, but the big Russian was back to holding his peace, at least for the moment. That was okay; it would only take a moment to finish this up.

"If there are no further questions," Jack said, "then there's only one more thing to add. Namely, that while all this is going on, the gravity gradient is getting steeper and steeper. Until it's finally so steep that nothing, not even light, can escape…

"...Which is why we call them black holes."

"Very nice, Adler." Medvedev was smiling through his beard now. "A pretty story, but it has been told before. Two hundred years ago, the Frenchman LaPlace imagined 'black stars' with escape velocity greater than the speed of light. Why not be so good as to share with us the fruits of your own intellect instead."

"Well, these aren't really *my* ideas, you understand," Jack said. "But the fact is, supernovas aren't the only way to make black holes. Every mass has its own cosmic point of no return—a lower limit on its size called the Schwarzschild radius. Beyond that, gravity takes over and collapses it down to a singularity. Shrink any mass small enough, and you get a black hole."

Medvedev smirked. "Even, perhaps, this?" He bent over abruptly. When he straightened again he was holding out a small lump of river-rounded rock.

"Huh? Yeah, sure," Jack said, eyeing the pebble. "Though it'd be easier to visualize if we start with something slightly larger. The Earth, say."

"By all means, choose what example you will." The Russian eased himself down opposite Jack, keeping the fire between them.

"Okay, well, Earth's Schwarzschild radius is about one and a half centimeters. So, if you could put the whole planet into some humungous vise and crush it down to a one-inch sphere, it would become a miniature black hole." Jack looked Medvedev in the eye. "With me so far? This is all just plain-vanilla relativity."

"No one disputes what you say, in theory," Medvedev bristled. "But where is the actuality? Show me this fantastic vise, this 'Schwarzschild machine' of yours. Let me create a singularity myself, purely as an experiment. Then I, too, will believe."

"You know that's impossible. The pressures needed are unimaginable, beyond anything we can even dream of today."

"Hah!" The Russian turned to his colleagues with a told-you-so grin.

Jack sighed. "But that doesn't mean it's *never* been possible. There was more than enough radiation pressure in the first instants of the Big

Bang to spawn PBHs—primordial black holes—of arbitrarily small size. And, as you know…"

"Yes, yes," Medvedev said, "I know only too well: it must therefore have been one of your famous PBHs that caused the Tunguska Event. All the generations of scientists who have struggled to understand this phenomenon of the Tunguska Cosmic Body are fools, fools or worse—futilely scouring the taiga for a meteorite that never existed. So claim the Three Wise Men from Texas University: Jackson and Ryan and Adler.

"But, Adler," Medvedev went on, "I say it is *you* who are the fool, coming all this way in pursuit of what was known to be folly when first published thirty years ago."

"Known? What do you mean known?"

"Simply that if your compatriots Jackson and Ryan had troubled to acquaint themselves with the geophysical evidence—evidence gathered painstakingly over the years by *serious* researchers—they would never have put forward their preposterous idea in the first place."

"Believe me when I tell you," Jack said, "that I've gone back and forth over your geophysical evidence, what little there is of it: seventy years of expeditions and you still haven't got a clue what the thing was. Was it a comet? A meteor?" He shook his upraised hands in mock dismay. "We don't know, we can't tell. Let's just call it a TCB, a 'Tunguska Cosmic Body,' and have done with it."

A frown crossed the Russian's broad features. "But this is standard scientific nomenclature—"

"Face it, Medvedev: calling the thing a TCB is an admission of defeat. It says you don't know what you're talking about, that your so-called 'evidence' is full of holes, inconclusive in the extreme. Except, of course, in those instances where it actually lends support to the Jackson-Ryan hypothesis."

"Support?" Medvedev snorted. "To what support do you refer?"

"Well, take the geomagnetic storm that Irkutsk Observatory tracked for hours following the impact. That effect could easily be accounted for by the right type of primordial black hole. At the same time, it just about rules out your own candidate for the Tunguska Cosmic Body. You guys from Tomsk have been pushing the TCB-as-comet theory for as long as anyone can remember. But comets aren't magnetic—they're mostly made of ice."

"A meteorite after all, then," Igor put in, to Medvedev's evident displeasure.

Jack turned to him. "Okay. Only now you're stuck explaining away another key piece of geophysical evidence: no crater. By Medvedev's own calculations, his TCB would've been the biggest thing to hit Earth in fifty thousand years. And base camp here can't be more than a mile or so from the epicenter. So why aren't we sitting at the bottom of a hole the size of the Grand Canyon?"

"As is well known," Medvedev said stiffly, "the lack of a crater is due to the event having been an airburst."

"An explosion kilometers up, resulting in *complete* volatilization of a meteoric body?" Jack said. "Sorry, I don't buy it. All right, maybe, if it was a stony meteorite. But you need a *ferrous* meteorite to explain the magnetism, and there's just no way that much iron could totally self-destruct."

He shook his head. "No, when you add it all up, the airburst theory begins to look like just another circular argument: the strongest support for it is the thing it's supposed to be explaining. 'No crater? Okay, then, must have been an airburst!' Call that evidence? Give me a break!"

"I see no reason why we must sit here and listen to this, this—" Medvedev began.

But Jack wasn't done yet, he'd saved the best for last. "And let's not forget who started this whole airburst business. One of Kazantsev's crackpot theories, wasn't it? That's some strange company you're keeping, Academician."

No one spoke. The only sound was the crackling of the campfire. Igor sucked in his breath but said nothing. Luciano choked on a laugh and covered his mouth with his hand. Medvedev glowered, his eyes far redder than could be accounted for by the pungent woodsmoke.

To so much as mention the mountebank Kazantsev in the same breath as the revered Academician was nothing short of scandalous. For it was Aleksandr Kazantsev who, fresh back from a 1946 inspection tour of the Hiroshima devastation, had startled the world with the claim that the 1908 Tunguska catastrophe had resulted from a similar high-altitude nuclear explosion — the explosion, in fact, of a nuclear-powered spaceship from Mars!

Medvedev had lurched to his feet now, and was standing there hunched over, still not speaking. The firelight cast his distorted shadow huge against the wall of Kulik's old cabin. In its eerie glow he bore the look — eyes widened, teeth bared — of a beast baited almost beyond endurance.

Jack wasn't about to back down. "Take your pick. Whichever hypothesis you choose, there's always some piece of your 'geophysical evidence' guaranteed to undermine it."

For a moment Jack thought the Russian was going leap the firepit and attack him physically.

Instead, in a voice shaking with barely-checked rage, Medvedev bellowed, "*Yes?* Well here is a piece of geophysical evidence I invite you to explain, Adler: your lack of a so-called 'exit event.'" He drew a deep breath. "If your ridiculous theory were true and the TCB were in truth one of your micro-holes, nothing could have prevented it from boring down through the Earth and out the other side, true? Your friends Jackson and Ryan said as much, predicting that it would come rocketing up out of the North Atlantic shortly after its touch-down here. Their 1973 *Nature* article, in fact, offers this retrodiction as a test of the whole hypothesis."

"Aha! So you *have* read it then."

"Oh, do not look so surprised, Adler. Of course I have read it. I enjoy science fiction as much as the next fellow." Medvedev smiled tightly. "But, here is my point. If your 'micro-hole' could cause such devastation on landing here in Tunguska, how could it not do so again on erupting up out of the ocean on the other side of the world?"

"Well —" Jack began.

But there was no stopping Medvedev now. "It should, in fact, have raised a catastrophic tsunami, not so? Vessels in the Atlantic shipping lanes should have been capsized by the shockwave. A wall of water fifty feet high should have gone crashing against the shores of Iceland and Eastern Canada — areas far more densely populated than Central Siberia, then as now. Why then do the newspapers of the time contain no reports of such a disaster?"

The Russian leaned closer, teeth bared in an unpleasant grin. "I will tell you why, Adler. *Because it never happened!* None of it did. To think otherwise is the worst sort of naiveté and scientific irresponsibility!"

All eyes were now on Jack, waiting to see how he would respond.

Jack chose his next words carefully. "Remember your Sherlock Holmes? The one where he says 'Once you've eliminated the impossible, whatever remains, however improbable…'"

"'Must be truth,'" Medvedev finished for him, "Yes, yes, this is well known. But what is your point?"

"Just this," Jack said in a low voice, "I don't think the thing ever came back out.

"I think it's still in there."

4 | Reacquisition

T *HAD* BEEN worth the wait.

Knox sat spellbound as a slideshow fit for a Senatorial subcommittee flashed across his NetMeeting window, telling the tale of an agency known as CROM.

The initials turned out to stand for Critical Resources Oversight Mandate. On its face, that fit right in with the parent Energy Department's mission statement. But the title was just more misdirection: the "critical resources" CROM oversaw weren't oil reserves or plutonium stockpiles, they were…people.

Specifically, scientists of the former Soviet Union, with the occasional Pakistani or North Korean thrown in for good measure. Scientists working in the so-called WMD disciplines—the old nuclear, chemical, biological Weapons of Mass Destruction mavens.

CROM was the little Dutchboy with his proverbial finger in the dike, trying to stem a brain drain of death-dealing expertise. Trying to keep privation-weary Russian and Third-World researchers from selling their souls and their secrets in the worldwide mass-destruction marketplace. Yet another silent struggle on the darkling plain of the war against terrorism, a war without victory or boundary or end.

None of which explained why some CROM operative was out there electronically impersonating consultants. But Knox thought he knew how to find out.

"Mycroft, great job. You really outdid yourself."

"My pleasure." Mycroft beamed back from the small face-to-face frame in the corner of the widescreen. "Will that be all, Jonathan?"

"Not quite." Knox hesitated. Normally, he'd have known better than to ask at all, but not this time. "When were you going to tell me how to find this CROM outfit's back door?"

"Back door? Jonathan, let me assure you—"

"Never bullshit a bullshitter, Mycroft. You didn't just cobble that presentation together on the spur of the moment. Every frame in the deck carried a DOE watermark."

"Um, yes, well, I was hoping you wouldn't notice that, actually. Those electronic signets are the very devil to remove without degrading the image itself. And given the time constraints—"

"Save it. Where'd you get it?"

"Are you sure you want to know this, Jonathan? Plausible deniability, after all."

"It's hereby waived. Just tell me how to follow the breadcrumbs, I'll take it from there."

Mycroft blinked but said nothing.

"I don't think you understand. I *need* to get into that site!"

"Want to hold it down a little, Jon? People are trying to sleep." This time the voice came not from the videoconferencing window, but from the corridor outside his office.

"Huh?" Knox looked up to see Richard Moses hulking in his doorway. "Oh, hi, Richard."

Most mornings, the Archon CEO's round, pleasantly plain face could be counted on to be wearing a puckish grin. That helped counter the initial impression conveyed by the crewcut, broken nose, blocky torso, and ham fists. Richard didn't really fit the somatype for a systems analyst; without the grin he looked more like a prizefighter gone to seed.

The grin wasn't there today. Richard kept his expression carefully neutral as he glanced back into the corridor and said, "He's right in here, Ms. Bonaventure. I'm sure Jon didn't mean to keep you waiting so long."

Knox sighed. "Richard, I'm right in the middle of something."

"Kill it." Richard drew an index finger across his throat. "Big client here to see you."

Back to work then. Knox turned back to Mycroft. "We'll pick this up later."

Mycroft frowned. "If we must. In the meantime, the primary site lists some external links that might merit a follow-up, once I break the encryption."

"Whatever, just so long as you tell me how to track down my email spoofer." Knox terminated the session and said to himself, "*God*, do I want to nail the bastard that pulled that stunt!"

Knox turned to face Richard again. He wasn't there. Instead, a young woman stood in the doorway. The same young woman last seen cooling her heels out at the reception desk.

Now that he could see her in the flesh, Knox revised his initial estimate. She was not striking; she was drop-dead gorgeous. A goddess in business casuals. Tall—at least five foot eight—with a figure more lithe than voluptuous…almost catlike. A mane of glossy dark hair framed the finely-chiseled features of her pale face: dark eyes, a straight, slightly upturned nose, and that mouth! A swelling red bow beneath, complemented above by a perfectly sculpted, slightly everted upper lip. A small moist highlight shimmered on that exquisite lipline.

And, behind those dark brown eyes. Something of an edge there. What would that be about?

"Mr. Knox? Marianna Bonaventure." When she spoke her name in that husky voice it was a poem. She held out her right hand and flashed an ID in her left—a holographic picture ID with the initials *CROM* emblazoned across the top.

There was the merest hint of a smile tugging at the corners of Marianna Bonaventure's perfect lips. "I've got a feeling I'm that bastard you wanted to nail."

✳

The goddess drove as if possessed by a divine madness. As if the New Jersey Turnpike had been designated her own personal Indy 500 for the duration of this Wednesday afternoon.

Knox had a pet theory that some people became cops just so they could do the things cops put other people in jail for doing. Marianna Bonaventure might not be a cop, not exactly. But she seemed to take the same characteristic delight in crossing over the line, in throwing her weight around in ways that would have had a mere civilian up on charges.

As she had done back at Archon. In short order, Knox had found himself conscripted, requisitioned, whatever the fuck the bureaucratic term was for it. And Richard, that wuss, had gone along with nary a peep of protest.

"Good of the firm, Jon," he'd said. "Don't want to go eyeball-to-eyeball with the feds here, Jon," and, "This'll get us on DoD's preferred-vendor list for sure, Jon." Not for the first time Knox was reminded that Richard Moses looked on him, along with the rest of the consulting staff, not as personnel, but as product. And CROM had anted up the sticker price.

Now, a scant three hours later, Knox was motoring through the Turnpike's lunar landscape toward Newark Airport, a new assignment, and an uncertain destiny, with a madwoman at the wheel and no clue as to what he was supposed to *do!*

Not that the last part was so unusual. Over the past fifteen years, Knox had grown used to the rush of inferential uncertainty—"Why this? Why me?"—that inaugurated every new client relationship.

One thing seemed certain: if all this "CROM" wanted was another lifer specialist, they'd have hired one. Instead, they'd opted to pay top dollar for a generalist, a card-carrying member of corporate America's homeless elite. There had to be a reason.

A reason that doubtless had to do with a little matter of identity theft.

Knox turned to Archon's new "big client," if that's what she was, and gave it one last try. "I don't suppose you'd consider telling me what you were doing screwing around with my email the past couple days?"

She made a face which on a mere mortal might have passed for a pout. Gauging how much to tell him, no doubt. Then she sighed, and, without taking her eyes from the road, began rummaging through her carrybag.

She pulled out a photo and handed it to him. "Do you know this person?"

A careworn blonde in a washed-out summer dress peered blankly out at him, nondescript cityscape wavering in the heat behind her.

"Who's she supposed to be?"

"Interesting turn of phrase," the client said. "She's *supposed* to be Galina Mikhailovna Postrel'nikova."

Try as he might, Knox couldn't map the image of this tired, middle-aged woman onto the vibrant girl he had known so long ago. The shot was blurred by the speed of the drive-by vehicle, but—could that be Galya? Had two decades of Soviet and post-Soviet privation so leeched the spirit out of what had once been a vivacious eighteen-year-old *Wunderkind*? Only a year or two separates a *devushka* from a *babushka*—a girl from a grandmother—as the saying goes. Still and all...

He frowned and tried to jog memories from half a lifetime ago. The first time he had seen Galina Mikhailovna Postrel'nikova— Galya, for short—she had been standing on the escalator of the Okty-abrskaya Metro station, comforting a frightened child.

...A child Knox had borrowed for the day.

Stevie Schumacher was four years old and cute as a button. Perfect for purposes of storming the bureaucratic barricades.

And three weeks into his year as a *stazhyor*, or exchange student, at Moscow State University, Jonathan Knox had just about had his fill of those barricades. Soviet officials were grand masters of red tape and procrastination, and those in the university Registrar's Office were no exception. Their whole purpose in life seemed to lie in devising new roadblocks to Knox's proposed program of archival research.

But the bureaucracy had a soft underbelly, and Knox had tumbled to it. Like most Soviets, its functionaries were suckers for little kids.

Knox was never quite sure why Soviet society, not otherwise renowned for its humanitarian proclivities, was so universally child-friendly. The political theorist in him guessed it had something to do with the regime's concept of the child as ideal citizen: dependent, obedient, infinitely malleable. His sociologist side saw it rather as a carry-over from the extended parenting endemic to Russian village life.

Whatever the reason, Knox saw an opening and dove for it. Gary and Anne Schumacher were pleased, if somewhat nonplussed, by the offer of free babysitting from a friend and fellow *stazhyor*. They never realized they could have charged Knox by the hour for the privilege.

Because bringing Stevie along on his rounds worked like a charm. Hardened Soviet timeservers softened and melted when Knox showed up with the tyke in tow. Small cellophane-wrapped hard candies magically materialized out of vest pockets and desk drawers. More to the purpose, administrative obstacles impeding Knox's access to *TsGAOR*, the Central Archive of the October Revolution, vanished just as miraculously.

All of which left Knox, his paper-chase completed in the record time of seven hours, with only the one last chore of delivering Stevie to his father at the Lenin Library in central Moscow. Since the bureaucratic scavenger hunt had led far out on the Sadovaya ring road, their best route back to town lay via the Metro station in nearby Okty-abrskaya Square.

Rush hour was still ten minutes away when Knox and Stevie walked through the double doors into the station's mezzanine, but a line had already formed in front of the ticket-checker. Knox gave the hall's ornate vermilion-and-white marble appointments only a cursory glance: once you'd seen one People's Palace, you'd seen them all. His attention was directed dead ahead, at the escalators. He'd been through Oktyabrskaya once before.

"We ride the train to Daddy now, Uncle Jon?" Stevie tugged on Knox's hand. Knox wasn't sure what accounted for all the enthusiasm—seeing Daddy or riding the train.

He chose the likelier of the two. "Yes, Stevie, we're going to ride the train."

"Goodie!" Stevie began jumping up and down.

He kept on jumping all the time they stood on the line. The abnormally slow-moving line. The ticket-checker, seventy years old if he was a day, was being a prick, officiously checking for anyone who'd forgotten to renew their monthly Metro pass now that September had started. A glance at the lengthening queue in front of the ticket booth made Knox glad he'd remembered.

"Stay with me now, Stevie." Knox retightened his grip on his still-hopping charge. Lord knew, even a grown man could find a trip down the Oktyabrskaya escalator somewhat, well, daunting.

At more than three stories below street level, the Oktyabrskaya stop was one of the deepest stations on Moscow's old Southwest line—sunk so far underground that workmen had died of the bends building it back in the 1930s. The depth was deliberate: in the pre-atomic era it had still been possible to hope that a metropolitan population might survive aerial bombardment, given enough air-raid shelters. And that's what Moscow's subway system was—a network of enormous air-raid shelters masquerading as rapid transit.

The escalators were the giveaway. They could all be re-geared at a moment's notice to run in one direction: straight down. The shafts the escalators plunged through were pitched at a dizzyingly angle to the vertical. And they all ran at *extremely* high speed. Conveyor belts, in other words, to shunt as many Muscovites as possible into the safety of the Metro's subterranean caverns if and when the sky rained death.

In peacetime, it still made for a scary high-velocity ride, like stepping off the edge of a cliff and plummeting down, down into the bowels of the earth. Even veteran straphangers sometimes blanched at the brink of the Oktyabrskaya escalator. And this was going to be Stevie Schumacher's first time.

Preoccupied by what lay ahead, Knox paid scant attention when it finally came time to flash his pass at the wizened blue-capped checker. He and Stevie were halfway to the escalator when an outraged croak came from behind. Knox felt the pluck of arthritic fingers at his sleeve and turned to find himself face to face with the ticket-checker again.

The old man was mouthing a stream of rapid-fire, spittle-punctuated Russian at him. Something about his ticket.

Hadn't the geezer seen it? Knox retrieved the little cardboard booklet that held the monthly transit pass and flipped it open again. This only incensed the old man further. Glancing down, Knox saw why: the pass he held was for August. He must have forgotten to swap it out when he bought the new one yesterday. Did he have the September pass on him? He patted down his pockets distractedly. Where he could have left the damn thing?

Three stories below, the 4:54 screeched to a halt at the platform.

"Train!" Stevie cried out joyously. Suddenly his little hand had wriggled free from Knox's grasp and he was gone.

Knox watched in stunned disbelief as Stevie dodged between legs on a beeline for the shaft. His paralysis lasted only an instant. Then he shoved the ticket-checker out of the way and took off in hot pursuit. A whistle blasted behind him, not half so shrill as the little boy's first screams. Stevie was on the escalator!

"Stevie!" he yelled. He couldn't make out Stevie's small form in the crowd, but he could tell from the shrieks echoing up the shaft that the child was already some distance down and moving away rapidly. If he should fall on the racing stair...

"Stevie, hang onto the rail!"

Knox elbowed through the line and flung himself onto the crowded escalator. Now he could see Stevie as well as hear him, maybe halfway down the long shaft, still screaming at the top of his lungs. And he could see something else as well.

From the platform far below a young woman in a jeans jacket, hardly more than a girl herself, had run onto the down escalator. Pushing and shoving through the homeward-bound commuters, ignoring their oaths and imprecations, she was working her way up against the tide.

She reached the terrified child, scooped him up in her arms and hugged him tight.

Stevie flung his arms around her neck and collapsed with a sob. Together the two rode the rest of the way down to the safety of the platform below.

To Knox, still shaking with reaction, the sight bordered on the beatific. With her backlit honey-blond hair, the glowing serenity of her face contrasting with the concern in her emerald eyes, the young woman seemed an icon of the Madonna come to life there in the depths of the Moscow Metro.

Galina, the way Knox had first seen her, the way he would always remember her: Galya, holding a child.

✳

Marianna took her eyes off the rear end of the minivan she was tailgating just long enough to check on her latest acquisition, her resource and last resort. No change; Jon Knox was still sitting there in the Viper's passenger seat, not moving a hair, not saying a word. Other than the occasional sharp intake of breath in response to one of her road-warrior maneuvers, she hadn't heard a sound out of him since she'd handed him the picture of Postrel'nikova maybe five minutes ago. He'd spent all that time just sitting there, gazing at the image with preternatural intensity.

That gaze, she'd learned, could look right through you. The hooded gray eyes lent an air of uncanniness to an otherwise presentable enough face.

More than presentable. Pretty good-looking actually, in an older-guy kind of way. A nice smile, a kind smile, the little she'd seen of it; he'd been sort of grim since she'd acquired him. He looked fit enough, too, considering he spent his days behind a desk. Oh, and those socks didn't really go with his slacks. Most likely hetero, then: the straight guys she knew *all* seemed to dress in the dark.

"You okay?" she said.

"Hmm? Yeah. Or I will be if you'll keep your eyes on the road!" he added in a tight voice.

Marianna swerved to avoid the eighteen-wheeler. "You got so pensive there."

"I guess. It's just I'm having a real problem figuring out why Galina, of all people, should have shown up on CROM's radarscope."

"I'm really not at liberty to discuss—" Marianna began, but the Archon resource wasn't listening.

"Lord knows she's smart enough," he went on, half to himself, "Brilliant, even. But all her research was in MHD, magnetohydrodynamics:

stellar magnetospheres, fusion power generation, that sort of thing. Nothing with a military application. Nothing that could hurt people...

"...Nothing that could hurt children."

He wasn't staring at the picture any more. He was staring at her, as if trying to read an explanation in her face.

"So, I guess I've been sitting here," he said quietly, "trying to figure out how just about the kindest, most loving person I ever met could have become the target of a counterterrorist witchhunt."

"Counterterrorist?" This was getting too close for comfort. "What gave you the idea—"

"Counter-proliferation, then," he cut her off, his voice not so quiet now. "Whatever you call it, it's insane. Ask anyone who knows her: Galina would die before she'd sell blacklisted technology to the monsters. And there just isn't any other way she could've wound up in Reacquisition's crosshairs, now is there?"

Marianna swallowed. He wasn't supposed to know any of that. None of it yet, and some of it never. What *was* it about this case? Each time she started getting it back on track, it blindsided her from a new direction. Now even the Archon option was spinning out of control on her.

"You *are* Reacquisition, aren't you?" he asked. "Not Interdiction?"

"If I was Interdiction," she snapped, "we wouldn't be having this conversation!"

"That's something, anyway." He sounded as if he understood what turning the case over to Interdiction would mean: don't make any long-range plans—like, for the weekend.

"So," he continued, "that would make you one of Aristos's direct-reports. His second-in-command, maybe?"

"Listen, I don't know how you came up with this stuff, but it *had* to involve violating the National Defense Security Act seven ways from Sunday."

"Actually, you handed me that one yourself, when you had your daemon forwarding email to *reack-2*. And while we're on the subject of culpability..." He showed her his smile again; it didn't look so kind now. "You'd best be packing a warrant or two. You could be looking at maybe five counts of wiretapping and mail fraud, not to mention as-sorted breakings and enterings. Uh, back in lane, please."

She crossed back over the white line in *plenty* of time to keep the frantically honking semi from rear-ending them.

Look on the bright side, Marianna told herself as she nosed out a BMW to make the Newark Airport exit: the Archon resource was definitely living up to his advance billing. Maybe what Pete persisted in calling her crazy scheme had a shot at working after all.

5 | Interview with the Shaman

"I**T'S STILL IN** there." Dr. Jack Adler repeated his mantra over and over as he trudged up the spine of the Silgami Ridge. "I know it's still in there."

"You spoke, Professor Adler?" his hiking companion asked in accented English.

"Just talking to myself." Jack glanced over at Dieter Hoffman, Professor of Ethnography at Hamburg University and the expedition's resident Siberian folklorist, trying to gauge whether the older man might be ready for a rest break. With his wrinkled cheeks and snow-white beard, the lean, ascetic German looked to be well into his sixties, yet so far he'd hardly broken a sweat. If anything, Hoffman's eagerness for the climb only seemed to increase the closer they approached the summit, and their goal.

Jack sighed and went back to metering out shallow breaths, his unwelcome doubts beating in time to each one of them.

Hell, it's *got* to be in there. But—

But can I *prove* it?

Jack got that sinking feeling again. His one chance of confirming the Jackson-Ryan hypothesis rested with the Superconducting Quantum Interference Device he'd lugged halfway round the world with him. And the SQUID was malfunctioning. He should be back at base camp right now, nursing his sick machine, instead of trekking through the taiga en route to some improbable meeting.

An impossible meeting, if you took everyone else's word for it—impossible to arrange, that is. The man he was going to see had not consented to speak with a Western scientist—indeed, any scientist—in twenty years or more. Still and all, the chance to speak with the last living eyewitness to the Tunguska catastrophe! So Jack had dutifully put in the request. He'd been more surprised than anyone when it was granted.

And now here he was, against all odds, puffing and wheezing his way to an interview with—

"What's this old guy supposed to be again, Professor Hoffman? Some kind of witch doctor?"

That stopped Hoffman in mid-stride. He turned and looked down his long, thin nose at Jack—no mean trick, seeing as Jack had three inches on him, easy.

Finally the older man said, "I believe the term you are groping for is 'shaman.'"

"Same difference, right?"

"Ah, well, if I may be frank, 'witch doctors' exist only in the overheated imaginations of your Hollywood screenwriters. A shaman, on the other hand, is a holy man—a practitioner of mankind's oldest religious tradition. He is a bridge between the Middle World of men and the Upper and Lower Worlds of the spirits. In short, he is the tribe's authority on, and emissary to, the wider cosmos."

"Sort of a primitive cosmologist, huh?"

"'Primitive' is hardly a scientific designation," Hoffman said, a hint of frost in his voice.

Jack sighed. Seemed he couldn't say word one without rubbing Hoffman the wrong way. And he needed the prickly little Prussian: no one else on the expedition was fluent in the Evenki language.

"In fact," Hoffman was still talking, "shamanism has as good a claim to modernity as, say, Christianity. It is still practiced throughout the world, in your own Wild West no less than here in Siberia. Though here, of course, is where the term itself originated."

"How's that?"

"*Shaman* is in fact an Evenki word, transmitted to Western scholarship via the early Russian anthropologists. Its root meaning is 'the one who knows.'"

"Knows what?" Jack asked.

Hoffman's lips quirked. "That, my dear Professor, is what we are here to find out."

✳

It took three rings before Jonathan Knox opened an eye on the unfamiliar dark of the Reston Hyatt hotel room. Triangulating on the noise and on the ghostly glow of the incoming-call display, he managed to snag his Treo handheld from its charger cradle on the third try. He thumbed the unit into cellphone mode.

"Hello?"

"Good evening, Jonathan."

Evening? According to the handheld, it was a hair past three A.M.

"Mycroft? I thought you'd be calling closer to, uh…" Closer to what? Six-thirty? Seven? Mycroft would've long since turned in by any civilized callback hour. Still, Knox supposed he should consider himself lucky the old night owl had bent the rules even this much, agreeing to lift Weathertop's ironclad late-night communications curfew, just this once. An honor of sorts.

Knox didn't feel honored, just groggy. He shook his head to clear it, flicked on the nightstand lamp, and tried again. "Is it done?"

"Already in your inbox, assuming you've got your email set to auto-fetch."

"Let me check." Knox switched the display to Snappermail and scrolled down the message list looking for Mycroft's return address. "Okay, looks like it's here. What now?"

"If you'll transfer the attachment to your memory card, I can talk you through installation and testing."

It took ten more minutes, and two false starts, before Mycroft finally pronounced himself satisfied.

"Thanks, Mycroft," Knox said. "Nice piece of work. Any problems getting it coded up?"

"None at all, other than timeframe. Why the rush, if I might ask?"

"I've got a meeting first thing in the morning. Could turn adversarial. *Will* turn adversarial, if the past is prologue. I couldn't see going in totally naked."

"The best defense, eh, Jonathan? Well, I'll be here and standing by, should you need me."

"I appreciate that, Mycroft. But I'm really hoping I won't."

✳

The view from the top of Silgami Ridge was almost worth the climb. From up here, Jack could see the whole of the Cauldron, as the early explorers had christened the valley of the Impact. What must this vast basin have looked like when Leonid Kulik first glimpsed it in 1927, before scrub pine and larch had scabbed over the scars on the land, obscuring the treefall pattern that radiated out to the horizon? Even now there was an eerie foreboding about the place.

Which made it all the harder to understand why anyone, holy man or not, would have chosen to live here. To live within sight of the disaster that had nearly claimed his life.

Yet that was what the man he'd come to see had done. Jack abandoned the vista, turned to look at the small encampment set back against the scraggly treeline. Just a cluster of huts dominated by a central *choum*.

That *choum* was an outsized, all-weather edition of Jack's own birchbark tepee back at base camp. With one curious extra. As Jack walked up to the dwelling, Hoffman was staring at the strange structure jutting out of its roof: a thin vertical pole with a rectangular frame lashed to it. The whole ensemble had the look of some Neolithic TV antenna, if you discounted the animal hide stretched across its frame.

"Think he gets MTV on that?" Jack nodded at the contraption.

Hoffman shot him a disapproving glance before looking up again. "This is really quite unique," he said. "I have seen such charms, but only in old photographs, never before in real life."

"What's it for?"

"The deerskin is a sacrifice to appease the storm god Ogdy, in order that he not send his thunderwings against this house."

"Thunderwings?"

Hoffman shrugged. "Mythical birds. They are said to be the size of a grouse, but with bodies made of iron. In Evenki legend, they are the effectuators of the storm god's wrath, sent forth to rain destruction on the Middle World."

"As in the Tunguska Event?" Jack couldn't quite hide his smile.

"This must all seem foolish to a man of science such as yourself, Professor Adler. But you would do well not to show it now. We are about to enter the home of someone who believes in it unreservedly."

With that, Hoffman faced the *choum* and uttered a stream of liquid vowels interspersed with harsh consonants, presumably a greeting in the Evenki language.

It had no visible effect. A minute went by, two, then Hoffman tried again. This time, rustling movement could be heard within. One corner of the tent flap lifted. Jack caught an impression of a small, dark, oval face, high cheekbones, dark eyes peering out at them.

"That can't be our guy," Jack said. The rawhide-clad man—no, woman—now emerging on hands and knees from the *choum*'s interior couldn't be a day over forty. Any eyewitness to the Tunguska Event would have to be well over a hundred by now.

"No, no, of course not. Let me see." Hoffman spoke again in Evenki, and this time received a lengthy response.

"Her name is Akulina," he translated, "an apprentice to the shaman, and his eldest great-granddaughter. She rejoices at the coming of Eagle."

Eagle?

At Akulina's urging, Jack crouched and followed her into the *choum*, with Hoffman bringing up the rear.

It was refreshingly cool inside after the midday heat. Cool and dark. What little sunlight managed to sift in through overlapping layers of birchbark was all but absorbed by the heavy deerskin hangings lining the walls. Only a single bright shaft slanted down from the smokehole to strike the floor and scatter dim illumination throughout the interior.

As Jack's eyes adjusted to the half-light, he could see they were not alone. On a small rectangular rug in the center of the *choum* he could make out a kneeling figure, hunched over, head down.

"He awaits us on his *dehtur*." Hoffman's whisper came from behind Jack. "A good sign, a very good sign."

"His what?"

"A *dehtur* is a prayer rug — a consecrated mat of worked reindeer hide. Within its confines are joined the three Worlds of the Evenki cosmos. Its presence here signifies that our host means to speak of sacred mysteries. As does his ceremonial dress — look!"

The shaman wore a robe of fringed rawhide, metallic talismans dangling from its many tassels. As Jack watched, he lifted his head and inspected his visitors through the eyeholes of a leather mask shaped to resemble the head of a bear.

With his apprentice's help, the shaman slowly got to his feet and removed the bear's head. The face that emerged from beneath it was almost as brown and leathery as the mask itself. A strong, square face bearing the ravages of time and pain and age.

But what caught Jack's attention were the eyes. Dark, almost black, they fairly shone with secret wisdom. What had those eyes witnessed on that long-ago morning?

And why was their probing stare directed now at Jack himself, as though seeking something deep within his soul?

Abruptly, the man broke into a toothless grin. He raised an arm and spoke several quavering, breathless syllables for Hoffman's whispered translation.

"Eagle, be welcome among us. I am called Jenkoul."

✳

"What's all this 'Eagle' business?" Jack finally asked Hoffman. Because it hadn't stopped with that first mention. No, all through Jenkoul's preliminaries — blessing of the visitors, blessing of the occasion, blessing of the raggedy prayer rug, for godsakes — seemed like every third word out of the old guy's mouth was something to do with eagles, each time accompanied by a significant glance in Jack's direction. "You sure you're getting that translation right?"

Hoffman made a face like Jack had just told him his baby was ugly.

"Yes, of course," he said stiffly. "It is basic vocabulary, after all,"—big emphasis on the *basic*—"entirely unambiguous."

"And he's definitely talking about me."

Hoffman chuckled unexpectedly. "Consider it a token of esteem, my dear Professor. Perhaps he takes you for a fellow shaman."

"He's not alone. There's any number of my so-called colleagues who'd agree with him."

"Shh," Hoffman said, and pointed. Clutching Akulina's arm for support, Jenkoul had risen from his prayer rug and was easing himself down onto a hummock of hide and fur piled opposite the *choum*'s entrance. From there, half reclining, the old shaman regarded his guests brightly and invited them to seat themselves. Following Jenkoul's lead, Jack settled back too.

With the opening ceremonies out of the way, it was finally time for the main event.

✦

"The sun of high summer rises early over the valley of the Stony Tunguska, but on that fateful morning I arose with it, for I had far to ride."

Jack leaned forward, watching Jenkoul's face, listening to his soft, breathy intonations alternating with the Teutonic precision of Hoffman's English translation. This was what he'd come for: the old man's firsthand account of the Event itself.

"I had journeyed into the heartlands many times before, Eagle, and always before my heart had rejoiced at their beauty. But on this day my heart was filled with dread. Were it not for my father's wish that I lead the southern herd to fresh pasture, I would never have ventured there. Not on that day. I was in mortal fear of the curse, you see."

Jack nodded, still waiting for Jenkoul to get to the good stuff. As far as cosmology was concerned, that did not include curses. Hoffman, on the other hand, seemed to be lapping this part up. He said something in Evenki that could have been a request for more detail. Leastways, Jenkoul gave them some.

"The curse of Ogdy, revealed at the solstice ceremonial. Revealed to Pilya, shaman of our clan, as he walked the spirit road for the last time."

Jenkoul shook his head. "Pilya. There are none like him today. Even in those days there were few who could peer beneath the skin of the world and behold its beating heart, as he could. And fewer still willing to give their lives to know the true way of things.

"He died, you see." Jenkoul sighed as if it had all happened yesterday, rather than nearly a century ago. "He gave warning of the storm god's coming and he died. The vision killed him, the horror of it stopping his heart." He sighed again and stared into the distance, at things only he could see.

Hoffman took advantage of the pause to lean over and whisper, "Not the vision. It was almost certainly the mushrooms that killed him."

"What mushrooms?" Jack whispered back.

"*Amanita Muscaria*, fly agaric—the Hindus call it Soma. The flesh is hallucinogenic, used by many cultures throughout the world to bring about a trance state. It is, however, also poisonous—not fatal in small amounts, but a large enough dosage could induce cardiac arrest."

Hoffman broke off then. Jenkoul was resuming his tale. "So you see, Eagle, I had reason to fear the heartlands. Still, what son would deny his father? So, early that morning I mounted my reindeer Onikan and set forth—"

"Hold on," Jack said. "He's seriously saying 'reindeer'? As in Rudolph?"

It took Hoffman a moment to get the reference. "Ah, your Santa Claus myth. Yes, Professor, reindeer as in Rudolph—the Evenkis ride them."

"Little low to the ground for that, aren't they?"

Hoffman ignored him and went back to translating. "The going was slow until we reached the Silgami ridge. There the rocky soil offered better purchase for Onikan's hooves. And with no underbrush to impede us—for only mushrooms and mosses grow well in the half-light that filters down through the treetops—it now seemed I would reach the southern herd at Churgim Creek by noon. For the first time that morning, I began to hope that I might complete my journey safe from harm, after all.

"Then, without warning, a shadow reared up before us. Onikan jerked to a halt, nearly pitching me over his antlers. At first I could not make out its true form; it seemed only a patch of deeper darkness against the forest gloom. Then it moved and revealed itself: a giant Siberian gray bear, twice my height and not ten strides away.

"Onikan stood trembling, eyes rolling, ready to bolt. I reached out a hand to soothe him, knowing that if the reindeer tried to run, the bear would be on us in an instant. It was only when my mount began to calm that I could spare a moment to regard the enormous beast before me, and ponder what to do.

"I was then only in my fifteenth summer, Eagle, but already I had learned much of the old ways, the wisdom of our people. And I knew that this lord of the forest must be paid the respect which was his due, the due of all his kind."

This last remark sparked a brief exchange between Jenkoul and his interpreter, all of it Greek, or rather Evenki, to Jack. When Hoffman spoke next, it was as a professor of ethnography, not a translator.

"Our friend here has touched upon an interesting point. The Siberian peoples, you see, hold very different attitudes toward the various predators that share their world. One, in particular, they have singled out for demonization, the one they regard as that worst, most malevolent of animals, the one they call the 'beast of evil heart'—the hated and reviled wolf."

"Hey," Jack said, "I happen to *like* wolves."

"Perhaps you would feel less sentimental, Professor, if forced to compete with them for pride of place at the top of the food chain." Hoffman held up a hand to forestall further protest. "In any case, I do not condone the opinion, I merely report it. And that only by way of contrast to the folklore surrounding the bear. Evenkis view the bear, you see, as almost a benign creature, one that seldom attacks without provocation and never kills without cause. Indeed, from his manlike mannerisms, upright stance, and manifest intelligence there stems a belief that the bear possesses something akin to a human soul. So strong is this imputed affinity that Evenkis have been known to address bears using terms otherwise reserved for kinfolk. Which is, in fact, what our friend Jenkoul had begun saying a moment ago."

Hoffman then turned for a brief exchange with the shaman, following which the story recommenced. "I faced the bear, speaking slowly and in deferential tones. 'Grandfather,' I said, 'let there be peace between us. Do not bar my way.'

"The Siberian gray shifted his stance, but made no other reply. I saw then I might have no choice but to kill him. I unsheathed my firearm and took aim at an eye. Hit him there and he might die before he could reach me. My finger was tightening on the trigger when something in the bear's manner gave me pause. He stood there, head to one side, as if waiting for ... for recognition, perhaps?

"The rifle trembled in my hands, as I realized what, or who, confronted me on that shadowed hillside. This was no ordinary bear at all. It was — 'Bynaku?' Sure enough, the ears pricked up at the sound of his true name. This was none other than an avatar of Lord Bynaku, Ruler of the Lower World.

"The spirit-bear drew himself up to his full height. He sniffed the air and took a step forward, waving his huge paws. I heard him speak then, growling *'Mot! Mot!'* — the words we Evenkis use to goad a reindeer into a gallop. The Lord of the Lower World was warning me back the way I had come. But why?

"My Churgim Creek encampment beckoned, its *choum* offering relief from the noonday heat, but.... but only the foolhardy ignore the counsel of a god.

"I bowed low, then steered Onikan around on the narrow path with the pressure of my knees. I twisted in my saddle for a last look back, but the Siberian gray was nowhere to be seen. In the place where the spirit-bear had stood, a single beam of early morning sunlight fell upon the mossy forest floor.

"What danger could threaten in this sacred place? Ogdy's curse? The heavens gave no sign of the storm god's displeasure. And yet I was suddenly filled with nameless foreboding.

"I could not desecrate the earthly abode of Bynaku with a shout. Instead, I bent forward and pressed my lips to Onikan's ear. *'Mot! Mot!'* I whispered.

"And we began to run."

✳

The story went on from there, of course. On to a flash of bright blue light, to peals of thunder, blasts of heat, miles of forest laid waste, etc. Far as Jack was concerned, it was all pretty much same old, same old. Nothing that hadn't been reported a hundred times before, and by observers in a better position to actually see the event. By his own admission, Jenkoul had been racing *away* from the Epicenter at the moment of the impact, after all.

Jenkoul must have read the disappointment on Jack's face. He pursed his lips. "In days long past, there were many who could have told you such things as I have spoken of, such things and more. They have all since departed on their journeys up the River of the Dead." The old man shook his head. "Still, they left behind record of what was known to them, that others might know it too."

Jenkoul levered himself up to a sitting position then, the better to fix Jack with another of his penetrating stares. "But what I would tell you now, Eagle, is known to me alone."

And, with that, the old man had launched into the most harrowing tale of all. Yet, despite the gruesomeness of the events and the pain Jenkoul was plainly experiencing on reliving them Jack could hardly keep from grinning ear to ear. For here it was: a gold mine of corroboration for his hypothesis. He was right, after all. Had to be. No other explanation could fit the facts.

The facts — was he getting them all? He quick checked his digital recorder, then sighed in relief. The indicator lights showed it still recording, still capturing this amazing story for posterity.

Finally Jenkoul was done. Jack waited to see if he had anything more to offer. But no, he had leaned back into the pile of furs again and closed his eyes, resting from his exertions.

Or not. Jenkoul's eyes opened again to narrow slits. "Eagle," he said, "it is fitting that you should know your own part in this. As I have told you my fate, so I will tell you yours. You have only to ask."

Jack hesitated, unsure what to make of this. Before he could decide, Hoffman intruded on the silence with a response. Presumably in the affirmative, since Jenkoul began to speak again.

"It was at the solstice festival five summers ago. For one last time I tasted the sacred mushrooms and walked in spirit the crooked path to the Lower World. There, I was met by One who had guided my footsteps all unseen since days of my youth, yet who only now revealed himself to me once again: Lord Bynaku."

Right, the old guy's familiar, or whatever—the spirit bear who'd supposedly saved him from the impact.

"We talked through all the space of a fleeting summer night," Jenkoul went on, "And in that time beyond time, Bynaku showed me many mysteries. But the last was greatest of all. For he showed me how, in the final days of the Middle World, he, Bynaku, would send forth Eagle, lord of the winds, wisest of creatures, to find the lair of Ogdy's all-devouring Wolf.

"I am old," Jenkoul said. "My spirit readies itself for its final journey on the River of the Dead. But before I die, I longed to look upon Bynaku's Eagle. Eagle, who will confront Ogdy's Wolf, not with might, but with wisdom."

Jenkoul struggled to sit up and look Jack once more in the eye. "And now, Eagle," he whispered, "You have come."

✳

Jack was still trying to think how to respond when he felt Hoffman's tap on his shoulder. "Professor Adler? It grows late. We must rejoin the group."

Jack glanced at his watch: after five already. Where had the time gone? But Hoffman was right: factor in the hour or so it would take them to get down to the rendezvous point, and they'd just make it before the Land Rover left for base camp.

Leavetaking was quick and painless. Until the last, that is, when the old shaman laid a palsied hand on Jack's arm and said, "Go forth, Eagle, find the Wolf. Stop Ogdy's evil before it can devour the world of men."

"I—I'll try." What else could he say? The look in the old man's eyes was so desperate.

Outside Akulina was preparing the evening meal over a bed of coals. Jack waved her a good-bye and waited for Hoffman to join him.

"Ready to go?" Jack said, then, "Anything wrong?"

Hoffman's face held a curious mix of emotions, chagrin dominant. "I am afraid you have wasted your time, and mine, Professor Adler."

"What makes you say that?"

"Well, that last part was complete and utter rubbish! And casts doubt on all the rest." Hoffman's face showed red against his white beard. "Prophesying the end of the Middle World, as if shamanism were a chiliastic religion, like Christianity. There is nothing, nothing whatsoever in the Evenki oral tradition to hint of such a Manichean battle between powers of light and darkness, nor of Eagle and Wolf as those powers' surrogates. From the point of view of ethnology, I fear all this material is worthless."

"Worthless? What about the vigil in the Great Swamp, the encounter with—"

"Oh, please, Professor Adler, do not pretend you lend any credence to *that* account. Why, the whole thing was obviously nothing more than a mushroom-induced hallucination."

"Actually, that account may have furnished a key to the Tunguska mystery itself."

"Clearly delusional," Hoffman said. The way he was looking at Jack made it unclear whom he was referring to.

"No, really, I'm serious."

"Of course you are. Next, you will claim that you are in fact this Eagle savior-figure sent from Bynaku to confront Ogdy's Wolf."

"I'll admit, I don't get that stuff about the Eagle. What's it supposed to mean? That I'm an American, maybe? Eagle's the symbol of America, after all. But, still, I can't be the first American the guy's ever seen."

"And yet you are so typical an American," Hoffman said around a sneer. "You trouble to master no language but your own. Not even to learn the meaning of your own name."

Jack said nothing, just looked at the German ethnographer.

"Your name—Adler," Hoffman said.

"What about it?"

"It is the German word for Eagle."

6 | Our Ship Comes In

AFTER AN EARLY breakfast topped off with two hours of what the client euphemistically referred to as "check-in"—a battery of security probes stopping just this side of a full body-cavity search—Knox was ushered into the august presence of Euripedes "Pete" Aristos, Director, Reacquisition Working Group, DOE Critical Resources Oversight Mandate.

Aristos turned out to be a heavyset, balding, shirtsleeves type, whose taste in office décor ran to Greenbar Baroque: he'd had his headquarters suite furnished almost exclusively in randomly situated piles of computer printout.

The man himself was talking on a headset and worrying with a lightpen at a high-definition display that took up most of the rear wall. Right now, that datawall was showing a channel map of the Chesapeake Bay spangled with blinking points of light done in tasteful shades of fire-engine red. Aristos was playing connect-the-dots with the lightpen in synch with whatever the headset was telling him. Without turning, he waved his visitors toward chairs stacked with the ubiquitous printouts. Marianna unceremoniously dumped the contents of her chair on the floor, and motioned Knox to follow suit.

"I keep telling him it's the paperless Third Millennium—wake up and save the trees," Marianna whispered, leaning toward Knox conspiratorially. She was making an effort to be friendly this morning. "But Pete's old school," she went on. "He'd rather live with this clutter than try to assimilate textual information from a vertical surface."

"He could get a thinline display," Knox said. "Pricey, but it would lie flat on his desk."

"Don't think I haven't tried," she began, then broke off when her boss turned to face them.

"Knox? Pete Aristos." Aristos held out a beefy hand. "Marianna take care of you? Get you a coffee?"

"I'm fine, thanks."

"Okay." Aristos slipped off the headset and settled into his chair. "Everything you're about to see and hear comes under the Homeland Security boilerplate you just—" He paused to cock a quizzical eyebrow at Marianna, who nodded. "—you just signed. Nothing leaves this room, got me?"

"Check."

"Marianna, do your thing." Aristos handed her the lightpen. He rolled his chair to one side and beat a brief tattoo on the detachable keyboard resting in his lap.

Marianna rose and walked behind the big desk. In response to Aristos's keystrokes, the map of Chesapeake Bay covering the rear wall gave way to the seal of the United States Department of Energy, hovering over a Day-Glo-on-midnight Top Secret banner.

"We're under some time pressure here," Marianna began, "so I'll skip through the intro pretty quick." If she knew or suspected that Knox had already seen most of it, she wasn't letting on.

"As you may have already gathered, Jon, the Mandate is a branch of the Energy Department, attached to DOE's National Nuclear Security Administration. But it also dotted-line reports to Homeland Security…and, of course, those field agencies with operational responsibilities."

The datawall now showed an organization chart. On it all roads led to CROM, including some originating from agencies with household three-letter acronyms.

"CROM was created back in the mid-nineties as a DOE carve-out from the Nunn-Lugar Cooperative Threat Reduction program," Marianna continued what sounded like a well-practiced pitch. "But, whereas CTR proper focused on the material aspects—working with the Russians to decommission weapons production facilities and secure or destroy fissionables—CROM was tasked with what NSA General Counsel Elizabeth Rindskopf had called 'the human dimension of non-proliferation.'"

Marianna was prowling back and forth in front of the datawall. Her feline movements held far more fascination than her lecture material, most of which Knox knew already.

"When the Soviet Union formally ceased to exist on December 21st, 1991," she was saying, "the military-industrial complex it left behind was the second largest in the world capacity-wise, and *the* largest in terms of population. The nuclear weapons program alone employed over a million workers, housed in ten secret cities. Not shown on any map, known but to God, the USSR Ministry of Defense, and the CIA. Just one of these cities stored more weapons-grade plutonium than the stockpiles of France, Great Britain, and the People's Republic of China put together."

With a pass of the lightpen, CROM's org chart yielded to a polar projection of the former USSR, ten red stars all a-twinkle. "More to our point, this 'nuclear archipelago' was home to some ninety thousand weapons scientists and engineers. While chemical and biological warfare never achieved quite this level of urban planning, adding in their staffs would increase those numbers by fifty to sixty percent. Over half of them now living below any Third World poverty line you'd care to draw."

Marianna took a breath, then continued. "Enter the Initiative for Proliferation Prevention, IPP for short. Overshoes and kerosene space-heaters to keep guards at their posts. Food stamps for physicists. Urban renewal in Sarov, Snezhinsk, Zheleznogorsk, all the secret cities. Anything to keep Russia's weapons experts from selling their services to the rogue nations of the world. Quite simply, that's us. CROM *is* the Initiative for Proliferation Prevention. Among other things."

The box labeled "CROM" was back, now sporting a smaller IPP rectangle inside it. "The intent back in '94 was just to provide administrative support for the Initiative. Didn't turn out that way. There's more to the 'human dimension of non-proliferation' than food-stamps and workfare. If you think it's hard repurposing a neurotoxin or a thermonuclear device, try retraining the scientists who created them. Even now, IPP has moved less than ten percent of the target population out of WMD research and into the civilian economy. Meanwhile things just keep on getting worse for the ones left behind."

Behind her, the datawall filled with stills and clips of soup kitchens in Tomsk-7, picket lines in front of the Arzamas-16 weapons lab, hunger strikes at the Primorskii nuclear power plant, a march on the Ministry of Atomic Energy in Moscow to demand unpaid wages.

Aristos turned to look Knox in the eye. "Don't go getting all choked up there, Knox. These are the same guys that thought the Cold War was the glory days. You know what the other Ivans used to call them? The 'chocolate-eaters'!" He snorted. "Special shops and hospitals, trips abroad, exclusive resorts, first class all the way. Now that they're standing on the breadlines with everybody else, 'course they bitch and moan about it."

"Still, there's no denying that these resentments represent a very real danger," Marianna resumed smoothly, "when harbored by a population with marketable skills in mass destruction. By the turn of the century, disaffected scientists posed a greater proliferation threat than did the lax security on the materials they produced. Dozens of outlaw states, and more than a few well-heeled terrorist organizations, were offering top dollar for WMD expertise on the hoof."

Aristos added, "Bottom line, IPP alone wasn't getting the job done. Everybody knew it, nobody gave a shit."

Marianna seemed used to integrating her boss's interjections into her presentation. "That changed come nine-eleven."

September 11th, 2001 — the day everything had changed. As for the change in CROM, that was reflected in the org chart, where the IPP box had now been joined by one labeled Compliance.

"Don't be misled by the name. Compliance's main responsibility is to monitor the movements and activities of the twenty thousand or so individuals in Russia, the CIS, and elsewhere who pose the highest proliferation risk."

Now the wall was showing flyovers of multiprocessors in serried ranks, fisheyes of banks of workstations staffed by analysts in office casuals and headsets, lingering close-ups of room-filling climate-control and uninterruptible-power installations—all the paraphernalia of a large IT operation, served up to impress visiting Congress-critters and other dignitaries. Knox yawned.

"Satellite feed, communications intercept, media analysis, physical surveillance," Marianna narrated, "—it all flows into Compliance for cross-correlation and action recommendations."

"And," added Aristos, "as a sideline, they keep tabs on the KGB."

"It's not called that anymore, is it?" Knox said. "Don't you mean the, uh, FSB?"

"Don't I wish!" Aristos said. "Russia's Federal Security Service is working *with* us on this. No, I mean the good old Ka-Geh-fuckin'-Beh, pardon my French." He twitched a smile in Marianna's direction, then turned back to Knox. "See, not everybody made the cut when they transitioned to a kinder, gentler police state. Some balked. Others just plain weren't asked—Soviet-era excesses, that sort of thing."

"And, not being the sort to 'go gentle into that good night,'" Marianna added, "they've banded together into a so-called 'shadow KGB.' A cabal dedicated to restoring the dictatorship of the proletariat—and, not incidentally, their own privileged positions within it."

"But, Dylan Thomas aside," Knox said, "how is any of this CROM's concern? I'd have thought you had your plate full just with the proliferation problem."

Aristos shook his head. "The shadow KGB *is* the proliferation problem, Knox. Nobody else has got the contacts to set up these deals. I'm talking close working relationships with global-reach terrorist networks stretching back three, four decades. The scientists are just merchandise; it's the KGB does the sales and provisioning."

"And," Marianna picked up her cue, "it's largely due to their craftwork that Compliance loses track of as many disaffecteds as it does.

When that happens, it's up to our working group to reacquire the targets." The org chart was back, having grown a third rectangle labeled "Reacquisition."

"It's breadth versus depth." Marianna ceased pacing and hiked herself up onto a corner of Pete's desk, improving Knox's view of well-turned leg no end. "Compliance is in charge of the big picture. Reacquisition focuses on individual cases."

"Such as misplaced magnetohydrodynamicists?"

"Marianna filled you in on that part, huh?" Aristos shot her a vaguely disapproving side-glance. "Actually, MHD only rates a yellow alert. The magnet guys wouldn't even be watch-listed if it weren't for the Tokamak connection. You know about that?"

"About Tokamaks? They're, um, magnetic bottles, aren't they? Electromagnetic arrays that generate a containment field for plasmas of subatomic particles. Pinch the plasma, and you've got thermonuclear power generation. That's the theory, anyway; I don't think it's ever worked in practice." Knox, the closet popular-science buff. "If they've got any military application," he finished, "I don't know about it."

"Turns out they do," Aristos said. "It's called a pure-fusion bomb — a fissionless H-bomb."

That made sense: A normal thermonuclear device used a plutonium trigger — in essence, a small atom bomb — to generate the million-degree heat needed to jumpstart the fusion reaction. But a really tight magnetic pinch might achieve the same effect. The yield would be small, maybe no more than a kiloton or two. But with no radioactives on board...

"Jesus Christ! The damned thing would be undetectable."

"Yeah, your ideal suitcase bomb, if anyone could figure how to build one." Aristos shrugged. "Hasn't happened yet, far as we know. But pure-fusion tech in the wrong hands would be destabilizing as all hell. And nobody's about to take chances anymore. So CROM adds magnet guys to the watchlist, and, when Compliance loses them, we get to go find them."

"Which sums up the Reacquisition mission as a whole." Marianna was nothing if not adept at keeping a meeting on track. "It's gotten easier since the Russians started playing ball after nine-eleven. Between us, we've cranked the flood down to a trickle."

A trickle—that didn't sound so bad. Knox relaxed ever so slightly.

"Too bad these days even a trickle can kill you." Aristos sent an evil grin his way.

"Still," Marianna hurried on, "most often, it's much ado about nothing: a radiology technician off on a lost weekend with her best friend's husband, or an assistant biolab director attending an out-of-area conference unannounced. Stuff like that."

"And sometimes it's not," Aristos again. The man seemed to positively delight in stoking Knox's already considerable consternation.

The datawall behind Aristos now showed a close-up of a somber, donnish-looking gentleman in winter coat, fur hat, and handcuffs. Its caption read: Ivan Alekseyevich Kruglov, former head of the Arzamas-16 nuclear weapons lab, reacquired Tbilisi December 20th 2002 en route to Teheran.

"We call them 'proliferation threats,'" she said, "'proles' for short. Nice Orwellian touch, don't you think?"

Kruglov's image telescoped down to a thumbnail in the upper left-hand corner and another took center stage—Marina Aleksandrovna Golytsina, chief of toxicology, Bayun-17 black lab—then another, and another. By the time the sequence had run its course, the entire data-wall was filled with miniature mug-shots of "reacquired" fugitives, a rogues gallery of Russian science.

"These, of course," Marianna voice-overed, "are only the ones we managed to reacquire while in transit. Them, we hand off to Russian or CIS authorities for the actual arrest and detention, under a codicil to the Cooperative Threat Reduction program. If, on the other hand, a prole is located only after the buyer's taken delivery, reacquisition gets problematic. In that case, the file is turned over to Interdiction for final disposition. We point, they click."

A new rectangle took its place on the org chart, displayed in half-tone, presumably to signify that Interdiction was in the organization but not of it. Sure enough, dotted lines ran from it out of the CROM frame entirely, to terminate in the external "field agencies with operational responsibilities"—a case study in the matrix management of mayhem.

Knox shifted in his chair. "And 'final disposition' involves what, exactly?"

Aristos exchanged a glance with Marianna, then turned back to Knox. "We could tell you, but then we'd have to shoot you," he joked. At least Knox hoped it was a joke.

"Which brings us back to me," Knox said. "From what I've just seen of your IT ops, you're up to your bikini briefs in systems analysts. What do you need *me* for?"

In response, Marianna called up a new slide, blank except for security markings and three names:

- Viktor Il'ich Komarov
- David Yakovich Dinershtein
- Galina Mikhailovna Postrel'nikova

"Like you said earlier, Jon, it's all about magnetohydrodynamicists. These three in particular. CROM is trying to reacquire them as we speak."

She did a creditable job of pronouncing the names, then filled in the details: "All three are Ph.D. laureates of the All-Union Institute for Magnetohydrodynamics in Moscow—doctorates awarded '89, '98, and '90 respectively. All involved in Tokamak research till its defunding in 2001: Postrel'nikova and Komarov as staff at Akademgorodok, Dinershtein as a postdoc at Mendeleyev in St. Pete. On IPP maintenance thereafter. Last sightings: Komarov, in Lisbon, February 11th a year ago; Dinershtein, in Cherbourg, September 3rd, same year; Postrel'nikova, lower Manhattan, just two days ago."

That explained the non-alphabetical listing: order of evaporation.

Marianna turned from the wall display to look straight at Knox. "Part of the reason you're here is your personal relationship with one of the subjects—Postrel'nikova. In addition, though, there's another, even more promising connection..."

"The name 'Rusalka' mean anything to you?" Aristos asked.

Knox furrowed his brow. "Um, something out of Russian folklore. Ethnology 101. It's a, a mermaid of sorts, I think."

"Really? Didn't know that." Aristos flicked a smile on and off.

"Anyhow, that's not the one I meant. *Rusalka*'s a ship. A ship registered to Grishin Enterprises International, Arkady Grishin's conglomerate."

"But a *rusalka* isn't your standard-issue Hans Christian Andersen-type mermaid." Knox had remembered the rest of it. "More a kind of water demon. She entices sailors into the depths and drowns them. Hardly an auspicious name to give a boat."

"Tell me if this looks auspicious to you." Aristos tapped at the keyboard in his lap. The CROM org chart went away. In its place, the 3-D image of a ship now floated in the datawall behind him. "'Luxurious' doesn't even come close. You name it, she's got it: helipad, banquet hall the length of a football field, nailed-up downlink from the Sviaz-12 geosynch satellite—the whole nine yards. You sure you never heard of her? She was in all the papers when she called on New York this week."

"Guess I've got to start reading the shipping news. But that time-frame is suggestive."

Marianna nodded. "Uh-huh. It was during *Rusalka*'s New York layover that Galina, or someone posing as Galina, got herself disappeared."

"You're suggesting Galina was abducted by someone on *Rusalka*?"

"Hell, no—she *arrived* on *Rusalka*." Aristos ran fat fingers through thinning hair. "They extracted her right off the roof of a downtown skyscraper. Caught Compliance with their pants down. No sightings since. The ball's in Reacquisition's court."

Marianna's cheeks looked flushed for some reason. "There's more to the story than that," she said. "You flashed on it yourself yesterday, when I showed you that snapshot. The extractee was almost certainly not the same Galina Mikhailovna Postrel'nikova who boarded *Rusalka* on June 27th in Cherbourg."

"But, whoever she was, she disembarked, right? So why all the interest in the ship?"

"Common denominator. The first two, Komarov and Dinershtein, were routine disappearances, not extractions like Galina. But there's a *Rusalka* connection there too, if you go looking hard enough." Something in Marianna's tone said she was the one who'd gone looking.

"So, if Galina never really left…"

"Uh-huh," she said. "We're guessing all three of those proles are still onboard."

"What's Galina doing on a yacht, anyway?" Knox asked. Precious little luxury in the lives of Russian physicists these days, if CROM's stats were even halfway accurate.

"For public consumption?" Aristos shrugged. "Taking a cruise with an old flame, is all."

"Wait a minute… not Sasha?" So that's why they'd called him in.

"Right the first time. Arkady Grishin's second-in-command, heir apparent, and, by a strange coincidence," — this time Aristos' broad grin seemed genuine — "your old drinking buddy, Aleksandr Andreyevich Bondarenko."

Sasha.

This assignment sure was raising old ghosts. First Galina, now this: the specter *par excellence*, the memory Knox had consigned to oblivion lo, these past twenty years. The friend he'd never intended to make in the first place.

Making friends with Russians in the waning days of the Soviet era was contraindicated for an American exchange student. The xenophobia was mutual, to the point where the only Russians eager to hang out with foreigners were dissidents or, worse news, KGB snitches. Either way, they spelled trouble.

Trouble was exactly what Jonathan Knox didn't want. He'd pretty much resigned himself to a solitary ten-month tour, to moving wraithlike through Soviet society, a detached, immaterial observer.

Meeting Galina in the Metro made short work of his plans for immateriality. Stevie's adventure on the escalator had raised his clinginess index to where any attempt to disengage him from his rescuer threatened another squalling fit. For her part, Galina didn't seem to want to let go either. The three of them wound up riding together all the way into central Moscow. With the little boy perched on her lap in the rocking subway car, the young woman even managed a hesitant, whispered, getting-to-know-you conversation with Knox. It was as if all her ingrained Soviet wariness of foreigners had melted away in the presence of this foreign child. As if childhood were a country unto it-self, any of whose natives could claim dual Russian citizenship.

If Galya was shy and soft-spoken, the friend who met them at the Lenin Library station more than made up for it. Aleksandr Andreyev-ich Bondarenko—"Sasha" to his many friends—was large, loud, and dauntingly gregarious. Born and raised in Bratsk, north of Lake Baikal, he epitomized the expansive, wide-open character Siberians are justly famous for. Even before Galina could break from his embrace to make introductions, Sasha was holding out a hand to Knox, his face crinkling in a grin so wide it almost made his eyes disappear.

"Aleksandr Andreyevich Bondarenko," he announced in a voice ex-uberant enough to draw stares from passers-by on the Metro platform.

Knox gave the beaming, sandy-haired stranger a dubious once-over. Young, perhaps only a year or so older than Knox. Taller and thin-ner than your average Russian, with broad peasant features redeemed from plainness by the lively intelligence shining out of his blue eyes and the way his mouth kept breaking out in a slightly gap-toothed grin.

What the hell. Dismissing the stray paranoid thought that this whole Metro episode was some elaborate KGB sting, Knox reached out and shook the extended hand.

"Jonathan Knox. Very pleased, Aleksandr Andreyevich." Paranoia or not, it was best to keep the relationship at the arms-length formality that went along with the first-name-plus-patronymic form of address.

"But, no, you must call me Sasha." The Russian offered the ultimate ice-breaker: the diminutive version of his first name.

"Jon," Knox said, looking dubiously at his new, contraindicated friend.

As it turned out, he needn't have worried; Sasha and Galina were neither dissidents nor informants. Like physics students the world over, they were almost wholly apolitical, and so caught up in their own complementary lines of research—Sasha going for his doctorate in astrophysics at Moscow State, and Galina a teenage prodigy in mag-netohydrodynamics at a small, specialized institute across town—as to spare little interest for anything else.

Knox had read enough pop science—layman's guide to relativity and such—to keep pace with his friends' enthusiasms. The late-night sessions in Knox's Moscow State dorm room sparkled and swirled with quasars and solar magnetospheres, neutron stars and black holes — the whole outré bestiary of *fin-de-siècle* astrophysics — as Sasha and Galina took turns grappling with the mysteries of the universe like cosmic tag-team wrestlers.

And, if conversation ever flagged on the cosmological front, the three could always fall back on that time-honored staple of Soviet discourse: the latest rumors.

And *what* rumors! In the perfect informational vacuum engineered by the authorities, the merest scrap of hearsay would inflate and distort into breathless, Byzantine extravagance.

"Here is one you cannot have heard, Dzhon," Sasha would say, and then proceed to spin some improbable yarn about how the entire Soviet space program was being run on contraband microelectronics smuggled in from Silicon Valley.

But even Sasha's best rumors paled by comparison with the one Knox himself had heard in a gypsy taxicab driving in from Sheremetevo Airport, the day of his arrival in August 1984. According to the cabby, the official reports that Yuri Andropov had succumbed to kidney failure in February of that year were lies, plain and simple. In reality, the then-General Secretary of the Communist Party and former KGB Chairman had been assassinated in his sickbed, stabbed through the heart by an unidentified hospital worker, who had thereupon promptly self-destructed.

The only time Sasha ever topped that one, it wasn't with a rumor at all. It was with a mystery.

The occasion was pineapples. Knox had gotten in the habit of making the trek up from the archives to the US Embassy about once a week. If nothing else you could chow down on a reasonable facsimile of a cheeseburger at the snack bar, and sometimes there were delicacies to be had at the small commissary down in the basement. That day, a bitingly cold, clear day in mid-February, he had struck edible gold: pineapples! A whole binful of the succulent tropical fruit had been delivered that morning, and there were still three left by noon. Knox bought two.

The pineapples were a roaring success — with Sasha in particular.

He got a faraway look in his eye and reminisced how, as a child in Bratsk, he had once gotten close enough to a pineapple to actually *smell* it.

"And does the taste live up to what you remember of the smell?" Knox wanted to know.

Sasha's grin made his words all but superfluous. "Live up to? It fulfils and overfulfils, my friend."

"Must have been hard," Knox mused, "growing up with so few luxuries — so few necessities, even. Vitamin C and all that, they're kind of essential."

"A hard life, yes, Dzhon," Galina said. She came from Tomsk, on the edge of the great central plateau. "But also Siberia can be a magical place for a child. Have you heard, for instance, of 'the whisper of stars'?"

Knox shook his head, saying nothing that might interrupt her. He loved to listen to Galya speak. Russian was a beautiful language in any case, but in her warm, gentle contralto, it became a song.

"Far out on the taiga, in the dead of winter, it grows very, very cold. Cold enough that a breath quickly freezes in midair. So quickly it makes a little tinkling sound. The whisper of stars, it is called." She sighed, remembering. "It is enchanting."

"Also cold enough that you dare not drink a glass of tea coming straight in from outdoors," Sasha teased. "Or your teeth will crack."

At a look from Galya, he relented. "No, truly, our frontier is a land of marvels — wooly mammoths perfectly preserved in the permafrost, prehistoric fishes still alive in the depths of Baikal. Legends of giant subterranean rats and ghost wolves and thunder gods bringing down the wrath of heaven. And, of course, the greatest wonder of all…"

Galina wrinkled her nose. "Please, no, Sasha. Not that old tale again."

"Galya grows tired of hearing me speak of this." He winked at Knox. "And yet it is the reason I study cosmology. How could the search for the secrets of the universe not be in my blood, when I was born less than five hundred kilometers from the epicenter of the mystery itself?"

And he told them then of Tunguska. Of a meteor strike with no meteor, of a ring of fire-scorched, blasted trees stretching for thousands of hectares in every direction, but no crater. Of his meeting there with an ancient Evenki shaman.

A shaman who claimed to have witnessed the thunderwings of the god Ogdy splitting open the sky and plummeting to earth.

And who, on learning that his young visitor yearned to know the secrets of the stars, had opened his medicine pouch and, from it, brought forth a very special gift...

"Knox? You still with us here?" The voice broke in on his reverie. He refocused his attention on an impatient-looking Aristos, hunched forward with his meaty forearms on the polyplast desktop.

"I don't see what good I could do you," Knox said at last. "I haven't seen either Sasha or Galya in going on twenty years. I for sure never knew Sasha'd gone on to scale the heights of Russia, Incorporated. Not what I'd have expected from an astrophysicist." Though Sasha had always seemed well-connected. And the brave, new post-Soviet world had seen stranger success stories.

"You didn't try to keep in touch after you got back?" Aristos asked.

"Sure, we sent letters back and forth, for a while. The visits from your friends in the 'field agencies' didn't help matters any."

"That's just standard FBI exchange-student follow-up. And it worked: when we scanned for someone who could get to Bondarenko, out pops your name. Anything else? Beyond the letters, I mean."

"Nothing," Knox said. "Things were going to hell in a hand basket by then. *Perestroika* and *glasnost* were triggering the whole revolution-of-rising-expectations thing. I always thought we'd get back in contact after the dust settled." He shrugged. "Never happened."

"Well, Knox, you're in luck. *Rusalka* docks in Baltimore this afternoon with Bondarenko aboard. Your reunion's all set for tonight."

"Grishin Enterprises is hosting a gala at the Kennedy Center," Marianna elaborated, "A benefit for one of Grishin's pet causes: *Mir i Druzhba,* his Peace and Friendship Foundation. Half the movers and shakers in Washington will be on hand for extra helpings of peace and friendship. You too, thanks to the email correspondence that put you back in touch with Sasha."

Ignoring his glare, Marianna handed Knox an invitation featuring a hologram of the GEI Ourobouros and his own name in raised lettering. "Appropriate attire has already been delivered care of your hotel room. Questions?"

"You bet," said Knox. "How about we start with: are you *kidding?*"

7 | Mythologies

"THE GERMAN WORD for Eagle." Back home again at base camp, Jack Adler was going back over the day's events for an audience of one.

"And you are certain Hoffman never told the old shaman the meaning of your name?" Luciano Carbone asked.

"He swore not." Jack shrugged. "Acted insulted I'd even think such a thing. I guess it's some sort of ethnographic Prime Directive: never reinforce the natives' belief system. Or challenge it for that matter."

"And what of your own belief system, Jack? Was *it* challenged by Jenkoul's tale?"

Jack rose from his borrowed camp stool and looked around. The silhouette of base camp's main lodge showed dark against the sunset sky. Off in the distance, he could hear the muted rattle of his diesel generator, faithfully holding the SQUID's temperature within operating range, reminding him of work still undone.

"Didn't realize I'd been talking so long," he said. "It's getting late."

"Nonsense." Luciano glanced upward to where towering thunderheads shone red and gold in the last rays of the sun. "At home in

Bologna, we eat dinner later than this. You do not evade the question so easily. What, if anything, might modern physics have to learn from an Evenki shaman?"

"Well, I'll tell you one thing, if you set aside all the mumbo-jumbo, that old guy's a pretty credible witness for the Jackson-Ryan hypothesis."

"But you just finished telling me his stories did not contain anything new."

Jack nodded. "They didn't, not about the Tunguska Event, anyway. But there's one part I haven't told you: Jenkoul went back."

"What, back to the Epicenter?"

"Sounds crazy, doesn't it? I mean if something'd come within a whisker of killing me, you can bet I'd stay the hell away from then on. But Jenkoul's clan had kind of figured him for their new shaman, even young as he was, on account of what he'd been through and all. And it wasn't like they didn't need one. But better to let Jenkoul tell you why in his own words."

As he'd been doing all along, Jack scanned through his recording of the interview, till he'd found the part he meant to play for Luciano. Once again Jenkoul's quavering tones alternated with Hoffman's accented English:

> *The ring of fire burned itself out,*
> *The sky purged itself of choking haze,*
> *Yet still the world remained unhealed.*
> *Neither winter's snows nor spring's floods*
> *Had power to leach from the land its lingering malignancy.*
> *Summer's new growth came up warped and scabrous,*
> *All creatures feeding upon it sickened and died.*
> *Strange, oozing lesions afflicted the reindeer,*
> *And those of my own clansmen straying too far into the lands now under*
>   *Ogdy's curse.*

Jack hit the pause button. "It got kind of ritualized in the retelling, I guess. But, to make a long story short, exactly one year after the Event, Jenkoul returned to the heartlands. And built him a sweatlodge in the middle of the Great Swamp, and sat down and waited for this Ogdy to show up."

"Forgive me, Jack," Luciano said, "but all this sounds simply like more of what you have already called 'mumbo-jumbo.'"

"That's because you haven't heard the rest of it yet. Once you do, I think you'll agree it's a dead-on accurate recollection."

"But, Jack, a recollection of what?"

"Of what it'd be like to be standing at the Epicenter when the micro-hole came zooming right straight up underneath you."

The god comes, the god comes.
The earth trembles in fear at the coming of Ogdy.
The earth rises and falls beneath my feet, like waves of water.
My place of purification is overthrown, my lodgepoles topple.
The god comes.

Jack paused the playback again,. "I don't know about you, Luciano. But, what with the ground shaking and the sweatlodge collapsing, it sure sounds like an earthquake to me."

"But, but the Epicenter has been surveyed by every seismographic instrument known to science. Nothing of the sort has ever been observed, ever."

"Oh, sure — now. But, remember, it took twenty years to get anything like a scientific expedition in there. If there *was* a primordial black hole circling round and round inside the Earth all that time, chances are its orbit would've degraded by then, down to where any seismic effects would have been undetectable — by 1920s equipment, at least."

"And you are saying that, by the time we arrive here with our vastly superior instrumentation, it has receded even further."

"Uh-huh. Five, ten kilometers down by now, I'd guess. But my point is, Jenkoul went out there a year after the event itself, in the summer of 1909. Back then you'd have measured the thing's closest approach to the surface in inches, not miles. Now, picture a five-billion tonne gravitational point-source plowing up through solid rock at thousands of klicks an hour, up to within a few meters of the surface.

This is more your area than mine, Luciano—what's that going to give you?"

"Mmm. Compression and shear, certainly. And on a massive scale." The little geologist tugged at his goatee. "I understand what you are saying, Jack: this could perhaps account for Jenkoul's earthquake. Even so it hardly constitutes definitive proof of your black-hole hypothesis."

"Hang on." Jack advanced the recording to the next bookmark. "We're not done yet."

The god calls out.
Blinding-bright, his tongue lashes the sky.
His roar echoes off the hills, the heavens ring with it.
Ogdy is calling his avatar from the Lower World.
The earth at my feet burns at the touch of his fiery tongue.
The god calls out.

Jack stopped the recording there. "Hoffman says that's all shaman-speak for a lightning bolt, one that may have just barely missed frying our friend, in fact."

"But, Jack…lightning at midnight? From a cloudless sky?"

"That's a tough one, all right. But, in a way, it's maybe the key to the whole thing."

"How so?"

"Well, these preferential lightning strikes say to me that whatever's coming at Jenkoul is carrying a whole lot of charge, electric or magnetic. I'm betting magnetic, on account of the object's age."

"What would age have to do with it?" Luciano asked.

"Given enough time, an electrically-charged object would neutralize itself by attracting opposite charges. And my hole's had the whole lifetime of the universe to do it in."

"But magnetism is even worse in that regard, no? The force must always cancel itself out, since every magnet possesses two poles of opposite charge, north and south."

"Nowadays, sure." A faraway look glowed in Jack's eyes. "But there *was* a time, a long, long time ago—within an eyeblink of the Beginning itself—when things could've been different. That's when the primal superforce broke down. And, when it did, it tied the fabric of spacetime in knots."

"Knots?"

"Uh-huh." Jack nodded. "Very peculiar knots. Particles with an unpaired magnetic charge, a single pole—what we call monopoles. I think that may be what my hole's made out of."

"So, you believe the Tunguska Cosmic Body to be a black hole with a magnetic charge?"

"Not just any magnetic charge. A single pole without an opposite to offset it: a north, say, with no south."

Luciano whistled. "That would be much more powerful than an ordinary magnet."

"Uh-huh. Powerful enough to call down lightning out of a clear sky. Powerful enough to've trapped the thing here in the first place."

"Yes, yes, now that you say it, I am eager to hear of this—your solution to the 'exit event' problem. You told Medvedev that your black hole must have remained within the Earth. But you did not explain how this is possible. Should not its speed have carried it out the other side?"

"Should have," Jack conceded, "always assuming nothing slowed it down first."

"But, Jack, what could slow something so small and yet so massive? My understanding is that it should have passed through the atmosphere *and* the solid earth with no resistance at all."

"The earth, yes. But the atmosphere's a whole different story. One that starts with Hawking radiation."

Luciano's face showed a flicker of recognition, but Jack would've bet that was more due to Stephen Hawking's name than to any familiarity with the weird quantum process the man had discovered. A process by which black holes could give off particles. Radiation, in other words, heat. And the smaller the hole, the more particles it'd give off.

"Just take it from Steve Hawking," Jack went on, "my micro hole'd be plenty hot. Surface temperature into the *billions* of degrees. Hot enough to strip the electrons off any nearby atoms on its way down...and leave an ionization contrail that'd put an Airbus-II to shame."

"The 'bright blue tube' reported by the eyewitnesses," Luciano said.

"Exactly. But now watch what happens when you add a monopolar magnetic charge in on top of the radiation effects: the hole's magnetic flux-lines are going to be sticking radially outward, like the spines on a Koosh ball. And the ions it's churning out aren't going to want to go crossing those lines of force. They're going to latch onto the hole instead, and hang on for dear life. Get dragged along with it, sped up till they're going faster than the speed of sound. And that means—"

"Sonic booms," Luciano said half to himself. "All along the flight path, as the individual air molecules break the sound barrier." Then he snapped his fingers. "That would explain the cannonades that accompanied the object's descent."

Jack nodded. "Plus, when that trailing column of superheated air slams into the ground, it's going to destroy everything for miles around."

"All the Tunguska phenomena, then."

"Right," Jack said, "but those are all just side effects, compared to the main event."

Luciano stared at him expectantly. "Which is—?"

"Air-braking!"

"Air-braking, Jack?"

"Sure. See, the atmospheric drag just keeps piling up and up. It's like the micro-hole's this humongous broom, sweeping tons of atmosphere along in front of it, and every additional gram just slows it down more. Slows it down maybe to below escape velocity, to where it can't climb back up out of Earth's gravity-well anymore."

Heeding the god's call, the Avatar arises.
Night-walker, Spawn of Darkness, Beast of Evil Heart,
From the Lower World he arises.
Insatiable, All-devouring, he arises.
He seizes me.
His monstrous jaws engulf my head,
His great claws pin my feet,
As wild dogs tear at entrails of their kill, so the Wolf tears me limb from
*   limb...*

Jack clicked off the recorder. "Final piece of the puzzle," he said. "I'll admit, that one's not so obvious. But it's got to be the tides."

Luciano raised an eyebrow. "The tides, Jack? As in the oceans?"

"Uh-huh. Tides are just a byproduct of gravity, after all—more specifically, of how gravity grows stronger the closer you get to its source, and vice versa. Take the moon, for instance: its gravity pulls strongest on the piece of ocean nearest to it, so the waters right underneath the moon get lifted up relative to the Earth as a whole."

"But there is also a tide on the opposite side of the Earth, is there not?"

"Right. The waters there are furthest away from the moon. They feel its gravity the least so they tend to stay in place. But since everything else on Earth is getting pulled at more, it's as if that part of the ocean humps out away from the moon. When all's said and done, you wind up with two standing waves of seawater moving through the oceans at twelve-hour intervals."

"The tides."

"Uh-huh. Now picture that same effect, only generated by a gravitational point-source like my micro-hole. The mass is a whole lot less, but so's the distance. Now, figure Jenkoul stood maybe a meter and a half, two meters tall. And figure back in those days the hole came to within four-five meters of the surface, with him standing right over it. That'd mean—" Jack closed his eyes to do the math. "Um, call it a difference of about one full gravity between the crown of his head and the soles of his feet."

From the look on Luciano's face, he wasn't seeing the implications.

Jack tried again. "Think of it this way: say our friend the shaman weighed eighty kilograms. A one-gravity differential top to toe is going to feel like his head's been clamped in a vise while a hundred and seventy-five pound weight dangles from his ankles."

That came across loud and clear. Luciano gave another of his low whistles. "Poor Jenkoul, no wonder he felt he was being torn apart by monstrous teeth and claws! Lucky for him it was over in an instant."

"Except it wasn't," Jack said. "Not by a long shot. Oh, sure, the hole itself would hit its apogee and be gone in milliseconds. But the aftermath...well, Jenkoul barely made it back out of that swamp alive. In the days to come he nearly died of a raging fever, huge sores all over his body. He showed me the scars. Toothmarks of the Wolf, he called them."

"And this too can be explained, I assume?" Luciano said.

Jack shrugged. "Radiation burns, pure and simple. I told you, that hole is *hot*. As close as it must've come to the surface back then, it's a wonder it didn't— What's the matter, Luciano?"

"Nothing, Jack, nothing. It's just that, well, you must admit Jenkoul's version was far more…poetic." The little Italian sighed. "I suppose I am something of a romantic. Some part of me hates to see all the mysteries of the world fade in the light of prosaic scientific explanation."

"Read your Keats; there's beauty in the truth, too. The world's got more than enough mysteries as it is. Me, I'll take all the explanation I can get."

Jack chuckled then at his friend's crestfallen look. "Oh, come on, Luciano. You didn't seriously believe there was a *real* Wolf out there waiting for me, did you?"

✳

The long subarctic summer day was dying. Through thickening light, Yuri poled his canoe along the Khushmo's densely wooded banks, occasionally checking distance to the target on his handheld's Global Positioning display. Five kilometers still to go, and upstream at that. But drought had shrunk the swollen torrents of spring to a gentle flow. The river in mid-summer could no longer offer much resistance to a determined traveler.

Low as it was, the Khushmo still ran fresh and clear, its waters so limpid that the enormous trout drifting motionless in its deep pools seemed almost to be levitating in midair. Above the river's near-invisible surface, swarms of gnats hovered in clouds dense as evening mist. Beaver paddled through the twilit water, breasting the canoe's wake on the way to their lodges. From either shore choruses of birdsong floated out across the tranquil current, swelling toward one final crescendo against the onset of night.

The peace of the river and the Siberian summer evening was lost on Yuri Vissarionovich Geladze. He had no use for wilderness. Cities were where he needed to be. Cities were the home of the well-off, the comfortable, the human sheep. And, so, the natural hunting ground of the human wolves who preyed on them.

The stray thought prompted him to glance down to where his four-legged passenger—accomplice, more properly—lay sedated beneath the concealing tarp, in a steel cage that took up half the canoe. Prompted him to think, as well, of the strange implement he had been given to do the job. Needless complications of a simple business, all in the name of making the death appear an accident.

An accident! Yuri shook his head. Accidents, disappearances without trace—his employers simply had no appreciation of the *uses* of violent death. A killing should instill fear, should intimidate the living even as it silenced the dead. All this effort to ensure that the act would not be known for what it was went against Yuri's grain.

Other than that, the plan was sound. Grishin Enterprises had managed the logistics with customary efficiency, even here at the ends of the earth. Rumor had it that Grishin himself had spent time out here some fifteen or twenty years ago. Though what he could have been seeking in this emptiness was beyond Yuri's imagination.

No matter, imagination was hardly an asset in Yuri's line of work. The client's business was his own...until and unless it affected Yuri's.

The pole found bottom again. A flex of muscle propelled the craft soundlessly forward through the hush of evening.

Beneath its canvas shroud, the wolf in the cage dozed fitfully.

8 | Press Gang

THIS WAS NOT the moment Marianna would have chosen for the final recruitment drive. The Archon resource was perched on the edge of the government-issue visitor's chair, voice tight, jaw muscles clenched. None of this seemed to've registered on her boss, though: Pete was plowing ahead regardless.

"Lighten up, Knox, this is no big deal." Pete was trying his best to sound persuasive, give him that much. Too bad his vocal apparatus wasn't built for it. "Hey, you eat some caviar, drink some vodka, talk old times, the government picks up your per diem. Piece of cake."

"Why don't I believe that?"

"You're right, Jon," she put in, before Pete could make things worse, "there's more to it than that. With any luck, Sasha will let something slip that'll point us to Galina."

Those gray eyes probed her a moment. "Look, I'm only saying this one more time: there's no way on earth the Galya I knew would've sold out to your so-called shadow KGB. But, okay, say she did. Say she's in it up to her earlobes. That'd have to mean Sasha is too, right? So, why would he just go and rat her out?"

"It's a long shot," she admitted, "But you do have a personal relationship with both subjects; it would only be natural for you to ask about her. Plus, your dossier's pretty bulletproof. There's nothing to connect you to CROM, and we're the only ones they're worried about. No one else even knows Galina's missing."

Too complicated by half; it sounded like she'd made it up on the spot. It didn't help that she had.

Marianna turned the warmth of her smile up another notch and tried again. "And, there's always the chance your friends don't really know what they've gotten themselves into. Not the whole of it, anyway. I'd like to think not; Sasha seemed like a nice enough guy from his e-—I mean, I think he still has good memories of the old days, back in Moscow."

That struck a chord. The resource—no, get used to calling him Jon—was thinking about it at least. Now if her boss would only cool his jets.

No such luck.

"I'll level with you, Knox," Pete said. "There's no way we can move in on GEI with what we've got. The trail's gone cold on Galina, and other than that Grishin's squeaky-clean. No links to the oligarchs, no Mafiya ties, nothing."

"I didn't think anybody made it to the top in Russia these days without the one or the other."

"Tell me about it. Fact remains, except for maybe these low-level proles,"—he waved at the bullet list of Russian names still displayed on the screen behind him—"we haven't got squat on Arkady. And he's too high up the food chain to go in on spec. If we come up empty, his friends on the Appropriations Subcommittee'll skin me alive. Marianna too."

"We don't know that you'll turn up all that much, Jon." Marianna tried to get things back on track. "But anything beats sitting around on our hands."

"But I'm a systems analyst; I've never worked undercover in my life. You've got to have better options you can put in place."

"Not by tonight," Pete said. "And *Rusalka* sails tomorrow. Tonight's our last shot at inserting an operative."

"'Inserting an operative.' That sounds ominous."

"Just craft-speak for a pleasant evening's conversation," Marianna said quickly. "All we need you to do is get some feel for whether or not our magneto-troika are still Grishin's guests. We'll take it from there."

"If that's all, why not just 'insert an operative' when *Rusalka* docks in France, or wherever?"

"Too long a lead-time," Pete said. "Lots could happen between now and then."

"Between now and when? What does a vessel like *Rusalka* do—twenty knots? She'll be in Europe the end of next week."

"She's rated for twenty-eight knots, tops," Marianna corrected, "but that's irrelevant. *Rusalka's* not a passenger liner. She's got no schedule to keep. Over the past eleven years, the summer voyages have averaged a month and a half in length, with a max of three in 1997."

Pete tapped a few keys and the datawall backed up these statistics with overlaid charts of *Rusalka's* North Atlantic peregrinations as far back as 1993.

"That puts us into mid-September, earliest," he said. "If Grishin's planning something, we need to know now."

"But what does *Rusalka do* out there?"

Pete shrugged. "World's biggest floating tax dodge. She's GEI corporate headquarters, so the longer she stays at sea, the harder it is for the IRS-types to keep tabs on Grishin Enterprises."

"She's also part oceanographic research vessel," Marianna added. "Arkady Grigoriyevich fancies himself something of a patron of the arts and sciences." That elicited a snort from Pete.

"Actually," she went on, "they've done some pretty decent science. Published a detailed seismographic survey of the entire Newfoundland Basin four or five years ago. What she's been doing out there since is anybody's guess. Sometimes she steams in slow circles. Sometimes she just sits on station. And summer isn't the only cruise she makes. Altogether *Rusalka* spends eight or nine months out of every year sailing the North Atlantic."

"Off topic," Pete cut in again. "Look, Knox, we're getting wind of something big going down. It's looking like September'll be too late. If we're going to move against GEI, now's the time."

"It's really not much we're asking, Jon," Marianna said. "You talk to people for a living. That's all we want you to do here."

"This is certifiable no-risk." Pete and his two cents again. "Hey, when's the last time somebody got whacked in the Kennedy Center?"

"It's for your country, Jon," Marianna said. "And for Galya, too. It's not too late to save her."

"Who knows?" Pete leaned forward. "Work with us on this and we might even cut Sasha a break, if he's not in too deep."

Jon was silent for a bit.

"Let me see if I've got this straight," he said finally. "You want me to sell out an old friend on the off chance that, if I do get him to betray himself, you *might* go easy on him? Why should I believe that? Based on what? So far, you've purloined my email, press-ganged me personally, put Galina under surveillance, Lord knows what else. I just don't see any basis for trust here, folks, much less a working relationship. I'm sorry, but you're going to have to do your own dirty work—you seem perfectly capable of it."

He'd been looking at her as he spoke, but now he shifted his gaze to Pete. "As for my participation, the answer is no."

Pete's face was set hard, unmoving. Only his eyes still gave signs of life, as if glaring out from behind a mask. Marianna knew that look only too well.

"Pete," she began, "Maybe if we just—"

"Marianna, would you excuse us please?"

"Pete, are you sure...?" Don't do this.

"Leave us. Now."

✳

Was it Knox's imagination, or did Aristos grow in size as he put on a textbook intimidating stare and leaned across the desktop?

"I don't think you appreciate the situation here," he said.

"I'm sure you'll enlighten me in your own good time, Pete. Mind if I check my voicemail first?" He already had his handheld out and was punching in the speed-dial code Mycroft had given him last night.

"Won't work in here." Aristos waved an arm. "The whole building's shielded. Why'd you think we didn't just confiscate that gizmo at the door?"

"Score one for CROM, then." Knox shrugged and repocketed the little device. "So, okay, go ahead. I'm listening."

Aristos settled back in his seat. "What you've got to realize is, your Russian friends winding up in detention isn't necessarily what you'd call your worst-case scenario."

"Sounds pretty bad-case to me." Especially when those terrorism-related detentions had acquired a nasty habit of stretching on indefinitely. "Why, Pete? How were you planning on making it worse?"

"They could wind up dead." Aristos's eyes didn't move from Knox's face. "Sasha, right away. Galina, soon as we reacquire her. Look, Knox, it's not the way I like to do business, but one phone call and Bondarenko goes home from the Kennedy Center in a body bag."

Could he mean that? Lord knows, the government had grown more than usually cavalier about due process ever since the World Trade Center attack.

Aristos was still looking into Knox's eyes. "Now, you tell me: doesn't playing ball with us on this work out better all around? Better for your friends. Better for you, too, if it comes to that."

Knox repressed an urge to swallow—no telling what biometric scanners this room came equipped with. "I'm sure I don't need to remind you," he said, "there's a whole office full of witnesses back in New York that saw your little gopher drag me off to D.C."

Aristos grinned unpleasantly. "Oh, there's lots of stuff can happen short of Interdiction. There's tax audits and investigation of actions in restraint of trade and indefinite detention as a material witness and such."

He splayed his hands on the desk and levered himself to a standing position, eyeing Knox like a water buffalo about to charge. "Goddammit, Knox! All we're asking is, you go *talk* to the man!"

"Okay, that should be about enough." Knox rose and addressed the empty air. "Mycroft? You getting all this?"

"Five-by-five, Jonathan," a voice issued from the desktop speaker.

Aristos jumped as if bitten by a snake. A window popped open on the wall-filling display behind him to reveal a thrice-lifesized image of Mycroft's smiling face.

Mycroft had let his image-enhancing software dress him for the occasion: he was resplendent in black tie and gold-lamé tuxedo jacket against a background of green baize tables and crystal chandeliers. A game of baccarat was in full swing behind him—very Casino Royale.

"I'm forgetting my manners," Knox said, reseating himself and putting his feet up on a convenient, ottoman-sized stack of printouts. "Euripedes Aristos, meet my associate Finley Laurence—Mycroft to his friends. "

Aristos stared at his datawall in disbelief. "How the fuck—" He began, then stopped when Knox withdrew his handheld from his jacket pocket again.

"I told you that can't work here," he sputtered. "No fucking way you could've called out!"

"*I* didn't call out, *you* did—or rather your console here. Among my handheld's undocumented features, it can broadcast infrared, using the same protocols as most standard detached keyboards. I had Mycroft preload it last night with a keystroke sequence that instructed your own systems to set up an outside link. We've been online, logged into a Net-Meeting session on Archon's server, ever since you and I started this heart-to-heart."

Aristos's face darkened. He looked as if he were trying to choose from among a repertoire of possible retorts. The one that finally came out was: "Shit!"

"Yeah, it's a bitch," Knox commiserated. "Oh, just so we know where we stand: I'm going to forget all about this conversation if you will. It's that, or read the transcript on the front page of tomorrow's *Washington Post*."

He got to his feet. "Time to be going—no, don't bother getting up; I can see myself out." He looked Aristos in the eye. "I trust there won't be any unpleasantness if I just leave the way I came in?"

Aristos shook his head sullenly and spoke the permissions into his headset mike.

Knox paused at the door and smiled tightly. "Pete, It's been real."

He closed the door quietly behind him and was gone.

✳

"Okay," Pete said into his headset, then broke the contact. He scowled at Marianna. "That was the front gate. Elvis has left the building."

"I figured as much," she said. "Are you going to tell me what went down in here, or do I have to guess? And why'd you let him walk, for Christ's sake? We've only got till tonight."

Pete wasn't meeting her eyes. He mumbled something inaudible, cleared his throat and tried again. "You were right," he said.

It was like pulling teeth, but Marianna finally pried the whole story out of him. She didn't know whether to laugh or cry. She'd had a gut feeling that strong-arm tactics were going to backfire with her Archon resource. This surpassed all expectations.

Left to her own devices, she could've talked Jon around, she knew she could, what with the looks he'd been giving her. But no, Pete had to go get into a testosterone tourney.

She sighed and stood up. "Well, okay then, I'll just have to go round him up again."

"Goddammit, Marianna, sit down! You're not going anywhere."

"But, Pete, don't you see? We need him back, now more than ever. He's just proved he's the right guy for the job."

"How do you figure that?"

"Admit it: it took brains *and* balls, the way he skonked you." She tried hard to keep a straight face as she said that, she really did.

"Skonked *us*, Marianna. *You're* the one that waltzed that walking security risk in here."

"All I'm saying is, I'm more convinced than ever: this whole thing could work. I've just got to talk to him again."

"Talk to him? The way he left here, we've seen the last of him. And that's my *best*-case outcome."

"You put a tail on him, didn't you? Tell me you did that much, Pete."

"Yeah, we're tracking. He phoned for a limo on that damned—" A disgusted look flashed across Pete's face. "He headed into the city," he said finally.

"Where? To do what?"

"Smithsonian. That's where he got out, anyhow." Pete shrugged. "Maybe he's just taking in the sights. —Where are you going? I told you to stay put."

"Where do you think?" She was already halfway out the door. "Dulles is just five miles up the road. He could have gone straight there and caught the next flight back to New York. He didn't. So, maybe he's still thinking about it. Still thinking things over. I'm going to find him and see if I can talk him back in."

"Won't happen. Not when you've only got—" Pete glanced at the timestamp in the upper left corner of the datawall. "—nine hours left on the clock."

"I've got to try. There's still time to reacquire him, time to fix this." That sounded good—calm, confident, competent: the sort of image she always tried to project to CROM's male-dominated hierarchy. Privately, though...

There's still time, she repeated to herself, but Pete was right: it was running out fast. She couldn't help thinking that her boss had just dumped her whole investigation into the shitter. And any chance of stopping Grishin with it.

9 | Ghost

THE UNIVERSE-SEED COMES *into being vested in inconceivable heat and light and beauty. No physics can describe it. Poetry comes closer: "Infinity in the palm of your hand and eternity in an hour." Yet it is more than even Blake could know or say. It is all of space and time encapsulated in a nexus of infinite density and infinite power and infinite fecundity. It is the source, the wellspring, the place where everything begins.*

To Dr. John C. Adler, to any cosmologist really, it was the Holy of Holies. And now here he was, thirteen billion years hence, sitting on a small blue speck circling a dim ember of that long-ago glory, straining to catch the faintest echo of creation's final chord.

And failing utterly.

Jack tossed on top of his bedroll—it was too sweltering to climb in—haunted by the specter of imminent defeat. Tonight even contemplation of the Infinite seemed powerless to quiet his churning thoughts, or break his mind free of their downward spiral.

To make matters worse, every time he was on the brink of dozing off, the generator would cycle on and haul him back to wakefulness.

Finally he sat up, pulled his boots on, and crawled out of his *choum*.

The endless subarctic twilight had given way to full night. Jack gazed up into darkness lit only by the ancient light of faraway suns. He heaved a sigh, then walked over to the table holding his laptop. Reached up to the sixty-watt bulb he'd strung on a cross-pole and tightened it in its socket. If the generator was going to keep him awake all night, the least it could do was supply the light needed to make the insomnia productive.

With yet another sigh, he sat down to resume his computer-mediated contemplation of the misbehaving SQUID. The laptop was still reporting all systems nominal, no repeats of last night's "hiccup."

Jack glanced over at the breadbox-sized insulated housing that contained the business end of the Superconducting Quantum Interference Device. Please, *please*, let it not be the SQUID. He'd all but signed his life away to get the highly experimental, half-million-dollar instrument released on loan from IBM's Watson Research Center.

It *had* to be working!

And no reason it shouldn't be. The device was so sensitive to magnetic anomalies that, until he'd programmed the computer to ignore them, it had been tracking the near-Earth satellites passing overhead in their polar orbits. If the SQUID could do that across a hundred or so miles of empty space, what were a few miles of permafrost and solid rock?

A problem, evidently. The thing had already produced one false reading late last night. Jack hadn't been awake to see the "ghost" go tracking across the display. Coming on top of three days worth of jet-lag, the dust-up with Medvedev had completely done him in. It had been all he could do to start the calibration run before dragging himself into the *choum* and falling into a dreamless sleep.

But the SQUID, unsleeping, claimed it had tracked...something.

A fluke. Had to be. Some glitch still lurking in the initialization routines, maybe, or the detection software itself. Sure, the signature matched his models for an object "orbiting" far down within the Earth. But that was the only thing that did match.

Deep as his quarry must've sunk by now, only the merest whisper, the slightest scintilla of distortion in the background geomagnetic field would mark its passage. His "ghost," on the other hand, was tracking way too big, or way too close.

This had all looked so good on the drawing board back in Austin. What the hell was going haywire out here in the field, where it counted?

Jack pondered a moment more, then got up to retrieve his Stetson from where it lay on the packed-earth floor of the *choum*. Logic wasn't working, he might as well try magic. He put on his lucky hat and snapped the brim.

✦

The flashing of the GPS told Yuri he had arrived. He found a secluded spot to beach the canoe, got out, and hauled it up on the Khushmo's pebbly bank…slowly, so as to minimize the noise its bottom made scraping along. Then he straightened and stood listening.

At first all he could make out were the night calls of birds or beasts in the depths of the devil-take-it forest. Then he heard it, far off: the faint chug of a diesel generator.

The sound that would guide him the final half-kilometer or so to the killing ground.

A few things to do here first. Puffing and grunting, Yuri rolled the canoe on its side and eased the heavy steel cage out onto the bank. Its rank-smelling occupant uttered a low complaining growl, but continued to doze. No problem; Yuri had just the thing to wake it up.

A shake of the cage, and the sleeping beast shifted around enough to pin the haunch of one hind leg up against the bars. Perfect. Yuri withdrew a hypodermic from its shockproof sheath and administered the shot.

Now, one last thing. He slid the weapon case out from under the canoe's single seat and, by the light of his flash, peered at the strange implement it contained: a set of spring-loaded metallic jaws, not unlike a miniature bear trap. Except that where any normal trap would have a stylized zigzag of teeth, here the metal had been shaped into replicas of real ones—a gleaming row of incisors bracketed by wickedly-curved canines.

A perfect match for those of the wolf now slowly awakening in its cage.

Yuri's own steely grin made it a threesome.

✳

Jack's lucky Stetson seemed powerless against whatever Siberian voodoo had jinxed his instruments. His vision was beginning to blur from fatigue: he could barely make out the diagnostic readouts on the laptop's display. Still he pushed himself. It was something simple, he was sure of it. Something so obvious he'd laugh out loud once he had it figured out.

He cocked an ear then. Had that been a sound from over in the trees? He sat stock-still, hardly breathing, listening for the snap of a twig, an animal cry, anything.

Nothing.

Jack shook his head to clear it. Darkness, fatigue, and solitude were conspiring to play tricks on his mind. Maybe he should bag this, try to get some rest. Things would make more sense in the morning, after whatever he could salvage of a night's sleep.

Exhausted as he was, he nearly missed it. He was just reaching out to close the laptop's lid when a flicker caught his eye. The Proximity Alert icon was flashing in the upper right corner of the screen. He froze midway through the motion that would have sent the computer into sleep mode.

Proximity Alert?

A glance at the menubar timestamp confirmed it. The exact same time, to the second, as last night's "ghost" event. Jack felt tiny hairs rising on the back of his neck. This was no ghost—not twice in a row like clockwork.

There was something down there!

A click, and the icon expanded into a window. Columns of figures scrolled by, too fast to read. Jack frantically typed in the key-sequence for graphical display.

And there it was! The little blip tracked across the screen for an instant, then was gone.

He hit replay. Gaped in disbelief. Hit replay again.

It was *real!*

Jack only realized he'd been holding his breath when his lungs began clamoring for air. Only knew how broadly he was grinning once his face began to hurt. Hoots of laughter echoed off the trunks of the pitch-pines. Real. *Real,* by God!

Real. But—so close? Jack reviewed the numbers: judging by the signal strength, the thing was less than three kilometers down. That just didn't seem right.

Jack had expected to find his mini-hole in a relatively stable orbit within the Earth, an orbit tracing a series of looping curves like a pattern on a Spirograph. An orbit that, hopefully, would from time to time crest here far beneath the permafrost of Tunguska, where the whole thing began.

He had *not* been prepared for the improbable regularity of the orbit, or how little it had degraded in nearly a century. It was almost as if some external force had been at work on his micro-hole, truing up its trajectory, holding it up or even hoisting it, maybe?

No matter. He'd work all that out in time. The important thing was that he'd found it.

And *what* a find! Jack was suddenly filled to overflowing with a wild elation. He could see himself ascending the stage of Stockholm's Konserthus to receive the Nobel Prize for Physics from the hands of the King of Sweden.

Then he sobered. He'd spent years refining the theory, designing the experiment, sweating the details, pulling together the funding. Years ramping up to this culminating act of discovery.

And, in all that time, he'd treated the whole thing as an intellectual exercise, scarcely giving a moment's thought to what the discovery itself might mean.

For, if it was true—and the proof was right there on the display in front of him—if the Tunguska Object was a primordial black hole still trapped within the Earth, then it represented a terrible danger to all life on the planet. To the planet itself.

What would they—what could they—do about it?

Distracted by the exhilaration of his discovery, distraught at its implications, Dr. Jack Adler did not even notice as a second figure stepped into the circle of light cast by the naked sixty-watt bulb.

10 | A Visit to the Smithsonian

EEP TIME. ITS texture is the granular trickle of sand through the fingers; its signature sound, the echoing of footsteps down marble corridors, past doorways opening onto the light of other days.

Out on Constitution Avenue the heat and noise were building toward their midday peak. Here, inside the Smithsonian Museum of Natural History, the cool and the quiet were all but sepulchral.

Jonathan Knox stood before a window into Earth's past: the Ancient Seas diorama, with its teeming, thrashing life arrested at the height of febrile intensity, its serpentine proto-whale arching for the never-to-be-completed kill. He peered into the empty eye of the archaic predator and felt how narrow a gap separated them, measured against all the annals of the Earth, and he shivered at the spectral touch of Deep Time.

Contemplating that trackless, bottomless emptiness, the mind could cease its manic twitching, could view the tumult of the present from the chill, calm perspective of the ages. Knox needed that; the events of the morning had rattled him. He needed to distance himself from them before he could think what to do.

One thing was clear: the confrontation with Aristos had settled nothing, nothing at all. Knox grimaced, replaying that final scene. He'd let himself get too involved, lost his objectivity—never a good thing. The key was to see with the other's eyes, then find the right word, *le mot juste*, the word that shifted the focus toward a mutually-acceptable vision.

Instead, he'd only made things worse, letting Aristos bully him into playing the old game of who's got the bigger, uh, hammer.

He'd won a round, but so what? The game went on. The same old game frozen at mid-move in the paleozoic pageant before him. The game no one ever really won in the end.

The game that had, evidently, caught up two old friends in its coils.

Sasha and Galya… It had been a long time since he'd thought of them, even in passing. A long time since he'd wanted to. Did they really have a claim on him after all these years? And, if so, was aiding and abetting CROM any way to make good on it? Would he be saving them or destroying them?

Not that it mattered. Humiliating Aristos had slammed the door on any chance of persuading CROM to go easy. He couldn't save Galya and Sasha now, no matter how much he might want to.

And, in Sasha's case at least, Knox wasn't sure just how much he might want to. Not given the way they'd left things, almost twenty years ago.

It was to have been Knox's final night in Moscow. A night late in the month of May. Moscow State University's Lenin Hills campus—in his mind's eye forever glazed with ice and snow—had come into bloom. A time for final exams and farewells.

As the last long late-spring twilight blued into dusk, with incongruously balmy breezes wafting in the open window of Sasha's dorm room, the three friends had toasted one another's health, peace, and eternal friendship.

At some point in the endless rounds of vodka, Sasha had brought forth his "most prized possession"—a thick, crudely-bound document entitled *Kak vyigryvat' druz'ei i vliyat'sya na lyudei*. The greatest book he had ever read, bar none.

There was something about that title. Knox's eye strayed to the author's name — Deyl Karnehgi — and he choked back a laugh just in time. Sasha was holding a bootlegged, photocopied Russian translation of Dale Carnegie's *How to Win Friends and Influence People*. Sasha had always seemed unusually adept at getting the bureaucracy to disgorge a desired result. No wonder!

The festivities were winding down. Around ten p.m. Galina excused herself to go study for an eight a.m. final. But not before giving Knox one achingly warm embrace that left him wondering ever after what might have been.

Sasha insisted that the two of them party on, watch the sun come up on their last night together. Knox could always sleep on the plane.

The spirit was willing, but the flesh was weak. Knox had been up late carousing the night before. By midnight he was bone-tired and ready to crash.

"Don't worry," Sasha told him, "I have something here that will help us stay awake. And entertain us besides." He rummaged through his desk drawers and brought out a small, crudely-carved wooden box containing two dried shreds of brownish fleshy-looking stuff.

"I got them back home last summer, on a canoe trip up to the site of the Tunguska disaster. From that old Evenki shaman I told you about — Dzhen-something. Eighty years old, if he was a day. And still sharp as a pin, for all his wild stories about seeing the Thunder God plant his lodge-pole in the Stony Tunguska heartlands. He took a liking to me, I think, and when I told him I was studying the stars, he gave me these."

Sasha picked up one of the shreds and held it to the light. "If I *really* wanted to walk out among the campfires of the Upper World beyond the sky, the old man said, this was the way the shamans did it."

"Did it work?" Knox eyed the shriveled brownish lumps dubiously.

"I do not know, Dzhon. I have only these two, and have been saving them for a very special occasion."

Knox shuddered with more than the mausoleum chill of the Smithsonian's Ice Age Hall, recalling just how "special" that occasion had become. How he had missed his flight the following morning, and the morning after that. The USAF captain who served as Embassy physician had diagnosed him with food poisoning. And he was ill, true enough, albeit with a sickness not of the body but of the soul. As the ensuing weeks, and months, and years were to show.

Just then his handheld rang, offering welcome distraction.

"Hello?"

"It's Mycroft, Jonathan. I hope I'm not interrupting. I have something you need to hear."

"No, no—no problem. I was just finishing up here, in fact. Getting ready to come home." As he spoke the words, Knox realized they were true. He had irrevocably closed the book on Sasha and Galina, abandoned them to whatever it was that fate, or CROM, held in store.

But Mycroft was still talking. "Do you recall the external links I found on that CROM website? The encrypted ones?"

"Mmm, vaguely."

"Well, accessing the CROM machine this morning gave me the keys I needed." Mycroft paused for breath. "Jonathan, those links led to an intranet site inside the Russian Embassy. A site maintained by some entity called the 'FSB.'"

"Sure, that's their, ah, Federal Security Service. What about it?"

"You're their featured attraction."

"Come again?"

"Your name and address, a none-too-flattering likeness, and a caption in Russian. Babelfish translated it as 'Detain and interrogate.'"

"Detain and interrogate? For what?"

"I couldn't be certain. But almost the entire site was devoted to 'the business of G. M. Postrel'nikova.' Does that mean anything to you?"

"Yeah, sure, the G. stands for Galina—a friend I haven't seen for twenty years." And now never would again.

"And, Mycroft? I hate to tell you, but your Babelfish is misfiring again. That word it translated as 'business'? I'm sure it's *delo* in the original, and that can mean any number of things: 'Business' is one, but in this context the best translation would be…" Knox trailed off as the implication hit him.

"Jonathan, are you still there?"

"It means 'case,'" he said. "As in criminal case — the FSB's investigation into Galina's disappearance."

"But if you haven't seen this person in twenty years, then why—"

"I don't *know* why!"

His shout echoed off the vaulted marble ceiling, loud enough to startle the two other men sharing the hall with him. They quickly turned back to the display cases they'd been inspecting, but not before Knox had managed to get a good look at them.

They didn't look much like your typical mid-week museum-goers. If anything, they looked more like museum specimens. The big guy with the sloping forehead and thick-muscled frame, for instance, could have stepped right out of the Early Man exhibit upstairs. And his smaller companion — thin, sharp-featured, with glittering, furtive eyes that slid away when Knox returned his stare — he would've looked at home among the shrews and voles of the Rodentia collection.

And, now that he'd seen them, Knox realized he'd been seeing them all along. They'd been with him, hovering at the edge of noticeability, ever since Ancient Seas at least, maybe since he'd entered the museum.

Mycroft was saying something. "You seem to have come to the attention of some powerful instrumentalities of late, more's the pity."

It came back to him then: detain and interrogate.

"Listen, Mycroft, I've got to go."

Knox pocketed his handheld and swallowed hard. It was probably pure coincidence. This whole CROM thing had him jumpy enough to start seeing patterns where there were none. And even if it was the FSB, what could they do to him here in the heart of D.C.?

Still, no sense taking chances. Knox began to sidle toward the exit, past case after free-standing case filled with shards of pottery and small bronze medallions, all inscribed with graceful loops and whorls. Something called "The Enigma of Linear A."

Any other time, he might be interested. What interested him now, though, was that his shadows had picked up the pace. Perhaps ten feet behind him, and closing. With the exit arch still thirty feet away.

He was just debating whether to make a run for it, when he saw something that stopped him cold. There, beneath the exit sign, stood an all-too familiar figure, waving to him.

✳

Marianna raised her arm and called out, "Jon, over here!"

What a time she'd had reacquiring him. The Smithsonian was just too damned big. Marianna felt like she'd been tramping around it for hours. She must've passed that damned stuffed African elephant three times by now. Why couldn't the guy have gone to a bookstore or a bar or the goddamn Lincoln Memorial, for godsakes? Why'd it have to be this barn?

It was only as she'd circled the Rotunda once more that the special-exhibit poster finally registered. "The Enigma of Linear A." No time right now, but it was here through the end of September; maybe she'd come back and scope it out some other day.

Or... What the hell. As well look for Jon there as anywhere. She studied the floorplan she'd downloaded to her handheld. Past Pacific Cultures, left at the Mighty Marlin...

There, in the center of the special exhibits hall, stood case after case of priceless artifacts. What had they done, moved the whole Iraklion collection here for the month? They would have loved this, Mom and Dad both. Marianna brushed at the corner of her eye.

When she looked up again, she saw him: Jonathan Knox.

And beyond him, two FSB foot-soldiers, to judge by the dark suits and dour expressions. They looked for all the world like the sweepers for an abduction op.

Shit! Jon was going to be spoiled goods for sure if he showed up at the gala tonight with the smell of the Russian Federal Security Service all over him. Or failed to show up at all.

She beckoned to him. Even the FSB wouldn't try picking him up if he were in the company of an eyewitness. *Look at me, dummy!*

He did. He stopped short and stared at her.

"Over here!" she called again.

Then she watched, dumbfounded, as he turned tail and bolted for the far exit, with the FSB in hot pursuit.

11 | The Beast of Evil Heart

NTENT AS HE was on his discovery, Jack still sensed someone hovering behind him. He whirled to see —

"*Shit*, Igor! You damn near scared the hell out of me!"

There in the glare of the single bulb stood the young biologist from last night's campfire, the one with the shy grin and the hip-flask of "mosquito repellent."

"What're you doing out here in the middle of the night, anyway?"

"Forgive me, Professor Adler." Igor Zaleskii shuffled into the clearing. His grin wasn't working tonight. In its place he wore a hangdog expression.

"What's wrong?"

"Please understand, it is none of my doing, but..." A sigh of Russian proportions. "Academician Medvedev complains that your diesel generator keeps the entire camp awake. He insists you leave still tonight. I am to help you pack."

"What? Leave? But, but he can't do that!"

Igor sighed again. "It is already done. The Academician has radioed to the authorities at Tomsk University denouncing the noise and, ah, other disruptions you are causing as an obstacle to the progress of the expedition. They in turn contacted your own Texas University administration."

It was Jack's turn to sigh. "And they caved, right?"

"Beg pardon?"

"My guys back in Austin, they went along with it, didn't they? Anything not to rock the boat."

Igor just nodded, eyes downcast.

"That's okay. I've got a little boat-rocker of my own here—a major find, I think. Just let me finish my analysis, and we'll see who's standing in the way of progress. By tomorrow, I should—"

"Tomorrow? No, no, impossible. The helicopter will be here for you in an hour." Then Igor blinked. "Did you say major find? Is it—that is, may I be permitted to know?"

"Just let me square things with our fearless leader first." Jack glanced over at the SQUID and the laptop, its display still alight with the raw data of his discovery. "Damn! This couldn't have come at a worse time. Are you positive Medvedev won't keep till I've wrapped things up here?"

"I think it best you talk to him now. I shall watch over your equipment for you until you return."

"Well, okay. But no touching, promise?"

"Do not worry. Go now, and…" The shy grin made a brief reappearance. "Good luck!"

"Thanks." Jack smiled back. Hell, it wasn't the kid's fault if Medvedev had him doing his dirty work for him. On impulse, he whipped off his Stetson and set it on Igor's head. "There you go. Them as guards the gear, gets to wear the hat."

"Oh, yes, please." Igor beamed, managing to look even more boyish than usual. "I like cowboys!"

✳

Yuri was in luck. The target—wearing that same foolish, wide-brimmed hat from the photographs—sat with his back turned in the middle of the clearing, hunched over a computer screen, oblivious to what awaited. The element of surprise should more than make up for any awkwardness with the unfamiliar weapon.

He checked to be sure he was holding the device as instructed. Arming it had been a chore in its own right. A wolf's jaw could exert a pressure of fifteen hundred pounds per square inch. Simulating its bite required setting and locking three separate spring mechanisms, each requiring all Yuri's strength. And that in total silence not fifty meters from the kill zone, since the weapon was too dangerous to carry armed through the tangled underbrush.

No need for silence or subtlety anymore, though. Three swift paces carried Yuri across the clearing, to where the target was just beginning to turn and rise from his seat. One hand clamped the mouth shut and tilted back the head. The other pressed steel jaws against the exposed throat, depressed the mechanism's release, then wrenched back as it slammed shut.

Yuri was an accomplished knife-fighter, well versed in the close-quarters kill, but even he was surprised at the amount of blood. A knife leaves a narrow slit of a wound from which blood merely seeps or at most, when an artery is hit, jets out in a spray. But here the cruel steel teeth had torn one whole side of the throat out. Gore fountained from the severed carotid.

It would not do to be drenched in blood. The real wolf might—

Yuri released his hold and took a step back. Unsupported, the body fell and lay twitching.

He took a last look at the curious weapon before pocketing it with a grin. He would have to see about having one of these made for himself.

He wiped his hands on the fabric of his jacket. Now for the rest of it.

Yuri set about smashing the equipment spread out on the camp-table and the ground beside it. He was supposed to make the damage look haphazard, like the work of an animal. And how the devil was he supposed to know what that looked like? His employers would just have to be satisfied with his standard, manmade death and destruction.

The target was still trying to scream. Only a hoarse rattle gurgled through the mangled larynx.

Yuri looked up from his work, looked into the dying eyes. Take away the hat, and the man lying there didn't much resemble the snap-shots in the dossier. But then dead faces all tended to look alike, especially when contorted in such horror and covered in so much blood.

The one look was all he got. The damaged diesel generator sputtered and died. The single bulb winked out. Silence and night reclaimed one more tiny patch of light and purpose, merging it again into the vast, dark, meaningless wilderness beyond.

A moment more and the ragged breathing ceased. Only one thing left to do.

Yuri withdrew a bottle from a zippered pocket and uncapped it carefully. Holding it at arm's length, he splashed its foul-smelling contents around the campsite, careful not to get any of the liquid on the body itself, lest it overpower the coppery stink of coagulating blood.

He paused a moment then, listening. Vagrant breezes bore a faint sound in from the banks of the Khushmo. A low growling sound.

Good.

✳

Jack was halfway to the main camp when he stopped short and slapped his forehead. That's what he got for going off halfcocked. In his rush to confront Medvedev with his find, he'd neglected to bring along any of the evidence for it. All the tracking data, from last night and this, were still on the laptop back at his *choum*.

He retraced his steps. It would take no more than five or ten minutes to set up the printer and hardcopy the key observations. The delay would doubtless piss Medvedev off even more, but screw that! He'd come around once he understood the significance of the find, once he realized the danger posed by a miniature black hole orbiting inside the Earth.

Jack slowed to a halt again, struck by another thought: my God! Forget Medvedev—it was going to take the entire world scientific community working together to avert a global disaster!

Jack quickened his pace. He could see his *choum* now, through the trees, outlined by the light from the one small bulb. He could hear the rumble of the generator and...a crash?

Dammit! He'd told Igor not to touch anything.

He reached the edge of the clearing and froze. In the dim light, he could see someone, not Igor — a stranger standing there, a large man all in black. He couldn't see Igor at all, unless... could that be him lying on the ground? The light cut out then, but it sounded like the stranger was smashing Jack's equipment to hell and gone.

Jack's scream caught in his throat. Speechless with shock, he groped his way forward through the darkness.

✳

Yuri retraced his path, marking the trail with more of the reeking liquid.

The steel cage was sitting on the riverbank where he had left it. His eyes confirmed what his ears had already told him: the wolf was awake.

The beast was pacing the narrow confines of its prison, slavering, biting at the bars in its consuming hunger. The GEI expediter had assured Yuri that the wolf had been starved for three days in preparation for this mission. It was ravenous, ravenous enough to overcome its natural fear of man, ravenous enough to kill and devour anything in its path.

Now came the tricky part: releasing the predator without becoming prey. That was what the scent-bottle was for; it contained the urine of a she-wolf in heat. Yuri had laid down a pheromone-trail even a famished animal would be powerless to ignore. With luck, the wolf would heed that hormonal siren song and follow the spoor back to Adler's isolated camp before it could think of its hunger again.

With luck. Yuri's left hand unlatched the cage door and swung it open. In his right, he held a pistol. It would be a shame to have to kill the beast after hauling it all the way up from the staging area. And Yuri stood to earn a premium if no one suspected Professor Dzhek Adler's death of being anything but an accident. A gunshot now would forfeit that. Still, no sense taking chances.

The wolf emerged snarling from its cage, and turned to fix Yuri with its yellow glare. For a moment the two formed a dim-lit tableau on the riverbank, animal and man, kindred spirits, beasts of the evil heart.

The wolf sniffed the air, then turned and loped off along the scent-trail leading to Adler's camp.

＊

Jack found Igor lying beside the remains of the laptop. He knelt down, but even in the darkness he could see there was nothing he could do. Arterial blood pooled black in the starlight. It looked as if Igor's throat had been torn out. My God! What kind of animal would do such a thing?

He ought to say something: a prayer, a lament … *some*thing. No words came.

Jack's Stetson had rolled under the camp-table in the struggle. He reached to retrieve it, and placed it on Igor's chest. "He liked cowboys."

He straightened and walked over to the SQUID. His pocket flash played over a half million dollars worth of scrap and blasted dreams. He couldn't take it in, couldn't wrap his mind around it. *Why?*

He was still standing there numbly surveying the wreckage when a growl came from behind him.

He spun around. Caught in the flashlight's glare, a gigantic wolf stared back at him, no more than five feet away. The creature was sniffing at Igor's remains.

"Get away!" Jack shouted. He waved his arms. No effect.

Still shouting, he grabbed a spare tent stave and swung it over his head. The wolf looked up from his meal.

One hundred fifty pounds of claws and fangs hit Jack square in the chest, ripping and tearing. The wolf's stinking jaws stretched impossibly wide, inches from his face.

He lost his footing, toppled backwards, hit the ground. His head cracked hard against a corner of the case that had held the now-ruined SQUID.

It didn't feel like dying. Not really. More like drifting down, down, into an ever-widening vortex of light. The pain of the lacerations was receding, along with the rest of his bodily sensations. He let them go, let memory go, let go life itself. The small spark that was Jack Adler made ready to rejoin the universal radiance. The light flowed forth to welcome him home. He beheld it at last in all its splendor.

The seed, the source, the place where everything began — *infinity in the palm of your hand and eternity in an hour.*

✳

Even from the riverbank, Yuri could hear the howling. Good, the wolf was busy covering any last traces of his own visit.

Time to be going. He loaded the empty cage back in the canoe and made ready to push off. The return trip would be easier; it was all downriver to the helicopter landing area, and the sky was already brightening to the east.

In the far distance, Yuri could see flashlight beams playing among the trees. It had taken them a good five minutes, but the other expedition members had finally roused themselves to investigate the ruckus. With luck, they might even arrive in time to catch sight of the wolf. If not, well, the sound of its snarls and the tracks it would leave behind should be enough.

Yuri smiled grimly to himself: Grishin would have his "accident," and *Rusalka* would keep her secret.

12 | The Illusion of Choice

JONATHAN KNOX TOOK the stairs down to street level two at a time, conscious of the pounding of two, maybe three sets of footsteps behind him. Conscious, too, of the pounding of his own heart, the breath catching in his throat.

Making a run for it hadn't been such a hot idea, on the evidence. But what else could he have done? Especially once he'd seen that little CROM minx was in on it.

In on it? She'd probably orchestrated the whole thing from the get-go.

If he could just get out onto Constitution Avenue, hail a cab.

Knox double-timed across the Smithsonian's entrance foyer. Didn't dare look back, but the pursuit no longer seemed to be gaining on him. Maybe running hadn't been such a bad idea, after all.

He ran straight for the nearest exit, slammed a shoulder into the heavy bronze revolving door and shoved.

Then suddenly he was out, into blinding sunlight and sweltering midsummer heat. He scanned for a free taxi, but the drop-off drive was empty, save for a late-model black Lincoln sedan. And the two dark-suited men looming, arms folded, in front of it.

As he came out the door, they dropped their arms and started for him.

✳

"An abduction is the mirror-image of an extraction." The half-forgotten Ops 101 lecture replayed in Marianna's head as she pelted down the stairs, bringing up the rear behind Jon and the sweepers.

"In an extraction, the target is a willing accomplice; it is the environment that is hostile, comprising an active security cordon. In an abduction, the target is a victim, uncooperative, but the environment is neutral at worst, and all the abductors need do is keep it that way. This essential difference colors every aspect of operations, beginning with team size…"

That's what her subconscious had been trying to tell her. This wasn't going to be a one-on-one. What with sweepers, handlers, blockers, perimeter security, FSB could have fielded ten-fifteen guys for this op.

Marianna suddenly felt very alone.

Why hadn't Jon just stood his ground? The sweepers can't sweep you into the clutches of the handlers if you refuse to be swept. And she was standing right there. Together they could have toughed it out.

Unless… She skidded to a halt in the middle of the Smithsonian entrance foyer.

Oh, God! He thought she was part of it! Of all the dumb—

Through the glass of the revolving doors, she could see Jon paying the price for that little error in judgment. He was struggling to break free of two massive handlers, and having about as much luck as a two-year-old squirming in the grip of a grownup. Try as he might, he was being dragged inexorably toward the dark interior of a curbside limo.

Should she maybe flash her ID and break this up? CROM did have a working arrangement with FSB to presume upon. But, no, Grishin probably had half the FSB's embassy staff on his payroll. If she spilled the beans now, he'd know of Jon's involvement with CROM by nightfall.

But she couldn't just stand here and watch her whole case go down the tubes. Not while there was the slimmest chance of salvaging it. *Think!*

The outlines of a plan took shape, as despairing as anything she'd ever come up with. Well, okay, taking on a dozen armed FSB goons probably beat it out on the desperation scale. Marginally. Still, any chance was better than none.

She turned and sprinted out the side exit.

The heat hit her like a wall. She stood blinking in the glare, waiting for her eyes to adjust, and counting.

One, two, a possible three, four. A by-the-book abduction called for a perimeter security detail of anywhere from four to six operatives. Given how quickly FSB must've thrown this op together, Marianna was betting they'd opted for the lower limit. And there they were, trying to look as inconspicuous as their dark Sunday-go-to-party-meeting suits would allow.

Two were staked out on either side of the semicircular drive, guarding the limo into which Jon was just now disappearing. Way too close to approach, much less take down.

But one was positioned on the sidewalk a ways up Constitution, all by his lonesome. Perfect.

She cut across a strip of sunbaked lawn and onto the sidewalk. Felt in her shoulder bag for the Talon's hard black shape. Another non-leth. But that was a good thing: for all FSB's faults, they were rivals, not enemies.

Casually as she could, she glanced back over her shoulder. *Shit!* They were packed up and ready to leave. Trying not to rush it, she continued walking toward her target.

The beefy stake-out guy looked her up and down—once with suspicion, once more with appreciation. Then he dismissed her and went back to scanning his sector. Just a woman.

Nearly there now. Behind her she could hear a car door slam, the big Lincoln engine turn over. She'd just run out of time.

The perimeter guard looked surprised when she stepped in close and twisted the handheld out of his grasp. Not as nearly surprised as he looked when she rucked up his shirtfront, pushed her Talon StunGun deep into his bare belly, and depressed the trigger for a full five seconds. Three hundred thousand volts *will* surprise you.

Oof! Marianna barely caught him as he slumped. His involuntary muscle spasms made it even harder to support him, but she needed his bulk to screen her from his compatriots half a block away. He made little mewling noises as she shoved a shoulder under his ribcage and, gasping, took the dead weight on her back.

Now came the tricky part. CROM's uneasy alliance with FSB extended far enough to have worked out a common set of codes governing operations like these. Let's just hope they used the same codes for FSB-only ops.

Still propping up the big guy as best she could, she lifted the handheld she'd swiped from him, and punched in what she hoped was the code for *Mission Abort*.

✳

To Knox, it was as if someone had waved a magic wand.

One instant he was in the back seat of a black Lincoln, straining for breath against the hand clamped over his nose and mouth, struggling to free his arm, now bared to the elbow, from the viselike grip of a man wielding a sinister-looking needle. And the next—

All around him, everybody's handheld began warbling at once. And the next—

He was sprawling flat out and face down on the cobbled surface of the drop-off drive. A screech of tires behind him, a blast of gravel-laced backdraft, and he was all alone.

Or not quite. He could hear the rhythmic click of heels on pavement now. He raised his head, enough to watch two shapely legs walk up and come to a halt in front of him.

"Jon," Marianna said, "looks like you could use a hand. And a lift."

She knelt and helped him up. He stood there a moment, leaning on her, catching his breath.

"You okay walking?" she said. "My car's about a half a block away. I could go get it while you rest here."

The thought of being left alone again sent a chill down his back. "No, no, I'll be okay."

As they walked along, gradually picking up the pace as Knox grew steadier on his feet, Marianna filled him in on the identity of his would-be abductors, and how she'd won his release.

"It all depended on them being pros," she said, "drilled and disciplined enough to scuttle the op first, and ask questions at the post-mortem. Else you'd be in the chair right now, spilling your guts."

She stopped talking, then, looked at him. Gradually it dawned on Knox that she was waiting for him to say something.

"Uh, thanks, I guess."

"You guess?"

"Well, face it, Marianna, you're the one that got me into this."

"Not me. That fancy handheld of yours. I'm willing to bet FSB had their signal-intelligence guys trawling for your cellphone signature ever since you hit D.C."

"I thought only the cops could do that."

She shrugged. "The cops, and anybody else who's got the price of a GSM scanner."

They were in the car and heading for Virginia before he tried again. "Okay, I can see how FSB found me, once they were looking for me. But why were they looking for me? What was it got me into this mess in the first place?"

"Oh, that. They must've picked up on your email traffic with Sasha, and connected the dots to Galina from there. They're all over GEI these days, you know, like ravens on roadkill."

Knox bristled. "*My* email traffic with Sasha? I seem to recall it was *you* that hijacked my account and contacted him."

"Whatever."

"It doesn't make sense, though," Knox said half to himself. "I mean if CROM and FSB are in bed together, and FSB knows I've been working with you—"

"Not only do they *not* know that, if you claim it, we'll deny it."

"When would I claim it?"

"After they've picked you up again."

"Again? But I thought—"

"Thought what? That I've got nothing better to do than babysit you, when you're not even working with us? No, I'll ferry you out to Dulles, but that's it. After that you're on your own."

He was silent for a time. Then: "And I'm going to have this hanging over my head forever, you're saying."

"Well, yeah. Unless..."

"Unless what?"

"Unless, say, CROM were to leak it that we've already got Galina in custody. That'd dial down the heat some."

"And CROM would do that? Out of the goodness of your hearts?"

"I think you already know the answer to that one, Jon."

He sighed. "The gala."

"Uh-huh."

"But just the gala."

"Just the gala," she said. "I swear."

✱

"I'm back, Pete," Marianna burst through the office door. "I've got him stashed in the hotel. We're back on track for—"

She stopped in mid-stride: Pete was not alone. Across from the Reacquisition Director a blond, square-jawed matinee idol occupied her usual chair, a devilishly handsome grin gracing a face so photogenic as to approach caricature. With his carefully cultivated tan, athletic build, and long, straight, sun-bleached hair, the guy looked like a refugee from Venice Beach.

"Marianna," Pete looked up, "Say hello to Chris Renshaw, CIA."

"Hi, Chris. We met last year. I don't know if you remember, but I was in your six-week Covert Ops refresher." *I don't know if you remember, but you tried hitting on me.*

"Marianna. Of course." Chris rose and took her hand all in one fluid movement. "Pete and I were just talking about you — about the great job you've been doing on the Grishin thing up to now."

Up to where you can take it over?

"Chris," Pete said, "I need a moment alone with Marianna here."

"Sure thing, Pete. I'll wait to hear from you on this. Only let's not wait too long, okay? Clock's ticking." Chris strode to the door, turned and winked, then closed it quietly behind him.

Marianna whirled on her boss. "Pete, you—"

"Stop. I know what you're going to say."

"I'm saying it anyway. You are *not* handing my case over to that big slab of beefcake!"

"It's not your call. The sort of play we're looking at here, it's...well, it's just too risky. Even a seasoned field agent like Renshaw could wind up neck deep in shit."

"I've been on field assignments too, Pete."

"Only the one." His eyes bored into her. "And look how that turned out!"

"The review board is going to rule that a no-fault, and you know it. I can't believe you're going to throw that in my face now, and blow the best shot we've got at Grishin."

"Marianna," Pete's voice became a shade less gruff. He took a sudden interest in rearranging the documents littering the desktop in front of him. "Marianna, try to understand. You could have been killed. There are other ways."

"What ways? We've been all through that. Short of launching Tsunami itself, Interdiction won't work worth a damn. A search-and-seizure is going to turn up nothing, *nothing!*"

"It's one of the options on the table, is all."

She took a deep breath and released it. "Do you have any idea how *big* that ship is? Forget about hiding a couple of proles; they could have an entire Tokamak stashed away in there, and you'd never find it. Grishin'll just sit back laughing up his sleeve at you. And then turn around and call his friends on Capitol Hill."

Pete nodded glumly. That had to've hit home: next month's closed-door budget hearing was fixing to be an uphill battle as it was, no sense making it a bloodbath.

Marianna leveraged the opening. "Pete, you know it and I know it: this has got to be done undercover. And I've been working the GEI case since day one. Who else have you got that can come up to speed in the next seven hours? And please don't tell me it's Chris Renshaw."

"He's a good undercover man, Marianna."

"He's a bad joke, is what he is. The guy sticks out like a sore thumb.

He couldn't be more conspicuous if he had double-oh-seven tattooed across his ass!"

"You're not all that low-profile yourself."

"But my legend's already in place, Pete. And Phase II's just about a done deal. Sasha's already emailed Jon about the voyage. And that's another thing: Jon. Who else have you got that can run the Archon resource?" She broke off then.

Not soon enough. "Stop right there and let's think about that," Pete said. "Say this all works out per plan; you could wind up having to shack up with this Knox guy to maintain cover. This is Chantilly, not Langley. I don't assign my people to…" His face flushed dark; he waved a hand clumsily rather than finish the thought.

"To what? Work as whores?" Might as well get this out on the table too, take the bull by the horns, so to speak. No misplaced overprotectiveness was going to keep her off this mission. "That's not how it's going to go, and you know it."

She looked him square in the eye again and smiled sweetly. "Don't worry, Pete. I'll break his pecker off and feed it to him before I'll let him stick it where it hasn't been invited."

That had the desired effect. Pete coughed and involuntarily glanced down at his own crotch, making sure it was still safely barricaded behind the polyplast desk, no doubt. Nothing like a little symbolic castration to quell those bothersome pseudo-paternal impulses.

Pete cleared his throat. "You don't even know how he's going to take it. The guy's a civilian, for Christ's sake. You watch: he'll turn tail and run like a rabbit the minute he finds out what you've got planned."

Marianna *had* watched. It was not a pretty sight.

"He's not going to find out. Not till tonight. First he hears of it, he'll be standing right in front of Sasha."

Pete stared at her as if she'd grown horns. "Now, that's got to be the dumbest stunt you've ever pulled. He's going to fu-—screw the whole thing up if you do that."

"Then he fucks it up while we're still on dry land. Think of it as a pre-flight stress test. If he bails, we fold. But he won't. He's got no choice but to go along, and he knows it."

"You're saying Mission Rusalka's good to go."

She nodded. "I'd stake my life on it."

"You got that part right," Pete said under his breath. He shook his head, made the sort of face that goes with a bad taste in the mouth, then spoke the words she'd been waiting to hear.

"Okay, give it a shot. Only..." He ran fingers through his almost nonexistent hair.

"Only what?"

"Only... Jesus, Marianna, you're a hard case! What is driving you?"

Marianna made no reply. She looked down at her lap, to where her hands were clenched into tight, white-knuckled fists, as if crushing a windpipe or...

...Or clasping the sweat-slick pommels of a leather horse.

All unbidden, the sights and sounds of that spring afternoon flooded in on her. Once again she heard Coach Gheorghiu calling for the dismount in his nasal Bucharest accent. Felt again the rush of acceleration as her arms propelled her high off the pommel horse, the flexing of her legs as she braced for impact with the pad-covered hardwood floor. Watched as her guidance counselor Ms. Pettigrew forced open the gymnasium's heavy double firedoors, dabbing at reddened eyes with a Kleenex.

The moment her life had changed forever. A freeze-frame etched indelibly in her mind's eye. Could it really have been eleven years ago?

She should have been on that plane with them. Mom and Dad had even planned their twentieth anniversary trip to Thira to coincide with Carver High's spring break. But State was coming up at the end of April—the first rung on the ladder that maybe, just maybe, led to a slot on the US Olympic team. In the end, Marianna had accepted Marcy's offer to stay at the home of her best friend and gymnastics squad co-captain for the three weeks her parents would be gone.

Except now they were gone forever.

Somehow she'd pulled herself back together in time to enter college that fall. What was there to do, after all, but work? But she'd switched her major from literature to psych, with a concentration in Criminal Psychology. And she'd dropped gymnastics for martial arts: six hours a week private instruction that earned her a second-degree black belt in the same three years it took her to get her accelerated degree. Scuba diving, flying lessons, computer programming—anything she could think she'd need.

There was a family trust fund. Not huge, but enough that, on graduation, she was free to follow her heart in choosing her life's work.

But is it really freedom when you have no choice?

For there was never any doubt where her road would lead. She would combat the evil of terrorism. The evil she had come to hate with every fiber of her being. The ruthless, pitiless evil that had taken her parents, her Mom and Dad, from her. From her, and from each other.

Love dies.

Hate never does.

13 | Puttin' on the Ritz

"**Y**OU CLEAN UP nice, Jon."

The familiar female voice had come from the interior of the stretch limo. Ducking his head to get in, Knox saw Marianna Bonaventure reclining against Moroccan leather, a strapless taupe confection in brushed silk complementing her now-upswept dark hair.

"Uh, you too," he said, too nonplussed for gallantry. "I didn't think you were serious about coming along."

"Wouldn't miss it for the world."

"But why? It's not like I'll need a minder the way your techies've got me wired." His House of CROM summer tux had enough electronics sewn into the linings to set off an airport metal detector. "Anyway, won't having a bona-fide CROM agent, however decorous, on my arm tend to blow my so-called bulletproof cover?"

"Not a problem. As far as Grishin and company know, the agent in question is out of the picture. Permanently."

"I'm sure you'll tell me what that means when we get a moment alone together." Knox gave her an inquiring look. When that didn't work, he added, "Come to think, we've got one now."

She got quiet. He hated when she did that; it meant she was metering how much truth to dispense this time around.

Finally she said, "Okay, I was there when 'Galina' got extracted. Not the in-charge, but I'd called it, so I got to observe. And it damn near got me killed. Did get me killed, as far as the opposition knows. Thrown down an elevator shaft." She shivered. "Look, could we talk about something else?"

"I don't know that I've got anything to match that," he said. "I mean, client relations can get strained at times, but it's always stopped short of defenestration. Until now, that is."

Talking usually soothed Knox's nerves. This conversation was having the opposite effect. Which served to remind him...

"Incidentally," he said, "speaking of potential bodily harm, did you—?"

"All taken care of. I talked to Pete, and you're off the hook with the FSB." She patted his hand. "Now, why don't you just relax? Four or five more hours and it'll all be over but the debrief. Think past it—think about your next assignment. London, isn't it? Tell me about that."

"Well, there's this bank..." He launched into a disquisition that, with Marianna's promptings, continued until the floodlit marble facade of the Kennedy Center hove into view off the limousine's starboard bow.

The John F. Kennedy Center for the Performing Arts illuminated the humid Washington dusk like a king-size bug-zapper, the oranges and blues of its floods luring in all manner of lepidopterous nightlife, resplendent in chitinous tuxes and diaphanous evening gowns. Knox and Marianna followed the shimmering throngs into the Hall of Nations, along its sixty-foot high, flag-draped length past the limpid blues of Maro's *Transfiguration*, down to the Grand Foyer.

Performances at the Center's six theaters had been canceled for the evening at Arkady Grishin's behest, so that the *Mir i Druzhba* gala might be held in the cavernous, red-carpeted Grand Foyer—a single continuous space as long as the Washington Monument was high, presided over by Robert Berks' monumental bust of John Fitzgerald Kennedy. Directly across from JFK, a string quartet was entertaining on the raised landing out in front of the Opera House, the musicians re-

flected in the eight floor-to-ceiling panels of Belgian mirror flanking
the entrance. One entire glass-fronted wall of the Foyer gave out on the
softly-lit gardens of the River Terrace, and the Potomac swirling in the
darkness beyond.

"That's him—Grishin," Marianna nodded her head toward a gray-
haired, distinguished-looking gentleman in his mid- to late fifties
standing at the center of a small knot of gala-goers.

They'd said the man was an avid sailor, and he certainly looked
like an outdoorsman of some stripe, with those rugged good looks and
ruddy complexion. But he also looked completely at ease in this draw-
ing-room milieu. Tall, slim, and immaculately tailored, sporting a dazzling smile, Grishin was holding forth to an audience that included,
far as Knox could tell, at least two United States senators and a Cabi-
net officer. Rising on its pedestal behind Grishin, the eight-foot-tall,
rough-textured bronze head of JFK looked on in mild bemusement at
the spectacle of a Russian magnate captivating the cream of Beltway
society.

Knox was surprised that the man of the hour hadn't drawn more
of a crowd. Then he saw the wall of muscle—a ring of swarthy, dour-
looking bodyguards—cordoning off the elect from the uncommon
herd.

Knox had to strain to catch what Grishin, through his interpreter,
was saying: "But in order to be a true friend and partner in the war
against terrorism, Russia must first and foremost be herself again.
What kind of honest dialogue can exist between our two great nations,
when one side is only parroting back what the other wants to hear?
No, my dear friends, Russia must find her own true voice once more."
Yadda, yadda. Rumor had it the GEI chief was weighing a run for the
Russian presidency next time around. If so, he'd come a long way to
stump for it.

None of Knox's concern; he was here to find Sasha. He scanned
the faces in Grishin's immediate vicinity. Where Arkady Grigoriyevich
went, could his right-hand man be far behind?

With Marianna in tow, Knox homed in on a familiar frizz of straw-
blond hair protruding above the artfully coiffed and coutured hubbub.

Sure enough, Sasha it was, standing beneath one of the Orrefors crystal chandeliers, his back to the crowd.

Sasha seemed oblivious to the glitter all around him. Totally lost to the world, in fact. Gesticulating wildly and uttering a stream of rapid-fire Russian in what seemed a manic conversation with himself. Terrific! He's gone and snapped under the strain.

Then Knox spotted the headset tucked behind his old friend's ear, and the hair-thin wire trailing down the side of his neck. Connecting, no doubt, to a cellphone base unit tucked in a shielded jacket pocket, where its microwave radiation would be less likely to fry his brain. The Sasha that Knox had known in Moscow hadn't even had a phone line to call his own. This paragon of pervasive teleconnectivity was going to take some getting used to.

Knox reached out to tap Sasha on the shoulder, and found his arm arrested in mid-arc by a hard, hairy hand. The hand belonged to a short, squat, Transcaucasian-looking individual. More hired muscle. The man released Knox's wrist, wagged an index finger at him, then pressed that same finger against his own lips.

"Shhh," quoth the torpedo. Evidently Mr. Bondarenko was not to be interrupted while engaged in his phone conversation.

The small disturbance had, however, registered on Sasha's peripheral vision. He broke off talking to the air and turned to see what was going on. A smile spread across his face as he sighted Knox. He spoke two words of dismissal into his lapel mike, one to his bodyguard, and stood there arms outstretched.

"Dzhon!" He crushed Knox in a bear hug and pounded him on the back. "I am so happy you could come. It is so good to see you after all the years."

"It's great to see you, too, Sasha," Knox said as soon as he could breathe again. He stepped back a pace. It was like stepping back twenty years in time. It was still Sasha. Still the same improbable mix of candor and cunning, open-heartedness with an eye to the main chance. Still his friend.

"You don't look a day older," was all Knox could think to say.

"Nor you, my friend, nor you." Sasha gave him a playful punch on the arm. He seemed altogether energized by the reunion.

"I'm forgetting my manners." Knox put his arm around Marianna's waist. Surprisingly, she snuggled against him for a moment.

"Marianna," he said, "this is Aleksandr Andreyevich Bondarenko, the old friend I told you about. Sasha, I'd like to have you meet—" What was that cover name again?

"Ms. Marianna Peterson," Sasha finished for him. He took Marianna's hand in both of his. Thought better of it and gave her a hug, then kissed her on either cheek for good measure. "I feel I know you already. Dzhon has told me so much about you."

Hmm. At that afternoon's briefing, Marianna had filled Knox in on some, by no means all, of the email correspondence conducted in his name over the past few days. If it had included any glowing references to herself, she'd neglected to mention them.

Sasha was still talking to Marianna. "Really, though, my dear, you must speak to Dzhon. He entirely forgot to tell how beautiful you are."

"You're too kind, Mr. Bondarenko." Marianna colored prettily. What sort of paramilitary training enabled that fine-tuned a control over the facial bloodflow? "Both with your compliments and with your wonderful invitation."

"Call me Sasha, please. We will be spending enough time together to become old friends, too."

Something about that last exchange didn't quite track. Knox was about to ask about it when Sasha turned back to him.

"So, Dzhon, a consultant? I had expected to find you a Harvard professor by now. Did you never complete your thesis?"

"Wouldn't advertise it if I did. In the consulting game, a doctorate's superfluous at best, downright suspect at worst."

"You never told how you got into this work. It seems a great distance from *Sovietologia*."

"Not so great as you might think. It's a long story, but the crux is, it all comes down to language. Moving from Russian to UML just means swapping one set of formalisms for another. But how about you, Sasha? Deputy director of Russia's third biggest conglomerate sounds like a far cry from cosmology, too. What's that all about?"

"As with you, it is a long story. The details are perhaps not so very interesting, and there will, in any case, be time to discuss later. For now: well, you claim it is only a short step from Sovietology to systems analysis. Permit me to say the same of the transition from astrophysics to high finance. Except magnitudes become even more astronomical." He winked.

"But I fear we have ignored your lovely companion too long." He turned to Marianna. "Forgive us please, my dear. There are years of catching up to do."

"Don't stop on my account, uh, Sasha. Jon and I are still so new to each other, every old friend is a chance to learn a little bit more about him. This mysterious Soviet past of his is only the latest puzzle piece." As she spoke, Marianna casually slipped back into Knox's embrace. It felt like she belonged there, warm and soft, cuddly when she wanted to be.

The scent of her was intoxicating. The distraction made it harder to focus on broaching the subject of Galina. And doubly hard to fathom what Sasha said next.

"We can wait until we are aboard to give such matters the attention they deserve, dear Marianna. We shall have all the time in the world then to bare the secrets of this poor man's soul."

Then he turned to Knox and said something even less comprehensible: "I trust you are all packed? I must apologize for the early departure, but *Rusalka* sails with the morning tide."

"Um," Knox said.

"We wouldn't miss it for the world, Sasha," Marianna took up the slack. "It's *so* kind of you to offer to sail us to Jon's next assignment."

"Nonsense, Marianna! When Dzhon emailed me that he must start work in London next month, how could I do otherwise? True, our big boat is much slower than a transatlantic jet, but I think you will find her far more comfortable. And, besides, there is someone aboard who cannot wait to see you, Dzhon! No less so than I." Sasha punched his arm again.

So that was what she hadn't been telling him. He was being shanghaied! Still, there was a way out of this. If he could just get Sasha to admit…

"Someone waiting to see me?" he began, "Is it —"

Is it Galina? he'd been about to ask. He couldn't. His mouth was suddenly otherwise engaged. The kiss Marianna gave him was long and luxuriant, exactly the way he'd been imagining it from the moment he'd first laid eyes on those exquisite lips. And none the less enjoyable for being totally contrived. Talk about *una cosa di biznes*.

"Oh, Jon," she breathed in his ear, "won't this be romantic?"

✸

"Next time you're thinking of pulling something like that," Knox said once they were alone in the limo again, "Some sort of advance warning would be nice."

"Oh, you mean the… call it a qualifying exam, Jon. I needed to see how you react to unpleasant surprises."

"I'm a systems analyst, remember? Unpleasant surprises are my stock-in-trade."

"Anyway, it worked, that's what counts. And it's not like you weren't going to London anyway. Thanks for the backup, incidentally."

"You're welcome. How'd I score?"

"Mmm…B plus. But it'd have dropped to a C if Sasha had caught that look on your face."

"You're referring to my justly famous 'Oh, Lord, the client's just gone off the high board and the pool's been drained' expression?"

"That's the one—do it for me again."

"Maybe later." Knox was a little too apprehensive about recent and possible future developments to keep up his end of the repartee. This was turning out to be radically different from any assignment he'd ever undertaken before. Turning out to be personal in the extreme, for one thing. There'd be no maintaining his carefully constructed façade of professional objectivity on this one. Would that impair—had it already impaired—his judgment?

Then, too, Marianna's assurances to the contrary, there was a strong undercurrent of physical danger here, an irreducible element of risk in setting foot on some strange vessel bound for God knows where. And none of it strictly necessary, if all CROM was trying to do was ascertain Galina's whereabouts.

That reminded him: "Why did you sidetrack me back there just when I was getting Sasha to open up about Galya?"

"I got the impression you kinda liked it," she said. "But, since you ask: there's no hurry on that any more."

She leaned in closer. Knox could feel the warmth of her again, could smell the way it was sublimating her perfume, the mingled aromas of Chanel and Marianna wafting from her décolletage. Close enough to kiss, not kissing—no encores for that part of the performance tonight, evidently. Still, her proximity alone was enough to cloud his higher faculties.

"Thanks to you," she purred, "there's no hurry at all. We'll have two operatives inserted by tomorrow morning."

✳

Arkady Grigoriyevich Grishin looked about him at the polished wood and brass appointments of his palatial headquarters suite and smiled. It was good to be back aboard *Rusalka*, good to be sailing with the morning. Over the past decade, he had come to feel more at home on the sea than the land.

He shook his head. Strange sentiments for a Russian. Like Antaeus, Russia had always drawn her strength from Mother Earth, from vast land armies, from peasant stock stolid and enduring as the eternal land itself. Hemmed in by her lack of warm water ports, denied ready access to the open ocean, for most of her history Russia had turned her back on the sea. Even Peter the Great had striven against that geographical destiny in vain, his dreams of a fleet come to naught. Only the Soviets, by dint of Herculean effort, had succeeded in making Russia a naval power—and that only in the past half-century. It did not come natural, even yet. Mastery of the seas was still too new and too alien to strike a responsive chord in the national psyche.

Grishin chuckled at the irony. For fate had decreed it would be on the high seas, from this magnificent vessel, that Russia would change the course of history.

The maritime clock on the mantel chimed five times. Five bells, two-thirty in the morning. It didn't seem that late. Grishin rose from behind his ornate leather-topped desk and poured himself a splash of Stolichnaya XX from the bottle on the sideboard. He stood there running his hand over the gleaming mahogany, imbibing its warmth and luster through manicured fingertips.

Changing the course of history... How many obstacles had he already overcome in pursuit of that goal? Even this evening's fête had its small part to play in the plan. All his pet Senators had come out for the GEI gala, as why would they not? Their fawning attendance was, after all, merely the outward and visible sign of that inward and spiritual grace conferred by soft-money contributions. The cash, funneled in through various fronts to choke the coffers and campaign war-chests of his unwitting allies in the American Congress, had had the desired effect: the federal watchdog agencies investigating GEI's affairs were being kept on a very tight leash, and would be for at least the next two or three months. Ample time to bring the Antipode Project to fruition. And then CROM and the rest would simply not matter, not matter at all.

Grishin frowned then, recalling how close a thing the CROM business had been. But who could have known, back when Komarov and Dinershtein first took up permanent residence onboard *Rusalka*, that anyone—anyone at all—would take notice? It was not as if these were biochemical or nuclear specialists. From a counter-proliferation perspective, tracking magnetohydrodynamicists made as little sense as shadowing veterinarians.

Still, that one slip-up had nearly brought the whole soaring edifice of the Project crashing down in ruins. Two weeks ago Security had confirmed that CROM was sniffing out this slenderest of leads, their inquiry spearheaded by one particularly tenacious analyst.

But the diversionary disappearance had come off brilliantly. Now CROM had what it was looking for: an overt extraction to investigate. To investigate, but never to resolve. For days, weeks—for all the time left to them—they would be haring down that false trail, seeking a woman whose very blood and bones had been reduced to their component atoms.

A false trail that led far from *Rusalka*, where all the while the real Galina was safely sequestered, free to complete her vital work, never suspecting she, or her alter ego, was the object of a nationwide manhunt.

And, best of all, the ruse had drawn their over-inquisitive CROM analyst out into the open, into the ambush. Two flies with one slap, as Yuri put it.

Yuri—that one bore watching. No principles, no convictions, no allegiances to any cause higher than money. A common mercenary. Or, give the devil his due, a most uncommon one. Principles aside, no one could dispute his effectiveness. Already, this afternoon, he had reported back that the Tunguska operation had gone off without a hitch.

That the last possible leak had been plugged.

Worth drinking to. Grishin drained his glass and poured himself another.

It would have been so much simpler in the old days. The very notion of American scientists tramping unhindered around the remote Siberian wastes would have been unthinkable to begin with. Now, his compatriots fell all over themselves making the Americans and their dollars welcome, like so many piglets pushing and shoving to suckle at the teat of the New World Order. How had it all gone so wrong?

That, at least, he could answer. He spoke a command and resumed his seat to watch the leather desktop retract, revealing the holotank beneath. Within its depths, sparkling like some improbable dendritic crystal, a computer-generated chronogram rotated slowly. A schematic encapsulating years of work by the Temporal Research group, depicting all of twentieth-century Russian history. And more.

For, though its main line charted the dates of key events in a deep, glowing blue, this was no simple linear chronology. Instead, from each of history's hinge-points there sprouted one or more offshoots in hues ranging from somber red to pulsating green. These branches, forking further even as he watched, gave the construct as a whole the aspect of a magical tree—the World Tree of ancient proto-Slavic mythology, each of its brachiating limbs another might-have-been, another alternative path into the future. He knew each node, the root of each sub-tree, by heart: Lenin's cerebral hemorrhage in 1924, Stalin's murder of Kirov a decade later, Beriya's arrest following Stalin's death, Chairman Andropov's premature demise in 1984, the failed 1991 coup attempt. So many, many places where things might have gone just a little bit differently.

Grishin rose to face the globe-girdling serpent of the GEI logo filling most of the opposite wall. He lifted his glass.

"To the glorious past," he said, his voice a whisper. "The past, and the even more glorious future…"

He took a single sip, then raised the glass again to finish the toast.

"And to the place where they meet."

Part Two
Rusalka

...all I ask is a tall ship
And a star to steer her by.
— John Masefield, "Sea Fever"

14 | Hull Number Forty-Seven

A T A HUNDRED thirty-three meters from stem to stern, *Rusalka* was more boat than any berthing facility on the Potomac could handle. Instead, she was anchored off GEI's private pier in Baltimore, a good hour and a half drive up from D.C. through Friday morning rush-hour traffic.

Or not. Knox looked down on the vehicular snarl radiating outward from the construction site at the Beltway/I-270 merge, and gave thanks for friends in high places. Several hundred feet high. He caught Sasha's eye through the door separating the cabin of the Grishin Enterprises helicopter from its cockpit. Sasha swiveled in the copilot's chair and grinned down at the bumper-to-bumper traffic. He mimed a "Whew!" of relief. Better them than us!

In the seat to Knox's right, Marianna was sipping at a latte, and idly tracing the veins in his hand with her index finger. The tiny tingle made him shiver. Pretending to be a couple with Marianna felt so natural that Knox found himself wishing they'd gone for something a little hotter than the prim and proper lawyers-in-love look for their cover story.

Too late to switch now. Deferred gratification was the order of the day as they wended their way north to Baltimore on the morning after the gala.

Twenty minutes' flight time brought them over the rooftops and esplanades of the city's renovated harbor district. The waterfront was directly ahead now, all but empty at this hour, too early for the tourists, too late for the Bay fishermen.

The chopper angled out over the water. Only then did they see her.

Knox was prepared for large. *Rusalka* was *enormous*. Out of scale. One hundred and thirty-three meters was just another number, another insubstantial abstraction. *Rusalka* made the abstract concrete—she was one-and-a-half times the length of a football field. Her gleaming white shape dwarfed the lesser yachts riding at anchor in the Inner Harbor, and transformed the shops and restaurants of the nearby marina into mere model-railroad accessories. She looked for all the world like a cabin cruiser that had somehow found its way into a backyard swimming pool.

Sasha tapped the pilot's shoulder and made a circle in the air. The pilot obliged by coming in low and orbiting the gargantuan craft.

Close up, *Rusalka* was an improbable multi-layered wedding cake. Her streamlined superstructure rose five decks high to a flying bridge ninety feet above the waterline. Half the top deck was given over to silvered skylight. Expanses of the same one-way glass fronted the bridge, and what looked like a observation lounge one deck below it.

The vessel just went on and on, yet there was grace in the gigantism too. The whole ensemble was sculpted into such sleek, backswept lines as to give *Rusalka* the look of cutting through the waves even as she rode at anchor.

"Seventy-five crew," Sasha shouted to Knox over the roar of their descent, "and ninety staff, counting administration and research."

Some of that headcount was coming into view as the copter circled. At white-linened tables scattered across the aft deck below them, a couple dozen senior management types and attendant one-rung-downers were breakfasting *al fresco,* preparing for another day of directing the fortunes of Grishin Enterprises from this, its self-contained floating headquarters.

One last, lingering look, then they touched down on a helipad just forward of the superstructure.

Marianna and Knox followed Sasha across a sunwashed arrival deck and into the cool and comparative dark of a vestibule hung with medieval tapestries and lit here and there with the glowing golds and rich browns of miniature Orthodox icons.

A heavy glass portal hissed shut behind them, sealing them all inside. Point of no return.

"Passports, please." Sasha held out his hand. "Must get you checked in." He walked the documents over to a guard stationed inside the entranceway.

Knox turned his head for a last wistful glance at the helicopter, their sole remaining link with dry land. It was gone. Could it have lifted off again once they'd disembarked? No, they would have heard the racket, even through those inch-thick tempered glass doors. Where...?

Then he saw where: it was disappearing below decks. The helipad they'd landed on must ride on an elevator-platform. The whole structure, with the copter still sitting on it, was descending into the hold below, allowing the two halves of a second, previously-retracted deck to slide out and close over it. Wow!

"Coming, Dzhon?" Sasha had finished his transaction with the guard. He saw what Knox was staring at, and grinned. "Best not to leave our chopper sitting out in the sun all day."

Sasha ushered his guests across an expanse of black marble flooring inlaid with the Grishin Enterprises logo—the Ourobouros fashioned of laser-cut jade this time, girdling a globe of lapis lazuli oceans and bottochino continents—and into an elevator at the rear of the welcome lobby.

The lift compartment's walls, ceiling, and floor were a medley of chrome and backlit Tiffany glass, the overall effect resembling a ride inside an art-deco jukebox. A ride so smooth that Knox was still waiting for them to start moving when muted chimes announced their arrival at accommodations deck, one flight up.

As to accommodations, Sasha knew his friend's reticence in affairs of the heart well enough not to bother inquiring as to the precise developmental stage of the Knox/Marianna relationship. Instead, he had elected to cover all bases: he showed his guests to two adjoining staterooms with a connecting door.

Their luggage having arrived ahead of them, Knox and Marianna were left to settle in. Sasha's special guided tour of *Rusalka* wouldn't begin for another twenty minutes.

Knox checked out his new digs. Outsized portholes, illuminated shoji screens taking up the top half of the inboard wall, and that king-sized platform bed sure looked inviting. He was tempted to slide under the matte gold comforter and make up for the sleep he'd lost to the late-night briefing at CROM Central. Rather than give in, he walked over to where his suitcase rested on a luggage stand at the foot of the bed.

Marianna had told Knox not to bother packing: CROM would put something together for him. Knox had gone along on the general principle that the client is always right, especially when they're volunteering to do the work. What that left him with, though, was a suitcase full of unfamiliar paraphernalia. Thank God he'd thought to bring his own toothbrush.

"Marianna? What's this all about?" he called through the open connecting door.

She came to the doorway and looked. "Oh, that." Then she motioned him out of the room and down a corridor to the outside. With the crew preparing for departure and most of the GEI headquarters staff already at their desks, they had the deck nearly to themselves.

"It's not safe to talk in there till I've deployed countermeasures," Marianna said, sotto voce. She leaned against the rail, morning breezes toyed with her hair. "Now, you were saying?"

"What am I doing with a wetsuit in my valise?"

"That's just standard emergency kit for any blue-water operation."

"Aristos isn't seriously expecting *Rusalka* to go under, is he?"

"Jon, the thing about covert operations is, nine-tenths is just contingency planning. Don't let it get to you."

"Okay, sure. SOP, if you say so." Did she actually believe this no-big-deal bullshit she was feeding him? *That* was scary. "Even so, what if they'd gone through our luggage and asked what we were doing with all that stuff?"

"We'd have said it's for scuba diving when we call in at the Azores. But they wouldn't ask, Jon. That's what makes you such perfect cover for this mission. Everyone's convinced we're just a systems analyst and his girlfriend."

"What do you mean, *just* a systems analyst?"

✷

Rusalka's observation lounge sparkled with chromed surfaces and Susan Puleo metallic fabrics. It reminded Knox of something. The vast technoesque space looked almost like—

Yes, there in the middle of the scalloped ceiling hung the mirrored sphere emblematic of an upscale discotheque. It lacked only the strains of Gloria Gaynor's "I Will Survive" blaring from the B&W sound system to complete the ambience. The post-Soviet Russians were making up for lost time, but to date they'd only gotten as far as the seventies.

Beyond the mirror-ball, the lounge was fronted by a wall of tinted glass giving out on a panorama of Baltimore Harbor. Between inpouring and reflected dazzle, it took Knox a moment to realize there was someone else in the room with them, seated on one of the L-shaped settees.

"Marianna, Dzhon," Sasha said, "I have the pleasure to introduce Ms. Naomi Cutler, senior editor for *MegaCraft International* magazine, who joins us on our tour today. Naomi, please to meet Marianna Peterson and Dzhonathan Knox, friends sailing to Europe with us."

"Are you along for the ride too, Ms. Cutler?" Knox asked the tall, athletic-looking brunette who had risen to shake hands with them.

"Naomi, please. No, just passing through. Not that I don't envy you the voyage."

"Perhaps you know of *MegaCraft*, Dzhon, Marianna. One of only two magazines in the world devoted exclusively to megayachts. Naomi is here researching a possible article."

They took seats, then waited while a white-liveried steward filled coffee and juice orders from an espresso machine *cum* minibar on wheels.

"*Spasibo*," Knox thanked the steward for his *espresso doppio*, then turned to Naomi. "An article? Is *Rusalka* news, then?"

She thought a moment before replying. "Could be. This is just a preliminary walk-through. If I like what I see, I'll come back with a photo crew next month and give her the full treatment."

"You mean all this…" Marianna's gesture took in the lounge and beyond "…might not measure up to your editorial standards?"

"Not that, exactly," Naomi said. "It's just we need to be convinced this boat has, well, lived down her past."

"Naomi…" Sasha began.

"Come on, Sasha. You know it's true."

"Have you been holding out on us, Sasha?" Knox asked, adding in his most melodramatic, what-evil-lurks-in-the-hearts-of-men baritone, "Could this big, bright boat of yours be harboring some deep, dark secret?"

He'd meant it as a joke, so it was kind of surprising how flustered Sasha got. "What? No, no, Dzhon, nothing of the sort. Naomi merely refers to certain, ah, unfortunate episodes in *Rusalka*'s history, prior to her acquisition by Grishin Enterprises."

"'Unfortunate'?" Naomi laughed. "That's cute, considering how she went from princess to pariah in the space of two years."

She turned to Knox and Marianna. "You've got to understand, from the moment Oskarshams laid the keel in 1987, *Sharifa* here was destined to be one of the crown jewels: third biggest private yacht in the world, ever. Add to that the mystery surrounding her owner…"

"What did you call her? Sharifa?" asked Knox.

"Uh-huh, *Shaika Sharifa*—*Queen Sharifa*. That was the rumor, anyway. As far as the yard was concerned, she was just Hull Number Forty-Seven. Those Swedes can be silent as the grave even when the owner hasn't insisted on total anonymity… and he had."

"But *MegaCraft* had a theory as to the owner's identity?"

"Well, the name alone was a pretty strong circumstantial," Naomi said, "if you know your Middle Eastern royals. But the clincher was when the yard stopped work on her as of August 5th 1990."

Knox got it then. "Not the Amir of Kuwait? What a bummer! Losing a boat like this *and* a kingdom, all in the same week." Oskarshams had suspended work the same week Saddam Hussein's tanks had come rumbling across the Kuwaiti border.

"Actually," Naomi lowered her voice, "losing this boat might have helped *save* the kingdom. The Amir needed all the in-area friends he could get at that point, and scuttling the Sharifa newbuilding went a long way toward mending fences with the Saudi royal family."

Knox furrowed his brow but said nothing.

"Too big," she elaborated. "At four hundred thirty feet length over-all, Sharifa was large enough to rival the Abdul Aziz, King Fahd's four hundred eighty-two-footer."

Knox chuckled. "No sense sticking a finger in your new best friend's eye, eh? So, what then? Grishin stepped in and bought her at fire-sale prices?—No, wait, the timing's all wrong for that. Wrong for any kind of sale, I'd guess, with half the world's potential buyers hunkered down dodging SCUD missiles."

"Uh-huh. When all was said and done, there was only one deal on the table." A look of distaste crossed Naomi's face. "Though I'd like to think the Amir never would've gone for it if he hadn't needed the cash for, uh, public relations."

"Of course!" Knox snapped his fingers. "The anti-Saddam PR campaign that brought Congress onboard with the military option." He looked about him. This vessel was a living link in the chain of events that had led to Operation Desert Storm. "What was wrong with the money?"

"Sad story. The only taker was a US junk-bond king with a scheme to convert *Sharifa* into a floating casino. He rechristened her the *Buona Fortuna* and steamed her across the Baltic into Gdansk for the interior work. All done on the cheap. A real schlock job, too: mirrors and red velvet galore."

"Your basic French Provincial bordello effect," Knox supplied.

Naomi sighed, as if taking *Sharifa*'s fall from grace as an affront to the megayachting community at large. "*MegaCraft* wouldn't touch her after that. To think we'd been holding our Spring '92 cover for her at one point."

"I must commend your, ah, journalistic diligence, Naomi," Sasha said. "Is it permissible to ask how much of such speculation you will include in your final article?"

"I look forward to talking with you about that, Sasha," she said smoothly, "Anyway, the story gets better from there on out. By early '92 the deal had fallen through and the boat was back on the block. And this time the high bidder was none other than Arkady Grigoriyevich —yes?"

Sasha nodded.

"The price would have been right," Naomi went on. "Grishin Enterprises *might* have shelled out thirty-five million, tops. Add another twenty for this latest refit, and it's still bargain basement—less than half what she's worth."

She glanced at Sasha for confirmation again, but none was forthcoming.

"Anyway, after the sale, she disappeared off everybody's radarscope. All we knew was the new owner had renamed her one more time, ordered up a minimal makeover—mostly just ripping out the gaming tables and installing office sets and labware—and put her to sea in late 1993. Where she pretty much stayed till the start of the new millennium."

"Well," Knox said, "even billionaires need a hobby, and oceanography's as good as any."

"I suppose." Naomi gave a noncommittal shrug. "Be that as it may, it's only over the past three years that they've finally gotten around to doing a proper rehab."

"Restoring the soul of a Queen, so to speak," Knox mused.

Naomi Cutler looked into the middle distance. Thinking, perhaps, about how that line would look emblazoned across the cover of *Mega-Craft International* magazine.

✳

After an hour of traipsing through one gilded chamber after another, Knox was suffering from opulence overload. It was like nothing so much as a very high-end pub crawl, without even the consolation of liquid refreshments.

As to that, the spirits were willing, but the schedule was taut: *Rusalka* was making ready to catch the morning tide, while MegaCraft Lady was booked on the noon flight out of BWI to Orlando. The helicopter that ferried Naomi out to the airport would have to rendezvous with *Rusalka* again as the vessel passed Annapolis.

The logistics were just tricky enough that they were getting tight on time. And with both salon deck and the oceanographic laboratory still to go.

"It is impermissible not to see the banquet hall before you leave us, Naomi," Sasha told her. "It is the centerpiece of our new *Rusalka*!

"But you, Dzhon and Marianna," he turned to them, "will have an opportunity to attend a dinner party there in three days. Why not save it as surprise? I will show you our lab instead."

So it was that the group split up. A few whispered words into Sasha's lapel communicator summoned up Igor Savchenko, *Rusalka's* lean, graying first officer. Savchenko was deputized to escort Naomi up for a look at the salon deck, and then on to Arkady Grishin's offices; the owner had expressed interest in meeting the *MegaCraft* editor and would personally see her off.

"Looks like this is goodbye, then," Naomi said, glancing at the time, "I'll have to airlift out as soon as I'm done up top. Sasha, we'll talk; I think there's a story here. Marianna, Jon, it's been nice meeting you. I wish you all a bon voyage." She shook each of their hands in turn, then she was gone up the broad spiral staircase.

Knox was sorry to see her go. There had been considerable entertainment value in watching Naomi keep Sasha on his toes. Why hadn't they gone with an enclosed-bow design like everybody else? What's with all the bearskin rugs and ponyhide upholstery—couldn't they at least *try* to be a little PC? One tough customer. If this kind of grilling was what you got with a walk-through, it's a sure bet Sasha wasn't looking forward to the impending "full treatment."

"So, Sasha, the corporate offices are up on salon deck?" Marianna asked on their way down to the lab. "I'd think you'd want the guest cabins up there for the view."

"The problem is roll, Marianna. Placing VIPs such as yourselves lower down on main deck minimizes discomfort."

"Roll? Oh, of course, the way the ship rocks from side to side. I keeping forgetting we're on a ship; *Rusalka's* just so *huge!*"

Sasha winced. "'Yacht' or, possibly, 'boat,' Marianna. Never 'ship,' please. 'Ship' refers only to merchant or military vessels."

"But, ship or boat or whatever," Knox said. "Is seasickness really a problem? I'd have thought a vessel like this would have God's own stabilization system."

"Not one system, Dzhon—two. First, Intering tank stabilization down in the hold, like on the biggest cruise ships. Conventional stabilizer fins on top of that. Except these are not so conventional: Old ones used gyroscopes; *Rusalka*'s are next-generation Trac digital stabilizers from American Bow Thruster. Two sets. You know about this?"

Knox shook his head.

"State-of-the-art: solid-state sensors embedded in the hull, constantly monitoring vessel's roll and pitch, and feeding data to microprocessors that optimize fin angles in real time. *Rusalka* feels the water she moves through."

"Sounds very cool." Knox loved technotoys.

Sasha turned to Marianna and smiled. "Between Trac and Intering, *Rusalka* guarantees you smooth sailing, Marianna. Dramamine not necessary."

"I'd really like to see that Intering system too sometime," Knox said, as they came to a halt before a watertight double door marked "Oceanographic Laboratory" in Russian and English.

"Just big U-shaped tanks filled with seawater, Dzhon." Sasha shrugged. "Pumps transfer water into the arm of the tank on the side opposite to the vessel's roll, and the counterweight damps movement. Nothing much to look at, and the hold is dark, dirty, hardly fit for sightseeing."

Off limits, in other words. Could they be hiding something down there?

"In any case," Sasha was still talking, "I think you will find what we have here much more interesting." With that, he punched digits into a keypad set in the jamb and the panels slid open to reveal *Rusalka*'s ocean sciences lab.

✳

But for its lack of windows, Knox would've been hard put to tell the lab from the salons and skylounges they'd just left. No Bunsen burners or Bakelite-surfaced workstands for GEI's researchers: late-model workstations were scattered about the vast, high-ceilinged space with all the artful randomness of tables at a sidewalk café. The lighting was subdued throughout, save where a spot illuminated yet another Ourobouros crest, inlaid in the center of the far wall above an unmanned reception desk.

Sasha followed the line of Knox's gaze. "Jorgamund, the Midgard Serpent," he said. "In Norse legend, Odin released a snake into the sea, where it could thrive. It grew so great that in time it encircled all of Midgard, the world of men, and bit its own tail. Most appropriate here: our researches also help the ocean, and its creatures, to thrive."

Knox frowned, trying to recall the Elder Eddas as filtered through the prism of Marvel Comics. "Um, I thought Jorgamund was one of Loki's three monstrous children. And Odin hurled it into the sea to keep it from devouring the Earth."

"Must not read *too* much into legends, Dzhon," Sasha said.

They walked past ranks of neat and tidy lab benches. Too neat and tidy. None of the real engineers and researchers of Knox's acquaintance would have lasted a day in such an antiseptic environment. Where was the clutter of a working lab, the Slavic equivalents of empty Jolt Cola cans and half-eaten pizza slices?

"Sasha? What goes on in here? Anything?"

"Seismometry, Dzhon. All quiet now. You should have been here six-seven years ago, before we finished our North Atlantic survey. We still keep a few seismologists on staff—there are always seaquakes and volcanic eruptions to investigate—but the focus of our work has shifted to the other three sections. Come."

Sasha steered them around the reception desk toward one of two glass doors set in the interior wall. Through the tinted glass, Knox could see a second room lined with more workstations, but this time sporting the bric-a-brac of lab apparatus too. Like the first lab, this one was all but uninhabited at the moment—precious little for an oceanographer to do in port, Knox guessed—but at least it had that lived-in look.

"And here, our *pièce de résistance*." Sasha pointed to the left as the party entered.

They turned to see a floor-to-ceiling aquarium occupying most of the inboard wall. Behind a giant slab of acrylic, in a luminous blue the color of the sky at dusk, there floated an armada of jellyfish, glowing iridescent in the ultraviolet-tinged light. The huge jellies—a plaque identified them as sea nettles, *Chrysaora fuscescens*—drifted like strange, amorphous extraterrestrials. The aliens were accompanied by flotillas of their smaller cousins, exquisite miniatures blazing like gems in the UV illumination.

"Specimen tank, for marine biologists," Sasha said. "A big brother of the aquarium up in our skylounge."

Knox peered into the tank's depths. It looked as if…yes, through the glowing water, he could trace the contours of another dim-lit laboratory, a mate to the one they were in. The sealed tank must go through the dividing wall into the other lab, so researchers on that side could observe its goings-on too.

Speaking of researchers, he could just make out someone in there, outlined against the light of a computer screen as he—she?—rose from behind a workstation and walked up to the other side of the tank. The whitecoated figure stared at the visitors for a long moment, probably having no better luck making out individual features through the layers of thick glass and twilit seawater than Knox'd had. Behind him, Sasha lifted a hand to wave. A whitesleeved arm waved back from the other side, then pointed to a door on the left.

"Come," Sasha urged Knox and Marianna toward an exit opposite the one they'd come in by. "Someone you must meet!"

He herded them out and into yet another lab, in time to see…

She was just emerging from another door further down the room. Then she was running up and throwing her arms around a startled Knox.

Galina!

"Ah, Dzhon! *Skol'ko lyet? skol'ko zim?*" How many years has it been?

"Galya…it's been a very long time indeed. Far too long!" He pulled back to look at her.

The years had etched character into the face he remembered, but could not dull her innate vivacity. In the joy of this meeting, she fairly glowed, her green eyes alight and sparkling with barely held-back tears.

Her honey-colored hair tickled his neck as she hugged him yet again. Simply no comparison with the woman whose image Marianna had showed him his first day on the assignment, that bleach-blonde ringer captured in CROM's drive-by snapshots.

Knox sobered at the thought of CROM, remembering there was an ulterior motive behind this happy reunion. Remembering that standing right behind him was...

"Marianna, I'd like to have you meet Galina Mikhailovna Postrel'nikova, an old, old friend from Moscow. Galya, this is Marianna Peterson. Marianna's my, uh..."

"Companion," Marianna filled in smoothly, holding out her hand, "Never mind about Jon; I can see you're not 'old, old.'" She sounded friendly enough, but there was something of the cat who ate the canary in the smile playing about those lovely lips.

"Very pleased." Galina took Marianna's hand in hers, oblivious to any dire consequences her unexpected appearance might bear with it.

They were clear enough to Knox: Galina was the smoking gun. With her presence aboard *Rusalka* confirmed, CROM had Grishin dead to rights. Interdiction would swoop in, impound the vessel, and frogmarch the lot of them off to jail.

Knox experienced a flash of relief. He was off the hook, no need to go through with the rest of it now. They'd be back in Chantilly closing out the GEI file by nightfall.

His relief mixed with melancholy as he looked into the smiling faces of his soon-to-be incarcerated friends. Galina's joy at seeing him seemed as unalloyed as Sasha's had last night.

Why? he asked Sasha mutely. Why did you just hand her to us on a silver platter? Where are the secret rooms and shoot-outs, the poison pellets and plans for world domination—all the melodramatics his imagination had been conjuring up ever since this damn assignment began?

Why did you make it so easy for me to betray you?

Though it was all anticlimax now, they continued to go through the motions. Playing their parts as VIP tourists, Knox and Marianna let Sasha show them around the rest of the lab, beginning with the section they'd first seen Galina in.

Knox read the sign on the door. "Seafloor tectonics? What were you working on in here, Galya?"

"Was not working, Dzhon. Not as member of *Rusalka* staff. Sasha lets me use workstation for email, and to edit articles, and for monitoring experiments left running back in Akademgorodok. Otherwise, am just like you—passenger aboard most beautiful yacht."

"Great! Marianna and I could use some company while Sasha's off charting the course of Grishin Enterprises." Knox suppressed a grimace as he said that; no telling where Sasha would be twenty-four hours from now, but it wasn't likely to be the commodious GEI corporate suites up on salon deck.

Rather than risk letting his chagrin show, he turned his face away. And found himself looking at the other face of the specimen tank he'd first spotted Galina through. The jellyfish swirled in the artificial currents, their carefree drifting mocking his preoccupations.

Through intervening layers of water and glass and *Chrysaora fuscescens* he could just make out the seawater-chemistry apparatus in the room they'd left moments ago.

✦

Knox hung back as their little tour group walked out the lab's forward door and down a short connecting corridor. He was getting that feeling again. The one he got when something wasn't adding up according to his subliminal calculus. Something about the way the space was laid out back in the lab. He glanced back over his shoulder but the glass door was already sliding shut behind him.

Looking around, he saw they were headed back to the same reception lobby they'd come in by some two and a half hours ago. And on their way back out to the helipad.

Where a tall, dapper figure in navy-blue blazer and white linen slacks was standing with his back to them, waving a farewell to the departing helicopter.

"Ah," Sasha said. "I thought we might find him here. Come say hello to your host."

Arkady Grishin turned toward them as they approached and smiled questioningly, icy blue eyes peering out of a tanned, genial face.

"Arkasha," Sasha switched to Russian, "I would like to have you meet my friend Dzhonathan Knox. I knew Dzhon in graduate school, in Moscow. By luck, his consulting agency has posted him to an assignment in London starting next month. I have taken the opportunity to invite him and his friend Marianna Peterson to accompany us on the Atlantic crossing."

A shadow seemed to flit across Grishin's face.

Sasha didn't notice. In English he said, "Marianna, Dzhon, please permit me to introduce to you Arkady Grigoriyevich Grishin, CEO and Chairman of the Board of Grishin Enterprises International."

"Ms. Peterson, Mr. Knox. Pleased to make your acquaintance." Grishin's English was quite passable, but he didn't seem comfortable speaking it. Releasing Marianna's hand, he turned to Knox and asked "Moscow, yes? You speak Russian, then?"

Receiving a nod, he continued in that language, "I would have greeted you sooner, had I known you were aboard. But I confess not to have foreseen any guests at all on this summer's cruise." Grishin flashed Sasha an enigmatic look.

Sasha swallowed. "Only for the run to the continent, Arkasha. Two weeks, three at most."

Grishin turned to Knox. "If you have known Sasha for so long, then you must know how impetuous he can be. In this case, I regret that it is impossible..."

All at once Grishin's eyes hardened. Though their surface affability never wavered, sparks of cold fury now churned in their depths. What could Knox have done to merit all the bad vibes from a man he had only now met? Short of setting him up to be clapped in irons, of course, but Grishin couldn't know that, could he?

Then Knox realized that the arctic glare was aimed, not at him, but over his shoulder. He turned to see what Grishin was looking at. And saw Galina just emerging on deck.

The moment passed. By the time Grishin turned back to Knox, his sunny cordiality had returned, rekindled as if by an effort of will. But its warmth never reached the cold blue eyes, nor thawed that wintry stare.

"Well, it is settled then," Grishin said. "Now that you have been reunited with Sasha and Galina Mikhailovna here, you must of course come with us. Welcome aboard."

✳

From main deck, Knox watched the weirs and jetties of Baltimore harbor slide by, shimmering in the midday heat. The gray bulk of Fort McHenry was receding minute by minute into the haze of distance, taking the land of the free and the home of the brave along with it.

What was CROM waiting for? Knox turned to his "companion," looking for signs of imminent action, seeing none. Marianna stood beside him close enough to touch, not touching. Lawyers-in-love was good cover for impromptu working meetings. It was just that he had no idea what was left for them to be working on.

"Uh, seems like we've accomplished about all we could have hoped for here, no?"

"Eyeballing our wayward prole?" She grinned. "That part did go quick, didn't it? Kind of surprising, the way Sasha just trotted her out like that."

"Maybe not as surprising as you think."

"Meaning?"

"Didn't you see how pissed Grishin was when we showed up with Galya? Maybe no one told Sasha he was supposed to be keeping her under wraps. Which means maybe he wasn't in on that disappearing act back in New York either."

"Maybe." Marianna didn't sound as if she cared much one way or the other.

"So, anyway, about time to call in the cavalry, no?"

"You're kidding, right?"

"Uh, I don't *think* so."

"Because this is absolutely our best shot at finding out what Grishin's up to."

Uh-oh. Where had he seen that kind of gung-ho attitude before?

Knox was beginning to get a queasy feeling in the pit of his stomach. "Marianna, don't take this the wrong way, but..."

"But what?"

"But this wouldn't happen to be your first field assignment, would it?"

"I've been mission-rated going on two years now." A defensive note had crept into her voice. "And nobody's got as much sweat-equity in this case as me. I *earned* this."

"That's not what I asked."

"*And* I'm a good enough field agent to've saved *your* ass back in D.C., remember?"

Knox said nothing, just waited for her to settle down.

She sighed. "Okay, yes, it's my first real field assignment. Not counting that business in New York, of course."

"Ah!" Her being a woman had kept him from spotting it sooner: the junior-exec-out-to-make-good syndrome...and overcompensating for a previous screw-up, to boot.

"What's *that* supposed to mean? I'm still the one Pete put in charge of this mission."

"I was there too, remember?" Knox thought back on their post-gala meeting with the Reacquisition Director. Thought back on Aristos's ill-concealed grin as he'd walked them through their pre-mission briefing. The bastard hadn't even bothered to pretend this cruise hadn't been on the agenda from the get-go. But he'd also offered a possible out.

"Pete gave us a specific objective, as I recall," he said, "Confirm Galina's onboard and call in the troops, preferably before *Rusalka* leaves U.S. waters. Well, I'd call what we've got here mission accomplished. And we seem to be in process of leaving U.S. waters just now, in case you hadn't noticed."

She turned to look aft at the noon-hour traffic crossing Francis Scott Key Bridge. "Galina's just the tip of this iceberg," she said, half to herself.

"Look, Marianna," he said, talking to her back now. "You know better than anybody what Grishin's capable of. Are you ready to run the risk we won't make it back with what we already know?"

She turned to face him again. "Given what we do know, what makes you think Grishin's just going to let us leave?"

"How about calling in, at least? You know, touching base?"

"No way. Feel free to swim back to Baltimore and report if you want, but we break communications silence only at discretion of the agent-in-charge. And the AIC is me."

"Guess again, Marianna. Last I looked, I wasn't part of your chain of command."

"I'd have thought you especially would want to stick it out, Jon. If your friends really are innocent, the only place you stand a chance of proving it is right here on *Rusalka*."

He had no ready answer to that.

She smiled sweetly then, her couples-mimicry routines still going full blast for the benefit of any onlookers. "Besides, a transmission right now would have them at our throats a lot sooner than CROM could intervene. Our best option is to lie low and see what else we can find out."

"Such as?"

"Such as what they've got Galina doing."

"Some nefarious MHD research? No sign of any magnetohydrodynamics in the lab today."

"Somewhere else, then."

But he had stopped listening. A mental Rubik's cube spun and clicked, all six faces resolving suddenly to uniform colors. So, that's why…

"Jon? Hello?" Marianna was talking to him. He blinked and looked at her. "You went away there for a minute," she said.

Knox was opening his mouth to respond when Sasha came up and slapped him on the back. "Hey, lovebirds! Time for lunch! Must eat, keep strength up!"

✦

Rusalka steered for the main channel of the Patapsco and gathered speed. It was past one by the time she rounded Swan Point and entered the broads of the Chesapeake proper. All through the afternoon she plied the calm, sun-flecked waters of this, the largest inland tidal body on the Eastern seaboard, the drowned nether valley of the Susque-hanna.

The long day waned, the slow moon climbed, the last streaks of sunset faded from the sky. It was nearing midnight and moondown when they passed beneath the Chesapeake Bay Bridge at the mouth of the great estuary. On the Virginia coast the Cape Henry light gleamed and was gone.

From his vantage up on main deck Knox watched a small motor launch pull alongside in the dark, matching speed and course with her giant sister. An access door swung open midway along *Rusalka's* shimmering flank and a Jacob's ladder clattered down to the smaller craft. Oblique angle and dim blue light made it hard to be certain, but Knox could have sworn that someone, something, just a darker blot against the general darkness really, was clambering up hand over hand, toward the open hatchway. By the time he'd rubbed his eyes, whoever it was, was gone.

Ship's bells chimed eight times: midnight. The Bay pilot, job done, descended the rope ladder to the deck of his launch, then turned to flip a salute at the bridge high above in the starlight. Dancing its assigned measure in the stately old pavane of ships putting to sea, the pilotboat arced away from the great vessel and sped back toward the lights of home.

Her gleaming bulk shuddered imperceptibly, her engines thrummed a deeper note, as *Rusalka,* alone now under the stars, made for the open sea.

15 | Patterns

"**Y**OUR PARDON, COMRADE Director." An intercom window popped open on the wall-sized display, Merkulov's squint-eyed, broad-featured face filled its frame. "You asked to be informed the moment Geladze arrived back on board." The high-pitched, tremulous voice didn't seem to go with the thick lips and pendulous jowls that produced it, as though *Rusalka*'s security chief were a badly-dubbed character in a foreign movie.

Arkady Grishin looked up at the interruption, pushed back from his console. "Thank you, Vadim Vasiliyevich. Please send him to see me immediately."

"Very good, Comrade Director. You may expect him at the headquarters suite in five minutes."

"No, not the headquarters. The hour is late. I will see him here, in the Residence."

A look of surprise flashed across Merkulov's fat face as the window closed. The security chief himself had never been invited to Grishin's private quarters. Few ever were.

Russians by nature abhor an information vacuum, and GEI's staff and crew were no exception. At any given time there were half a dozen rumors circulating as to what sybaritic splendors lay behind the case-hardened steel portal at *Rusalka*'s heart. None even came close to the truth.

Grishin's eyes roved around the blank off-white walls and Spartan furnishings of his quasi-monastic cell. A replica, complete to the smallest detail, of his old office out in "The Woods," as KGB Foreign Intelligence's suburban headquarters had been known. As such it offered a welcome refuge when the wretched excess reigning elsewhere throughout *Rusalka* began to cloy. And more than a refuge: a place to remember one's beginnings.

And one's ends. His gaze came to rest on the room's sole decorative touch, an outsized portrait of former Chairman of the State Security Committee, the late General Secretary of the Communist Party of the Soviet Union, Yuri Vladimirovich Andropov. A small brass plaque set into its frame identified the painting as having been presented to one Mstislav Platonovich Gromov, Major KGB, for meritorious service and exemplary commitment to duty.

The artist had captured the deep-set, watchful eyes well enough that they seemed to demand such service, such commitment, still.

Ah, Yuri Vladimirovich! We shall redeem the faith you reposed in us. As you shall redeem ours.

The heavy steel door slid back to admit the other Yuri, Geladze. *Rusalka*'s master computer had tracked his movements by the radio-frequency locator badge he wore, just as it tracked the movements of everyone else aboard the vessel. Almost everyone else. It was the two exceptions that had occasioned this late-night meeting.

"Welcome back, Yuri. I trust you had a pleasant flight?"

The Georgian just stood there, not deigning to respond. Unless that noncommittal grunt counted as a response.

Grishin ignored the impropriety. "Yes, well, it seems we have a small problem here. Unexpected American guests. Sasha took it upon himself to invite two friends to accompany us to Europe." A keystroke brought up names and images on the wall-sized screen.

Here, too, Yuri withheld comment, though he studied the faces on the wall with predatory intensity.

"Foolish, of course." Grishin shook his head. "Especially now that we are so close to our goal. I was going to have them put ashore again, when I saw they had already encountered Galina Mikhailovna."

"Ah," Yuri said, as if much had just become clear. "Your orders?"

"For the moment, only to watch. Much as he may deserve it, it would not do to upset Sasha unduly while his efforts remain essential to success. And, in any case, final disposition of this matter is better left until after Mr. Knox and Ms. Peterson have disembarked in London. There can be no point in calling unnecessary attention to ourselves."

"Only watch, for now," Grishin repeated. "After all, where can they go, what can they do that we will not learn of, here on *Rusalka*?"

✳

Rusalka steamed on through the night, past the towering Chesapeake Light fourteen miles east of the mouth of the Bay. Knox watched its strobes, the last signal fires of land, disappearing astern.

He leaned over the rail and peered down into the darkness. Breathed deeply, filling his nostrils with the sharp tang of brine. The vessel's bow cleaved the dark water cleanly, churning out patches of sizzling, starlit froth that merged into her phosphorescent wake. The gentle rise and fall was mesmerizing, an ocean-going version of highway hypnosis. Come, drift along with me, the midnight sea murmured, just drift along and leave trouble far behind…

"Jon?" A voice came from behind him. Trouble was back.

He turned to see Marianna framed in the pantographic doorway. Or, almost see her.

"I'm not sleepy yet," she said. "Think I'll take a turn around the deck before packing it in."

There was something subtly wrong about the way the light was playing around her backlit form. He rubbed his eyes and looked again as she walked up to him.

"Don't worry, your eyes aren't going on you. This outfit is made out of a high-refraction nano-block synthetic. It's hard to keep in focus." She wriggled mock-coquettishly to illustrate, leaving moiré afterimages on his retinas. "Why, in some lights I'm practically invisible."

"How come we're whispering?"

"Force of habit. I already swept our staterooms and put the bugs to sleep."

"And the Catwoman get-up?"

"Goes with the midnight-prowl thing."

"Want some company?"

"Sorry, no." She looked down and adjusted something on a belt studded with matte-black tool holsters, "Even two would be a crowd."

"In that case, how about a roadmap?"

"Come again?"

"Do you have any idea where you're going, or what you're looking for?"

She shrugged. "Whatever they've got Galina working on, wherever that is."

"In some sort of secret lab, right?"

"Call it that. As to finding it, I was planning on running a standard reconnaissance sweep. Why? You've got a better idea?"

"You hired a consultant. The least you can do is let him consult."

She half-smiled. "Be my guest—consult away."

"Step into my office." Knox took her arm and escorted her back down the corridor to his stateroom. "You did say we're okay to talk in here?"

In response, Marianna knelt and pried out a section of the platform bed's toekick base. She pointed to a silvery disk maybe half an inch in diameter clipped to the bedframe.

"The walls have ears," she said. "Japanese manufacture, wireless, self-contained. Fits anywhere, hears everything. Five in your room, one in mine." Marianna made a small moue to show what she thought of being rated the secondary target.

"All of them convinced we've gone to bed for the night. Like this." She grinned and flipped the disk over to show a small black chip epoxied to the back. "A phase inverter: takes any incoming sound, computes the inverse wave, and pumps it out, a hundred-eighty degrees out of phase. The net output vector is white noise. It's the same noise-cancellation technology that the Navy's been installing for the deck crews on aircraft carriers."

She replaced the panel. "Can't just leave it at that, of course. Grishin wouldn't have gone to all this trouble if he didn't expect to hear *some-thing*. So this base-unit in here…" She led him through the door connecting the two staterooms and into her bathroom, where she pointed out what looked like a compact WaterPik recharger sitting atop the cosmetics shelf. "…broadcasts an overlay signal that the phase inverters *will* pass on to all those waiting microphones."

"What does it broadcast?"

"Just something CROM Countermeasures whipped up for the occasion. Typical night sounds, snoring and such — all synched to a built-in timer."

"I don't snore."

"No one ever does," Marianna said. "Anyway, trust me, we're covered. Now, what's this about a roadmap?"

"Process first, then product." Knox was determined to elevate his status in her eyes. Right now it seemed to be hovering somewhere between dinner companion and excess baggage.

"Whatever." Marianna shrugged.

"Okay. Start by describing our grand tour of *Rusalka* this morning."

"Well, Sasha basically showed us everything. Took us all over, bridge to barnacles. It all checked out against the schematics we got from Oskarshams." The Swedish yard's vow of silence did not extend to Interpol. CROM's liaison had secured their cooperation, and their deck plans, months ago.

"Yeah," Knox said, "I'd been going back over them in my head, shortly before you made your entrance and put an end to all rational thought."

That earned him a brief smile.

"So, anyway, did anything stand out?" he asked.

"That research facility, of course. It took up a healthy chunk of one whole deck."

"Right, the lab. Now, for the next part, we need some light." He sat on the edge of the bed and switched on the headboard lamp. "And that pad and pencil. We'll do this scientifically."

"Here you go, Mr. Science." She fetched the items from the nightstand, then sat down alongside him.

"Okay. So, describe the layout of the lab."

"Um, a big box, subdivided into four rooms."

"So, a bird's eye view would give you a rectangle with an 'H' inscribed in it, divvying up the interior into two big rooms and two smaller ones." He scribbled on the pad as he spoke. "More or less like so, right?"

She leaned over to see what he had sketched:

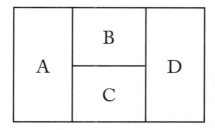

"An artist, too? Yep, that looks about right. Where's the problem?"

"Well, for starters, why so big? It seemed like they had way too much room in there for the amount of work they had going on."

"Grishin's legendary largess." She shrugged again. It made her petite breasts jiggle slightly beneath the jumpsuit and cast a disconcerting aura of stray lightbeams into the surrounding air. "Maybe it's to impress visiting VIPs like us. It works for that, and it's not like he can't afford it."

"But then why carve it up into four separate rooms?" Knox was fighting the distraction of having her so near. His ability to stay focused when in the throes of a presentation was no less the stuff of legend than Arkady Grishin's munificence, but this was pushing it. "If impact's what they're after, one continuous space would be lots more impressive. Why not lose the partitions?"

"You mean the firewalls?" She leaned against him as she studied the diagram. Inadvertently maybe, but she stayed that way. "But that's regulation laboratory construction, Jon."

"Or protective coloration. But let it go for a moment, and reconstruct what we did in there."

"We came in through a door here." She pointed halfway up the left side of the outer rectangle. "That put us in this first wide room with the big GEI crest on the wall and the mothballed seismographic lab — the one you labeled *A*."

"Keep going."

"Sasha took us around through this firedoor down here into the room you marked *C*, at the bottom of the drawing. Mostly seawater chemistry and aquatic biotelemetry in there. Oh, and that big specimen tank, the one with all the jellyfish. They used it instead of a wall to divide Lab *C* from Lab *B*, this other little lab room up here at the top." She tapped at the paper, leaning even closer. "You could look through the aquarium from one room into the other. That was how we spotted Galina."

"Or she spotted us."

"That's right, Galina saw you first and waved, then ran to join us. We all walked through into Room *D*, your other big room, and met her halfway, right here." Her fingertip rested on the right side of the rectangle.

"And that gives us enough to hazard a guess at the location of your secret lab."

"How?"

"Try this: visualize the layout again. Now, didn't it strike you that the two firedoors seemed too far apart when you looked at them from outside, in the long room?"

"I'm not sure I... no." She shook her head; her dark hair shimmered in the lamplight.

"I think maybe the middle section is divided into three rooms, not two. Here, look, this isn't to scale but it'll give you the idea." Knox erased part of the diagram and redrew it:

"That can't be right," Marianna said. "We looked straight through the specimen tank from *C* into *B*. We saw Galina standing on the far side of the glass, in the middle of that other lab. If your Room *X* was between us and her, how come we didn't notice it?" She snickered. "Or is it supposed to be full of jellyfish?"

"Let me answer that question with a question: how can you spend half of every working day in Pete's office and not see what it is they've done here?"

Her dark eyes half closed as she mulled it over. Then: "Oh, God! Not a *datawall*?"

"Close enough." That little highlight was playing about her upper lip again. Marianna was enchanting. Also very well armed. Knox set aside his fantasies and continued his exposition: "Sitting behind maybe three feet of real water and real jellyfish."

He sketched that in.

"One half-tank each in Lab *B* and *C*?" Marianna asked. "With what, videocams hidden behind the display scrim and broadcasting a view of the other lab in real time?"

"Not really. Pete's datawall is just a convenient analogy, a way to get the point across. No, I think what we've got here is a much older, simpler technology: a conjurer's chamber. Did you ever see that trick where a magician takes a box, shows it's empty by opening the front and the back so you can see his hand through it, then closes it and pulls out a rabbit?"

"Sure. Standard smoke-and-mirrors."

"Right, literally: there's a mirror set at an angle inside the box, with a rabbit hidden behind it. You only *think* you're looking through the box to the other side. Actually the mirror's bending light around what the magician doesn't want you to see."

He showed her the results of his sketching. "Now, what we've got here is probably two big Fresnel mirrors, one on the back wall of each half-aquarium. Those mirrors angle the light down to two more in the space below the lab and then back up and out. Anyone looking through those two half-aquariums is actually looking around Room *X* in the middle. Any imperfections in the displays are hidden by tinted glass and lighted water. Smoke and mirrors, like you said."

Marianna shook her head. "I don't buy it. Why would Grishin go to all that trouble just to hide a room? It's his boat; he can do anything he likes, right out in the open."

"Except he's got visiting dignitaries parading through here all the time. That's the beauty part: hide everything in plain sight. That way, if there's ever any trouble, you've got legions of blue-ribbon witnesses ready to swear you're pure as the driven snow."

Knox thought a moment more, then added, "And maybe they get off on it, pulling the wool over people's eyes, I mean. If I had a billion or so to play with, it's the sort of thing *I'd* do."

"Maybe that's my problem with it," she said. "The whole scenario sounds a lot more like you than Grishin. I co-authored the psych evaluation on Arkady Grigoriyevich, and, believe me, that's one serious dude. Whereas *you*..."

"Don't say it." Knox cut her off before she could bring up the Aristos incident again. "I didn't mean Grishin himself. More than likely, Sasha put him up to it. Now, Sasha I could definitely see running a scam like this. His favorite short story is Poe's 'Purloined Letter.'"

"The original hide-in-plain-sight scenario," she mused. Difficult as Marianna could be, it was nice working with a client who actually *got* most of his literary allusions for a change.

"So, is that what put you on to this?" she said.

"One of the things. Anyhow, the theory's easy enough to test—all we have to do is figure out where the entrance to the hidden lab is and stake it out."

"Why wouldn't it be through one of these other four rooms?" Marianna leaned across him to tap the paper. Her hair smelled faintly of lilacs.

"Well..." Knox maneuvered his arm around to where it was just barely touching her thigh. "There might be some sort of exit into the main lab, maybe concealed behind that big GEI crest in Room *A*. I doubt they'd use it for anything but emergencies, though."

"Why not?" She inched in a little closer.

Knox was finding it increasingly hard to concentrate. "Simple logistics: you wouldn't want people constantly trooping in and out of your secret room, messing up the illusion. No, if it were me, I'd run an entrance shaft down through the decks above it."

"But that would make a visible bulge in the walls of all the rooms it passed through."

"Bring it right down through the point where four rooms come together and it shouldn't amount to more than a bump-out on each inside corner. Where it passes through the corporate suites, you could pretty much stick it wherever you wanted—not a whole lot of public access up there. Down here on main deck you could, I don't know, maybe hide it in a closet? After all, the whole shaft only has to be wide enough for a single person climbing a ladder."

"Shafts again," Marianna said in a low voice. She was sitting close enough that he could feel her shudder. More loudly she asked, "Any chance it passes through one of our cabins? That would simplify things—just go in from the side."

"Sorry, no. They gave us outside staterooms—for the view, see?" Knox pointed to the star-filled sky beyond the porthole. "The shaft would have to be just about amidships. We'll have to leave home base to get to the entrance."

"And where's that?"

"Let me think." Knox tried to visualize the design of *Rusalka*'s decks. "Somewhere on bridge deck, I'll bet—probably the chartroom. We could check the schematics on the laptop."

But Marianna was already up off the bed, standing at the doorway.

"Actually," she said, "I had something a little more proactive in mind. C'mon, it'll give you a chance to brush up on your Russian."

✳

Marianna dialed her fool-the-eye leotard into high-refractivity mode and eased herself up the rear companionway to bridge deck. She emerged into a service corridor so dimly lit she had to wait a moment for her eyes to adjust. The lookouts must value their night vision; the wheelhouse down at the far end of the passage looked even darker.

She glided down to the doorway and peeked in: sure enough, only a smudge of reddish illumination from an exit sign conspired with the phosphorescent glow of multiple status screens to hold back the night. If it weren't for the low murmur of voices, she'd have been hard put to tell that Jon was in position, running interference with the bridge crew as he "brushed up on his Russian."

Rusalka's bridge was fully computerized: standard watch-complement on the graveyard shift was only one junior officer and a seaman first class. And even they had very little to do between visual scans of the horizon every other minute or so. Jon's arrival bearing a thermos of hot tea from the galley must have seemed a godsend to the bored crewmen. Not to mention he was happy to help them while away the empty hours between midnight and dawn with the rambling conversation Russians loved. Manna from heaven.

Marianna retreated back down the corridor to the doorway she'd bypassed a moment ago. This was it: the chartroom where, if Jon's guesses panned out—and guesses were all they were, really—she'd find the entrance to a secret lab.

Whose existence itself was just a guess.

Why was she going along with this fishing expedition of Jon's, rather than following standard reconnaissance procedure? For that matter, what had she been thinking of on the bed, back there in his stateroom? Not that it hadn't been nice, being close enough to a man to feel the warmth of his body without getting groped. Okay, maybe a little groped.

Come on, Marianna—focus!

Well, as fishing expeditions went, this one wasn't going to take all that long. It wasn't really feasible to scour the chartroom for hidden doors and secret passages anyway, not with crew on duty less than fifteen feet away. She'd just stake the place out with a spyeye and leave it at that.

Her spyeye was a self-contained camcorder no bigger than a largish cufflink. At that size, it had no bits to spare for processing or storing high-definition images. Instead, its motion sensor simply triggered whenever a human-sized shadow crossed its light-sensitive laminates and then dumped a timestamped gray-scale to non-volatile memory. It couldn't even televise these simple images to a receiver in the stateroom; like most of the monitoring devices Marianna had brought with her, it was a passive, nontransmitting collector. Not only did it have to be manually installed, but it would have to be manually retrieved again before they could access its captured data. Very low-tech, but it got the job done with no telltale signals for GEI's counterintelligence to detect.

She paused in the chartroom doorway, peering in. The visibility was marginally better in there, thanks to a single overhead lamp rheostated down almost into the infrared. By its murky light she could make out an antique-looking wooden chart table standing in the center of the room. The table's twenty-first century equivalent—a flatscreen display plotting the vessel's course in real time via a GPS feed—took up half the rear wall. The forward wall was blank save for a connecting passage to the wheelhouse. A curtain had been drawn across that doorway—night vision again—and through the heavy fabric she could hear muffled voices. She smiled: Jon continuing his diversionary chit-chat with the bridge crew.

Marianna scanned the chartroom again. Not just eyes, instruments too this time, looking for cover for the spyeye. It had to be tucked away out of sight, yet positioned where it could take in as much of the alcove as possible.

It was in the course of this second sweep that she discovered someone had beaten her to the punch.

All but invisible behind a ventilator duct screen, though obvious to her EM detector, a videocam was panning back and forth, covering the room from its vantage above the wheelhouse door. Grishin's CI boys were keeping tabs on *something*, that's for sure. Could it be that Jon's whole precarious pyramid of assumptions had somehow been correct?

Thank God she hadn't just barged into the chartroom. One more step and she'd have been on candid camera. She slipped back out of the doorframe into the passageway. She needed to time out and rethink this.

From its electromagnetic signature, Grishin's videocam was a broadcaster rather than a wired device or a self-contained collector. Reaching down, Marianna withdrew a tunable video receiver from her toolbelt. Most of these commercial surveillance units transmitted in a narrow frequency band. Nothing. They must have jiggered it. Try a harmonic. Easy, now. There.

On her receiver's postage-stamp display there took shape an image of the chartroom as seen from the perspective of the ventilator duct. Wide angle coverage, all right, but centered on the map table. That put the doorway she'd been standing in just off camera. She couldn't have been spotted from where she stood, thank God!

There were ways to befuddle video surveillance, but it didn't do to overuse them. She'd need such subterfuges when she actually entered the chartroom. And she was no longer planning on doing that tonight, not when there was an easier way to get what she was after. Readings of signal strength and orientation from several angles told her she could pick up the videocam's transmissions from her stateroom. She'd only needed to know they were there.

Thank you, Arkady Grigoriyevich! Rather than deploying her own spyeye, Marianna could piggyback off Grishin's.

She locked in the frequency and restashed her receiver. She was just turning toward the stairwell when she heard a new voice join the bull session on the bridge. Its grating timbre and curious accent hovered at the edge of recognition. She crept down to peer into the gloom of the wheelhouse again. One shadowy figure loomed over the rest. The mate and crewman had fallen silent, but Jon was still talking, still trying his best to engage all comers and buy her more time.

The stranger offered no reply to what Jon was saying, just grinned. The ruddy light from the exit sign glinted off two steel canines. And, with that, Marianna knew him.

She felt her nostrils flaring, her lips skinning back to bare her teeth. It was the man who'd thrown her down the elevator shaft from the top of 17 State Street!

✳

As Knox entered the stateroom, Marianna looked up from her laptop. "Are you okay?"

He was warmed by the look of concern on her face, though at a loss to explain it—she'd had the hard part. "Sure. Why, what's up?"

"Do you know who that was up on the bridge just now?"

"The big guy? Said he's a contractor from the Georgian Republic."

"You get a name?"

"Yuri. He didn't give a last name. Even getting that much was like pulling teeth. Hardest man I've ever tried talking to. I can't say I'm looking forward to repeating the experience."

"Well, don't," she said. "In fact, if you see him coming, run the other way. He's a contractor, all right—as in contract killer. You remember the guy I told you about, the one I tangled with back in New York?"

"No shit…that's him?" Knox's stomach churned. He'd been close enough to reach out and touch the man. Or vice versa. "You sure?"

"Let's just say I've seen that winning smile before."

"The steel choppers? Used to be, back in the old Soviet Union, they were a pretty common dental appliance. I didn't think porcelain was still in such short supply, though."

"Maybe with this Yuri guy it's a fashion statement." She twitched the corners of her mouth in imitation of a smile. "What was he doing up on the bridge?"

"I got the impression he was looking for me—and you. Almost the only talking he did was to ask where you were. I told him I'd left you sleeping down in the stateroom. That I'd be down there myself if it wasn't for a migraine so bad it made me want to die."

"What did he say to that?"

"Nothing. That was when he grinned."

✦

Marianna turned back to her laptop and finished linking the video receiver to dump its purloined signals to non-volatile memory. No coding required; CROM's systems folks had installed half a gig of prefab software components on the little machine, and all she had to do was cookbook the right mods together. With a final flourish, she set up a simple motion-analysis routine to flag the frames where someone walked within range of Grishin's chartroom videocam.

She leaned back in her chair and stretched. "Now we wait," she said, stifling a yawn. "If you're right about the chartroom hiding an entrance to the lab, we'll pick up shift change activity, at least."

"*If* I'm right?" Jon sat down on the edge of the bed just across from her, looking vaguely crestfallen. "The surveillance camera didn't convince you?"

"It's pretty circumstantial," she began, then relented. "Okay, okay, I'll admit it looks like you're onto something. It's only..."

"Only what?"

"Only I'd feel better if I knew how you did it. This inspired guess thing, I mean. Was it something you saw? Something you heard? Why didn't I notice it? I was on the tour too."

"It...it's not all that easy to explain." He seemed at a loss for words, for once. "Things just didn't...fit somehow."

"Things? What things?"

"Sasha, for instance. He was trying too hard, too much indirection." Jon's expression evoked the disdain of the professional prestidigitator for the feeble effects of the rank amateur. "In particular, that whole business with Galina looked a little, um, staged. That, and the geometry of the firedoors being off, like I said."

"But that's, like, nothing." She stood and confronted him, hands on hips. "You're saying you took a bunch of disconnected impressions and deduced the presence of a hidden room?"

"It's what I do." He shrugged. "Not all the time, not reliably, but sometimes things just sort of, well, click for me. 'Knox's onboard pattern-matcher,' they call it at the office."

"Okay." Marianna sat down beside him on the bed, mulling it over. "Whatever you did, it worked. But sometime you're going to have to tell me more about this pattern-matching business."

"Trade secret." Jon grinned. "Incidentally, at times like this, it's customary to turn to the consultant and, in a voice atremble with awe, exclaim 'Wow, you must be a trained analyst!'"

"Wow," she mimicked, "you must be a trained analyst!"

Then, without knowing quite why, she leaned over and kissed him full on the mouth.

Quickly as the impulse had come, it was gone. She pulled back from him, her half-closed eyes flew wide open again, to see Jon looking as startled as she felt.

Then she was up off the bed and standing on the opposite side of the room. From there, arms folded, she said, "So, what do we do next?"

He said nothing, just stared at her. It occurred to her then that her last question might be subject to misinterpretation.

"About your secret lab, I mean," she said, so as to leave no doubt.

16 | Idyll

IN THE END, what they had done was table the matter and go to bed. In separate cabins, more's the pity.

Knox had drifted off to sleep that night thinking about her kiss. Even when they reconvened in Marianna's room at eight-thirty the next morning, his lips were still tingling with the memory of it. All too brief, yes, but soft and warm as the one she'd hushed him with at the gala, and far less premeditated. Even now he could see the way the silken sheen of her lip gloss had been blurred by the momentary contact…

"Earth to Jon." Marianna raised her voice, jolting him back to reality. "Jon, do you read me?"

"Hmm?" he managed.

She sighed. "I was saying, if you're not going to help out here," — she jerked a thumb in the direction of the laptop sitting on her dressing table — "then how about you go rustle us up some coffee and O.J.?"

Knox would have been more than pleased to help her review the hijacked surveillance video, if only they could've focused on the few potentially interesting sequences already earmarked by the motion-sensing routines. But no, Marianna was going strictly by the book, which meant slogging through all seven hours' worth of image capture, ninety-five percent of it featuring an empty chartroom. Even with intermittent fast-forwarding, the exercise held all the fascination of watching paint dry. Knox didn't even try to hide his relief at being assigned to the breakfast-procurement detail.

They'd left the curtains drawn in their staterooms. Natural enough, given what they were up to, but it meant the brilliant sunlight out on deck took Knox by surprise. He shaded his eyes and walked to the rail.

The sky was a bowl of crystalline blue deepening almost to violet at zenith, and unblemished save for a few small puffs of cloud gleaming far off on the horizon, so white they seemed lit from within. Out beyond the forward wind-baffles a stiff breeze was embroidering the ocean-top with lacy whitecaps. Knox took a deep breath of fresh, sea-scented morning air. Invigorating. He really should go back and drag Marianna out here.

He was not alone in his enjoyment of the moment. At scattered intervals all along the rail, casually-dressed men and women stood in clusters of two and three, chatting, smoking, nursing cups of steaming liquids — tea, most likely — or just quietly contemplating the ensemble of sea and sky. Members of *Rusalka*'s headquarters and research staffs, no doubt, delighting in a spectacular Saturday morning.

And, well apart from all the companionable little groupings, a solitary, black-garbed figure leaned against the rail. Looking, not out on the beauty of the morning, but down the length of the deck, directly at Knox. Noticing that Knox was looking at him, Yuri grinned back. Bright morning sun sparkled on his bared canines.

✳

Marianna answered the door at Jon's knock. "Perfect timing; I was just done with the scan."

"Oh, that looks good," she added. Jon was balancing a tray laden with carafes of coffee and juice, a basketful of breakfast pastries, assorted miniature jam pots, and two table settings bearing the GEI crest.

She cleared a space. "Here, set it down on the dresser."

"Thanks. I didn't have anything this ambitious in mind, but the steward in that little outdoor dining nook wouldn't take two lattes and an orange juice for an answer." He poured coffees and handed her one. "Evidently word's gotten around that we're Mr. Bondarenko's special guests. Everyone's keeping an eye out for us, including your friend Yuri."

"I know. I was watching him watch you before." She took a sip from her cup. "If he stays on us like this, it's going to complicate things."

"What sorts of things? Did you find something?"

"I'll let you tell me." Better he should draw his own conclusions. "Three of the flagged sequences are routine: mate comes in from the wheelhouse every couple hours to check position against the chart, stuff like that. The other two are, well, something else entirely. Here, take a look; see what you think."

She clicked on the hotlink for the third of the five motion-detection incidents. In response, the display filled with a freeze-frame of the chartroom, shot from the by-now familiar perspective of Grishin's spy-cam. A timestamp in the lower righthand corner read 06:29:57 July 31.

"Ready?" She tapped a key. "It's showtime."

The digits of the timestamp came to life and began registering the passage of seconds and minutes once more. The camera resumed its slow circuit, left to right and back again. Then, with a quick blur of movement, someone entered the shot, stage left.

"Notice he's come in off the access corridor," Marianna pointed out, "not from the bridge. Whoever he is, he's not standing watch."

The new arrival was a tall man in his mid- to late thirties, wearing a checkered shirt and jeans. The grainy, available-light image wasn't good enough to resolve more than a broad-brush abstraction of the face: a receding hairline, a fringe of beard, a heavy brow sheltering weak, tired-looking eyes. The tired look could be due the early hour: the timestamp said this scene had played out at half past six in the morning.

"Anyone we know?" Jon asked, whispering as if they were spying on the man in real life.

"I don't think so. Watch, here's where it gets interesting."

The man stood still for a moment, looking back the way he'd come. Another few seconds to make sure no one was about to push the curtain aside and come in from the bridge. Then, with a series of jerky movements, he was standing behind the antique chart table looking down, its dimly-lit surface illuminating his features from below.

"The action's a little stop-motionesque," Marianna said. "Camera's only transmitting five frames a second. Makes it hard to see exactly what he does here. But the result's clear enough."

The man's right hand fumbled around under the tabletop. Whatever he was looking for, he found it: the heavy wooden table slid forward three or four feet as if on skids. The man braced himself on the table's edge, then disappeared down behind it. A few more seconds and the table eased back into its original position.

Marianna halted the playback. "That's it. After half an hour, the whole operation repeats in reverse: table moves back, guy comes up, slides it into place and leaves. Want to see that?"

He shook his head. "This here's enough to clinch it: we've just watched somebody visiting our hidden room."

Marianna nodded. "That's what it looks like, all right. Still, I'd feel better if we'd caught the actual shaft entrance on camera."

"Be thankful we got as much as we did. Look at the camera angle—whoever set this up didn't want the shaft, they wanted full-face on anybody going into it."

"Which should make it more interesting," Marianna said, "when I try that myself."

✳

"What?" Knox wasn't sure he'd heard right.

"Oh, not right away. We've got to rough out their duty schedule first. It's that, or run the risk of bumping into a staffer or two when the time comes for me to pay a call to your secret lab."

"You had me worried there. We're going to need lots more data capture before we even think about that. Figure on forty-eight hours worth at least, maybe seventy-two just to be on the safe side." The way Knox saw it, a day without breaking and entering was a day without the threat of imminent death or dismemberment.

Marianna was still putting her laptop back in auto-record mode when the doorbell chimed. She shot Knox a look that said: whoever it is, get rid of them. He walked to the door, hoping it wasn't Yuri making a housecall.

He relaxed when he heard the voice booming from the other side: "Dzhon, Marianna! Do you plan to stay in bed all Saturday?"

"Hi, Sasha," Knox opened the door to find his friend standing there in knit shirt and shorts, "You're looking kind of casual this morning."

"Ancient Slavic custom: *vik-ehnd*," Sasha deadpanned. "Perhaps you have heard of?"

"You guys invented the weekend too, eh?" Knox grinned, but remained standing in the threshold, blocking entrance to the room. He turned his head and said "Honey, look who's here!"

"Good morning, Sasha!" Marianna waved from the desk.

"Truly, a good morning, Marianna—too good to waste sitting indoors. I have come to say that, if you two will hurry, we can play some golf."

Knox turned to face him again. "Don't tell me you've got eighteen holes squirreled away below decks."

Sasha grinned. "Even better, Dzhon. *Rusalka* has a driving range at the aft end of lab deck. Very popular with senior cadres, especially on Saturday morning. But I have succeeded to reserve a half hour slot for us, beginning in…" He consulted his watch. "…fifteen minutes."

"I'm up for it. But I think Marianna mentioned something about going for a swim. Didn't you, honey?" The term of endearment still rang false in Knox's ears, even on the second try. But maybe such awkwardness was in character for lawyers-in-love.

"I did have my heart set on doing a few laps, especially after that dinner last night." She patted her tummy. "Why don't you boys go on without me? Just come by the pool and get me when it's time for lunch, okay, dear?"

Then she smiled as if to say she was too much the consummate professional to let all this "honey" business make *her* self-conscious.

✴

Marianna waited until Jon had hustled Sasha off before turning her attention to the laptop again. A few minutes more and she had it configured to continue recording while feigning sleep mode. She locked it down, got up and stretched. What next?

She walked over to a porthole as big as a bay window and drew back the curtain. Jon was right: it was a beautiful day out there. And he'd more or less committed her to putting in an appearance at the pool. What the hell...relax and enjoy it.

She stepped through the connecting door into her own stateroom to change. Briefly weighed wearing a one-piece consistent with her semi-staid cover story, but rejected it in favor of a medium-hot black bikini. Do her good to get out from under this "honey" persona for a bit.

Marianna paused in front of the full-length mirror to check for overall effect. Not bad. The scanty bikini bottom accentuated her long legs and tight butt. And they, in turn, diverted attention from her less-than-generous endowment up top—legacy of a puberty sacrificed on the altar of gymnastics. She frowned, then stuck her tongue out at the image.

Completing the ensemble with sandals, a wrap, and her carrybag, she pulled the door closed behind her and walked down the passageway to the outside. Let's see, the pool was all the way aft on accommodations deck. She strolled along with her hand barely brushing the rail, basking in the warmth of the sun after being cooped up in the air-conditioned interior.

Rusalka's outdoor saltwater pool was twelve meters long, three-fifths the width of the deck. With most of the GEI staff off duty for the weekend, it was a popular spot. Especially with families, to judge by the little tow-headed kids splashing and squealing in the roped-off shallow end; Marianna hadn't realized there were marrieds-with-children aboard. The deep end was grown-up territory, though: drink service, at ten A.M. no less, as well as a sauna cheek by jowl with a traditional Russian *banya*, and maybe twenty Solaris chrome-and-teak chaises longues in two concentric semicircles fanned out around the diving board.

Most of the chaises were already occupied by sunbathers, but Marianna spotted an empty one and headed for it, past seeming acres of sallow, slowly broiling Slavic flesh. Regardless of age or girth, all the men were wearing those skimpy little bathing suits one saw on European beaches. Most of the women had on something less revealing, though a daring few had gone the other way entirely and followed the men in wearing only a thong-like bottom, sans top.

Well, when in Rome…no, not really, but she did shrug out of her wrap; no sense in being *over*dressed. She leaned on the aft rail and looked down. There was the golfing area Sasha had been talking about. In fact, there were Jon and Sasha waiting their turn to tee off. A light breeze was tousling Jon's brown hair. Taken together with the bit of tan he'd gotten on his face and arms yesterday, it gave him an uncharacteristically outdoorsy look.

"Jon, hi!" she called and waved. She struck a slightly self-conscious pose, and was rewarded when his initial startlement segued into an appreciative once-over. Boobs aren't everything.

Her pleasure was short-lived. While she'd stopped to preen for Jon, someone else had scooted into the last available chaise. Served her right.

She briefly considered just spreading a towel out on the deck, but the no-skid surfacing in the pool area was some sort of roughened, distinctly uninviting resin. When in doubt, run a standard reconnaissance sweep: she strolled down the aisle between the pool's rim and the inner arc of chaises, looking for an opening. Emphatically *not* looking at the occasional bare-breasted Earth Mother, supine and glistening with sunblock.

She was working so hard to avoid staring with envy at the *Frei-Körper* fanatics she almost missed noticing that one of them was staring at *her*. A statuesque honey-blond wearing only wraparound mirror-shades and the obligatory thong. Now that she got closer, it looked like…"Galina?"

"Good morning, Marianna." Galina smiled and rose to a sitting position that only made her breasts more prominent. She shifted around to make a little room on her chaise. "Sit, please?" she invited, patting the empty spot beside her.

"Thanks," Marianna said, squeezing in, "I won't crowd you long. I really just need a spot to stash my bag while I take a dip."

"*Nichevo*—Is nothing. Always difficult to find a place here on weekends. Pool is very popular."

"I'd noticed. That wouldn't have anything to do with the scenery, would it?"

Galina looked puzzled for a moment, then she got it. "This?" She arched her back demonstratively, and laughed. "No, no, is not like that. This is Siberian thing. We love sun, but get so little. Can never have too much. So, naturally, when there exists possibility…"

"You kind of let it all hang out, hmm? But even if it's just sun-worship, I'm surprised Sasha isn't up here fending off the, uh, worshippers."

"Sasha? Sasha cares little for what I do." Galina sighed.

Marianna wasn't prepared for the look of sadness that came over Galina's face then. "What's wrong, Galina? Is it about Sasha?"

"Sasha? No, no, I think perhaps it is about me." Another sigh. "I had hope, when Sasha first invited me aboard, that we begin again, make new start. But he must work so hard. Always so busy, always so tired. Too tired to…" Her voice trailed off, leaving an eloquent, if somewhat jiggly, shrug to complete the thought.

"But you and Sasha look so happy together," Marianna blurted out.

"Look happy?" A single tear ran out from behind Galina's mirror-shades and worked its way down her cheek. She wiped it away angrily. "Look, perhaps. But not feel."

She just sat there then looking down at the deck, shaking her head.

"There, there," Marianna patted her on the back, not knowing what else to do. This sort of situation arose so seldom in the normal course of counter-proliferation operations.

"Is all right, Marianna." Galina sniffled. She raised the shades to dab at her eye with a corner of her beach towel. "I have my work still. Important work. Is also possible to live for that, to believe in that."

Any other time, Marianna would have lunged at an opening like that: oh, really, Galya? And just what is this all-important work? Come on, you can tell *me*.

Now she found she couldn't. Instead, sitting there with her arm around the disconsolate woman, ignoring the curious stares of the other sunbathers, she found herself considering—for the first time, really—the possibility that she'd been wrong. Wrong about Galina, at least. Galya seemed so openhearted, so sympathetic, so…lost. She was either for real, or the most accomplished actress in the world.

And somehow Marianna could tell she wasn't acting. No one could fake that longing, that utter desolation at love's ending. Marianna knew that for sure. Knew for sure what Galina was going through, where she was coming from. After all…

Love dies.

✳

Knox continued staring up at the rail after Marianna left. Becoming infatuated with the client was definitely contraindicated, but—

Sasha tapped him on the shoulder and broke the spell. "Dzhon? Our turn." A couple of stocky GEI execs were just vacating the practice tee.

Three sides of that tee were enclosed with lucite wind-baffles, the fourth was open to the sunlit, whitecapped ocean. The whole North Atlantic had become a driving range, an all but inexhaustible supply of Arkady Grishin's Titleist EcoSure biodegradable golf balls sailing off *Rusalka*'s stern, roughly in the direction of Newfoundland. There were no range-markers, of course. Instead, a small, self-contained radar unit located beside the tee computed the distance for each shot.

Sasha was tall for a Russian of his generation, as Knox was for an American. That meant Knox had a good two inches on his friend, a height differential that gave him a longer moment arm, and hence a more powerful swing—as long as he didn't have to hit anything smaller than the Atlantic Ocean.

"One hundred eighty-seven point six yards," a synthesized voice announced in response to Knox's last drive. The talking ball-tracker came with the golf balls, and the wags at Titleist had given its speech synthesizer a bit of a brogue. Grishin had yet to have it reengineered for Russian.

Which reminded him: "How do you say 'Fore!' in Russian, Sasha?"

"*Chetyrye*," Sasha replied, head down, addressing the ball.

"Not the number 'four.' I meant—" Knox stopped and grinned. Sasha was just yanking his chain.

"*Fore!*" Sasha shouted, and shot. "Same word in Russian, Dzhon. As is well known, this expression is actually coming from old proto-Slavonic, meaning…"

"One hundred sixty-six point three yards," the Scottish radar unit barged in.

"So, my friend," Sasha said, switching topics apropos of nothing in particular, "do you still follow events in Russia as before?"

Knox eyed his friend warily. Was that just idle chit-chat, or the prelude to one of the long, lugubrious heart-to-hearts Russians were so fond of? Knox wanted no part of any such soul-baring right now. It wasn't just that he'd yet to sort out his own feelings toward this man who'd befriended him, and nearly destroyed him, two decades ago. There was all that latter-day CROM baggage added to the mix. Had Sasha betrayed him back then? Was Knox betraying him now? Better to steer the conversation in another direction altogether.

"Follow events? Not really, Sasha, or I'd have known more about *your* meteoric rise. Come to think, you still haven't told me how this whole Grishin thing got started."

"My association with Grishin Enterprises International, you mean? It began by purest chance: I was administering a small Bratsk research institute in the early 1990s. 'Administer' is perhaps not the right word. My role was more one of trying to keep the staff housed and fed."

Knox nodded. Things had been tough all over back then, and had gone from bad to worse since. But if anyone could finesse the bare essentials to keep an institute going, it was Sasha.

"Anyway, Arkasha at that time was just beginning his 'roll-up,' as you call it, of materials sciences enterprises throughout Russia, under Yeltsin's privatization policy."

"Materials sciences labs, I could see—that's how GEI got its start, after all—but an astrophysics research outfit?"

"Please, Dzhon, permit me to finish. Bratsk institute was specializing in degenerate matter studies. Sounds like any other kind of material, yes?" Sasha laughed. "In those days, all of Russia was like a land rush in your Wild West: take first, ask details later. By the time Arkasha discovered that we studied only stellar interiors, neutron stars, and so forth, it was too late."

"Meaning you were already on the inside, and making yourself as insidiously useful as ever." Knox chuckled to himself. How could he have ever seriously doubted that Sasha would somehow finagle his way to the pinnacle of New Russian success? "You always did strike me as being as much a hustler as a researcher, Sasha, what with your..." He trailed off.

Sasha grounded his club and looked up. "Sorry, Dzhon—With my what?"

With your *How to Win Friends and Influence People*, Knox had been about to say, thinking of that bootlegged copy Sasha had shown him once. But that had been on their last night together in Moscow, and he definitely did not want to relive that episode here.

He tapdanced instead: "I'll bet Grishin never knew what hit him."

Sasha looked at him curiously but said nothing. Knox spent the rest of the match steering the conversation back onto safer ground. Even as they strolled up to the pool toward noon, he was still regaling Sasha with golfing stories. Metaphysical golfing stories. Tales of Michael Murphy and his mystical pilgrimages with Shivas Irons across the links of Burningbush Country Club. Meditations on how the inherent frustrations of golf made it a spiritual discipline par excellence. Working hard to keep things light and airy and inconsequential.

They found Marianna, laps done, sunning herself poolside. She was lying flat on her stomach with the string of her black bikini top undone in the interests of a continuous tan.

"Hi." She raised her head. "How was golf?"

"Good, good," Sasha said. "Better for Dzhon: he won."

"If you're looking for Galya," Marianna said, "she's gone up to the outdoor buffet to get us a table. We're supposed to meet her there."

She fumbled with the loose ends of her bikini top. "Jon, could you help me with this?"

Knox knelt to refasten her. Yielding to the moment and the smoothness of her sun-warmed skin, he pushed the lawyers-in-love envelope by leaning over and kissing the nape of her neck.

Whoops! There went his own spiritual discipline. She smiled up at him. Didn't necessarily mean anything, though. With Sasha watching, she might just be staying in character.

Weird situation: another unadvertised peril of covert operations. Trying to *become* intimate with her, while pretending to *be* intimate with her, meant he could never be sure exactly where he stood. Though there was that impulsive kiss last night…

✳

Regrettably, the afternoon held no more such unguarded moments, full though it was with an assortment of other delights. The evening brought cocktails and dinner, followed by a private screening of some forgettable first-run film in the full-sized theater up on salon deck. Sasha, for one, seemed not to want the day to end, but even the second-in-command of the mighty Grishin Enterprises International was powerless to hold back the clock. By the time they'd trooped up to the skylounge for a nightcap, things were winding down.

The clock on the wall read quarter to three in the morning. It wasn't quite that late: The time had been set two hours ahead at midnight to compensate for *Rusalka*'s eastward movement. Still, it was into the wee hours, whatever the time zone.

Knox glanced over to where Marianna was curled up in one of the lounge's overstuffed leather armchairs, the glass of Chardonnay beside her untouched. After a full day of sun and sea air, she was about as tuned into the conversation as were the anemones and angelfish dancing in the tropical aquarium behind her. And Galina had been gone since before dinner—something about checking in on an experiment in progress back home in Akademgorodok.

Knox drained his Dewar's. "How 'bout it, Sasha—call it a night?"

If Sasha heard, he gave no sign. He, too, was quietly contemplating Marianna's drowsing form, swirling the drink in his glass. When he did speak, it was to say, "Your friend, Dzhon, is most lovely. So full of energy and life. Quite charming, truly."

"She's far too good for me, that's for sure," Knox said, and then—because it was expected, and because it was true—added "Galya's looking terrific, too."

Sasha drained his fifth?—seventh?—Stolichnaya of the evening. "If you say."

"Do I detect a note of—how do I put this?—ennui?"

Sasha sat there, head down, staring into his now-empty glass. "Time can bring to an end even the closest relationships, Dzhon," he said in a barely audible voice. He cleared his throat before adding, "You especially would know that, being divorced yourself."

"So you're saying you and Galya…"

"Our association is still one of friendship and professional collaboration," Sasha enunciated carefully. Whatever the exact count, he'd had a *lot* to drink. "But no more than that. Not for years."

"Gee, I'm really sorry to hear—" Then it hit Knox. "Wait a minute. How'd you know I'm divorced?"

"Oh, as to that, GEI's corporate intelligence is quite thorough. They checked you out as soon as I received your first email. I know all about you, Dzhon: your divorce, your work at Archon, how you abandoned your Soviet researches for a career in systems analysis…"

Sasha heaved a sigh. "All about you. Even about the consequences for you of that night, the night we sampled the shaman's gift."

"Sasha, that's all blood under the bridge."

"Please, Dzhon, painful as it is, I must say this: I am most sincerely sorry for what happened, for the harm I caused you. Had I only known…"

"It's okay. Really. It's not like I died or anything." Though for a while there, he'd wished he could.

"Not okay, Dzhon." Sasha was shaking his head. "How could I have been so stupid? But I thought then you had simply experienced what I did—the beauty, the wonder of it. For me, it truly was as the old Evenk had promised: a journey out among the stars." He sounded as if he'd be ready to sign on for the magical-mushroom mystery tour again, given half a chance.

"Maybe it was for me too, at first. Except, where you saw cosmology, I saw quantum reality."

Knox had been hooked on quantum mechanics ever since encountering his first pop-science rehash back in high school. It was as if the Uncertainty Principle had resonated with some deep-seated yearning that the world not be totally deterministic, totally predictable—that there still be some room left for mystery in the universe, if only in the realm of the very small. He'd lacked the heavy-duty math skills to advance much beyond the level of an educated layman, but he got far enough to revel in the theory's quasi-mystical implications.

Until that last night in Moscow, when those implications walked up and bit him in the ass.

"It *was* beautiful, in the beginning. But after a while it all turned...bad." Knox shuddered, remembering. This was not a good idea. Not if he wanted to sleep tonight.

If only you hadn't left me all by myself. If only there'd been someone, anyone there to talk to me, talk me through it, talk me down. He'd spent an eternity alone in the darkness, powerless to wrench his gaze away from Chaos and Old Night, away from the wriggling horror the world had dissolved into. Only as dawn broke had he finally found his way back to—or, by an effort of will, reconstructed?—a recognizable cosmos again.

"But I did not leave you, Dzhon." Sasha's whispered response was Knox's first hint that he'd said at least part of that aloud.

"Huh?"

"It was you who left, perhaps two hours before sunrise. I should have stopped you, but..."

Knox hadn't thought much about the events of that long, unendingly dark night in nearly two decades. Had, in fact, invested a good deal of psychic energy in not thinking about it at all. But now that Sasha mentioned it, he could vaguely recall waking up back in his own dorm room.

If you could call it waking when the nightmares didn't stop.

"I went looking for you, of course," Sasha was still talking, "as soon as I was able. But by then you were gone. I foolishly assumed you had taken a taxi to Sheremetevo and flown home. You never said anything in your letters."

Sasha looked truly miserable now. "I only learned the truth this past week. Your stay at the Embassy clinic, how you dropped out of graduate school. Dzhon, my friend, I ask your forgiveness."

"For what it's worth, you've got it. But really, Sasha, there's nothing to forgive."

As he spoke the words, Knox couldn't help wondering if Sasha would find it in his heart to be as forgiving, when the time came.

17 | Buy-In

"**Y**OU DON'T LOOK so hot, Jon," Marianna said as Knox shambled into her stateroom for their three P.M.

Actually, he felt okay, considering he hadn't gotten to sleep till sunrise. The late-night with Sasha had left him with too much to think about, and no way to turn the thoughts off. Things he'd avoided thinking about for years, and now he remembered why. He'd felt like shit when he'd dragged himself out of his cabin shortly before twelve, but an afternoon of basking in the restorative rays of the sun had pumped him back up to maybe eighty-five percent.

"I wouldn't mind the insomnia so much, if only I could sleep through it." He smothered a yawn. "Course, the way they keep changing the time around doesn't help." *Rusalka* was running full bore almost due east; the two hours they'd already moved the clocks ahead translated into one twelfth of a day in lost sack-time.

"Are you sure you're up to this?"

Knox nodded cautiously, trying to synch the movement with the residual throbbing in his head. "I'll manage. Let's do it."

He could tell she was getting antsy, not to mention heartily sick of faking a becoming ineptitude at skeet shooting, archery, and all the other paramilitary recreations *Rusalka* had on tap. It must have been a relief for her to come back to the stateroom and review the nearly forty hours of data they'd captured, courtesy of Grishin's own chartroom surveillance arrangements.

"So, altogether that makes three shifts in a day and a half," Marianna summarized the findings. "Three visits, more like, each lasting about half an hour: one at six-thirty yesterday morning, then again at six-thirty in the evening, finally, the one at eight-thirty this morning. With me so far?" The clipped efficiency of her wrapup was rendered slightly incongruous by the fact that she delivered it wearing nothing more than a body-hugging yellow sunsuit.

Knox nodded again. Not to be outdone, he was attired in swimming trunks and a windbreaker. As far as he was concerned, all client conferences could be like this: nubile, scantily-clad young females, and not a three-piece suit in sight.

"At least now we know where Galya had dinner last night," he said.

"Uh-huh. I was kind of surprised to see that, but it was her pulling the evening shift, all right."

Knox waited, but Marianna didn't elaborate on why she found Galina's involvement so surprising all of a sudden.

"What about our early riser—the guy in the checkered shirt?" he asked, referring to the man they'd watched descending into the shaft on both mornings. "Could he be one of your missing 'magnet guys'?"

"Hmm. Take away the beard and it could be Komarov. We'll put a name to the face some other time. Right now there's something else we need to focus on."

Knox straightened up and did his best to look alert. "Which is?"

"The duty schedule. I mean, twelve hours between the first two visits, then fourteen hours till the third? What's going on? When's the next one going to be?"

Through the fog of sleep deprivation, Knox glimpsed the outlines of an answer. "Um, let's try flipping the perspective here. What if whatever they're working on isn't onboard this ship?"

"Boat," Marianna corrected, then: "How does that explain anything?"

"Take another look at the timing: six-thirty A.M. and P.M. yesterday, then today it jumps to eight-thirty A.M." He paused for effect. "Now, what happened at midnight last night?"

"Oh, right. They reset the clocks."

"And the spycam's on ship's time," he said. "The two-hour discrepancy between yesterday's interval and today's is just an artifact of *Rusalka*'s own passage through the time zones. If you shift your point of view, and think of the secret lab monitoring something at a fixed point on the globe, then whatever it is repeats every twelve hours…at, um, half past eleven GMT, morning and evening."

"So, the lab should empty out as of nine tonight?"

"Uh-huh, and stay empty till, uh, ten-thirty tomorrow morning."

She smiled at him. "Thanks, Jon. Sounds like I go in tonight at midnight."

That brought Knox full awake. "Huh?"

"Well, sure." She kicked off her sandals and draped one languorous leg over the arm of her chair. "Seeing as how you just proved there won't be anybody in the lab then. What'd you think this was, some theoretical exercise? I've got to come up with an action plan here."

Uh-oh! Served him right for showing off. "Hold on. I didn't *prove* anything."

"What do you mean? You yourself said—"

"I know what I said." Knox swallowed: he'd created a monster. "It's just—do you know the old engineering joke, the one that goes: If you need a straight-line fit, plot only two data-points?"

Humor was a consultant's secret weapon, a guided missile that sailed in under the radar, bearing insight as its payload. Would it work here? Help the "client" appreciate just how risky it was to go off half-cocked like this?

Marianna laughed. Then frowned. "You're saying we still don't have enough hard data to move on this."

"Not enough to trust our lives to. And, from what you've been telling me about the dark side of Grishin Enterprises, that's exactly what we'd be doing."

"But we've tracked three occurrences already." Marianna had both feet back on the floor now; she was leaning forward, re-engaged.

"My point exactly: we've got three dots on a page, and you're trying to connect them up into the Mona Lisa. You'd know better if—" He stopped himself before he could complete the thought: *if this weren't your first field assignment.*

"What about your 'pattern-matching' thingee. That's just connect-the-dots too, isn't it?"

"No. It's subconscious. Whatever its other failings, the subconscious mind has a firm grasp on reality."

"And I don't, you're saying?"

"I'm just saying we don't know how real this supposed duty schedule is. Until we understand what's really going on down in that lab, we won't know if the timing of the visits isn't just random chance, like a roll of the dice. But you're thinking like a gambler, convinced the last roll influences the probabilities on the next."

"So, we wait for what—total certainty? That's not an option, and you know it."

Oh, Lord! Another client hell-bent for disaster, and intent on taking him with her.

"All right, here's an option for you..." Knox took a deep breath. "I'll go."

✸

"Come again?" She had to fight to keep from laughing.

"Face facts: I'm a better observer than you. It's what I do for a living. *And* I read Russian, fluently. Stands to reason I could pick up the same amount of information in maybe half the time. That alone cuts the risk by fifty percent."

The remarks rankled, but Marianna was damned if she'd show it. Just like a, a...consultant!...to try getting you so mad you started saying stupid stuff and wound up doubting your own competence.

Sweet reason, then. "Even if what you say were so, Jon, it wouldn't work. One of us has got to be in the wheelhouse distracting the bridge crew. And, as you just finished pointing out, your Russian's a lot better than mine."

"Find a way to improve the odds, then, if you're so set on doing it yourself."

"Why are you making this so goddamn difficult? Can't you be a team player for once?"

"Believe me," he said. "You don't want that. Unless the only thing CROM hired me for was my entrée with Sasha."

He paused, as if waiting for her to say it wasn't so. Don't hold your breath, Jon.

"Anyway," he went on, "if there's any value added I can contribute here, it's because I'm *not* a team player."

"How's that?"

"I'm trying to give you an objective assessment of our chances. I couldn't do that if I was part of your chain of command; I'd be worrying about who I was pissing off, how I was screwing up my year-end review, my chances for promotion—all the things worker bees have to get past before they say word one.

"So, no, don't think of me as being on your team, Marianna—think of me as the umpire."

Marianna held her head in her hands. It wasn't enough that she was working the biggest case of her career—hell, the biggest case in CROM's history—all by herself. No, she had to have the hired help questioning her authority at every turn. Umpire, indeed.

Still, she needed him to make this work. Not looking up, she said, "Okay, final offer: we hold off till eight-thirty tonight and see if that duty cycle of yours still checks out." Not much of a concession there; she had to wait for dark anyway.

"If it does, we go at midnight," she finished. "Hey, at least this way you get another data-point for your collection."

"And if it doesn't—check out, that is?"

"Then we need a new theory, and congratulations: you've bought yourself a whole 'nother day's delay.

"But if it *does*," she went on, "if Galina's evening visit comes off right on schedule, I want you behind me a hundred percent on the follow-up, agreed?...What?"

"Has it even occurred to you to prepare for something going wrong?"

"Ease down, Jon. I've done my homework." Most of it anyway. As for the rest, well, no time like the present. "I just hadn't gotten to the contingency part, is all. But now that you bring it up, how's this? You play lookout again, but this time we rig you for sound: wearable microphone and an ear insert for reception."

She crossed to her dresser and rummaged through her utility kit.

"Then," she said, "I go in with the earphones on. You've got a mate to my call-box on the mike unit. You chat up the bridge crew like before, only now you've got a panic button just in case. Hit it, and I'll tune in and hear what's going down in time to run for cover."

He eyed her sharply. "You're making this up as you go along, aren't you?"

She thought about bluffing, but what was the use? He was reading her like a book.

"Uh-huh," she said. "Have I got your buy-in anyway?"

He looked dubiously at the microelectronics resting in the palm of her hand. After a long moment he reached out and took them from her.

"You're the client. Just make sure you record everything. And, Marianna?"

"Um?"

"Nothing, just...try to think *patterns*."

✳

Buy-in was on Pete Aristos's mind, too. Had been for the whole drive in to D.C. And all the way up to the top floor of the Forrestal Complex, the Energy Department's headquarters.

He stepped off the elevator and scanned the nearly-empty hall in search of his target. Then he was striding purposefully toward the small, gray sparrow of a man standing by the entrance to the executive conference room.

"Ray," he blurted out, even before he got to within handshake distance, "tell me you've got Gallagher onboard with this thing."

Raymond Hartog, Director of the DOE Critical Resources Oversight Mandate, gave a dry chuckle. "Hello to you, too, Pete," he said.

"Oh, yeah. Sorry, hi," Pete said. "Well, what about it?"

Ray tilted his grizzled head back a bit, the better to look his subordinate in the eye. Then he put on his dour Dutchman's frown, and said, "It's still a toss-up, Pete. I can't make any promises."

Shit! What *can* you do? Pete knew better than to voice the thought aloud, of course. But some echo of it must have crossed his face, because when he reached for the door handle, Ray laid a hand on his arm.

"Pete?" A warning note crept into the reedy voice. "When we get in there, you're to follow my lead, understood? You talk if the Secretary asks you a direct question, or if I hand off to you. Other than that, you're scenery. Got it?"

"Jesus, Ray, there are lives at stake here! And likely a whole lot more!"

"Your Ms. Bonaventure knew the risk she was taking. And she'd better not be wrong about the whole lot more, either. We're going to look bad enough if we're right!" Ray's next words came out in a strained near-whisper. "Now, we're going to play this my way, or not at all. I say again: have you got that?"

"Got it." Pete had seen it before: there was something about breathing the rarified air of the higher bureaucratic altitudes that eventually killed off the little gray cells. Ray had held out as long as most, maybe longer. But if he could really seriously fret about appearances in the face of a threat to national security...

Pete sighed and shuffled to one side, letting Ray ease the heavy oak doors open just wide enough to stick his face in.

"Ray!" The raspy voice issuing from the other side was one part septuagenarian, two parts drill instructor. "Get in here!"

Following his boss into the gymnasium-sized conference room, Pete couldn't help but notice how Ray hunched his thin shoulders, like a dog about to take a whipping. Pete looked up and saw why.

There, at the far end of a mahogany table long enough to bowl on, sat Helen Artemis Gallagher of the Boston Gallaghers, former Junior Senator from the Great State of Massachusetts, and, by the grace of God and the patronage of the President, for the past seven months Energy Secretary of these United States of America.

Pete had only ever seen her at the bimonthly DOE all-hands get-togethers. It was different being in the same room with her. Up close, her steely gaze was more than a match for the iron-gray of her close-cropped hair. Tough as nine-inch nails was the word on the street, committed to twisting Department policy into whatever shape the exigencies of Administration politics dictated.

Ray swallowed and said, "Good afternoon, Madame Secretary."

"Sit down, Ray," she replied, "You too, ah, Pete. We haven't got all day. You know everybody, right?"

"Uh-huh. Hi, Nate. Hi, Don." Ray flashed a tentative smile at the two men flanking the Secretary.

Pete just nodded. He knew them, if only by reputation. The bald, bearded guy in bifocals and shirtsleeves perched on Gallagher's right was Nathan Hornstein, Deputy Administrator for the Defense Nuclear Nonproliferation program and Ray's immediate superior. Across the table from him sat *his* boss Donald Scatizzi, Undersecretary for Nuclear Security, his substantial girth camouflaged by a tailored natural-linen suit. Mutt and Jeff, the two were called—less for their physical contrast than their complementary talents: Hornstein, the Department's top nuclear-technology dweeb; Scatizzi, its master negotiator.

"So," Gallagher said, "what brings you boys in from the boonies on a Sunday afternoon? What's *this* all about?" She tapped a polished fingernail on a three-ring binder lying on the table in front of her. Its cover bore the words *Operation Tsunami* over a DOE sigil and the requisite security notifications. "Make it good," she went on. "Make it worth missing my grandniece's birthday party."

"I'm sorry if we've interrupted your weekend, Madame Secretary," Ray began. "This was the only open slot on your calendar before your Far East trip. As to the reason for the meeting, it's all spelled out in the executive summary—"

"I've read it. I don't see the urgency. Tsunami's a contingency plan, no more—right?"

"Well, yes, in a manner of speaking. It's just that we feel we, uh, may need to be in a position to action that contingency in the near future."

"The near future," Gallagher echoed. "When, exactly?"

Ray's Adam's apple bobbed again. "Uh, this week?"

"This week?" She turned Hornstein's way. "Nathan?"

Hornstein got the message: these were his people, his problem. He peered over his spectacles and fixed Ray with a gimlet stare. "Correct me if I'm wrong, Ray, but what you're advocating here is that the United States commit an act of piracy."

Ray flushed all the way up to the hairline. "Um, I realize it might look that way on paper, Nate. But, uh…" He looked to Scatizzi for support, but the Undersecretary was busy studying the intricacies of the conference table's grain.

Hornstein slid a sheet of paper over to Gallagher. She picked it up and began reading from it. "Interception of a foreign-flag vessel on the high seas. Boarding, in international waters, with the option of commensurate response in the event of resistance. Inspection with a view to—" She set the paper down. "Now look, guys, I'm no admiralty lawyer, but this sounds like it'd be out of bounds on Lake Michigan."

"Madame Secretary?" Pete jumped in before Ray could cave altogether. "Can I say something?"

"*Some*body better."

"Grishin Enterprises is under suspicion of trafficking in WMD expertise, three counts. I've got operatives in place aboard the target vessel right now, trying to make that case stick. If they do, we've got to be ready to move or we could lose the evidence *and* my people." And one of those people is Marianna.

"What Pete is saying," Scatizzi said, still not looking up, "is we have reason to believe GEI is violating international covenants on nonproliferation to the detriment of US national security. We'll want to coordinate with our NATO partners, of course. But the only remedy available to Grishin Enterprises themselves would be to bring suit against the United States government before an international tribunal. Under the circumstances, I'm confident that tribunal would find for us."

"It's the same as a raid on a terrorist base, Madame Secretary," Ray chimed in. "Bigger than most, maybe, but no different in principle." If he was pissed at Pete for talking out of turn, it didn't show.

"What about the Russians?" Gallagher asked. "A boat belonging to one of their nationals, flying their flag? They may not sit still for an interdiction, no matter how justified."

"I was on the phone with Vitali Rumyantsev all Friday afternoon," Ray said. "He's IPP coordinator for the Russian Republic—the guy on the receiving end of the Proliferation Prevention funding stream.

He's not in love with the search-and-seizure concept, but he's even less thrilled by the prospect of an aid freeze. The way we left it is, as long as we can keep this from becoming a national sovereignty issue, the Kremlin will pretty much stay out of it, limit itself to proforma soundbytes. You know: 'We do not support, but will not oppose'—that sort of thing."

Pete waited, but Ray had evidently said all he was going to. Judging by Gallagher's expression, it hadn't been enough.

"Madame Secretary? There's something else."

"Go on." She favored Pete with a this-better-be-good look.

"Well, I don't have Ray's kind of access, understand. My contacts are more at a worker-bee level. But—" He took a deep breath. "It's just I get the sense the Russians wouldn't be all that bent out of shape if we took Grishin down for them."

"The head of their third largest corporation?"

"Hard to believe, I know. It's just that last March we hosted this joint CROM-FSB workshop out in Chantilly. You know: 'get to know our Russian partners for peace'—touchie-feelie, team-building type stuff. So, five o'clock Friday rolls around, and some of us head over to Sully Plaza for drinks. I wind up sitting around, shooting the—that is, talking to Volodya Kalugin. He's in charge of reack ops for Greater Moscow. Seems like a good guy."

"What's your point?"

"Well, we must've been on our third round or so when, out of the blue, he starts talking about how their head honcho's got this wild hair up his, uh, nose. On account of he's really got it in for this one oligarch, but it's like the guy's untouchable. Too connected, too well protected."

"Protected from the Russian government?" Scatizzi sounded incredulous.

"I'm just telling you what the man said. But there's more: Volodya leans over and tells me, in this real low voice, that there's some kind of bad blood between the *Prezidyent* and this guy, from way back. From when they used to work for the same firm back in the old days."

"The KGB?" Gallagher arched an eyebrow. "And you think he was talking about Grishin?"

"I can't say for sure. Background checks have turned up zip for links between Grishin and the KGB, shadow or not. But think about it: the Russians know CROM's been sniffing GEI over. How much of a stretch is it to read this whole thing as a tactical leak?"

"You're suggesting," Gallagher said slowly, "that your Mr. Kalugin divulged this, this—oh, hell, it's not even information, is it?—these hints and innuendoes deliberately, on orders from his higher-ups?"

Pete shrugged. "It's the way they've always done business—you know, rumors and all."

"So," Gallagher steepled her fingertips, "We might, in fact, be doing them a favor. We'd have to confirm that informally, of course. But if it turns out they want it bad enough. Hmm."

She got to her feet. The rest of the room rose with her.

A smile crinkled her cheeks for the first time. "Okay, boys, you've got my buy-in. This has still got to go to the top of the tree, you understand. But the Man's been looking for a quid pro quo, now Moscow's listening to reason on the Moldava situation. Crazy as it sounds, an act of piracy could be just what the doctor ordered."

18 | Night Moves

MARIANNA CHECKED HER wristtop: midnight. Jon'd had long enough to engage the bridge crew in conversation. Her teeth worried her lower lip as she dialed her trompe l'oeil jumpsuit into blur mode. Then, a shadow among the shadows, she climbed the back stairs to bridge deck and slipped into the passageway leading to the chartroom.

Now came the tricky part: knocking out Grishin's spycam long enough to get in and get out. Phase inverters were marvelous things; any waveform was fair game for nullification. They'd even begun installing big ones under the office buildings in downtown LA to damp down earthquake tremors. Marianna had nothing so elaborate in mind for her miniature version; canceling the signal from Grishin's surveillance camera would be quite enough, thank you.

She couldn't leave it at that, of course. Grishin's watchers would get suspicious if their monitors went blank all of a sudden. No problem; by now Marianna's laptop contained hours (and hours and hours) of filched images showing an empty chartroom, including a segment from this same time last night. On her postage-stamp display, she overlaid the real-time transmission with the sequence she'd edited out of the recordings. She began making final adjustments, trying to synch up the two image streams. Everything—the lighting, the fall of the shadows, even the animated timestamp in the lower righthand corner (with today's date patched in, of course)—everything had to match perfectly. Not even a frame-by-frame postmortem could uncover the deception, or they'd be cooked.

She was nearly there when she heard something, the creak of a floorboard sounded like, coming from the wheelhouse at the end of the passageway. She froze, her pulse pounding in her ears. More creaks, then a shadow flitted across the half-open wheelhouse door. In a moment, its owner would poke his face into the corridor and see her. Her suit's camouflage might be enough to hide her from a casual glance in dim light, but not from careful scrutiny.

Praying she'd gotten the feeds synchronized right, she hit the key that canceled out the signal from Grishin's spycam and spliced in her own substitute. Now the watchers should be watching chartroom images twenty-four hours old, so Marianna's present-time incursion should remain, to all intents and purposes, invisible.

That was the theory, anyway. And she had no choice but to test it. One more glance toward the wheelhouse, then she took a deep breath and stepped across the threshold into the chartroom.

No alarms, no scuffle of booted feet in the passageway; even the shadow-man from the bridge seemed to have lost interest and returned to his post. Phase One, complete: she'd made it as far as the chartroom.

Next step: Grishin's hijacked video-surveillance transmissions had recorded a protocol of sorts for gaining entry to the access shaft. At least they showed that, prior to descending out of camera view, Galina and her associate had each run a hand along the rim of the map table. Now Marianna's gloved fingers followed suit.

A concealed toggle snicked and the table slid back to reveal a one-meter square aperture in the parquet flooring. Marianna was now looking down three decks to a brightly-lit room. The shaft itself remained in darkness until she located a switch for a line of emergency bulbs. Their light reflected off the steel rungs running down one wall.

Marianna braced herself and placed a foot on the first rung. She climbed down till her eyes were on a level with the shaft's rim. Now what? The switch that moved the chart table back was out of reach, three feet above her head. A quick scan located its mate on the shaft wall. She flipped it, then ducked down into the shaft as the heavy table slid back into place.

One more thing to check, now that she was finally out of sight and earshot. Tightening her grip on the ladder, she activated her throat mike and earphones. Her ears were suddenly filled with bridge-crew chatter, indistinct for the most part, and in Russian to boot, though Jon was coming in loud and clear.

"Jon?" she cut in, "it's me. I'm on my way down to the lab, but I want to test our linkup first. If you can hear me, don't answer. Just give me three seconds on your panic button."

A steady beep came back at her.

"Okay," she said, "reading that five-by-five here. Beep again if you need me." Marianna switched her earphones back off—too distracting—and began her descent, sight unseen, through the salon and accommodation decks.

In the final ten feet, the rungs gave way to a free-standing ladder, then she was setting foot on tiled flooring. She looked around to see if she had company. Nobody in sight. And it wasn't as if anyone could hide in this glare. So far so good.

Phase Two, complete. Marianna was now standing in *Rusalka*'s secret heart.

She checked the indicator lights on her toolbelt, humming "She Came in Through the Bathroom Window" under her breath. All recorders were in the green, documenting her visit on their designated swaths of the electromagnetic spectrum…and watching for anyone who might be watching her.

On that score, none of the lab's EM signatures telltaled the presence of spycams like the one up above. Grishin must not want the lab's interior imaged anywhere else on *Rusalka*, not even at his watchers' posts. Good thing, too; she'd come prepared to jam such transmissions, but doing so would set an upper limit on her time here. What internal surveillance did exist was rudimentary: easily-countered motion and infrared sensors. A textbook example of what was known in the trade as "Maginot Line" security—lots of capability, all of it directed outward. A suboptimal configuration, as her incursion was even now demonstrating.

Marianna began running a standard recon: cover all bases, observe everything, disturb nothing. Not that it was easy to avoid bumping into things in these close quarters. Hiding a third room in a floorplan built for two hadn't left space for much more than two banks of workstations separated by a narrow walkway.

Those workstations were impeding her intel-gathering along with her freedom of movement. They made up the bulk of the lab equipment, and, unlike a physical test stand or measuring device, there was little clue to functionality in the Cyrillic acronyms populating their displays. Her handheld included a small Russian lexicon, but it was survival vocab only. Neither it, nor her night-school Russian, were a match for the cryptic scientific shorthand in use throughout the clandestine lab.

Jon was right, damn it! He would have been better at this than she was. Oh well, like he'd said: when in doubt, record everything. As if that weren't just commonsense tradecraft.

And she could go it one better. Marianna unsnapped a tool holster and extracted the NSA's contribution to the interagency proliferation-control effort: a matte-black device maybe two inches square by an eighth of an inch thick and trailing a hair-thin antenna. Now for the secret lab's local area network; she traced the coax out of the nearest workstation till she found a likely spot to conceal the little bug, then she clipped its retractable collar to the LAN. Nice and non-invasive, but all the signals flowing among the lab's computers would be captured, compressed, and dumped to storage on a five-day rollover. Now she was definitely recording everything, and would continue to do so even after she left.

What was Jon's other piece of unsolicited advice? Oh, right—think *patterns!*

One pattern, at least, was obvious. A single word repeated over and over on the displays: АНТИПОД. The handheld was no help, naturally. Marianna wrinkled her brow. She knew enough Russian to know that this was not a native Russian word; must be some sort of foreign cognate. Wasn't there an English equivalent? Not "Antipod"—"Antipode." Meaning the opposite end of the Earth from wherever you happened to be standing. What the Brits used to call Australia. She shook her head. Didn't suggest anything. Just one more data-point, as Jon would say.

Make that one big data-point. Fully three quarters of the lab equipment was dedicated to monitoring or controlling this "Antipode" thingee. There were readouts for what looked like nuclear reactor status (currently online, running at two-thirds of max), geophonic graphs tracking the seismic surround (nominal now, but with a blip some three hours ago), gravitometric readouts (ditto on the blip), half a dozen other telemetric technologies... all of them labeled АНТИПОД. Whatever the Antipode facility was, it was a nuclear-powered major piece of work.

Marianna paused before a display with a green light slowly pulsing above it. It showed a wire-frame sphere, and something within it. Three of the cyan arcs making up the wireframe were bolder than the others—equator, Greenwich Meridian, International Dateline? Looked about right. Assuming the sphere was supposed to be the Earth, then... what was *that*?

Beneath the turning, transparent surface of the blue wireframe globe was inscribed a rosette of red semi-ellipses, tilted at an angle, looking for all the world like the looping flower-petal designs she used to trace with a Spirograph when she was a kid. A small yellow light winked halfway down the brightest arc. Charting some sort of subsurface magma flows? She couldn't begin to guess. The questions were accumulating far faster than the answers.

A countdown box bearing the АНТИПОД label occupied the upper righthand corner of the screen. It was reading ten hours and change to go till... something. Marianna mentally adjusted for ship's time. Bingo! This clock was ticking down to 1145 Zulu. Whatever was slated to happen then, there would be somebody here to see it; the event was synched with the next scheduled check-in by Galina's checker-shirted colleague.

But what event was that? The countdown included the phrase *vysshaia tochka*. Marianna puzzled out the Cyrillic again. She'd been studying Russian off and on ever since starting with CROM, but day job demands made it slow going. Let's see, *tochka* was a dot or a point, and the other word—a quick check with the handheld—was "higher" or "superior."

"Superior dot"? Try "higher point," "highest point," something like that. Like, say, the cusp of one of the ellipses in the display? Marianna glanced at the wireframe diagram again. If that little yellow marker were going to hit the high point on the red ellipse in ten hours time… But, no, it was moving way too fast; it had shifted position visibly while she was standing here and would be at the top of its current arc in minutes, not hours. Maybe only some of the arcs counted?

She shook her head—no time for this now. Save it for the postmortem. Marianna turned and continued down the narrow aisle between the workstations, heading for the far end of the lab.

Where she found the one thing that seemed out of place amid all the electronic gear: a small steel box, about the size of a wall safe, but bolted onto the outside of the bulkhead rather than built into it. It looked for all the world like a microwave oven, even down to the rotisserie platform visible behind its glass door and the potholder gloves hanging beside it. How homey. The oven was empty, though, and its door was locked.

She did a one-eighty and began her return sweep.

Finally, she struck pay dirt: a previously-unnoticed display, bearing the ubiquitous АНТИПОД legend, held a schematic of what looked like an airlock. Could Antipode be a space station? But, no, an accompanying chart entitled *vneshneye davleniye vody* was displaying numbers in units of… what looked like an abbreviation for "atmospheres." *Vody*, she knew, was the genitive for "water," and, prompted by the fact that they were measuring something in atmospheres, Marianna guessed what the handheld confirmed: the phrase meant external water pressure. Lots of water pressure—hundreds of atmospheres—judging by the readout.

Antipode wasn't in outer space. It was miles below, at the bottom of the ocean.

Just as she was mulling the implications, something gave out an earsplitting, fingernails-down-a-chalkboard shriek.

Marianna whirled and crouched. What the hell *is* that? Her gaze darted round the room. Nothing there. The sound was coming from …from everywhere, it seemed.

She was getting ready to hightail it on the chance she'd triggered some alarm, when she caught a flicker of movement behind the glass door of that strange little wall safe. At the same instant the shriek cut off and, in the sudden silence, she heard the safe make a small popping sound, as if venting air. There was something in it now, something silvery. She could see it dimly through the glass, rotating slowly on the little turntable. It hadn't been there before; the rotisserie hadn't even been moving.

She walked over and inspected the safe where it joined the wall. Just as she'd thought, the box was a sealed unit. No way anything could've gotten in from that side. So, where had whatever-it-was come from?

For that matter, what *was* it? She couldn't make out more than a hazy shape—the glass door was fogged with steam or cold. The little safe, or oven, or whatever, still felt cool to the touch, but she couldn't be sure through her gloves, and she wasn't about to take them off.

One more mystery for her collection.

✽

"With utmost respect, Pyotr Fillipovich, why now?" Grishin's words were civil enough, but his tone belied them. It said he would gladly have reached out and wiped that insolent grin from the ferret face floating in the darkness of *Rusalka*'s headquarters suite.

Regrettably not possible: Pyotr Fillipovich Karpinskii was a good thousand miles away in his *dacha* on the outskirts of Moscow, and a videoconferenced persona makes a poor substitute for the real thing when intimidation is the purpose at hand. In the end, Grishin was reduced to glaring at the datawall and mouthing empty formalities. "With all due respect, how can you propose to reopen this question now, with implementation at most only weeks away?"

Karpinskii matched Grishin's glare with one of his own. "Comrade Director, I consider it my duty to give the full Council one last opportunity to rethink its decision, before it is too late."

"And the rest of you are in agreement with this?" Grishin's gaze swept the other five faces, each framed in its own window on the wall-filling display. Vlasov, Parkhomenko, Batkin, Tikhonov, Zaporozht-sev—all the members of the Council for National Resurrection had heeded Karpinskii's call for one last teleconference, one last thrashing through, one last second-guessing of the Selection. All of them save Prilukov, who had begged off pleading indisposition…meaning he was drunk again.

"We have agreed only to hear, Comrade Director, only to listen. In a spirit of collegiality." Batkin slurred his words, but not from in-ebriation. The drooping mouth that marred his distinguished, if elderly, good looks was a reminder of the stroke he had suffered at the begin-ning of the year.

"Forgive me, but there is nothing to listen *to*, Andrei Romanovich." Here, at least, Grishin need not feign civility; Batkin, with his long years of service, had more than earned it. Still, some things needed say-ing all the same. "The alternatives have all been ruled out. Those closer in are suboptimal in the extreme. Those further out, well…"

He turned to the man who till now had been sitting quietly in the suite's second most comfortable chair, watching the proceedings with an air of detachment. "Sasha, explain it to them. Again."

"Uh, comrades," Sasha began, "It is as Arkady Grigoriyevich says: the further back we go, the more protracted the target acquisition, and the slimmer the safety margin. Worse, the uncertainties multiply. The-ory suggests that many otherwise promising hinge-points are simply unexploitable."

"Theory!" Karpinskii spat the word out. "Precisely my point. Three and a half billion American dollars down the drain. Twelve years of ef-fort. And even now all we have is *theory?*"

"Not theory alone, Pyotr Fillipovich," Grishin said. "You are forget-ting the probes."

"Probes? Puzzles you mean! Riddles which only Bondarenko here claims to understand. You give us paradoxes, when what we need are results." Karpinskii's fist, out of frame, could be heard to thump the table. "Permit me to suggest, Comrade Director, that perhaps you are not pressing your research cadres hard enough toward attainment of those results!"

"Calm yourself, Pyotr Fillipovich. This is Nature herself with which we deal. She will not click her heels and snap to attention simply because you command her to." Out of the corner of his eye he glimpsed Sasha's nod of approval. But that was small consolation when the Council itself remained unconvinced.

He faced them down, one by one. "Whom then would you propose? Beriya? That drunken butcher?" His temper, held in check till now, flared at the thought of the old NKVD chief. "You know as well as I, he spent his days on his knees licking the excrement off Stalin's boots, and his nights cruising the streets of the capital in that black ZIL of his, looking for adolescents of either sex to molest. Is *that* your exemplar for the New Russia we seek to build? Khrushchev did us all a favor by having him shot."

Grishin lowered his voice. "Now, Andropov, on the other hand," he began, then broke off as his wristtop computer emitted a mellow tone.

His irritation at the interruption gave way to anticipation: another probe had arrived! Perhaps even the one they had all been waiting for. But he couldn't drop off the call, not with the Council still sitting on the fence like this.

"Excuse me a moment, comrades." He muted the voiceline, then turned so his lips were shielded from the videocam: "Sasha, I must remain here and put this issue to rest once and for all. Will you go and retrieve the message for us?"

With a nod, Sasha rose and fumbled his way through the darkness in the direction of the door.

Grishin pressed a call button. "I will have Yuri join you there."

Sasha paused with his hand on the knob. "That should not be necessary, Arkasha. I can be there and back again in no time."

"Indulge me, Sasha. Safe is safe."

✳

Knox was entertaining the mate with reminiscences of other midnights in Moscow, when who should come tripping up the main stairway to the bridge, but... "Sasha? Good evening."

Sasha spun at the sound of his name. "Dzhon?" he asked, peering into the gloom, "Is that you? They keep it so dark up here by night."

"What brings you up here so late?" What indeed? Sasha had been headed in the direction of the chartroom when Knox had hailed him.

"You will excuse me, Dzhon. There is something I must attend to." Sasha turned back toward the passageway.

Knox took a deep breath and hit Marianna's panic button. After a brief pause, the unit in his ear whispered, "Jon? I'm here. What's up? Can you talk?"

Knox cleared his throat, trusting the miniature mike to pick up what he said next. "Uh, Sasha? As long as you're going in to check out the maps anyway, would you mind showing me how to operate the zoom on that position display?"

✳

Down in the lab, Marianna let out the breath she'd been holding. When the panic button went off, her first thought had been that *Rusalka* security had somehow detected her presence in the off-limits area. But it was only Sasha out for an evening stroll. She was still safe. Grishin wouldn't send his second-in-command to do his wetwork for him, would he?

On the other hand, Jon had said something about maps. That meant the chartroom. If Sasha was headed that way, he could have business down in the secret lab. It might have nothing to do with her, but that wouldn't help if he caught her flatfooted.

She shrugged and resumed her recon sweep. But she mentally added one more item to her to-do list: see if there's a hidey-hole in here somewhere, just in case.

After all, safe is safe.

✳

Three decks above her, Sasha had paused at the entrance to the passage. "The zoom, Dzhon? I fear I do not know myself. Perhaps one of the mates can assist you." He turned away again.

"Um…" Knox's mind raced, trying to come up with something, anything to stall with. "You know, Sasha—" He broke off at the sound of someone else clumping up the stairs. What now?

Midnight's perfect, Jon, Marianna had said. The next check-in's not for hours yet. The place'll be dead — no one in the wheelhouse but the watch. Yeah, right. Grand Central Station's more like it.

The new arrival hove into view at the top of the stairs...

Knox hit the panic button. Hard.

✳

Marianna's second sweep had fetched her up in front of the wall safe again. The glass of the door had cleared by now, and through it she could see...what?

The vaguely cylindrical thing lying on the now-motionless turntable had the sheen of stainless steel, but there was a strange, half-melted look to it, as if it had been pulled like taffy. Marianna thought she could see distorted symbols embossed on the gleaming surface, but the angle was all wrong; no way she could make them out.

She was debating whether to risk jimmying the door's lock mechanism, when Jon's second alert of the evening sounded in her earphones. He shouldn't play with that panic button; it was making her nervous.

Not nearly as nervous as what came next.

"Yuri!" Jon said, extra loud for her benefit. "What a pleasure to see *you* again!"

Oh, shit! Marianna swallowed and moved the search for a hideaway to the top of her agenda.

This had just turned serious.

✳

Sasha was on the point of entering the chartroom proper by the time Knox had gotten over the shock of Yuri's sudden appearance. "Hey, Sasha," he called out, "wait up!"

"Was there something else, Dzhon?"

"No, nothing much. It's just that — you know, it occurred to me we never did finish our talk. About your career change, I mean."

"Yes, what about it?" Sasha glanced at his watch.

"Do you ever miss it? Astrophysics, I mean?"

"Ah, well. But of course. Now is a very exciting time for cosmology. I try my best to follow the most interesting developments, in what leisure I can spare from my duties."

"So, what's grabbing you at the moment?"

Sasha thought it over, but not for long. "A joint Indian-Canadian proposal to use the Hubble's successor for experimental verification of the Smolin hypothesis." Behind him, Yuri shifted his bulk impatiently. Sasha held up a hand and the disturbance stopped. "You know of the Smolin hypothesis, Dzhon?"

"No. But it must be a pretty big deal to catch your attention this far from launch. That new Webb space telescope isn't scheduled to go up till—when is it?—fall of 2010, I think." He took a step back in the direction of the wheelhouse, willing Sasha to follow.

"Spring of the year after. Launch date has slipped again." Sasha still wasn't budging from the chartroom doorway. "And, yes, the Smolin hypothesis is a 'big deal'—a theory of cosmological natural selection."

"Must be the engine noise, Sasha. It sounded like you said 'cosmological natural selection.'"

Sasha nodded eagerly.

"What, you mean like: 'Al Einstein, meet Chuck Darwin'?"

"Yes, only without the silly nicknames, Dzhon." Sasha wagged a finger at him. "Survival of the fittest—among universes."

"Enlighten me."

"It is very simple, really. Smolin—must be of Russian descent with such a name, *ne pravda-li?*—Smolin theorizes that our current universe is the product of evolutionary processes. And he begins with a good, solid astrophysical question:

"Why is the universe full of stars?"

✷

Marianna had to grin in spite of herself. English or Russian, Jon was never at a loss for words. His stock-in-trade, he'd no doubt say. Good thing, too—he was buying her precious minutes in which to find concealment.

And that was proving more difficult than anticipated. The cramped space of the lab combined with the glare from the overheads to leave Marianna-sized shadows in short supply, and her refractive jumpsuit was useless in direct light. No handy broom closets or storage lockers. Not even a large cardboard box. C'mon, c'mon!

✳

"This is sounding like the sort of discussion that goes down better with a cup of tea," Knox was saying. "I think there's still half a thermosfull up forward."

"Oh, very well." Sasha chuckled and followed him. He paused at the entrance to the wheelhouse and looked back. "Yuri, would you please see to this business for me?"

Shit! Out of the frying pan, into the thermonuclear holocaust.

Knox retrieved his thermos bottle and swished it round. "Um, no, this is going to be cold," he improvised. "Think we could ask your friend here to trot down to the galley for a refill?"

He crossed back to the passageway and held the thermos out to Yuri. The Georgian regarded it as he might a live snake, then shot a questioning look at Sasha.

"Please, Yuri, oblige us. I can handle matters here."

Yuri looked for a moment as if he might protest. Then he glowered, yanked the thermos from Knox's hand, and set off down the stairway.

"Okay, I'll bite," Knox said when they were alone again. "Why *is* the universe full of stars?"

"Simple, simple question," Sasha said, half to himself. "Too simple for astrophysicists to trouble their heads over. But the answer? The answer turns out to be not so simple."

"It's just basic physics, right? I mean, pack enough hydrogen together, you get a star."

"Ah, Dzhon, but how basic is that physics? Many parameters in the fundamental equations appear arbitrary, yet they must all be tuned to just the right values to yield a cosmos full of light and life."

"Such as?"

"Take your own example of packing hydrogen together to make stars. For gathering matter into star-sized clumps, the gravitational constant must be set just so. Too weak, and the whole universe remains just thin gas. Too strong, and it recollapses again into a Big Bang singularity before any stars have a chance to be born. Either way, the universe is dark and dead."

"Well, okay," Knox conceded.

"Many such parameters are left undetermined by the Standard Model of quantum theory. String theory, too. Value of nuclear-binding force, masses of subatomic particles, relative strengths of fundamental forces. All of these must be fine-tuned, in complete independence of one another, for 'basic physics' to support star formation. No, Smolin calculates probability of a star-filled universe coming into existence by chance at one in 10^{229}!"

"So, the odds are googles to one against?" Knox whistled. A one followed by two hundred twenty-nine zeroes. That was way, way more than the number of atoms in the known universe! "Definitely not the way to bet. What does that leave—the Hand of God?"

"Hah! In the old days, we would have unmasked you as a bourgeois apologist of crypto-mystical false consciousness!" Sasha's parody of Marxist-Leninist orthodoxy sounded almost as clunky as the real thing.

"Well, what's Smolin's alternative, then? If it couldn't have happened by chance, and you don't want to hear about divine intervention, what does that leave?"

"Evolution. As I said."

"Yeah, yeah, I heard you say it. But evolution of what?"

"Go back close enough in time to the moment of the Big Bang, and what do you find? A singularity. Dive to the center of a black hole, you find the same thing. Cannot, can*not* be coincidence."

"So every black hole singularity is actually the birth of a new universe somewhere else?"

"Exactly! And survival of the fittest then dictates that there will be many more universes able to produce black holes than universes that cannot."

"And producing black holes takes stars, right?"

"Most assuredly. Except, of course, for very littlest ones formed in the Big Bang itself."

"Very littlest whats? Black holes? I thought they had to be big as suns. Oh, hey, wait a minute…" Knox struggled to recall the details of other midnight conversations two decades ago.

Sasha spoke not a word. Instead, he laid a finger alongside his nose, smiling impishly.

Now, why the hell? Knox knew that look, though he hadn't seen it in going on twenty years: it meant Sasha'd already said too much. They had somehow managed to stumble into his friend's conversational discomfort zone. In cosmology, no less. What did really little black holes have to do with anything?

Sasha was looking at his wristtop again. "And now, Dzhon, I really must go."

And Marianna still hadn't confirmed she was safely under cover.

Because she wasn't. She scanned the confines of the secret lab a third time, looking with mounting apprehension for someplace, anyplace. Her gaze ran over the equipment banks, the walls, the floor—

The floor! Was it a trick of the light, or was that group of four ceramic tiles slightly raised above the plane of the flooring? She dropped to her knees and ran her gloved hands over the surface. Yes, she could just barely feel a bump...

The thing was a camouflaged hatch cover.

There must be a control that raised and lowered it somewhere, but nothing obvious and no time to look for it. She tried to get her fingertips under the rim to gain purchase, but the plate was too close to being flush with the floor. Up, damn you, *up!*

"This whole business does remind me of something else, though—" Knox launched his final bid to keep the discussion going. "Hugh Everett's 'Many Worlds' interpretation of quantum mechanics."

"Ah, Dzhon, I knew you would find a way to bring quantum physics in. But I fail to see the relevance."

"Try it this way: how many black holes you figure there are in our own universe?"

"Mmm." Sasha knit his brows in thought. "Perhaps one black hole for every ten thousand stars, a hundred billion stars per galaxy, and a hundred billion galaxies. So, order of magnitude—say, one billion billions."

"A billion billion black holes, each of them spawning a whole new cosmos," Knox said. "And Everett's got the universe splitting in two every time anybody performs a quantum measurement. I didn't like that and I don't like this. Any way you slice it, it all adds up to a whole shitload of universes. And for what? No, give me that old-time re-expression of the vacuum any day."

He felt a tiny frisson of anxiety then. This was going to cost him again; in steering the conversation away from what Sasha evidently felt was shaky ground, he'd moved it onto some even shakier ground of his own. He sensed another bout of sleeplessness ahead, another night of staring into the void.

"Re-expression of the vacuum? Hah!" Sasha hadn't noticed Knox's momentary indisposition. "Metaphysical claptrap! Surely you cannot believe this?"

A voice came from behind: "There you are, Sasha. What has kept you? Must I see to this myself?"

Knox turned and, enunciating carefully for the sake of the microphone, said, "Ah, good evening, Arkady Grigoriyevich."

Go to ground, Marianna! Time's just run out!

＊

The man himself was on his way down! Marianna could hear the hollow clunk of Grishin's shoes on the rungs of the metal ladder. From the way he was wheezing, he didn't make this trip all that often. What could he be up to?

And what would he do if he found her? Best she could tell, Yuri was back from his tea-run. Even if she could get by Grishin, his personal hitman would be waiting for her at the top of the shaft.

Her wristtop's telltale was reading pulse and respiration way up. Her fingers scrabbled frantically against the edge of the floor plate, to no avail. She could hear Grishin's labored breathing getting closer.

In desperation, she pulled a utility knife from her tool belt and inserted its micron-thin blade into the crack. Gingerly, taking care not to snap it off, she levered the blade...and felt the hatchplate rise maybe an eighth of an inch. That would have to be enough. She set a small slot screwdriver against the raised edge, and pounded it with the heel of her hand, sinking it deep into the plate's plasticized substrate. She gripped the handle and heaved. *Please!*

Click! The upward pressure must have tripped a switch, because a hidden mechanism whirred softly and swung the plate up on its hinges, revealing an access tube with rungs leading down another level.

Yes! Thank God!

As Marianna lowered herself into the tube, her eyes swept the room one more time: everything as it had been; no trace of her visit. Then, pausing only long enough to place a small hemisphere of lucite on the deck, she pulled the hatch-cover closed.

"Jon?" she whispered into her throat mike. "I'm clear."

Marianna crouched there in the darkness, watching the feed from the periscope on her miniature display. Watching Grishin step off the last rung of the ladder and stride across the lab. He barely glanced at the workstations, but headed directly to the sealed "microwave oven." She switched from fisheye to hemispheric and then to close-up mode, minimum distortion, max magnification. She needed to be sure she caught this.

Grishin punched seven digits into the keypad, too fast for Marianna to catch them all. Never mind, it was recorded. He reached for the insulated oven-mitts hanging alongside the unit and pulled them on. Then he opened the safe and withdrew its contents: that strange cylindrical object she'd glimpsed before.

Grishin's gloved hands rotated the thing back and forth around its long axis, to give him a better view of the engravings on its surface. Not good enough, evidently. Even with the object held right up to his eyes, Grishin seemed to be having trouble deciphering whatever message it bore. Finally he took his right glove off, walked over to a nearby electronic whiteboard and began making notes on its surface with a marker, puzzling out letter after letter.

He pocketed the object then, and stood for a moment examining his transcription. Marianna couldn't focus on what he had written from this angle, but, judging by the expression on his face, the result pleased him.

A quick swipe with an eraser, and he strutted to the metal ladder to begin his slow ascent.

Waiting, so as to give Grishin time to clear the access shaft, Marianna played her flash around her hiding place. One deck below her there was another hatch, identical to the one just above her head. What the hell, recon is recon. She climbed down. This hatch, too, yielded to her proddings, opening onto the top landing of a spiral stair in the midst of a cavernous dark.

She didn't have time for this. Couldn't even be sure if Jon was still on station—just incidental noises coming in over her still-live earphones now. Maybe just a quickie. She swept the coherent beam of her flash once through the chamber. The tight spot of light elongated and warped as it encountered a series of curved surfaces in the darkness. Marianna widened the beam and simultaneously pumped up the illumination to compensate.

The broad band of light fell on a strangely-shaped giant, part orca, part Yellow Submarine. A bathyscaphe, floating in a moonpool. But what a bathyscaphe! This was no dinky Trieste. It was a monster, the size of a small submarine. What could it be doing down here? How could they ever get it out to launch it?

Too many mysteries. Marianna's head was spinning. She needed to work this through with her pet "trained analyst." She smiled, remembering. But he was pretty good in that department, and—well, Jon had done pretty good all around tonight. For some reason, that last thought gave her an odd, tingly feeling.

Marianna climbed back up and out of hiding. A glance to be sure she was alone again, then she walked over to the whiteboard. Grishin had wiped the writing clean, but his hand had been heavy; the soft plastic of the electrolytic surface still held a faint imprint. Marianna squinted, tried different angles, couldn't make it out.

She thought for a moment, then pulled the flash from her belt again, switched the setting to UV, and played it over the surface. Trace residues of marker-inks fluoresced in the ultraviolet beam, transforming the empty whiteboard into a palimpsest of scrawls. One, the most recent, judging by the way it overwrote the others, stood out.

ПОИМКА 3/VIII 2247—a Russian word, *poimka,* unfamiliar

both to her and to her handheld, followed by a date and time, Cyrillic style: 10:47 P.M. August 3rd.

Less than forty-eight hours from now.

19 | Party Animals

THE FIRST INKLING Knox had that Marianna was back safe and sound was when she stuck her head in the door connecting their cabins.

"Come in here, Jon, we need to talk. There was some weird shit down there."

He stepped in and stopped. She was pacing up and down, unable to keep still.

"Are your microelectronic wards still in place?" Her agitation was making him nervous.

She walked into the bathroom to doublecheck. "The base-unit's reading all phase inverters in the green. Little Mr. WaterPik's playing night sounds for the benefit of our listeners. It's rigged for a separate audio feed, too. Want to hear what 'we' sound like?" If Knox didn't know better, he'd have said she sounded high on something.

"Stereo snoring? No, thanks." He spoke too late: Marianna had already hit a concealed switch on the WaterPik recharger.

The air was filled with audio of indifferent fidelity but fabulously prurient content. Was that supposed to be him and Marianna? Whoever CROM had hired to make the recording, they sure sounded like they'd enjoyed their work. And they sure didn't sound like lawyers-in-love.

Marianna blushed and switched the sound back off. "Whew! Distracting. Countermeasures really outdid themselves this time."

Knox's clever comeback died unspoken, slain by the look on her face. Her lovely face. The brown eyes wide, the glossy lips barely parted. He became aware that he was holding his breath, conscious that the two of them were standing there, inches apart, not speaking, as the seconds ticked by. He reached out. Something flared in her eyes.

"Listen, Marianna—" he began, just as Marianna pounced.

This was the kiss he'd been fantasizing about. And a whole lot more. Marianna was all over him, pressing herself to him as though life depended on it. Her outfit might scramble light rays, but, judging by the enthusiasm with which she was rubbing against him, it seemed to pass other sensations just fine. Not that that mattered; she was halfway out of it already.

"God, I hope you're straight, Jon," she gasped. Rather than wait for confirmation, she slipped a hand inside his pants. "Oh! Guess *that's* a big 'Yes'! Got protection?"

"Night table, my room," he managed. They maneuvered each other through the connecting door, down onto his bed.

Like the take-charge lady she was, Marianna preferred to ride on top. Knox took advantage of the, for him, unaccustomed underdog position to fondle her petite, beautiful breasts. Not for long, though: Marianna would brook no distractions as she worked to scratch her sudden itch. Gripping his hands with unexpected strength, she wrested them from her nipples as she reared back, sliding to and fro, urging—no, ordering—him on and on.

She pumped him dry, but had yet to find release herself. Discarding the spent condom, she erected him again with fingers, mouth, and *force majeur*, then resheathed him and reimpaled herself. For Knox, the experience had gone beyond sex by now. It was more like being assaulted by a multi-featured vacuum cleaner—one with the optional clawing and biting attachments.

After what seemed an eternity, she became utterly still, quivering, aglow with the endless incandescence of her orgasm.

✳

Marianna sat up and looked around in the dark. Quietly, careful so as not to wake Jon, she lifted back the coverlet and lowered her feet to the floor.

The time-display on the wall read 2:52 A.M. Its dim blue digits cast just enough light to make out where her jumpsuit lay discarded at the foot of the bed. She bent to retrieve the garment, then rose and tiptoed to the connecting door, breathing shallowly as she could, the reek of her own musk in her nostrils. Slipped through into her stateroom and, without looking back, eased the door shut and locked it behind her.

Into the bathroom. Shower on full force. Only then, when she was sure she couldn't be heard from the other room, did she allow herself to burst into tears.

✳

The morning sun shone through the curtains. Knox rubbed the sleep out of his eyes and rolled over. He reached out an arm in drowsy anticipation of finding Marianna's slumbering form beside him, but encountered rumpled, unoccupied bedclothes instead. He stretched and looked around him. Marianna was gone, the door to her stateroom shut tight. Hunh!

He got up, slow and stiff. He felt remarkably good, considering how much he hurt; last night's flood of endorphins had flushed out of his bloodstream by now, so there was nothing to dull the ache where she'd scratched his shoulders and chest. He shambled to the connecting door and knocked. Knocked again. He looked at the time: 8:23 A.M. She might be at breakfast already.

She was. When Knox got to the outdoor dining area twenty minutes later, Marianna, clad in sweats, was sitting at a table sipping orange juice. A magazine sat propped open in front of her, its pages fluttering in the wisps of breeze that managed to circumvent the wind-baffles. She returned his "good morning" without looking up.

Uh-oh. Cold, gray light of dawn syndrome.

Well, if there's no opening, make one. He glanced at the magazine's cover. "*Predprinimatel'*?" *Entrepreneur,* the mouthpiece of Russia's right-wing business community. "Your Russian really up to that?"

She made no response, just kept on flipping pages, too fast to be reading them.

"Marianna, what's going on? No, put the magazine down and look at me!"

"Jon, it happened. Let's leave it at that, okay?" Still no eye contact.

"But..." Knox was seldom if ever at a loss for words. Except around Marianna. "Listen, the next time we have a fight, you've got to tell me, so I can at least attend."

She was standing by this time, still looking past him. She looked beautiful in her sweats, her face still flushed from her morning workout. She looked beautiful in anything, and nothing. She said quietly, "We're not going to talk about it right now."

She met his eyes then, flashed him one of her endearing back-off-or-I'll-break-your-arm looks, and walked over to the aft rail.

✦

Marianna stood looking out at, but not seeing, *Rusalka*'s churning wake. She wasn't being fair. It wasn't Jon's fault she'd gone off the deep end last night. That damn Countermeasures recording had pushed her over the edge. And when the rush hit, Jon was just the nearest body equipped with a phallus. All her training and experience taught her to use whatever tools were to hand. Well, she'd gone and done so...

If only she hadn't been so damned horny to begin with! Had to've been that close call with Grishin in the lab. There were studies about that in the literature, weren't there? "Post-Imperilment Euphoria," they called it—PIE for short. Shared danger triggers the reproductive urge, and it's "Wham, bam, thank you Sam!"

If the acronym fits, wear it. She certainly felt as if she had "pie" all over her face this morning.

Shit, shit, *shit!*

The worst part was, she'd been starting to like the guy. Liked the way he'd kept his cool and run that conversational riff on Sasha last night, saved both their butts most likely. Not to mention the chutzpah it had taken to send Yuri out for tea!

And he'd wanted to go on the raid itself in her place. *Him* trying to protect *her*. Silly, but sweet.

Three weeks back in D.C. and all this would be a fading memory. Her problem, their problem, was to get through the next three days. No way could she deal with this now. She had to stay focused on the job at hand, keep things on a professional level.

And on that level, she needed him. For somebody who'd started out the quintessential fifth wheel, he'd made himself surprisingly useful. Especially that little pattern trick he did. She needed his input. Bad choice of words. She needed his *perspective* on the data she'd gathered last night.

Once she'd sorted it all out, she could see there was no help for it: She'd just have to set her feelings aside—or keep them in check, not sure which—for the duration.

She turned and walked back to the table where Jon was sullenly perusing the pages of *Predprinimatel'*.

✳

Knox had to keep reminding himself it'd only taken Marianna fifty minutes to reconnoiter the secret lab. You'd never know it from how much of the morning her interminable post-mortem had already chewed through. Of course, it would have gone faster if she hadn't insisted on freeze-framing the damned video every time another damned line of Cyrillic scrolled across another damned workstation screen, or on having Knox squint and translate the barely legible text. But try telling her that.

His eyes were watering in earnest by the time they got to the end, but he sat up and took notice nonetheless. Marianna had saved the best for last.

"And here's the final sequence: Grishin puzzling out that message on the cylinder," she said as she switched to the footage she'd shot from hiding. The presentation concluded with a still of the cryptic inscription itself glowing purple against the whiteboard in the UV light of Marianna's pocket flash: ПОИМКА 3/VIII 2247.

Show over, Marianna retreated back to the armchair in the far corner of the stateroom. Knox got the feeling that, if this meeting could have been held from the opposing baselines of *Rusalka*'s indoor tennis court, she'd have opted for that.

She sat erect in her corner chair, dressed in black jeans and a Hamilton College sweatshirt. Prim. Proper. Knees locked tight together. Not the slightest whiff of languor.

She was talking to him, at least, but she'd raised shields again. Back to day one: cool, neutral, businesslike. A normal client relationship, really. It was the last few days that had been atypical. To say nothing of last night.

Best not to think about that now — focus on the business at hand. "What's so important that Grishin couldn't wait to find it out?"

"You tell me. What does *poimka* mean anyway?"

Knox sighed. Playing Russian etymologist again. "It's a noun derived from the verb *poimat'*."

"You mean 'to understand'? — No, wait: that's *ponimat'*; *poimat'* means, uh, 'to catch,' right?"

"Uh-huh."

"Thanks. Thanks for that, and for all the interpreting, Jon. Good job."

"*De nada.* Not my usual line of work," — no more so than the rest of this assignment — "but, what the hey, Archon is a full-service consulting agency."

"So, it would be the act of catching, or capturing, or something?" She was back to business.

"'Capture' about sums it up. But capture what, and how? Let's see..." He glanced over at the laptop screen, but it had gone dark at the end of the sequence. "The date was tomorrow?"

"Yep, 10:47 P.M. Midway through Galina's regular evening shift, given we'll be on Azores time by then."

"Too much of a coincidence. That lab has to be involved somehow. Too bad there aren't any surveillance signals to tap into, like in the chartroom."

"Yes, but I'm beginning to see why not, and it isn't lax security like I'd thought." Marianna was talking more to herself than him.

"Whatever's going on is so super-secret Grishin doesn't trust anybody else to tend to it, has to go and do it himself. So it's for sure he doesn't want to go broadcasting images of it all over the boat. You could probably count the number of people who know what's going on in down in that lab on the fingers of one hand."

"Forget who knows about it; the question is how do *we* find out about it. You didn't by any chance leave one of your spyeyes behind last night?"

"Couldn't. Too much chance of it being spotted; you saw how bright it was in there. I did manage to bug their LAN, but that's not going to be much use in real-time: we'd have to reverse-engineer their interprocess communication protocols first, if we even can."

"What's our alternative?"

"Simple: deploy a full-video recorder in the lab just before this capture business is set to start, then extract it afterwards." She'd started thinking aloud again. "I'll need darkness for both, so we're talking nine, nine-thirty P.M. for the insertion, earliest."

"An hour before the balloon goes up? That's cutting it kind of close, isn't it? I don't like the thought of you going down there even one more time, much less twice in an evening."

"Can't be helped."

"Sure it can. Can't we access your LAN-bug remotely?"

"Of course. Hell, Pete could fire it up from his desk in Chantilly via satellite downlink."

"What's stopping us, then? Don't tell me the transmissions aren't encoded?"

Marianna emitted a ladylike snort. "Hello? Would it help if I told you the manufacturer's initials were N.S.A.? It comes standard with the latest in spread-spectrum pseudo-encryption—transmits each successive bit on a different frequency across a range of several megahertz. The receiver's got to be precisely synched or all you hear is noise."

"Where's the problem, then?"

"Like I said, it won't give us near the amount of information that video would. We can't sit here on our hands with God knows what-all going down and no way to surveil it. Agreed?"

"Would it matter if I said no?"

"Not really. So that's it then: the spyeye goes in at, say, nine tomorrow evening, and comes back out at midnight. That's going to mean two stake-outs on the bridge for you, or one really long one. How's your Russian holding up?"

"Plenty of chance to practice at the party tonight."

✦

To celebrate the inception of *Rusalka*'s summer research program, Arkady Grishin had decreed a formal banquet be held. With the ship's complement still halfway synched to US East Coast time, Grishin had indulged his own nocturnal predilections: cocktails and *zakuski* would be served at eleven, dinner would commence at the stroke of midnight, and the revelry was to continue till dawn. Knox, who had spent a summer in Spain as a young man and grown to love the late evening dinners in the open-air cafés of Madrid, was up for it. His kind of party.

Marianna had packed her own evening gown, but Knox had just taken CROM's potluck formalwear. He was still peering dubiously at the paisley cummerbund reflected in the full-length mirror when Marianna walked in through the connecting door.

"You ready, Jon?"

He turned to look at her, and kept on looking. She wore an ankle-length halter gown of black silk knit, its high neckline — only her shoulders were exposed — accentuating her long neck and upswept hair. The demureness of the cut stood in marked contrast to the way the fabric itself clung to her curves. A single wide gold cuff adorned her left wrist.

"Like it? It's a Donna Karan."

"Beautiful. But DKNY's not what comes to mind when I think of government-issue evening wear."

"It isn't — government-issue, that is. I've got a rainy-day trust fund I dip into when khaki threatens to take over my wardrobe altogether. Set to go?"

She turned toward the door.

"Did you remember to turn off the WaterPik?" Knox said, then stopped. He became aware his mouth was hanging open. "I can see why you didn't want tan-lines," he managed.

There was no back to her dress! With the single exception of the halter strap around her neck, all there was to be seen from crown to coccyx was Marianna. From the rear, it looked as if she had just stepped from her bath and wrapped a black towel around her rump — just barely around her rump. The lamplight caressed her smooth-muscled, perfect skin.

And she had him on a strict look-but-don't-touch regimen. A torment to almost make him believe in reincarnation: Knox simply hadn't done enough mean, rotten things in his current lifetime to merit such punishment.

✳

"Ready?" Knox was still looking at Marianna as he held one of the banquet hall's outsized French doors open for her. "Time to see what kind of a shindig the world's third richest Russian throws."

Then he turned to see what lay beyond, and fell silent.

Rusalka's banquet hall was as wide as the vessel's twenty-meter beam, and nearly double that span in length. To either side marble-colonnaded walls, their intercolumniations all of tempered glass, rose up and up, two full deck-heights, to skylights opening out on the evening heavens. From gimbaled fixtures in the munnions of those skylights there descended six starburst chandeliers of the same Austrian crystal as graced New York's Metropolitan Opera, save that these had been fitted with gyrostabilizers for use aboard ship. The chandeliers' subdued radiance blended with the glow of the skies above them: the stars of a summer night, with six galaxies hovering closer than the rest.

The far wall, a hundred feet away across the hall, was a single concave expanse of luminescent onyx veneer bonded to backlit Nomex substrate, with a huge replica of the now-familiar GEI world-snake coiled at its center. Unlike its mosaic counterparts elsewhere on *Rusalka,* this Ourobouros was three-dimensional, and…moving. Its great scales flashed as it sank fangs into its own tail, closing the loop around a slowly spinning, cloud-mottled globe. An enormous hologram, beneath which Grishin held court from a raised dais, smiling benevolently out over the throngs of senior corporate staffers and researchers that constituted GEI's latter-day service nobility.

Veteran of the occasional power-lunch at the Four Seasons that he was, Knox was still frankly dazzled. "In Xanadu did Kubla Khan a stately pleasure dome decree..." he recited to Marianna.

"'...Where Alph, the sacred river ran,'" she recited right back at him, "'through caverns measureless to man, down to a sunless sea.' Samuel Taylor Coleridge." Marianna had nailed it all right, as she did most of his references. Where was he going to find another woman like this, now that he'd gone and lost this one?

"Yeah, Xanadu..." He didn't quite succeed in keeping a note of plaintiveness out of the rest of his reply. "Just rotten luck that old Sam got himself interrupted in the middle of that beautiful opium dream. Now it's gone for good, no way to ever get it back again." If she read his intended meaning, she chose not to acknowledge it.

They moved out onto the parquet dance floor, where pseudo-glitterati swayed to the strains of Strauss waltzes and the rhythms of Motown shags—both equally foreign, hence equally cultured, to Russian sensibilities. Traversing the periphery of the crowded space, Marianna left a swirl of male admirers in her wake. Khrushchev's old dictum about humanity's face being more beautiful than its backside could have claimed few adherents among his countrymen here tonight.

Knox and Marianna found silver placemarkers embossed with their names at settings of Rosenthal china, Bacarrat crystal, and Cartier silver, all incised with the serpentine GEI crest. Beyond the tableware, an expanse of Damasque tablecloth sported a row of golden candelabras, each rising out of a Steuben crystal bowl filled with fresh orchids helicoptered in from the Azores that morning.

They also found Sasha, resplendent in a custom-tailored summer tux, chatting up the Grishin Enterprises CFO and her escort.

Sasha held Marianna's chair as—carefully, so as to reveal no more than Donna Karan had intended—she took her seat. He then sat down beside her and began spinning yarns of grad-school days in Soviet-era Moscow, including several starring Knox that were better left forgotten.

With this tete-a-tete in full swing beside him, Knox was left to his own devices. He would have struck up a conversation with the dinner companion to his right, but that chair remained empty even as the clock chimed midnight.

A breathless Galina arrived just before the first course. "Sorry to be so late, Dzhon. Only stopped to work an hour ago, and took time to dress."

Knox rose. "The results are well worth the wait," he said, and truly they were: Galina was wearing a short royal-blue sequined dress with spaghetti straps, its fit complementing her legs and bosom simultaneously. "Still, I definitely need to talk to Sasha if he's got you working this hard on vacation."

"Oh, no. Is not work really. Is—what you call it?—labor of love." She seemed elated about something. Giddy, almost.

"Sounds fascinating. I'd love to hear about it."

With the suddenness of a cloud passing over the face of the sun, Galina's exhilaration morphed into a feminine version of Sasha's sly "let's not go there" look. Time to change the subject again.

She beat him to it. "Men!" she said with a sadder smile. "Always talking of work. Never of important things, of family."

Knox shrugged. "There's not much to tell. I got married about five-six years ago. Didn't take."

"Why is this?"

"Lots of things. Started out okay, turned into a disaster. In the end we just decided to pull the plug. You know, the Second Law of Data Processing: 'When in doubt, reboot.'"

Galina looked blank for a moment, then: "Ah, yes, reboot—restart computer. Is Second Law? Serious?" She frowned. "If so, then what is First Law of Data Processing?"

"'Never put your tongue on a power supply.'"

That got the laugh he was hoping would ease them off this uncomfortable topic. But Galina was not so easily sidetracked. "Children?" she asked.

"No, thank God! Divorce is complicated enough as it is without custody and visitation rights to contend with."

"Children not complication, Dzhon. Children—whole purpose of life. My advice: have little boy, little girl, before too late." She glanced over his shoulder, to where Marianna was sitting immersed in conversation with Sasha, then looked him in the eye. "Not too late for you yet, I think."

She read something in his expression then. "Or, you two are having fight, perhaps?"

Was it that obvious? "To tell you the truth, Galina, I'm not quite sure what it is we're having. Nothing good, that's for sure." Where was the pattern in all the rained-out relationships of the past few years? And how had he managed to screw up yet another one before it even got started?

"But what about you, Galya?" he said, as much to get off this subject as anything. "I don't see any little ones tugging at *your* apron strings."

Her reaction seemed out of all proportion to his words. Her face crumpled and tears started forth from her eyes.

"Not possible," she said between sobs.

He sat there feeling helpless, watching her silently weep. "Galina, what's wrong?"

"Ach, Dzhon." She mastered herself with visible effort. "Had possibility to have such 'little one' as you say. Was already growing inside me. But was, was too *neudobno*—too inconvenient. Too busy with researches, too little money. And abortions free in state clinics."

Galina sobbed again. "How could I know? How could I guess this was only chance? Was coming infection, and then, and then—no more possibility, ever."

✳

The dessert service had been cleared away, replaced by champagne and vodka, magnums of Louis Roedrer Cristal alternating with liter bottles of Stolichnaya XX. Galina was already on her third round of the latter, evidently intent on drowning old sorrows in liquefied good cheer.

Moving with what seemed exaggerated caution, the waiters brought in the *solyen'ye*—little salty snacks that served as indispensable accompaniment to any serious Russian drinking party. Intricately-engraved silver trays were set before the guests, five to a table. On each tray, three small silvery model ships, freighted with Beluga caviar, sailed round and round on a bed of mist.

Knox found the small portion-sizes a bit out of keeping—he would have expected Grishin to dole out roe by the tubful. He looked closer; the silver receptacles were miniatures of *Rusalka,* dainty as Fabergé eggs, distorted laterally to increase their caviar-cargo capacity.

Further down the table a gaggle of geophysicists had begun whispering excitedly to one another. Something to do with the fish-egg carriers. Knox peered, blinked, rubbed his eyes—the little *Rusalka*s were floating on, were floating on...

Were floating on *nothing*! He bent to bring his eyes level with the tabletop, looked again. There was half an inch of untroubled air between the keel of each mini-*Rusalka* and the mist rising off a bed of crusted ice. Knox straightened again to look into Galina's slightly unfocused eyes. She giggled. The background whispering was rising to a general hubbub, spreading out to fill the room.

"You knew!" Knox accused Galya. "You knew this was coming, and you didn't tell me!"

He couldn't believe it. This was still years off, decades even. Wasn't it? He reached across the table and gently nudged one of the Lilliputian *Rusalka*s with an index finger. It felt cold, but no colder than the ice beneath it. It bobbled, then floated serenely away, unsupported.

Incredible! Room-temperature superconductivity!

"Is this it?" He raised his voice over the growing clamor. "What you're working on, I mean?"

"No, Dzhon. This what I working *with*!" She laughed overloud at his puzzlement, and finished with a hiccup.

All around them people were beginning to clap their hands, to pound the tables, to clink silverware against crystal in unison. Then they were rising to their feet, stamping, whistling, shouting "Oo-rah," calling for Arkady Grigoriyevich.

With a show of reluctance, Grishin stood and accepted the plaudits of the assembled multitude. Champagne corks exploded with the precision of a fusillade, and he raised his glass.

"Dear friends and associates, it is my privilege to welcome you to the Rusalka Institute's Summer Research Program. May this year's efforts on behalf of science and all mankind be crowned with success."

Grishin set his glass down. He had given his toast in English, but now he switched back to Russian. To his left Knox could hear Sasha translating for Marianna as the GEI chairman spoke.

"Some of you will have been wondering at the unusual *solyen'ye* servers which adorn our tables this evening, courtesy of Grishin Enter-prises' Materials Sciences Division." He paused to acknowledge scattered "Oo-rahs!" before going on. "For those among us who, like me," — a small self-deprecatory smile — "have not the slightest inkling how this miracle has been accomplished, our resident materials magicians have been kind enough to prepare this brief explanation."

Grishin donned half-glasses and began reading from a small placard in his right hand. "Since the discovery of the Meissner Effect in 1933, it has been well known that magnetism cannot penetrate a superconductor. Picture the lines of magnetic force surrounding a bar magnet: they emerge from one pole and wrap around to enter the other in a series of concentric loops. Since this magnetic field cannot pass through a superconductor, the magnet itself is forced to rise high enough above the superconducting surface to allow room for its field lines. The result is magnetic levitation — a magnet will float above a superconductor, or vice versa.

"At the outset, the Meissner Effect could only be observed in liquid helium superconductors, at a temperature within ten degrees of absolute zero. Then advances in crystallography and ceramics in the late 1980s made possible materials that superconduct at liquid nitrogen temperatures: seventy-seven degrees above zero Kelvin. Still, magnetic levitation remained a phenomenon largely confined to the laboratory.

"Now, GEI Research has fabricated alloys which superconduct *at the temperature of frozen water* — nearly two hundred degrees warmer — ushering in an era of superconductivity for the masses, superconductivity within reach of any household refrigerator! This breakthrough makes possible resistanceless electrical circuitry for power storage and transmission, maglev trains and other transportation, medical diagnostics of unprecedented accuracy, and, not incidentally —" Grishin set down his notes and grinned genially around the room "— the little superconducting *Rusalka*s that levitate your caviar to you tonight." He smiled at the renewed applause.

Knox joined in the encomium. Well, and why not? Even in the

Soviet era, the Russians had had a world-class metallurgical and materials research program. This latest advance, while breathtaking, was
perhaps predictable. With the rest of the room, he lifted his full glass of
vodka and drained it, Russian-style, in a single swallow.

Now the champagne and vodka began to flow in earnest, as guest
after high-ranking guest rose to extol the achievements of Grishin Enterprises and the virtues of its CEO. Russians never needed much of
an excuse to tie one on, and Grishin had given the crowd two excellent pretexts. The inauguration of the summer research season, coupled
with the unveiling of the miniature marvels of (almost) room-temperature superconductivity, had induced a state bordering on euphoria at
the crowded banquet tables.

Before embracing Christianity in the year 988 CE, Prince Vladimir of Kiev had rejected Islam by reason of its doctrine of total absti-
nence. "Drinking is the joy of the Russes," the Chronicle of Ancient
Years quotes him saying. "We cannot exist without that pleasure." The
revelers certainly seemed intent upon proving the wisdom of the good
prince's words tonight.

With the party now in full swing, Arkady Grigoriyevich Grishin
left the Olympus of his dais to walk amongst mere mortals.

A new wave of toasts began propagating down Knox's own table,
prompted by Grishin's arrival at its head. Then Galina was standing up,
perhaps a trifle more unsteadily than warranted by the residual pitch
and roll of the hyperstabilized vessel.

She raised her glass. "To our host, our leader, our dear Arkady
Grigoriyevich. Future winner of Nobel Prize!"

"Arkady Grigoriyevich!" voices in various stages of inebriation
echoed the refrain through the banquet hall.

"*Za nashego spasitelya!* Excuse, please—to Our Savior! Savior of
children, of whole entire world!" Galina was on a roll now. "With
Arkady Grigoriyevich to lead, very soon now we catch the—we cage
the, the—" her English having chosen this crucial juncture to desert
her altogether, she blurted out in Russian, "—*Tunguskii Vurdalak!*"

That was troweling it on a bit thick. Savior of the world? Chalk that
one up to the vodka. Then Knox noticed Grishin's eyes. They had gone

cold and hard over a smile held too long. What in Galya's tipsy hyperbole could have brought that on?

What was that thing she'd said at the end there? Something about catching or caging a something. The message on Grishin's cylinder the other night had said something about "catching," too.

But, catching a ... *Tunguskii Vurdalak*? What, pray tell, might that be? Knox listened for Sasha's whispered simultaneous translation, but none was forthcoming. He tried to suppress the effects of several glasses of vodka long enough to think this through.

The *Tunguskii* part was easy. It referred to Tunguska, one of the most godforsaken places in all of Siberia. Actually, that might be aiming too low; one of the most godforsaken places on earth was more like it. Knox's long-ago Soviet ethnography survey course had touched upon Tunguska, as briefly as possible. Hundreds of thousands of square miles of empty wilderness infested with reindeer, bears, wolves, and in the mercifully brief summers, mosquitoes the size of lapdogs.

But a *Vurdalak*? Not one of your garden-variety Russian words, that's for sure. Something out of folklore, maybe? He rummaged through musty mental storehouses of Russian vocabulary, unused lo these twenty years. When it finally came, inspiration flowed from an unlikely source: Knox yielded to no man in his encyclopedic knowledge of movie trivia, and he seemed to recall an early-1960s spaghetti-horror trilogy, including an episode entitled "The Vurdalak." Starring Boris Karloff. About, about ... let's see ... about some sort of Slavic ghoul or vampire or werewolf.

The "Werewolf of Tunguska"?

Knox looked up. The awkward moment had passed. Grishin was his affable self again, applauding and complimenting a blushing Galina on her splendid, if undeserved toast. Marianna was acting as if nothing had happened. They all were. Knox put the thought aside and rejoined the party.

But deep down in the subcortical recesses of Jonathan Knox's onboard pattern-matching device, "Tunguska" was ringing a bell.

An alarm bell.

20 | Alive!

HE ERA OF fire is winding down now, the elegance of energy congealing into gross matter. The temperature of the universe-seed drops below ten billion degrees after the first second. The attenuating nexus is barely energetic enough to synthesize even the simplest chemical elements. The work of filling in the periodic table must be left to the stars.

Jack Adler stirred in his sleep and moaned.

Half a million years out, ongoing expansion lowers the universe's temperature to a few thousand degrees absolute, cool enough that true atoms can precipitate from its charged particle plasmas. At a stroke, the heavens shed their pearly luminescence and don the utter black of night in mid-ocean.

"Jack? Can you hear me?" The oddly familiar voice faded in and out at the edge of consciousness.

...A night with no stars. The first starlight is still a billion years in the future. It will take that long for the early universe's trace inhomogeneities to gather hydrogen into stellar-sized clumps large enough to ignite under their own weight.

Jack wet his lips, tried to swallow. "Gone," he croaked. "All gone." He turned back toward the receding radiance, but too late, too late. The bright morning of existence was over. Its brief noon had given way to evening. The sun of creation had set, and all that was left now was a dance in the long afterglow.

And through it all, forged from the same gargantuan gravitational forces as are gradually molding gas into galaxies, the last primordial black hole, sole relic of the creation, sails outward through the darkness.

A darkness that fled as Jack pried gummy eyelids apart and fought to hold them open against the onslaught of day.

With the light, the voice returned too. "He is coming around, I think," it said.

Jack tried to focus, to resolve shifting patterns of shadow and glare into the shapes he knew must be there. He raised his head for a better look, stopped when he felt a warning throb at the base of his skull. It felt as if someone had been pounding away on that spot with a hammer and cold chisel — someone who might be coming back any minute.

He lay back, panting, his strength taxed by even this much exertion. Took a deep breath and wished he hadn't: the air reeked of disinfectant and rancid floor wax. Experimenting, he found his eyes had adjusted to the light, enough that he was able to take in his surroundings. A glance down confirmed what his sense of touch had already told him: his arms and chest were swathed in bandages. And he was lying on a simple, steel-framed cot, one of three lined up along one bilious green wall of a small, airless room. A soot-flecked window, closed tight despite the noon heat, gave out on blank brick wall. Could have been anywhere, or nowhere.

He looked up to find the owner of the voice. There he was, sitting on the next cot over.

"Luciano," Jack whispered hoarsely.

The little Italian geologist smiled down at him. "Yes, Jack, I am here."

"Where *is* here, exactly?"

"The university hospital in Tomsk. I came by to look in on you on my way home to Bologna. And not only I. A…a friend is here to see you too."

"Good to see that you are back with us, Professor Adler." A second voice, deeper and differently accented but no less familiar. "For a while we feared we might lose you."

Standing behind Luciano, hovering — threateningly? solicitously? — over Jack's hospital bed was… "Academician Medvedev? What are you doing here?"

"I came in to have this x-rayed." Medvedev's left arm was in a sling. "They seemed to have set it well enough back at the Vanavara polyclinic, but I thought it best to be sure. Then, too, I wanted to check on your progress. I have what one might call a personal interest in your recovery."

"Jack," Luciano said quietly, "say hello to the man who saved your life."

Moving slowly and gingerly, Jack managed to prop himself into a semblance of a sitting position without reawakening the throb in the back of his head. Damned if he'd listen to the tale of his improbable rescue — by Medvedev, of all people! — from flat on his back.

"So, when Igor did not bring you back," the big Russian was saying, "I went to your campsite to look for you. I could barely see a thing in the darkness, but I knew the growl of a wolf well enough, and its stink."

He paused, then said, "That was a foolish thing you did, Adler. Brave, but foolish, to challenge a wolf like that. I was almost too late to save you."

"How… how did you manage that, anyway? I thought I was a goner for sure."

"Hah! As to that, we Siberians have been dealing with wolves since before your Declaration of Independence was signed. Simple, really: a wolf's jaw is very powerful, true, but the superstructure of his snout is quite fragile. It requires only that you get the wolf to bite onto something and hold still long enough to smash a rock down on his nose. He then loses his appetite entirely."

"Bite and hold onto what?"

In answer, the Russian held out his gypsum-encased left forearm. "I wrapped my shirt around it as best I could. Even so, the beast fractured my ulna."

Not for the first time, Jack was reminded what *medved* meant in

Russian; the man must have the strength and courage of a bear to go with the rest of his ursine attributes.

"I…I don't know how to thank you, Dmitri Pavlovich," Jack began.

"Just Dmitri, Dzhek," Medvedev said. "There can be no such formalities between two who have faced death together."

Was that it? The reason Medvedev—or Dmitri, then—was acting so downright cordial? More than cordial: beneath the gruff exterior, the man seemed almost…friendly.

"As to thanks," he held up his good hand, "let us hear no more of that! As head of the expedition, I bear responsibility for the safety of all its members. Besides, can you imagine the paperwork involved in shipping home a dead American?"

Jack couldn't believe it. Medvedev had made a joke!

Quick as it had come, the flash of humor vanished. The Russian sat down heavily on the adjacent cot and sighed. "No, Dzhek. You owe me no thanks. It is I who owe you an apology: we have had our differences, but that is no excuse for making you camp alone in that isolated site. Especially with wolves about…"

"That's all right, Dmitri. How could you have known? If your Siberian wolves are anything like their American cousins, it's unusual for them to come anywhere near a human, much less attack one. Hardly seems natural…"

Jack stopped talking then, thinking about what he'd just said. His memories of that night—initially fuzzy and unreal, as if they'd happened to somebody else—had been gradually coming into focus as they'd talked. Now everything rushed back full force. It hadn't been natural at all! "My God!" he choked out, "Igor! My experiment!"

"Jack, are you all right?" Luciano asked.

"Huh?" Jack wiped at his eyes. "Yeah, I'll be okay. I was just remembering." Remembering what? Igor's death, the ruined SQUID, and something else—something important, something that kept slipping away again. It was something to do with…

"Dmitri, did you happen to see, well, anyone else at the campsite, besides me and Igor?"

Medvedev didn't answer immediately. A look of concern flashed across his face, to be echoed on Luciano's. When the Russian did speak, it was in tones usually reserved for talking to small children, or mad-men. "Your man who became a wolf, you mean?"

"Jack," Luciano said, "please, understand: for the most part your wounds were minor, less severe than Dmitri's, in fact. Of far greater concern were the injury to your head and its attendant hallucinations. It was only luck that the helicopter already happened to be inbound to the expedition site, or we might have lost you."

Medvedev gave Jack a sheepish grin. Luck had had nothing to do with it; that chopper had been part and parcel of the Russian's plan to send Jack packing.

Luciano was still talking. "Even so, it took two hours to ferry you back to Vanavara, another four for the med-evac to Tomsk. And, all that time, you were raving about your, your werewolf. About a man who had bitten Igor's throat out."

"Given the intensity of the delusion," Medvedev added, "we feared brain damage. But the doctors here assure me your MRIs show noth-ing more than is to be expected with concussion."

Jack made no response, just lay there, feeling trapped. They were dismissing what he had seen with his own eyes as some sort of trauma-induced hallucination. Somebody had gone to a lot of trouble to make his death, and the destruction of his experiment, look like a wild-ani-mal attack. And it had worked: even his friends, both the old one and the new one, had bought it.

And how could he blame them? It was all so wildly improbable. If only his head would stop aching so he could think. Why would anyone trek all the way to the wilds of Tunguska just to kill a cosmologist and trash his experiment?

His experiment, his find—could that be it? But it was potentially the most devastating discovery of all time. Why would anyone try to suppress it?...to suppress him?

No, it couldn't be!

But the more he thought—thought about how unexpectedly pre-cise the object's periodicity had been, the more he knew it was true: somebody had been tampering with the micro-hole's orbit. Didn't they realize how incredibly dangerous that was? How the wrong move could decelerate the PBH into a death-spiral to the core and bring the end in decades instead of centuries?

And how had they kept it secret? Any installation big enough to do the job would have been impossible to conceal from satellite surveillance. The whole world would know about it by now.

But somehow the world didn't know. Only he did. At least that explained why they'd tried to kill him.

What if they were still trying?

Jack raised his head. "Dmitri, there hasn't been any publicity about my...my accident, has there?"

Medvedev shook his head. "This is still Russia, Dzhek; old habits die hard. We notified families and home institutions, of course. And posted an update to the Tunguska webpage. But just the bare facts: wolf attack, two casualties—no names, no details. We had hoped that you would recuperate enough to participate in our final press conference and tell the full story yourself. But now that the expedition is over..."

"No, no press conferences just yet," Jack said. Then he processed the rest of it. "Did you say *over?*"

"Your doctors felt it best to keep you sedated for a time, hoping your mind might heal itself."

"How long? What day is this?"

"It is August 3rd," Luciano said.

"Five days?" Christ! They'd had nearly a week to find out he'd survived, and track him here!

Whoever *they* were.

"This year's expedition is over," Medvedev confirmed. "Luciano is, as he said, already leaving for home. As may you, of course, once you are recovered." He hesitated. "Though I had intended to offer that you stay at my *dacha* while you are convalescing. Only if you feel well enough, of course."

"I'm feeling better. Really." He couldn't stay here, lying in this hospital bed. It was only a matter of time till word got out that he had survived. And he couldn't just hop on a plane and leave the country: he'd have to show a passport first. That might be all the killers needed to find him again.

He couldn't let that happen. He had to stay alive, if only long enough to get the word out. No, Medvedev's offer sounded like the best bet.

Jack sat there, silently regarding his new best friend. *You saved my life, Dmitri. How'd you like to save the world into the bargain?*

21 | Raise the Titanic

GALINA FELT FLUSH with pride and anticipation, so excited that she hardly minded pulling the morning shift for the hopelessly hung-over Komarov. Today was the day: finally, Arkady Grigoriyevich had given the go-ahead for capture!

Somehow Arkady Grigoriyevich always seemed to know the opportune time for initiating the next step in this cascade of complex operations. What an honor to be working on this project with him. Really, he made one feel again as in the old Soviet Union. Hardships and privations, yes — though not on *Rusalka* of course! — but, with them, a conviction that it was all worthwhile. A conviction that imbued the simple business of life and work with a heroic quality so sadly lacking in post-Soviet Russia.

And, really, wasn't this magnificent Antipode Project an echo of those grim, glorious times, when, led by dread Stalin, Russia had stood alone at the hinge point of history and fought back against another darkness threatening to engulf the world? Russia had saved all of humanity then, had saved the future itself from the horrors of Fascism, at Stalingrad. And now, in the hours to come, they would do so once again. Her own generation's Stalingrad—Galina smiled at the monumental incongruity of the idea—and she had been chosen to serve.

She blinked back sudden tears and looked again at the readouts. The lights were still green, but flashing faster—almost turnover time. A glance at the chronometer confirmed it: 10:46 A.M. Vurdalak was approaching its Azores apogee.

"Apogee" indeed! An apogee was the point in an object's orbit where it was furthest away from the Earth. How could one apply the same word to an object that was "orbiting" entirely *within* the Earth, tunneling endlessly round and round miles below the surface? Still, what else to call these highest points in Vurdalak's subterranean trajectory, grazing the underside of the crust at twenty degree intervals, stitching an invisible sinuous ring around the planet? When this was all over, they would have to sit down and work out some new terminology.

The gravitometer was now tracking Vurdalak's brief transit of the capture chamber some two hundred kilometers northwest and three thousand meters down. Here, at the highest point in its arc, Vurdalak moved at its slowest, spending whole milliseconds within the cage before hurtling down again along its return path into the bowels of the Earth. Round and round and round it goes, but while it is here...

A chime rang out. 10:47 a.m.! *Vysshaia tochka!* Turnover! The stuttering displays changed from green to red. Miles under the sea, Antipode Station's computers stepped through the polarity reversal sequence one last time, preparing to impart one more small delta-vee to the visitor from outer space now lurking in the Earth's interior.

The north-polar electromagnetic hemisphere shut down; its opposite-charged counterpart came on line. In a single instantaneous repulsor burst, it discharged all the energy stored over the past twelve hours, speeding Vurdalak on its way with one last push. And that should do it, as her instruments were even now confirming. One more half-day wait, and then for Galina it would be—what was the American expression?—"showtime."

She yawned. No sleep last night. The party had continued till all hours. And why not? Why not welcome back the sun on this first morning of a world redeemed, reborn? She smiled remembering the festivities, remembering dear, sweet Dzhon, who could hardly have guessed what it was they were truly celebrating, strumming a borrowed guitar and leading them in ballads from the Great Fatherland War, from Stalingrad itself: "Dark night, only the bullets whistling over the steppe..." She hummed the old tune as she hit the powerdown button.

How long it had taken the dedicated crew and research staff of *Rusalka* to bring this dazzling success within reach. Four years just to find the location of the North Atlantic apogee. Studies of the throwdown pattern of trees at the Tunguska impact site could yield only an approximate angle of entry at best. In the end, it had taken *Rusalka's* meticulous seismographic survey of the undersea target area to finally detect those faint twice-daily tremors in the oceanbed that betrayed Vurdalak's subterranean passage.

Then came the construction work itself—just another undersea mining operation, as far as the world at large knew. But what an operation! Forty months to excavate the main Antipode chamber, using Remote Operating and Autonomous Underwater Vehicles to carve ten billion metric tons of rock out of the heart of an undersea mountaintop, and to install the nuclear generators that powered the station's enormous superconducting electromagnetic arrays. Ten more months for the ROVs and AUVs to drill shafts for the capture Mohole and the kilometers-long braking train. All that at crushing depths thousands of meters down. It never could have been done at all without Grishin Enterprises' vast resources and expertise in artificial intelligence and telemediated systems. Even so, the automated workforce had required constant on-site supervision in the main bathyscaphe.

Galina shivered. If they succeeded here tonight—and they must, please God, they must!—such a trip to the sunless deeps of the Newfoundland Basin awaited her as well.

And then, the Antipode installation complete, three more years of electromagnetic pushing and pulling on Vurdalak. Three years of exertion to slowly change the orbit of an object massing five and a half billion metric tons! There was, of course, no electromagnet on earth powerful enough to raise the beast—its weight the equivalent of fifteen thousand Empire State Buildings—against the force of gravity.

Not directly, at least. Instead, they had tricked Vurdalak into doing most of the work itself, by means of resonance.

Resonance was a wonderful thing, enabling micro forces to yield macro results. Soldiers march in step across a bridge and, if the cadence of their footfalls happens to match the span's natural resonance frequency, the whole structure begins to sway back and forth. Small pushes on a child's swing, delivered one after another at just the right time, and soon the little passenger is sailing high into the air, squealing with glee.

Her eyesight blurred again momentarily. To enjoy such simple things with a child of one's own! But fate had ruled that hers was to be a sterner joy: to secure a future for all the children of the world.

If only there was still time.

As it was, they had almost been too late — another few years of orbital decay and Vurdalak would have burrowed down to depths beyond the reach of their best technology.

She knew all too well the worst-case scenario that would then have ensued: Sasha's multimedia mission briefings had been only too graphic. Orbital degradation would increase exponentially as Vurdalak spent more and more of its time in the denser layers of magma further down. As it slowed, it would absorb more material on each circuit through the Earth. That, in turn, would slow it still further and increase its capture cross-section still more, in a fiendish feedback loop. Until at last it came to rest at the core.

Then its ghoulish feast would begin in earnest.

Estimates varied as to when the end would come. Two years? Five? In a decade at most the Earth would have been utterly consumed by the beast at its heart.

And what then? No more autumn forests of pensive birch and stately pine, or little girls to wander through them in search of secret glades. No more rushing springtime brooks with small boys fishing alongside their papas on the banks. Gone, all gone in the final gravitational cataclysm, as the whole Earth together with all its inhabitants, all its children, collapsed down into a sphere three centimeters wide and disappeared forever behind its own Schwarzschild radius, wrapping its event horizon about itself.

From then until the end of time, the lonely moon, sole mourner and funerary candle for a once-living world, would circle a mathematical point with the mass of the Earth, a mere space-time distortion moving in its usurped orbit around the sun, sailing ever onward through the eternal night. Galina shivered again in the perfect climate conditioning of *Rusalka*'s secret lab.

But—glory to God!—they *had* been in time! By means of electromagnetic pulses timed to resonate precisely with its orbit, they had gradually increased Vurdalak's velocity and, with that, its height at apogee. At first, the vampire had been too deep to be attracted or repulsed by the main electromagnetic arrays within Antipode proper. But this, too, had been foreseen: a kilometers-deep Mohole had been bored down through the base of the mountain housing Antipode Station. Smaller, but almost equally powerful electromagnets were then lowered into the shaft, coming at last within grappling distance of Vurdalak. Over the next thirty-three months, these satellite arrays had been gradually raised back up the Mohole, dragging the vampire along behind them, coaxing it ever closer to the containment chamber at the top of the shaft.

The operation would have gone much quicker, of course, if only they had been able to erect a twin to Antipode on the Tunguska impact site itself. She pictured two stations on opposite sides of the Earth, bouncing Vurdalak back and forth between them like some grotesque medicine ball. But, no—impossible! The Siberian apogee had been a good eight kilometers below the surface when they'd started, and trying to sink a Mohole down to reach it would have destabilized the permafrost. Any facility that tried such a trick would sink beneath a quicksand lake of its own creation.

Not to mention that the Tunguska site was hardly an ideal locale, given Arkady Grigoriyevich's penchant for secrecy. Ever since the fall of Communism, hordes of astrophysical researchers had taken to descending on it every other summer. In fact, the latest joint Tomsk-Bologna expedition had been there until this past week, once again scouring the Great Southern Swamp for the remnants of a meteorite that had never existed. Her heart went out to her fellow scientists, laboring under a misconception now nearly a century old.

Well, and who could blame them? The truth was so fantastic she had scarcely credited it herself at first. She recalled the long-ago evening she had first learned of it, that wintry January evening in 1986 when Sasha had announced he was returning to Bratsk, to take up an old research interest. An interest recently rekindled by an interview he had been summoned to, somewhere in central Moscow. Of the mysterious interview itself he would say nothing, only that it had been "official." But he could not stop talking about the ideas it had sparked in him.

"Galya," he had said, barely able to contain his excitement, "it would be the greatest single find in the history of cosmology. Will be, better to say. If only I could find the support! Someone will, someone must. Of that I am certain, for it has already happened. If only it will be *me!*"

And with this strange preamble he had gone on to tell her of stranger things yet: of a message from out of time, from the future. Of a tiny knot in the fabric of space, of a thing that was old before the stars were born, smaller than an atom, heavier than a mountain—the thing that had devastated Tunguska so long ago. She barely heard him, struggling as she was with her own feelings of devastation. For it had become clear as he spoke that nowhere in his plans was there a place for her.

"It will be difficult, Galya," he had said. "Possibly dangerous as well. It is better that you remain here in Moscow, complete your doctorate. Have faith, I will return for you."

And return he had, though only after she had long since despaired of ever seeing him again, after the trickle of correspondence had dried up altogether, after her increasingly frantic inquiries had been met with ever stonier official silence, after he had disappeared without trace into that still, white Siberian emptiness that had claimed so many others.

He had returned for her, but not as she'd hoped. In the spring of 1992, he had returned to recruit her for the Project. He had found the support for his research, he said. In a way, he had *become* the support: his key role in the new Grishin Enterprises *kombinat* permitted him to fund certain pet projects of his own. On a small scale at first, true, but that would soon change, once results were forthcoming.

None of it seemed to make him happy. If anything, beneath the businesslike exterior he seemed haggard, troubled. And distant somehow, as though the better part of him had receded behind some event horizon of his own. Only when he spoke of the Project itself did embers of the old enthusiasm, the old Sasha, glow briefly amid the ashes. More than anything it was a hope that, somewhere within the stranger he had become, there still lived the man she had loved that moved her to join him.

Long after that hope had died, love still kept her at her post. Love, not for a man, but for the children of the world. A world she was working to save.

A world that stood in desperate need of saving.

For it was true, all of it: having obliterated the heartlands of the Stony Tunguska, Sasha's primordial black hole had not tunneled through the Earth and out the other side. It had taken up an elliptical orbit within the lithosphere. An eighty-minute orbit with its eighteen apogees advancing completely around the globe once every twenty-four hours, revisiting Tunguska and the waters off the Azores and even less accessible places again and again as it slowly consumed the Earth's very substance.

It had become Vurdalak, gnawing in secret at the flesh of the world.

If only an expedition had been dispatched to the impact site immediately, they could at least have known. Even the rudimentary magnetometers of the time—no, even a child's compass—would have fluctuated wildly once every twelve hours, betraying the presence of the fiercely charged Vurdalak as it returned nearly to the surface at its Tunguskan apogee. But czarist Russia had been preoccupied with imminent war and revolution; no expedition had been sent. By the time the new Soviet government sent Kulik and his party to the epicenter for a proper geomagnetic survey, twenty years had passed. Years in which Vurdalak had slowly receded deeper into the Earth as its orbit gradually decayed, descending almost beyond the range of the second expedition's primitive instruments. All Kulik managed to capture in 1928 were a few feeble magnetic anomalies.

Elsewhere in the world, the chances of detection were even slimmer.

Most of the apogees occurred in trackless ocean or inaccessible wasteland. The North Atlantic site—the point where, had it been in the
cards, Vurdalak would have left Earth forever on its original trajectory—was actually more propitious than most.

Even here, though, and even at the outset, the local maximum in
Vurdalak's orbit had only brought it within twenty meters of the surface. That was still too deep to have much effect on North Atlantic
shipping, other than to play havoc with the bridge compass of the occasional passing vessel. As it submerged ever deeper over the years,
Vurdalak may have been responsible for one or more unexplained
World War I U-boat disasters, but otherwise it had spiraled slowly
down beyond the ken of man, sinking unnoticed into the sunless abyss.

And leaving behind so little evidence of its passing that, when the
Americans A. A. Jackson and M. P. Ryan proposed their primordial
black hole explanation for Tunguska in 1973, they were made a laugh-
ingstock. Even the otherwise splendid American television series *Cosmos* had the astronomer Carl Sagan joining in the chorus of derision.

It was doubtless this air of the ridiculous, still clinging to the PBH-
collision hypothesis three decades after its proposal, that drove Arkady
Grigoriyevich to keep the Antipode Project under wraps, at least until
the cat was safely in the sack.

Galina reddened then, remembering her vodka-induced gaffe at
last night's banquet. Arkady Grigoriyevich had been very angry with
her; she had read it in his eyes. But while she could understand Chairman Grishin's insistence on cloaking his great humanitarian effort in
such secrecy, she could not agree. The fruits of this magnificent achieve-
ment must belong to the whole world.

Soon they would. Not only would cosmologists have an opportunity to study at close hand that dream of twentieth-century physics—a
"universe in the laboratory"—but, in time, networks of undersea cables
would carry a stream of clean, inexhaustible power to all the peoples of
the globe.

Her workstation's powerdown cycle had long since completed. Galina shook herself and rose to leave. As she climbed the rungs to *Rusalka*'s bridge deck, she was already looking ahead to what the next twelve
hours would bring.

Just as no force on earth, not even Antipode Station's gigantic superconducting electromagnets, could have raised the black hole's Brobdingnagian bulk, so too none had the power to hold it in place against the pull of Earth's gravity.

But Galina, sorceress of magnetohydrodynamic enchantments, had one more trick in store for Vurdalak. In just twelve hours, she would sap the vampire's own diabolical strength to weave her incorporeal web.

22 | Departures

THREE METAL CHAIRS, a sofa that doubled as a cot, a console, a portrait of Andropov—Grishin's private quarters were austere, not to say ascetic, in their appointments. And dark. The Residence was situated well inboard of the vessel's hull. For reasons of security, of course, but it meant no portholes, no natural light to soften the glare of the overhead spots or lighten the gloom beyond their cones of illumination. Outside it was still broad daylight, late afternoon, the westering sun just beginning to gild *Rusalka*'s superstructure. Within this sanctum sanctorum at *Rusalka*'s heart it might as well be midnight.

Sasha felt rather than heard the heavy steel door slide shut behind him and lock into place. He experienced a brief surge of panic, as though he were trapped in that other room again, the twin to this one, in the Foreign Directorate's headquarters on the outskirts of Moscow. As though he were facing, not the urbane Arkady Grigoriyevich Grishin, but Colonel Gromov once more. Confronting once again all the brutal power of the KGB, with nothing to pit against it, no means of reclaiming his life from it, but a theory bordering on madness.

A theory of how a black hole might have been, might yet be, used to warp time itself. A theory summed up in a single mantra: "It must be true, it will be true—for it has already happened."

Sasha shook himself. The moment had passed. He was back on *Rusalka,* that other existence far away, fading into nightmare memory again.

He turned his attention to the figure hunched over the console. Grishin was staring at his datawall, at what looked like visuals of *Rusalka*'s chartroom.

"You sent for me, Arkasha?"

"Ah, Sasha, come in and sit down." At a spoken command the datawall went dark, save for a countdown box in its upper left corner. Grishin swiveled his chair around to face the desk and picked up a gleaming object that had been resting on its matte-black surface.

"Here, have a look at this." A crystalline note rang out as the lopsided metal cylinder skittered across the desk. Sasha caught it just in time to keep it from rolling over the edge.

"Is this the probe that I was—that you retrieved the other night?" Sasha rotated the object, squinting to make out the message cut into its distorted surface. "But, but this is the go-code for capture! Why was I not advised?"

"I informed Galina Mikhailovna. And her team. I judged that sufficient."

Still angry about that business with Dzhon on the bridge, then. Best steer away from that. "For—when is it? I can barely make it out in this light."

"Tonight." Grishin glanced at the countdown on his datawall. "Some six hours from now."

"But this is wonderful news, Arkasha! Simply marvelous!"

"Indeed, indeed it is. But there are complications. I fear the time has come to say goodbye to your friends, Sasha."

For "goodbye," Grishin had not said *do svidania,* literally "until we meet again." Instead, he had used the archaic *proshchai,* a word meaning "farewell" or "adieu," with overtones of "forgive me." Such an expressive language, Russian, marvelous in its subtle indirectness. Entire populations condemned to the camps in passive-voice pronouncements discretely omitting mention of those responsible. Even a death sentence need merely be hinted at.

A thin film of sweat coated Sasha's brow. "Arkady Grigoriyevich—"

"This was stupid of you, Sasha." Grishin's hand slammed the desktop. "Inexcusable. You knew we could not have outsiders aboard *Rusalka* once we entered the final phase."

Sasha swallowed, and began again. "Had I known we were so close, Arkady Grigoriyevich! But who could have guessed before the probe arrived?"

Grishin appeared not to have heard. "Sasha, I am very disappointed. What could you have been thinking?"

"Dzhonathan Knox is an old friend, from a time when things were more...simple. When he contacted me just before the gala, when I learned that he was bound for London, I—well, it was the heart that spoke, not the head." Sasha straightened a bit. "Even so, we have hosted Americans on *Rusalka* many times. Even as researchers in the public labs. Good cover, we decided."

"But never so late into the end-game. No, my friend, you have left us with no recourse but a burial at sea."

Sasha opened his mouth to speak, but no words came out.

"Let it go, Sashenka. Let Knox and his lady friend simply disappear. It is not as if they will hold it against you, in times to come."

"But here, in *this* present, I have their blood on my hands. There must be some other way."

"Hear me well, Sasha: I will not compromise the security of this operation for the sake of sentiment. Already there have been unfortunate incidents."

Galina's toast of the evening before? "None too serious, I think." Sasha tried again. "Could we not simply put them ashore?"

"Where, in Great Britain? Even running at full speed, *Rusalka* is sixty-five hours out from Southampton. A round trip would mean a delay of more than six days. And the probe does not say next week—it says now."

Grishin scowled. "No, if you insist on preserving your friends' soon-to-be meaningless existence, you must give me a real alternative."

"We could always airlift them out."

"I, too, had considered this. However, the coast of Europe is well beyond our helicopter's range. An airlift merely translates to a more elaborate, and more expensive, version of the sea-burial. Unless you thought, perhaps, to call in a VTOL." Grishin smiled humorlessly.

Sasha stared. "A Vertical Take-Off and Landing jet?" Arkady Grigoriyevich thought big, give him that much. But—"The helipad would buckle under its thrust."

"So, you agree it is impossible?"

"Wait, wait, there is another possibility: the Azores."

It was Grishin's turn to stare, coldly. "Go on."

"Two and a half hours flying time, easily within helicopter range."

Grishin hefted the probe cylinder absently. "And the reason you would give for this abrupt departure?"

"I will invent something plausible, Arkasha. Please, believe: Knox may be puzzled, suspicious even, but there will be nothing he can do in the time left to him—the time left to any of us."

Grishin tapped the metal cylinder against his teeth as he gazed into the middle distance, weighing alternatives. The tap-tap-tap was the only sound in the room. Sasha held his breath. The seconds-display in the countdown box flickered in his peripheral vision. Tap-tap-tap.

Finally, grudgingly: "Very well, see to it."

Sasha rose, effusing thanks and reassurances. Inwardly, though, something was nagging at him. Something in Grishin's manner, in his tone of voice just now, hadn't seemed quite right. There was something he wasn't saying.

He paused at the door and glanced back, seeking to confirm the impression, but Grishin had already turned to his console again. The audience was over.

✶

Vodka wasn't supposed to give you hangovers. Knox's head was splitting, notwithstanding. Where was truth in advertising when you needed it?

The poolside deckchair had been a good idea, though. The late afternoon sun was definitely helping—he'd missed out on the early afternoon sun, having risen only half an hour ago — and the sea breeze felt good on his fevered brow.

Wild night. Good to know the Russians hadn't lost their ability to party hearty in the wake of Communism's collapse. He frowned at a vague recollection: of standing on his chair at the banquet table, declaiming *Russkii Yazyk*, Turgenev's magnificent paean to the Russian language. Had he really done that? Good thing they hadn't gotten him started on the *Lay of the Host of Igor*.

He broke off his reverie as a shadow fell across his face. Someone was standing over him, blocking the warmth of the sun. Maybe if he just kept his eyes closed and didn't move, they'd go away again.

"Dzhon, are you awake?" The voice came from what, squinting, he now made out as a backlit Sasha-shaped silhouette.

What now? Can't a man just crawl off and die in peace any more?

"Dzhon?" Sasha sounded none the worse for wear, despite the night's carousing. "I regret to disturb you, but something has come up. Do you know where is Marianna? This concerns her as well."

Knox blinked his eyes against bright sunlight and sighed.

✳

Grishin waited until Sasha had left, then spoke into the console's microphone: "Run it again."

In response, the image of the chartroom swam back into view, accompanied by a conferencing inset filled with GEI security chief Merkulov's bloated face.

"And this is the recording from the night before last?"

"Yes, Comrade Director. I must apologize for the delay in finding this, but the image-analysis software that caught the anomaly is a low-level background function. It runs against offline dumps, and then only in time available. A forty-hour backlog is nominal, considering. In any case," Merkulov hastened to get off the sticky subject of the time-lag in detecting the incident, "as you can see from the timestamp, the discrepancy begins about ten minutes after midnight, and continues for the next fifty-five minutes."

"I see no difference."

"Precisely. It is difficult to see, or we would certainly have caught it in real time. But watch, as I enhance this sector." A glowing rectangle sectioned off and zoomed in on that quadrant of the image showing the flatscreen display hanging on the wall. What now filled the screen was a computerized chart of the North Atlantic, with a stylized ship symbol marking *Rusalka*'s current position. Grishin peered more closely, and suddenly he saw it.

"Run that sequence again."

At exactly 12:11 and 23 seconds by the timestamp, the little position marker suddenly jumped backwards along the line of *Rusalka*'s course—nearly five hundred miles backwards!

"This is our latitude and longitude as they were twenty-four hours earlier. Are you certain it is not a navigation-system error?"

"No, Comrade Director. The charting software is not malfunctioning; someone has tampered with the videocam signal. There is an almost imperceptible skip in the recorded image at the same transition point, just at the 0011 mark. And, on close inspection, the date-digit shows signs of having been altered, from August 1st to August 2nd."

"One moment. Did you say between midnight and one a.m.?"

Merkulov nodded. "0011 to 0103 hours, Comrade Director. Why? Is something wrong?"

They were straining at gnats after swallowing an elephant. He had paid his own visit to the lab in that same timeframe—yet the recording failed to show it!

"No, nothing." Grishin said finally. The fewer who knew how close they were to their goal, the better.

"Comrade Director, I need not tell you that this incident represents a grave breach of security." Merkulov looked uncomfortable, as well he should. "In such circumstances, procedure requires—that is, shall I inform your second in command as well?"

"Absolutely not! Sasha has enough to occupy him at the moment. In any case, there is no need: I will see to the appropriate measures myself."

He terminated the contact and sat back, thinking. In a way it was good the Americans had turned out to be real spies rather than foolish innocents who just happened to be in the wrong place at the wrong time. Sasha need never know that the outcome would have been the same regardless, that he himself had signed his friends' death warrants the instant he let them lay eyes on Galina.

Grishin smiled grimly. Sasha need never know at all. As far as he was concerned, Knox and Peterson would be safe in London. There would be nothing to trouble his subordinate's mind, or keep him from his work in these final days.

The smile remained as he spoke into the microphone. "Yuri? Report to the Residence, please."

Time to see about those "appropriate measures."

✳

"A volcano?" Marianna took Jon's hand and pulled herself out of the pool. "You're kidding, right?"

"Not me, him." He motioned to Sasha, standing a couple paces behind him. "It's his story; let him tell it."

She turned to Sasha and raised an eyebrow.

"It is true, Marianna," he said. "Only an hour ago our remote sensors detected new volcanic venting in the rift. Indications are it could be Mount Venus herself."

Venus was the highest undersea peak in the rift valley that bisected the Mid-Atlantic Ridge. Out there, the tectonic forces that had created the Atlantic to begin with were still active, still steadily ratcheting the Old World apart from the New at the breakneck pace of almost an inch a year. For the most part, such seabed spreading took place without much fanfare. Every so often, though, things heated up—literally.

Sasha's scenario sounded plausible enough. But, coming so near the appointed hour for the mysterious "capture" event, the timing was a tad too convenient.

Still, she had to admit Sasha was putting his heart and soul into the performance.

"Imagine, an event of such magnitude, with us here to observe it firsthand." He beamed. "We believe in time it could break the surface, become an island." And *Rusalka* had arrived just in time for the show. Things could not be more perfect, except: "My friends, I am afraid this means you must cut short your stay with us."

As if she hadn't seen that one coming. Still, all she needed was one more night. It was worth a try.

"But it all sounds so exciting!" she gushed. "I mean, a whole new island! Oh, please, can't we stick around to watch?"

"I regret not, Marianna. *Rusalka* must take up station at the site of the eruption, you see. Possibly for weeks—all depends." Sasha shrugged. "No, best you follow your old American custom and go while the going is good."

Jon surprised her then. "Okay, Sasha, we'll be packed and ready to go first thing in the morning." Marianna knew he'd been less than enthusiastic about her return engagement in the clandestine lab that night. Yet here he was, pushing to buy her the time regardless.

"No, no, Dzhon. Sorry if you misunderstood—even now *Rusalka* is making full speed toward the epicenter. By morning, we will be two hundred miles northwest of our present position, and out of flight range of the Azores."

Come to think, she'd noticed that course-change. It was about an hour ago; she'd had to switch chaises or lose the sun. Was that part of the volcano ruse too? Or did whatever they were hunting lie in that direction?

"So, you see," Sasha went on, "you really must go soon, within, um,"—a glance at his wristtop—"within the next three hours."

"You're really sure there's no choice?"

"There are always choices, Dzhon. Some cost more than others." Sasha turned to go.

"Whoa, Sasha—hold on a minute!" Jon grabbed his friend's arm. "You don't just drop a line like that and leave. In the good old days, that kind of opener would've kicked off an all-nighter." Way to go, Jon!

Sasha wasn't rising to the bait. "Alas, in these brave new days, I have responsibilities to tend to still." He shook his head and sighed. "But you are right, too, Dzhon—those *were* good days."

He engulfed Jon in a sudden bear hug, then held him at arms' length, looking at his friend as if he might never see him again. Sasha's eyes were bright as he said, "How I have missed those days, Dzhon, missed talking as we did the other night on the bridge. Talking so freely, so free of care."

He released Jon and shuffled off, head down, wiping at his eyes.

Jon looked after him for a long moment, then turned to her. "Remember what you told me our first day aboard? Something about how nine-tenths of covert operations was contingency planning?"

She nodded, barely listening, still thinking about ways to compensate for the suddenly foreshortened schedule.

"Well…" There was a strange look in his eyes. "I think one of your contingencies just eventuated."

✷

"This our ride, Sasha?" Knox waved a hand at the Colibri sitting silently on *Rusalka*'s helipad.

"Yes, Dzhon. Horta in two-three hours. Would you like to stow that in the meantime?" Sasha pointed to the knapsack riding high on Knox's back.

"Huh? Oh, no thanks. My handheld's in there somewhere. Thought I might dig it out and make a call to the home office en route, to let them know I'll be in London a few days early."

"Dzhon, again, I am sorry for the rush. There truly was no choice."

"You can make up for it by naming your new island after us, Sasha." Knox was feeling anything but jocular; he was just joshing on automatic. "It would have to be 'Jonathania,' though; there already are some Mariannas, I believe."

"That's with one 'n,' dear." Marianna said, poking him in the ribs. "And they're in the Pacific, anyway. I could do with a namesake closer to home."

"Dearest Dzhon," Galina embraced him. "I had so wished you to be present at this historic moment." Knox could feel her trembling in his arms. She was certainly worked up about something, though he doubted whether even the birth of a new Azore qualified as a historic occasion.

"And you, dear Marianna,"—a quick hug—"perhaps next time we sunbathe, you not be so…" Galina wrinkled her nose and turned to Knox. "How to say 'zastyenchiva'?"

"Bashful," Knox supplied.

"Not so *beshfool*, yes?"

Marianna blushed. "Wish I had more to be bashful about. But maybe next time, provided we can lock the menfolk in the brig for an hour or so."

"Send me email when you are settled," Sasha was saying. "We should not wait half a lifetime again to get together." His parting bear hug was hampered by Knox's knapsack. "What do you have in that thing, Dzhon? Pipe fittings?"

"Telescope," Knox improvised. "Not that there'll be much viewing off Canary Wharf."

"Well, then, you must most definitely sail with us soon again. Out here we have always stars. And you must join him, Marianna."

"We hope you'll come to see us in London first, Sasha. Stars or no stars."

Grishin had come up behind the group as they were saying their farewells. He extended his hand. "So good to have met you, Mr. Knox. I look forward to welcoming you aboard again in future." Then, in English to Marianna, "And you, my dear, you too must return to *Rusalka*. My little boat is only half so beautiful in your absence."

Knox frowned. Everything seemed so normal. Had he overreacted?

But, no—over Grishin's shoulder, he could see one more figure slouching toward the helicopter, flashing that trademark steel grin of his.

"*Gospodin* Knox." Grishin switched back to Russian. "I have asked Yuri here to accompany you to Horta. I trust it is no inconvenience. Despite modern telecommunications, at times we must still move atoms rather than bits around the globe. In this case, some seawater samples expected at Woods Hole the day after tomorrow."

Sasha looked surprised at this, but said nothing.

Knox swallowed. What wouldn't he give not to be right all the time!

Still, keep up appearances: "We would welcome Yuri's company, Arkady Grigoriyevich."

By the time they were ready to depart, the sun was setting. The Colibri powered up, its flashing rotors catching the last light of day. It lifted off, circled *Rusalka* gaining altitude, then angled southeast in the afterglow.

✳

Yuri Vissarionovich Geladze sat off by himself in a corner of the helicopter's passenger cabin. He sat in silence. He looked at the window, but not out of it: between the interior lighting and the stygian darkness outside, its glass was transformed into a mirror. From time to time he looked at his watch.

He stole a glance at the other two passengers. They were chattering away in English, a language not among Yuri's accomplishments. At most he recognized the occasional word: "*Rusalka*," "London," that sort of thing. Of languages, Yuri knew only Russian and the tongue of his native Sarkatvelo, which the Westerners insisted on calling "Georgia." But he did know how to read tones of voice, and faces, and gestures.

By all these indicators, this pair seemed strangely agitated. Almost as if they knew what lay in store. It might simply be his presence that unnerved them. Yuri was aware that he had this effect on people. Other than its occasional usefulness in business, he seldom gave it much thought.

No matter. All over soon. He looked at his watch again: 10:25. The helicopter had been flying low, barely skimming the waves, for the past twenty minutes — staying well under the Terceira radar. There would be no way to trace this flight back to *Rusalka*. Give it five more minutes, just to be sure.

The man first, he thought. The man who had sent Yuri to fetch tea that night on the bridge. Who had treated him like a common lackey.

Then the woman. A waste, that. Perhaps he would have the Colibri hold on station while he indulged himself with her first. He had not had such a beauty in some time. Women unaccountably did not like Yuri.

A beauty. Yet something familiar about her too. Where could he have…?

Time, or close enough. Yuri unbuckled his seatbelt. Rose from his chair. The .45 slid noiselessly from his shoulder holster.

The couple stopped talking. Now naked apprehension showed on their faces. Good! No more of this polite nervousness. But the strangeness remained, their reactions were still not quite appropriate. They now seemed *less* afraid than they should be. Perhaps they still did not see what was to come.

This next part was ticklish. Grishin had instructed him not to soil the helicopter's interior with blood, if it could be helped. Yuri took pride in his workmanship; the order would be carried out.

Pointing the gun at the man, the greater threat, Yuri shouted *"Door!"* above the roar of the engine. One of his few English words. He made twisting and yanking gestures with his free hand. The man understood, though he looked sick. He went to the hatch, undogged it, shoved it back.

Good! The woman was cowering to one side. The man was framed in the now-open hatch. All Yuri needed to do was aim carefully, steady himself against the helicopter's bouncing, and the upholstery would not be bloodied. He grinned, broadly.

Suddenly, he heard a shriek, to his right. Not a scream of fright, more like a war cry. At the same instant he glimpsed a blur of movement almost at shoulder height. Something or someone was hurtling horizontally through the air towards him!

He was turning to bring the .45 to bear on this new threat, when his elbow exploded in agony! He heard an awful snapping sound. The gun was jarred loose, went skittering across the floor. The man grabbed for it, but missed. It flew out the open hatch, into the night.

Yuri howled. The bitch had broken his arm! Kicked him! Kicked him with all of her weight behind the blow somehow.

Yuri ducked and a second kick only grazed his forehead. He would not be caught unawares again. He turned to face the woman. She was crouching in some sort of martial arts stance. No question now who represented the greater danger. Yuri had miscalculated, seriously. What he wouldn't give for his *gun!*

He roared and lunged for the bitch. Crashed hard into the seatback instead. As he screamed in rage, she delivered another blow, this time with the toe of her boot, this time to his ribcage.

The pilot was having difficulty compensating for the sudden

redistributions of weight. The copter tilted abruptly. The man fell out the open hatch. The woman hesitated a moment, then leapt after him.

Sliding across the deck, Yuri snagged a seatbelt in his remaining good hand, managed to hang on. Cradling his arm, forehead bleeding, he stumbled to the door. He looked down fifteen meters to the heaving surface of the sea but could make out no details in the dark.

"Lights!" he commanded hoarsely. "Take us lower!" The pilot switched on the big spots and angled them down, illuminating a wilderness of waves. Then—

"There!" The two of them, bobbing on the surface. The woman was struggling with the man's knapsack, trying to pull something out.

Yuri dogged the hatch shut and climbed forward into the unoccupied copilot's seat, wincing as he jarred his shattered right arm. He strapped in and pressed a red button built into the frame of a flatscreen display. Two panels in the forward fuselage slid back to reveal a brace of machine gun snouts. The Colibri dropped all pretense of being a civilian aircraft and owned its true identity as a helicopter gunship.

"Strafing run!" Yuri said. The machine guns' video sights were equipped with infrared. On the screen, in the crosshairs, images of two warm, fuzzy blobs stood out against the cold, dark water. What he wouldn't give right now for a rocket-propelled grenade or two! Yuri squeezed the trigger. The spotlit chop below pocked with splash-craters as the slugs hit the water fast enough to ricochet.

Now there was nothing to be seen. Did he get them? He looked in vain for bullet-riddled corpses floating amid the swells.

Yuri ordered the pilot to circle, circle again. The downdraft from the rotors kicked up the surf, obscuring what he most needed to see. Still nothing. No sign of the man or that *devil-woman*. He ached to get them in the machine guns' crosshairs. Especially her. He knew her now, something in her voice, her stance. It was that bitch who'd tried to interfere with the extraction in New York. But he had seen her fall!

Over the years, upwards of fifty men had died by Yuri's hand. He had never killed a woman before. Other than under contract, of course. Certainly not in revenge. Revenge upon a woman would be uncultured, not in keeping with the code.

Now, though—the devil with the Mafiya code! He longed to see the dark blood-blossoms sprout on her brow as the slugs sang into her braincase. Wanted it so badly, he could almost see the image forming on the sighting display.

He saw nothing but churning, spotlit water.

A minute went by. Five. Still the helicopter circled over the now-empty sea.

Finally, the pilot protested. "This is useless, Yuri Vissarionovich! Our fuel runs low. We must turn back to *Rusalka* now, or go on to Horta to refuel. They are dead in any case. If the bullets did not kill them, the Atlantic surely will."

Yuri peered out into the darkness, considering. Grishin would want him back on board in the hours following the capture, not sitting at some devil-take-it airport in the Azores waiting for the night crew to refuel the copter.

And...

Yuri was not a stupid man; stupid men do not last twenty years in the Sarkatvelo Mafiya. Till now, it had seemed the two Americans were engaged in industrial espionage, pure and simple. But with his recognition of the woman came a realization: the U.S. government was behind this! And it was not Yuri's place to decide what to do about that. Grishin would need to know, soon. Yet, if they were indeed being stalked by CROM, he ought not break radio silence to report that fact.

And...

His arm throbbed in agony. It would require attention soon if Yuri was to be of any use in the crucial hours ahead.

All these reasons, good reasons. Still, for a long moment, prudence warred with murderous vindictiveness, the brain versus the blood. Then—

He turned to the pilot. With his uninjured hand he traced a single arc in the air and then pointed back the way they came. He scowled.

"Devil take them! Circle once more. Then we go."

The helicopter executed one more slow, fruitless circuit of the dark sea, and then arced off back toward the northwest, back toward *Rusalka*.

As it departed, the roiled black waters of the North Atlantic subsided again into gentle, empty swells.

23 | Armageddon

VURDALAK FED.

Vurdalak would always feed. An entity defined solely by its ravenous hunger, Vurdalak hurtled along its subterranean trajectory, and it fed.

But there was so little to feed *upon!* Vurdalak's capture cross-section was only marginally wider than the diameter of an atomic nucleus. At subatomic scales the solid material of the mantle through which Vurdalak traveled was mostly empty space. Individual atoms were few and far between, and what few it consumed were as nothing compared to its mountainous mass. They could do little to assuage its insatiable appetite. Only when it had spiraled in to the very center of the Earth, where the atoms of the molten interior were densely packed, could it begin to feed in earnest.

Yet, for a time, the dynamics of its own motion forestalled that inevitable outcome. Although Vurdalak swallowed only a few atoms in its headlong plunge through the Earth, its passage influenced many more. Its immense local gravitational field reached out to draw in mass from the immediate vicinity all along its path, to collide in its wake.

The resulting shockfront at its stern yielded Zeldovich-Salpeter acceleration—a tiny push that, for a time at least, could counter the even tinier pulls of gravity and drag. Powered by its own self-made thrusters, Vurdalak would remain in a semi-stable orbit, for a time.

For a time, a time now well into its tenth decade, Vurdalak's augmented trajectory would keep it within capture range. The question was how to capture it.

On its travels through the Earth, Vurdalak traced out a delicate rosette, reminiscent of a rose window in a Gothic cathedral. But each petal of this rose, each orbital arc, took the shape of a flattened semicircle, half of an ellipsoid. This geometry was critical for capture: it meant that Vurdalak's speed was not uniform. Most of the time, the primordial black hole whizzed along like the subterranean *sputnik* it was. But there were two points at either end of the arc where it ceased to rise and hesitated before falling back. In this, its motion was not all that different from a cannonball fired into the sky at an angle: it goes up, it comes down, but for a moment there, at the maximum of the curve, it does neither. It slows and slows and then hangs in space for an instant before speeding up again on the return trip.

It was in these moments, when Vurdalak slowed to a crawl at the top of its curve, that it would be easiest to stop it entirely. Stop it and hold it.

It had taken thirty-three months of electromagnetic nudging, nearly three years truing up the orbit. But finally the local maximum of one of Vurdalak's arcs, its 22:47 apogee, was about to pass precisely through the center of Antipode Station's spherical superconducting electromagnet array.

✳

Galina sat at the master console in the now-crowded quarters of the secret lab, with Grishin hovering over her shoulder. She leaned forward and keyed in a single word: *Armageddon*. A strange, non-Russian word, that. A word from the Bible. She had looked it up: the final battle between Good and Evil, the fate of the world hanging in the balance. Galina nodded to herself; it fit.

Three thousand meters below, responding to her keystrokes, Antipode Station came on line.

Galina looked at the time-display as Antipode's enormous electromagnets powered up: 10:37 P.M. Vurdalak was still ten minutes downrange.

"Postrel'nikova here," Galina spoke into her mike. "Requesting verbal confirmation on array power-up."

"North hemisphere, nominal—temperature holding at minus two sixty-six degrees C," a voice whispered in her headset, followed by okays from the other monitoring stations.

She swiveled her chair and nodded to Arkady Grigoriyevich. All boards green. *Showtime!* Curtain going up in eight minutes on the most important performance of her life.

Vurdalak sped along its track, oblivious to what awaited.

Grishin nodded a confirmation: they were go for capture. Galina entered a penultimate keystroke combination. She licked her lips and leaned toward the microphone again.

"Commencing braking train configuration." It came out as a whisper.

Three kilometers down in the sunless depths of the Newfoundland Basin, there rose a mountain called Hope.

Mount Nadyezhda—Russian for "hope"—was the seamount whose summit, towering a kilometer and a half above the abyssal plain, cradled Antipode Station. And whose eastern slope was now the scene of frantic activity as automated systems responded to the keyed-in command.

Galina did not need her displays to visualize what was happening all along the undersea mountainside that Vurdalak would be climbing in just seven minutes thirty-two seconds. In her mind's eye she could see the superconducting toroids of the braking train rearing up out of their cryogenic armatures and locking into place. Now a strand of interlaced rings adorned Nadyezhda's shoulder, descending in a gentle curve from her mile-high crown to her foot. Nor did the annular chain end at the seafloor; from there it entered the Shaft, a borehole twice as deep as the mountain was high.

A thousand supercooled metal-jacketed donuts—widely spaced at first, but bunched closer and closer together as they neared the summit—were now aligning precisely along the final five kilometers of Vurdalak's upward track.

Timing was critical: for safety's sake, the superconducting toroids had to be cooled well below the near-zero ambient temperature. Before long, seawater would begin to freeze on the now-exposed rings. The accreting ice could do damage. Worse, as it expanded, it could warp individual braking rings out of alignment. The solution was to limit the exposure of the active elements as much as possible—limit it to the final seven minutes before capture.

But that tight a time margin could create problems of its own.

Galina's display flashed red! A twenty-toroid section in the middle of the braking train was not responding to the reconfiguration command. The assembly as a whole was a hundred percent overengineered; it could still perform its function if every other one of its component electromagnets were to fail. But it could not handle a continuous hundred-meter gap in the chain!

Six minutes till the onset of the deceleration run. But only four before she must initiate a scram, or the links in the chain would not have time to withdraw out of Vurdalak's way. They would be destroyed, and to no purpose! She poised a trembling finger above the *Abort* key, hoping against hope that the holdout units would join the rest of their own accord before time ran out.

"What is it, Galina Mikhailovna?" Grishin's voice startled her. She had forgotten he was standing there behind her. "Are we still go? We must make capture on this pass."

"Please, Arkady Grigoriyevich, there is no time to discuss this right now. I must *think!*"

Under other circumstances she would be shocked to hear anyone, much less herself, address the head of Grishin Enterprises International in such peremptory tones. As it was, she scarcely paid heed to what she had said. Or to his reaction. Her mind was racing frantically, like a squirrel in a cage. Must focus, focus…

Suddenly, for no apparent reason, she found herself thinking back to the banquet the previous evening. Back to something Dzhon had said there, some joke. What was it? Ah yes, his so-called First—or was it Second?—Law of Data Processing: "When in doubt, reboot."

Nothing to lose. Try it!

She keyed in the reset command and hit *Send*. Barely time enough left for this to work. *If* it worked. It would take a full minute to retract all the units back into their sockets, another to step through the restart procedure, yet another to raise the toroids back into braking position again—three minutes cycle-time in all. Three minutes before she would know if the recalcitrant links in her chain would move into alignment with the rest.

Please—*please!*—let it work.

Silence stole over the lab. All eyes locked on the countdown displays, watching the seconds tick down to the scram point. The three-minute mark approached, passed. Nothing... Still nothing...

"*Green! I read green!*" One of the techs, Voshchanova, screamed it out from down the row of workstations. Galina checked her own display: sure enough, the entire five-kilometer track was now showing as an almost-continuous string of little green dots from bottom to top. The last laggard units went from red to green even as she watched. They all winked merrily at her like a strand of lights on a *yolochka*, a Christmas tree.

She would sag with relief, but there was no time, no *time!* Two minutes thirty-two seconds remaining till Armageddon. "Powering up frontline toroids," her voice cracked as she spoke the words. She entered the keystrokes, hit return. They were committed now.

Sixteen hundred fathoms below, power began to course from Antipode's main nuclear reactor down the braking train. At the bottom of the shaft, the first ten decelerators came to life.

But *only* the first ten. The reactor's output was insufficient to drive all the toroids in the braking train and still have power enough for what else must be done. No matter: this had been planned for.

"Confirming frontline toroids at full field strength. One minute eight to go on the clock," Galina announced finally. She was surprised at how calm her voice sounded, now that there was no turning back. "Engaging deceleration sequence in five, four, three, two..." She entered one last command.

"Mark: 2246 hours." The cool, androgynous tones of a synthesized voice picked up where Galina left off. "Armageddon Phase One: Deceleration Sequence, engaged." The mission computer had now assumed control over all aspects of the final phase, status reporting included.

10:46 P.M. Sixty seconds to go. Vurdalak was still twenty kilometers out, closing at thirty-two hundred kilometers per hour, but slowing, slowing as the vertical component of its velocity vector dwindled to zero with the approach of apogee.

Enough time for a last check of the readouts: at t minus forty seconds, Antipode's gravitometric instrumentation was just beginning to pick up Vurdalak's signature propagating through the mantle beneath the seafloor. Now the SQUIDs were reading its magnetic profile as well. The geophones detected the first faint subterranean rumblings of the vampire's approach.

The final seconds ticked down. Galina glanced again at the *Abort* button, but that option was no longer available to her. Humans were now out of the loop, their biochemical reaction times orders of magnitude too slow to even observe, much less direct, what would happen next. The Antipode techs could only sit on the sidelines as their automated factotums decided the fate of the Earth.

Galina watched as the countdown went to t minus seven, t minus six, t minus five... All the years of preparation, all the effort, the sacrifice, now balanced on the fulcrum of this single instant. No time left for second thoughts now, no time for might-have-beens.

t minus three, t minus two...

Time, perhaps, only for a prayer. A simple prayer, remembered from long-ago summers spent with her grandmother. *Gospodi, pomilui.* Lord, have mercy, have mercy upon us.

t minus zero.

Vurdalak encountered the first toroid in the braking train. Things began to happen. Fast.

Everywhere else in the known universe, magnetic poles come in inseparable north and south pairs. Can't have one without the other.

But Vurdalak was a magnetic monopole. In effect, just one big south pole, with no north to offset it. And the operative term here, from the standpoint of field strength, was *big*.

The superconducting rings were oriented so that their own magnetic south poles faced downward, in the direction of Vurdalak's approach. Like-charged poles repel one another. As Vurdalak entered the first ring, its radial field plowed into the one threaded around and through the toroid. For a few milliseconds the ring resisted the hole's forward momentum, and, though the outcome of the struggle was never in doubt, neither did Vurdalak escape entirely unscathed. It was slowed, if only by a minuscule amount. It was also deflected, by an equally minuscule amount—just enough to aim it dead center toward the next decelerator in the chain.

The toroid itself did not fare anywhere near so well. If time had permitted, the irresistible force of Vurdalak's passage would have smashed it flatter than a tin can in a roller press.

Time did not permit; there were bigger, faster effects afoot than mere mechanical stress and shear. Move a magnet across a conductor and you get electricity. As Vurdalak traversed the first toroid, electromagnetic induction set a current to flowing in the unit's superconductive alloy. Like all the rest of the phenomena associated with Vurdalak, it was a very *large* current.

The toroid could not contain the sudden burst of energy. It flared and died, exploded like an apple struck by a bullet.

Exactly as intended. Unless the magnetic field collapsed the instant Vurdalak entered the ring, the micro-hole would be reaccelerated out the other side like a pip squeezed from an orange. That was emphatically not part of the plan. So, the braking-chain elements had all been deliberately engineered to self-destruct like this. After performing one last service...

The frontline ring survived just long enough to pump its induced electric current into the connecting cables, and from there to its as-yet unpowered siblings up the line. Vurdalak's velocity, blindingly fast in human terms, was as nothing to the lightspeed jolt of power now flowing up the braking train. A second toroid contributed its delta-vee of deceleration, was overmastered by the rush of power, and, like its predecessor, passed along this gift of energy with its dying gasp. Then another, and another.

t plus one. Vurdalak's own motion was now the only thing powering the braking train, and that with megawatts to spare. Courtesy of Galina's electromagnetic jujitsu.

Galina could only watch as her little progeny sacrificed themselves, overloading and expiring one by one. But not before their job was done, not before they had each exerted their tiny drag on the hurtling black hole.

t plus six seconds, *t* plus seven... Four and a half of the braking train's five kilometers now lay behind Vurdalak. In ruins. In the vampire's wake, twisted wreckage was strewn across Nadyezhda's eastern slope like the aftermath of one of Marshal Zhukov's epic World War II tank battles. Three years' toil, expended in the blink of an eye. If this did not work, could they ever find the strength, the resolve to begin again?

But it *was* working. Vurdalak's centrifugal force was decreasing as it slowed further and further. Now each successive link in the deceleration chain must exert an increasing percentage of its force upward. Slower, slower...

The mission computer spoke the words Galina had been waiting to hear: "Phase One: Deceleration Sequence, complete. Initiating Armageddon Phase Two: Positional Stabilization."

t plus ten. Moving at a crawl, its path virtually horizontal now, Vurdalak entered the containment chamber at the heart of Antipode Station. Alarms shrieked as gravitometers and SQUIDs registered its incursion, tracked it microsecond by microsecond as it approached the center.

The capture chamber's arrays of superconducting electromagnets were fully charged and waiting. Compared with the Tokamaks Galina had worked on most of her professional life, Antipode was simplicity itself. No need to provide for plasma containment: there would be no plasma to contain, only Vurdalak. No need to pinch the magnetic field to induce a thermonuclear reaction; this was not a reactor, but a cage. An invisible cage woven of lines of magnetic force.

A cage whose intangible bars now slid shut.

As Vurdalak crossed the center of the capture chamber, the giant electromagnets in its ceiling and floor slammed all their available energy into the primordial black hole. The repulsor array pushed against its gargantuan weight from below; the tractor hemisphere pulled on it from above. Secondary installations on the walls fore and aft countered the hole's residual forward momentum.

Vurdalak bobbled on the lip of the field, like a basketball in a rim-shot, and…ground to a halt.

Now the geophones took center stage, registering a truly awesome seismic shear as Mount Nadyezhda shifted and settled under the burden of Vurdalak's weight. Seismometers around the world would jump before the hour was up. The American anti-submarine hydrophone network would register the shock within minutes. The Antipode Project, wrapped in a cloak of silence all these years, would become an open secret in the next few hours.

But hours were not important now. It was the next few seconds that counted. If Mount Nadyezhda should buckle under the strain…

But the seamount was holding. Holding…still holding…the tremors dying down…yes!

The generated voice of *Rusalka*'s main computer announced, "Phase Two: Positional Stabilization, complete."

The djinn was trapped in Galina's magnetic bottle.

But for how long? The prodigious energies needed to bear a five and a half billion metric tonne load were generated by enormous superconducting toroids. These were "permanent" magnets, but they would stay permanent only so long as they continued to superconduct, and their ability to do so was under constant threat from the disruptive potential of the electromagnetic flux coursing through them.

To survive as superconductors, Antipode's levitation arrays had to be kept far, far colder than the ice-water transition temperatures of the little toy boats at last night's banquet. The colder, the better, for safety's sake, and Galina had chosen to chill the arrays to within seven degrees of absolute zero.

But maintaining such a deep freeze against the massive heat-leak of the containment operation ate power at a ungodly rate. The real-time output of Antipode's nuclear reactor couldn't satisfy the demand alone. And in forty-five seconds, plus or minus five, the stored power would be exhausted.

The superconductors would begin to heat up. Their magnetic levitation fields would fail. Unsupported, Vurdalak would fall.

But not back into its previous orbit. If it broke free again after having been halted in its path, it would fall nearly straight down, grazing the very center of the Earth.

That must not happen. The same highly-conductive nickel-iron core that gave rise to Earth's magnetic field would resist Vurdalak's passage, inducing orbital aberrations. The new trajectory would differ radically from the one they had spent years studying and shaping.

They might not be able to find the vampire again. And in the meantime, they would have accelerated the timetable for the doom they had hoped to avert.

No, they could not let go of this tiger they had by the tail. There would be no second chance.

The mission computer spoke again, a note of what sounded like exhilaration in its synthesized tones: "Thirty seconds to Armageddon Phase Three: Power Stabilization. Initiating fuel feed."

At six equidistant points around the circumference of the containment chamber, precision-machined nozzles dilated minutely. Hair-thin pressurized jets of deaerated distilled water rushed in and converged on the captive object.

Or tried to. Like all submicroscopic black holes, Vurdalak was *hot*. Bekenstein-Hawking radiation heated it into the *billions* of degrees. But that was at its microscopically small surface. Further out, say a meter or so, the temperature dropped to a comfortable few thousand degrees Celsius, not much hotter than your average blast furnace. Still hot enough, though, to vaporize the inrushing water and blast the superheated plasma back out again, toward the walls of its cage. Toward the ring of superconducting MHD generators standing ready to turn Vurdalak's heat energy into electricity via electromagnetic induction.

A brute-force, inefficient approach, and so what? The thermal energy was free and virtually inexhaustible, courtesy of Vurdalak. The superconducting magnets would, to all intents and purposes, last forever. There were no moving parts to wear out. And the power output was phenomenal.

Plug that output back into Antipode's main cryostats, and voilà!

—enough constant, real-time energy to maintain superconducting containment temperature indefinitely. Vurdalak would become its own jailer. Till the end of time, if need be.

That was the theory, anyway.

Galina was now sweating through the reality: only fifteen seconds now to power stabilization. She monitored the rising slope of the MHD output as it raced against the depletion of the stored reserves. Adjusted the fuel feed to compensate for unanticipated deviations from modeled ionization rates. Glanced at the countdown: ten seconds until Vurdalak would have to pull its own weight. Balancing, balancing... there!

Galina monitored power flow for a few more seconds before daring to believe. Vurdalak was producing power to spare: enough to maintain its magnetic bottle indefinitely, and—soon now, as soon as the undersea conduits could be laid—free, clean power to help light the world's cities as well. Until then, the radiators crowning Nadyezhda's summit would vent the overflow into the inexhaustible heat-sink of the North Atlantic, a bonanza for the energy-starved ecology of the Newfoundland Basin and its extremophile lifeforms.

"Phase Three: Power Stabilization, complete," the mission computer announced.

Galina was shaking with reaction. All the desperate gambles of the past hours and minutes and years had paid off. Now the final phase was complete. Her face felt wet. She realized she was crying, whispering *spasibo, spasibo*—thank you, thank you—over and over like a prayer. In Russian, of course, it *is* a prayer, a contraction of *Spasi Bog*, "May God save you."

She rose from her chair, turned, and, still sobbing, hugged a surprised Arkady Grigoriyevich. *Spasibo!* she told him. A cheer went up from the lab crew. They too were rising from their stations, slapping each other's backs, embracing, weeping openly, the men as well as the women. Galina had always admired the way Russian men were unafraid to express their deepest emotions.

Except for that cold fish, Komarov. Out of the corner of her eye Galina could see him still sitting in front of his display like a toad carved from stone, oblivious to the euphoria all around him, still monitoring the configurations of the containment field, or so it appeared from here. Still tapping commands into his keyboard. Why?

The mission computer's synthetic voice began speaking again: "Commencing Armageddon Phase Four: Acceleration."

If there was more to the announcement, Galina didn't hear it. She released Grishin, took a step back. Acceleration? Acceleration of *what*? "What is going on here, Arkady Grigorievich? There *is* no Phase Four!"

Receiving no reply, she turned back to her console. There, before her eyes, the field geometries were shifting. The warping of the containment field was subtle. Anyone else might have missed it entirely. But Galina had lived, eaten, slept, dreamed these configurations for the past five years. She knew that slight strengthening at the ninety-degree lateral was *wrong*.

She dropped into her chair again, summoned the gravitometric readouts to her display. No doubt about it: Vurdalak was *wobbling*, as if it were being bombarded somehow by some invisible force. The containment arrays were compensating as they were designed to do, producing the distortion that had caught Galina's eye. The resulting field-disposition remained meta-stable, but Vurdalak's spin, already within three percent of the speed of light, was increasing!

She could see the reason now: the SQUIDs were detecting eight individual streams of heavy ions entering the chamber from emitters not on any of the blueprints she had seen. Moving at relativistic speeds, the atomic nuclei were skimming the black hole's submicroscopic ergosphere with the precision of a particle accelerator and the momentum of a pile-driver. Each impact was minuscule compared with Vurdalak's titanic mass, but cumulatively —

Could that be why the automated announcement had called the mysterious fourth phase "Acceleration"?

Where could the beams be coming from? She called up the site-plans on her display, reviewed the familiar 3-D cutaways for the thousandth time: containment sphere, control room with its observation gallery for visiting dignitaries, antechamber and bathyscaphe docking facility — nothing out of the ordinary there. More keystrokes brought up the infrastructure schematics: life-support machinery, heat pipes, transformer bay, cryostats and power-converters, on and on.

She paused, then paged back to the schematic of the transformer bay. The vast space occupied most of one level. The display showed it sitting empty right now: no need to install the equipment before the cableships had laid the deep-water conduits that would connect Antipode to the global power grid. But was it truly empty? There was room enough in there to accommodate what her instrumentation was detecting: eight radially-mounted linear accelerators.

As this realization dawned, Galina glimpsed a flicker of movement in the upper righthand corner of her display. She tore her gaze from the station schematics and saw that a small red rectangle had appeared there unbidden. Yellow digits were inscribed in it, ticking off the seconds toward an undefined event still some fifty-three and a half hours in the future.

A countdown window.

She jerked at the touch of Arkady Grigoriyevich's hand on her shoulder. He was saying something.

"Galina Mikhailovna—Galya, if I may—you are to be congratulated on your success this day." He took her by the arm, urged her up. "Let us go to my office. It is time we had a talk."

As Grishin guided her toward the exit, Galina glanced back at her now-silent coworkers by their ranked workstations. With the sole exception of Komarov, who looked almost...exultant? the faces of her colleagues mirrored her own puzzlement. Each of their displays now showed an identical red rectangle. All of them counting down in unison.

53:36:13
53:36:12
53:36:11...

24 | Night on the North Atlantic

T HE SEA IS *calm to-night, the tide is full, the moon lies fair...*
The sea *was* calm tonight, its placid swells unmarred, save by a
small floating hemisphere of translucent plastic. A fiber-optic periscope.

As the helicopter thuddered off into the northwest, two heads
broke the surface.

Marianna pulled the regulator from her face. "About time. These
little pony bottles are only good for fifteen minutes tops." She ditched
the miniature airtank along with her weight belt, and inflated her lifevest.

"That's another one I owe that bastard Yuri," she muttered to herself,
watching the chopper's retreating running lights.

She turned to where Jon was pulling the ripcord on his vest. "That
was a good call, Jon. I don't like to think what might have happened if
you hadn't seen it coming."

"I didn't," he said. "Just a feeling I had."

There it was again, that weird...thing he did. "Your 'feeling' pretty
much saved our skins. All the dive gear in the world wouldn't have

done us any good stashed in our suitcases. You get any more feelings, you let me know."

"Speaking of skins, should we lose the street clothes and leave just the diveskins?"

"No, keep your pants on." Marianna smiled, but this was serious. "The outer layer of cloth traps a bubble of dead water between the wetsuit and the open sea. Any little bit of insulation helps; the seawater temperature out here can't be much above sixty degrees."

"Okay, got it. What next?"

"We activate the come-hither." Marianna fumbled below the waterline, switching on the locator strapped to her waist. Its buoyed antenna floated to the surface.

"Is it working?" Jon asked after a moment.

He had every right to sound anxious. It was very dark. Not even the lights of a passing ship on the horizon. Only her small box of battery-powered gear now stood between them and one of several unpleasant deaths.

She stared down through the dark water, willing the indicator lights to come on and confirm a signal lock.

"We're green," she said finally.

"And now?"

"Now we wait. Pete was going to keep a search-and-rescue chopper on standby at Horta just in case we wore out our welcome." That was the plan, anyway.

"Has that thing"—he pointed in the direction of the antenna—"got the range to reach the Azores? We're pretty low on the horizon. Sea level, in fact."

"We're not transmitting to the Azores, or anywhere else on earth," she said. "Direct uplink to the Telesphere satellite network. Not enough bandwidth or signal strength for voice, unfortunately, but enough to send our GPS location over and over to a predesignated transponder."

"How long before we know they're coming?"

"Let me think. We were maybe two thirds of the way to Horta when all hell broke loose. That puts us less than an hour out." She glanced at her wristtop. "It's 10:53 now. So, with any luck, home before midnight."

Keep it bright and cheery. They weren't really in trouble. Yet.

✳

Knox had lost track of how long they'd been in the water. Drifting on the long, slow swells, some distance apart. Not speaking, wrapped in their own thoughts. Trying not to move. Moving would just make them colder, and might attract predators. He'd had enough predators for one night.

After a while, Marianna broke the silence: "Okay, Jon. I give up. How did you know Grishin was going to have us killed?"

Knox wasn't sure he wanted to get into this, but it beat just sitting there, waiting. "C'mon, Marianna. You must've suspected something when you saw Yuri was coming along for the ride."

"By that time it was way too late. You knew as soon as Sasha told us we were leaving. How?"

"Well, you must have noticed how nervous he was."

"Anybody gets nervous when they're lying, Jon."

Present company excepted, he carefully didn't say.

When he made no immediate response, she took a different tack: "Was it how choked up he got toward the end there?"

"Huh? No. I hardly noticed that. That's just part of the whole Russian thing."

"W-what, then?"

She really wasn't going to let go of this, was she? Why *had* he flashed on the danger? Often as not, the insights seemed to come out of nowhere. Which made sense, considering.

He sighed. "It was...yeah. Do you remember the last thing Sasha said?"

"Um, something about how g-good it was to talk to you again, like in the old days?"

"Uh-huh, like we did the night before last, on the bridge. That conversation on the bridge, that was the key, somehow. Not what we were talking about—the fact that Grishin broke it up."

"You think Sasha was trying to t-tip you off about Grishin?"

"Hmm? No, that's the funny part. I don't think he knew Grishin was planning anything, anything more than stranding us in the Azores, that is."

"J-jon, you've lost me." There was a slight tremolo in her voice, as if she were trying to keep her teeth from chattering.

"I guess it all sounds pretty nebulous." At least to anyone who hadn't experienced that momentary rush of absolute certainty. "But I think Sasha must have picked up on his boss's intentions, on some subconscious level. He was uneasy about something beyond just having to lie to us, and he was broadcasting the anxiety. When he mentioned the business on the bridge, everything else just sort of fell into place. ...What? What is it?"

"Nothing. I'm just glad I didn't ask you b-before. Might not have b-believed you. Then where'd we be?"

They drifted in silence a while, watching the moon set. Finally Marianna said, "C-come over here, Jon. P-please."

Was she coming on to him again? After the way she'd jerked him around over the past two days, couldn't she at least give the wounds time to scab over? Ah, well. The most maddening thing about her was he couldn't stay mad at her.

"C-c-come on," she repeated. "I won't b-bite."

"Judging by past history that's not necessarily a valid assumption. Why, what did you have in mind?"

"J-just a little sharing of resources. I'd swim over to you, but the antenna might p-p-pull loose."

"We wouldn't want that." Hampered by the lifevest, Knox dog-paddled awkwardly to her. "What resources did you have in mind?"

"B-body heat," she gasped, throwing both arms around him and hugging him to her. "I'm *f-f-freezing!*"

She *was* freezing. At sixty degrees Fahrenheit, the Portuguese Current wasn't much colder than a swimming pool on Memorial Day. But that still left a forty-degree differential between water and body temperature. And cold water chills the body twenty-five times faster than ambient air at the same temperature. Prolonged exposure would suck all the warmth right out of them. Polypropylene wetsuits and outer garments could retard the process. They couldn't halt it.

The effect hadn't hit Knox as hard yet: his greater body mass made him a less efficient radiator. It was easy to forget just how small Marianna really was. Not right now, though — she was shuddering, and clutching him so tightly that his ribs creaked.

"P-primary heat loss is from head, chest, and groin," she said through clenched teeth, as if reciting a lesson learned by rote, or a prayer. "But head and neck area are the worst — maybe f-forty percent of the loss in a f-free dive — and our heads are out of the water. That leaves the other two." She pressed tight against him, shivering uncontrollably.

He withdrew his arm from around Marianna's waist long enough to read the time. 11:37. They'd been in the water less than an hour. Still a good six hours till sunrise. If S&R didn't find them soon, they weren't going to make it.

Could be worse. Hypothermia was preferable to dying of thirst or sunstroke. After a while you just stopped shivering. Then, you just stopped breathing. It was supposed to be like going to sleep.

Knox tried to get his mind off it. Normally, that would have been easy, or at least doable, with a beautiful woman in his arms. But, as the saying goes, "if you're not here with the solution, you're part of the problem." Marianna was definitely part of his problem.

They drifted, huddling together.

Knox tilted his head back as far as the lifevest allowed. Midnight on the North Atlantic. The Milky Way, the "backbone of night," arched above them. He recalled hearing that the naked eye can only distinguish three thousand or so individual stars. The evidence of his own eyes said otherwise: there had to be millions of them up there, tiny points of light against the blackness…

Just for a moment, his perspective inverted. As if he were looking, not *up* into the night sky, but *down*, down into a well of stars. As though he might lose his tenuous grip on the Earth and fall downward, outward into the clear, cold beauty of the night.

The universe was so vast and indifferent, the stars so far apart, so far away.

"About that past history…" Marianna was speaking almost normally again; the body contact seemed to be helping. She pressed her mouth against his ear, "Jon, we need to t-talk."

"No time like the present." Anything to keep those other, those cosmic thoughts at bay.

"Okay." Marianna took a breath. She trembled with more than the cold. The words came tumbling out in a rush: "I, I screwed up. Bigtime. I let—we got ahead of ourselves. My fault. I don't know what happened back there. Or I *do* know, but it didn't have anything to do with, with us.

"We j-just got ahead of ourselves, is all," she repeated, trembling again, holding him tightly, her warm breath tickling his ear. "If we make it out of this, could we maybe please go back to the beginning and start over?"

Lifevests and wetsuits pretty much ruled out anything more ambitious than hugging. They made do. Long before the search-and-rescue chopper found them, the hug had become an embrace.

Part Three
Antipode

Time will run back and fetch the age of gold.
— John Milton, "Hymn on the Morning
of Christ's Nativity"

25 | West with the Night

THEY COULD NOT seem to stop touching.

Setting his Dewar's down on the tray-table, Knox reached out to cup Marianna's chin and draw her face, her perfect face, toward his. Smiling, she abandoned the draft of her final report yet again. Abandoned herself as well to a lingering kiss in the subdued light of the Airbus's first-class cabin. Even when Marianna had turned her attention back to her CIA-loaner laptop, even when Knox had turned to look out at the sunset-tinged traceries of cirrus clouds off the portside wing, even then they were still holding hands.

They could not seem to stop touching one another.

In the twenty-odd hours since search-and-rescue had landed them on Faial Island, they hadn't had a minute by themselves or a moment to rest till now. With the nearest CROM presence twenty-five hundred miles away, Aristos had pressed the CIA into service. A Company stringer working out of Terceira had shepherded Knox and Marianna as far as Lisbon on a five a.m. TAP Air feeder-flight. From there they'd connected through to Paris and CROM's European headquarters.

Seven hours in the old stone building off the Quai D'Orsay had taught Knox more than he'd ever wanted to know about the art and science of debriefing. But in the end Pete Aristos had pronounced himself satisfied. An early CROM-chaperoned dinner at an outdoor café, then back out to Charles de Gaulle International for the evening flight to JFK.

Through the swirl of activity, despite all obstacles, they kept finding ways to maintain physical contact. An arm around a waist. Fingers brushing a face. A surreptitious pat on the derrière. They just couldn't stop touching one another.

Between sleep deprivation, complimentary beverage service, and Marianna's own intoxicating proximity, Knox was totally buzzed. Awash in a flood of fatigue-poison-induced free association. Even so, what he was feeling here, fading in and out, felt real to him—as though he and she had bonded indissolubly in those cold, dark hours before dawn. As if they were two complementary aspects of a single whole, like position and momentum in quantum theory.

He rubbed his eyes and looked down on the darkening, cloud-wracked Atlantic. *Rusalka* must be down there somewhere, well off to the southwest in the gathering dusk. What a difference twenty-four hours could make. For one thing, he was still alive. More alive than he'd felt in a long time.

Now if the damn plane would only stop bouncing around.

"You okay?" Marianna reached out to touch his cheek.

"Yeah, sure. It's just I'm what they call a white-knuckle flier. Know too much chaos theory for my own good."

"Listen, Jon, relax, try to get some rest." Her lips brushed against his cheek. "Don't worry, if the plane falls out of the sky, I'll protect you."

"You know—" He stifled a yawn. "Excuse me. You know, I'm starting to believe you could, at that." He smiled and closed his eyes.

"Got to bring you along on all my trips…" His voice trailed off.

✳

Marianna studied Jon's sleeping face in the muted cabin light. If only she could just drift off like that. Either that, or unburden herself of the knowledge that was keeping her awake.

But she couldn't. It was strictly need-to-know.

She'd thought the marathon debrief was over. They'd already escorted Jon out of the secure videoconference room when Pete asked her to hang back and told her CROM was green-lighting Tsunami. The air/sea build-up would have been set in motion by now, the clock already running on a thirty-six hour countdown to strike-readiness. It was out of her hands. Just this final, proforma report to finish.

And that would keep. Carefully, so as not to disturb Jon, she leaned over and stole a glance out the window. Through a spangling of frost-stars she saw the twilight sea. Pictured the gathering of forces that would greet tomorrow's returning sun in the still-tranquil waters far away to the south.

It wasn't just her data on *Rusalka*'s secret lab that had unleashed Tsunami. No, something big had gone down out in the North Atlantic the night they'd left the megayacht. Pete said the whole SOSUS hydrophone network had lit up like a Christmas tree shortly before midnight GMT. The cause: a major undersea disturbance, with its epicenter two miles down in the waters directly beneath *Rusalka*'s keel. The time: 2347 Zulu.

Move one time zone west to the Azores, and that made it—

2247 hours August 3rd. It *couldn't* be coincidence: the time, to the minute, that Grishin's mysterious message-cylinder had called for the "capture" of…something. Something, evidently very very *large*. Something Pete was determined to stop.

At the same time, Galina, who seemed so loving and sincere, was obviously in this up to her neck. What if it were something they were better off *not* stopping?

Assuming it was even stoppable.

In her dark mood, Marianna hardly noticed the piano solo playing over her headphones until it tinkled to a close. A brief pause, then a new selection started. She knew it from the opening chords: Andrea Bocelli and Eros Ramazzotti's "Nel Cuore Lei."

As the duet soared, her forebodings fell away into the dull sea below.

2247 hours August 3rd. The time, though hardly to the minute, that she and Jon had shared their first true embrace. She turned toward him, reliving last night—his calming presence, the unexpected strength of his arms, the warmth of him pressed tight against her in the frigid water.

She slipped off the headphones with Bocelli and company in mid-crescendo. Reached over to touch his face again, then held back for fear of waking him.

What *was* it with her? She'd had lovers before. This was different. She couldn't keep her hands off him. The sound of his voice, the feel of his hands on her, just the clean, masculine scent of him was enough to give her that warm, liquid feeling in the pit of her belly.

She knew next to nothing about him.

Without opening his eyes, he spoke: "Forty years old. Divorced, no children. And, no, not currently with anyone."

"You're awake!" *Eleven* years older. An eternity! What would they have in common? What would they even talk about?—No, knowing what to talk about never seemed to be a problem for Jon.

Then it struck her: again! He was doing it again, and to *her* this time!

"How did you do that?"

"Lucky guess. Like I keep telling you: it's this trick I do. Sometimes things just click into place." He yawned. "It's why I became a consultant instead of learning an honest trade, I suppose."

"What's it supposed to be? Telepathy?"

"Nothing so mundane. Pattern apperception. Seeing the net. 'Knox's onboard pattern matcher.' It comes and it goes," he finished drowsily.

"How does it work? Where did it come from? Tell me!" She'd been preoccupied last night, but damned if she'd let him off the hook this time.

He opened one eye. "I'm not sure I can, exactly."

"Come on, try. You've got me burning up with curiosity—here feel!" Marianna took his hand and pressed it to the warmth of her cheek. She briefly considered redirecting his answering caress a little lower, in through the folds of her blouse, up against her beating heart. No, best not to start something they couldn't finish. Couldn't finish here, that is.

She settled for just kissing his open palm, interspersing the touch of her lips with little flicks of her tongue. Then she bit the heel of his hand gently. Well, more or less gently.

✳

Wincing at the nip, Knox had a fleeting vision of the fate awaiting him: *Liebestod* by hickey. Nothing daunted, he reached out for her again.

"Unh-uh," she said, expertly fending him off. "Debriefing first, displays of affection later. Now talk!"

"You drive a hard bargain, woman. But, okay." He sighed and leaned back in the seat. "To begin with, Marcus and Evelyn Knox's little boy Jonathan was not always the paragon of personal and professional rectitude you see before you. There were times in my misspent youth when—"

He stopped. Marianna was staring at him. Knox had been shooting for levity, but it had come out sounding all wrong, not to mention *unbelievably* stilted. Tell it straight, Doc Friedman had always said. Don't hide behind the words, Jon.

It occurred to him then that, apart from Charles Friedman, M.D., Ph.D., Marianna was the only person he'd ever told this to. Or tried telling it to, while the distancing words that were his natural defense mechanism did their best to get in the way. Taking a cue from his erstwhile shrink, he backed up and tried to tell it straight.

"I was never much into drugs back in college. I mean, I guess I maybe did enough pot to keep me off the Supreme Court. But nothing really heavy-duty. Until the spring of 1985, that is, on what was supposed to have been my last night in Moscow."

He took a deep breath. "Sasha had these little pieces of, of mushroom, he said they were. Got them from some shaman on one of his treks into the wilds of the Tunguska Basin." There it was again, that godforsaken piece of real estate. Hunh!

"Siberia?" Marianna asked. "Most likely fly agaric, then. Was it red with little white spots, kind of like the mushrooms in a Disney cartoon?"

"No, all brown and shriveled up."

"Treated somehow, then. To reduce the toxicity." Marianna seemed to have all manner of familiarity with this topic, though whether from the perspective of the perpetrator or the gendarme he couldn't tell.

She looked at him sharply. "You don't mean to say you tried it? Jon! I had you figured for more sense. That stuff's not just hallucinogenic—it's poisonous!"

Christ! He didn't need this. Talking about the experience was stirring unwanted memories of the void, of a spiritual abyss infinitely deeper and colder than the physical one that yawned not five meters beneath his feet, just beyond the thin aluminum-alloy skin of the plane's underbelly. Had it gotten warmer in here?

"Listen, Marianna, maybe this wasn't such a great idea after all."

Her hand clasped his. "It's okay, Jon. It's just that—well, I get the sense this is something key for you, something core."

"And unless I bare my soul to you, our—what? our relationship?—could end up like my marriage? Is that what you're saying?"

"You see?" She shivered a little. "You're doing it again. When you get like this, it's like you can see right through me."

"Yeah, I've got to learn to stop doing that on the job. It upsets people."

"You're not on the job now, Jon. And it doesn't upset me, not really. But you've got to admit, it's...well, it's eerie."

"'What kind of a weirdo have I gotten myself hooked up with,' huh?"

"Thank God, you do strike out sometimes. That wasn't even close to what I was thinking." She interlaced her fingers with his and squeezed gently. "I'm just trying to figure out what you've got going on, is all."

"All right. I can't promise you're going to like it a whole lot, though."

Marianna said nothing, just sat there waiting, holding his hand.

Still he hesitated. In a sense, Jonathan Knox made his living telling stories—parables and analogies intended to help people acknowledge their situations, realize their opportunities, confront their challenges. He was always telling stories, all kinds of stories.

All except this one.

This story, he suspected, was telling *him*.

26 | Bell's Inequality

KNOX'S MOUTH FELT dry. His eyes swept over the plush appointments of the first-class cabin without seeing them. Or seeing them, but seeing *through* them too, as if they weren't there.

Seeing down through the world of appearances to the chaos churning just beneath the surface.

He swallowed. How did he explain it, make it real, to someone who had never been there? How could he phrase it so he didn't just sound crazy? Above all, how did he talk about it without conjuring it up, without losing himself to it again in the act of speaking its name?

He looked down to where his hand lay cradled in Marianna's, then up again into her warm brown eyes. The world seemed to regain form and solidity, the wriggling flux retreated to the periphery of his vision. He could do this. All he needed was a place to start.

He took a deep breath. "How much do you know about quantum mechanics?"

"Quantum mechanics?" The stare that Marianna had given him at the outset paled by comparison with *this* long, piercing look. "As in the Uncertainty Principle?"

"That's the place to start, all right." Knox made a conscious effort to relax. "The Uncertainty Principle: tell me about it."

"It's got something to do with, um, subatomic measurements, doesn't it? Like how you can't tell where an electron is at the same time you're measuring how fast it's going?" Her expression bespoke her puzzlement at the turn this conversation was taking.

"Right, the position/momentum complementarity. Very good. And now for the real question: just why is that?"

"Why is what? Why you can't determine the position and momentum at the same time?"

Knox nodded.

"Let me think. It's been a long time, but…isn't it because an electron is, like, so small that it takes a really high-energy beam of light, or whatever, just to get a fix on its location? So high that you wind up interfering with its speed and direction in the process." Marianna looked pleased with herself at having recalled even that much.

"So," Knox said, "a subatomic particle really possesses these two objective physical properties, position and momentum. They exist out there in reality, it's just that our instruments are too fumble-fingered to fix on the one without hopelessly screwing up the other. That about it?"

It was Marianna's turn to nod.

"Well, the good news is you're in distinguished company: Einstein himself thought the same thing. Spent the last twenty years of his life looking for the so-called 'hidden variables.'"

"And the bad news?"

"It's demonstrably dead wrong."

"Say again?"

"Back in the mid-sixties, a researcher name of John Bell designed an experiment. Bell's Inequality, it's called. Took over fifteen years before anybody could figure how to carry it out, but when they did, Bell's Inequality proved—proved, mind you—that our electron has *neither* a definite location *nor* a definite speed until somebody decides to look at one or the other."

Disturbing stuff, if you thought about it too much. As Knox had. He paused long enough to flag down a passing beverage cart. Considering what they'd charged for these last-minute seats, Air France could damn well spring for another Dewar's. He sensed it was going to take that much at least to get through this.

"Jon," Marianna said, "I'm sorry, but I'm not seeing the relevance."

"The relevance is that it makes particle physics a branch of psychology. — *Merci*," Knox told the flight attendant as she handed him his scotch. Marianna accepted a Chardonnay and sat peering into its depths.

He took a sip and resumed. "A branch of psychology. Think about it: here we have the best-tested, most reliable theory in the history of science. A theory, by the way, that's essential to the workings of everything from your laptop there, to these little seatback HDTVs for the in-flight movie. And what it's saying, when you get right down to it, is…"

Just spit it out, he told himself. She won't think you're any crazier than she already does.

"What it's saying, is: it takes conscious choices, by conscious minds, to make reality *real*."

That, in a nutshell, was what had attracted Knox to quantum mechanics in the first place. And what he found so profoundly disquieting about it now.

"Of course, most physicists don't think about it that way," he went on. "They just kick back and do the matrix math. The answer comes out on the money every time, so who gives a damn what it all means, right? Almost nobody ever comes to grips with it on a gut level, ever thinks about what the world would have to be like for quantum mechanics really to be true. Almost nobody thinks about the void of indeterminacy that would be lying in wait beneath the firmest bedrock. Almost nobody thinks about it at all.

"Except me," he said at last. "I do — I've been there."

✳

Marianna had gone to school in the no-nonsense, nose-to-the-grindstone nineties, when every third classmate aspired to be an engineer or an investment banker. Even so, she could relate. Dad had been a borderline hippie in his day, before Mom straightened him out. Some of his weirder friends were still back there, stuck in the sixties, walking wounded caught on an endless tape-loop of drug-induced arrested development. Others hadn't made it out alive at all.

"It lasted maybe eight, ten hours all told." Jon was talking again. "And included all the old can't-miss tour stops on your quintessential bad trip. You had your basic luminous snakes, your freeze-frame visuals, your disintegrating flesh—the whole nine yards. But in the end, there was only the void. A vast, seething flux of noise and formlessness and meaninglessness. No one there, not even me. What the universe looks like when nobody's looking.

"It was hell, I guess." He sounded infinitely tired. "A vision of hell —the ultimate mindfuck."

"But, Jon, it wasn't real."

"If it wasn't real, nothing is. The flux is the substrate, reality's ground floor. And, God help me, once I'd seen it I couldn't un-see it again. The flashbacks went on and on for months.

"After a while, it was like there was no fixed *form* to anything, nothing to hang onto, nowhere to rest. I'd be looking at something real and solid—a tree, say—and all of a sudden I'd just…lose the idea of it. The idea of its being a thing in its own right. It would become radically contingent. Not something out there; just something in my head. Just a few bars of melody emerging for a moment out of the background noise.

"It was as if I could feel the winds of eternity howling through my soul," he whispered miserably, "threatening to disperse me into streamers of indeterminacies and smear me out across the void."

He looked up. Beads of sweat stood out on his forehead. He swallowed. "Well, you wanted to know."

She'd seen men paint themselves into some strange corners before, but…but this was *Jon*, dammit!

He made as if to speak again, but she held a finger to his lips. "Hush," she said. "It's all right now."

Not knowing what else to do, she unbuckled her seatbelt and, putting her arms around him, rocked him back and forth. She could feel his trembling subside as he relaxed in her embrace.

"There's more," he whispered in her ear.

She drew back to look him in the face. He looked better. Still pale, but back in control again.

"Jon, you don't have to. I'm really sorry I…"

"Brought the whole thing up?"

She shrugged. Not what she'd been about to say, but close enough.

"Don't be." He tried to smile. "I'm not. Ever since then, it seems like I've been living out my life not letting anyone really get to know me. Because, well, really getting to know me would mean getting to know *that* about me."

He hesitated a moment, then said quietly, "I want you to really get to know me."

The kiss that followed left them both breathless.

✴

"Anyway, I still haven't answered your question." Knox was feeling better. Incredibly good, considering. The way he'd felt after some of his most intense sessions on Friedman's couch—as if the weight of worlds had lifted from his shoulders.

"Not now." Marianna held her face up for another kiss.

Sometime later, he tried again. Couldn't very well go this far and not finish. "It was a rough year, that next year. Hardly a day went by that I didn't think about…" He broke off, restarted. "It was friends got me through it, pretty much kept me alive, I guess.

"Then, somewhere along about four months after the trip itself, something really strange started to happen."

Seeing the look on her face, he added quickly, "No, no, not *bad* strange—that I already had. This was *good* strange."

"Good, how?"

"Remember I told you how I could all of a sudden just *lose* an object in the background flux? How a tree would stop being a thing in itself and merge with the surrounding chaos?"

Marianna nodded doubtfully.

"Well, this was like that, except benign, somehow. I could look at that tree and see its interconnectedness with its environment, see it as one strand in a much larger pattern. A universal pattern. One of my friends—she'd been there too I guess—called it 'seeing the net.' On the good days the whole world would become a seamless fabric woven of faerie threads. There weren't that many good days, but they almost made up for all the bad ones, got me through the nights."

He paused. "I'm saying this poorly. There may not *be* any way to say it right. At bottom it's a nonverbal, maybe a preverbal, experience. Kind of like what Pirsig meant by 'Quality' in *Zen and*—"

"—*the Art of Motorcycle Maintenance*? Okay, that helps some."

Lord, had Marianna read everything in his library?

She sat there a moment in silence, then: "And I can see it helped you. But, Jon, I've got to ask you: was it, is it real?"

"As real as…the other. At least it seems valid as far as quantum mechanics goes." The arcane theory had become his touchstone, his proof that he wasn't crazy. No more so than reality itself, anyway.

"That's what Bell's Inequality really showed, you know," he went on. "That the universe as a whole is a web of these interconnections. Phase entanglements, they're called. Everything bound to everything else, renewing the bond from moment to moment, instantaneously."

"Instantaneously? What about the speed of light? I thought that was an upper limit."

"For a material object or a message. Lightspeed doesn't apply here. There's no real information being passed around, other than mere existence. It's just a sort of a continual background murmur—'I am here, I am here.'"

"I am here," she echoed softly, leaning toward him again.

What a woman! Knox marveled. Marianna could make even quantum mechanics sound sexy. They did a little phase entangling of their own for a while.

✳

"Jon?" That breathy single syllable tickled his ear.

Something about Marianna's tone of voice snapped Knox back to reality, some note of regret coupled with resolve. He pulled back from her just enough to survey her face in the dimmed cabin light, and found the same mix of emotions there.

"Jon," she repeated, "if this 'seeing the net' thing of yours really works…" She took a deep breath. "…then could it work for us? Here and now?"

"What? With Antipode, you mean?"

"Uh-huh. Seems like the more we learn, the less we know. If there's really a rabbit in that pattern-matching hat of yours, now's the time to pull it out."

"It's not like I can turn it on and off at will. I don't summon the insights, they're just…there, sometimes." Knox executed a gesture midway between a shudder and a shrug. "If I could control it, I'd bottle it and sell it. And let the buyer beware."

Come to think, though, there *had* been something the other night. Something Galina had said, at the banquet. Something that seemed to resonate somehow with one of Sasha's old hobbyhorses — the one Sasha'd balked at talking about that night on the bridge.

"What is it?" Marianna said. "You went away again there."

"Hmm? Oh, nothing." Nothing that he was ready to share with her right now, that's for sure.

But even as he reached out to draw her close again, he found himself wondering: what in God's name did Tunguska have to do with really, really little black holes?

27 | Harm's Way

SILENCE AND STARS. Arkady Grigoriyevich Grishin sat in his darkened headquarters suite, facing its panoramic starboard window, watching night steal over the world. The stars were coming out, gems scattered one by one across a sable cloak. Only a faint smudge of twilight still lingered in the west.

The west, where his quarry had fled.

He glanced again at the strangely warped cylinder resting on the buttery leather of the desktop, glinting in the feeble glow of the dimmed display behind him. Looked at the distorted letters engraved in its surface, letters that spelled out an Air France flight number, an arrival time, and two foreign names.

Finally, he looked across the desk to where Merkulov was sitting, his slug-like carcass barely visible in the gloom. Even if Grishin hadn't cherished darkness for its own sake, he would have preferred it to the sight of his security chief. How could the man let himself go like that?

Realizing he had Grishin's attention—though doubtless not realizing why—Merkulov pursed his lips and spoke, his cracked tenor all the more jarring in the stillness. "Comrade Director, I recommend we drop this matter. Knox and Peterson will have surely reported in to their superiors by now. Whatever damage they could do has already been done."

"Wrong on two counts," Grishin said. "The probe tells us her name is Bonaventure, not Peterson. And your situation assessment is incorrect as well: they must still pose a threat, else why send the probe at all?"

Chastened, Merkulov held his peace. Not for the first time, Grishin wished he could discuss this with Sasha, whose understanding of such matters far exceeded his own. Regrettably not possible in this case, where Sasha's erstwhile friends were concerned.

Or, perhaps there was a way?

Grishin swiveled his chair around and uttered a command phrase that brought up a new window on the wall display. It showed Sasha sitting slumped in his chair with his feet up, scanning a report on a data slate.

"Good evening, Sasha. Are you busy?"

Sasha looked up, then took his feet off the desk and sat up marginally straighter. "Nothing that will not keep, Arkasha."

"Then perhaps you can help settle a disagreement between myself and Vadim Vasiliyevich here. He claims that simply touring the Antipode Control facility would be sufficient for someone to guess the nature of our Project. To me this seems highly implausible. What are your thoughts?"

Sasha chuckled. "Are we perhaps planning on conducting such tours at our next Fort Lauderdale open house?"

Out of frame, Grishin's hand tightened into a white-knuckled fist. That's right, sit there smirking, you fool! If not for your negligence, none of this would be necessary in the first place.

"Purely hypothetical," he said at last, "merely a new slant on our old debate about whether surveillance is required within the facility itself." Of course, events themselves had effectively answered this question in the affirmative, but Sasha couldn't know that.

"A slant that assumes full access to the lab, yes?" Sasha sat a moment in thought. "Hmm, even so I would guess not. Your hypothetical tourist would have to be a person of great perceptiveness to piece together the secret of Antipode from so few clues."

"What about, for instance, your friend Knox and his companion?"

"Is there something I should know, Arkasha?"

"Not at all. I only sought an example well known to you. Choose another if you wish."

"No, no, this will do. I really do not know Marianna well enough to judge. She seems very bright, but perhaps not so inclined to speculate. Dzhon, on the other hand, hmm."

"Yes?"

Sasha leaned forward. "You must understand, Arkasha, Dzhon knows half this story already, from discussions, er, many years ago. Perhaps he is not so ideal a subject for your thought-experiment after all."

"No, no, all the better. Please go on. Knowing what he knows, and then seeing Antipode Control, could Knox work out the rest? Our capture of Vurdalak?"

"He is not the same man I knew in Moscow. The years have changed him. He seems deeper, in some way." Sasha pondered a moment, then, "Under the conditions you have set—and given access to the historical records as well, of course—I cannot rule out the possibility that he might make an inspired guess."

"Well, well," Grishin said, "it appears Vadim Vasiliyevich has won our little wager. Thank you, Sasha, that will be all."

Sasha looked as if he were about to say something else, but the window closed on him before he could get it out.

So the Project *did* stand in danger of being compromised—if, in fact, its secret had not been penetrated already. Or, no, what was it Sasha had said about the need for access to the historical records? Presumably including that infernal Jackson-Ryan article—that made sense. And his two fugitives might not have dug it up it yet. There could still be time!

Merkulov broke in on Grishin's thoughts. "Excuse me, Comrade Director, am I then to order spycams installed in Antipode Control?"

Sitting neglected in the darkness, the security chief had concocted his own interpretation of the just-completed call. Dead wrong, as usual —the buffoon would not know subtlety if it walked up and kicked him in the testicles! Ah, well, we must make do with the tools we are given. If one has no plow...

Grishin shook his head in resignation. "No, Vadim Vasiliyevich, it is far too late for that."

Then his voice strengthened with resolve. "At the same time, it is imperative that this situation unravel no further. You will arrange to have Knox and Bonaventure met when they deplane in New York."

"Uh, by 'met' am I to assume you mean—"

"Take whatever measures you think necessary—the Little Odessa Mafiya should be well positioned to deal with this—but stop them!"

"Are you certain, Comrade Director? With so little time to prepare, we must opt for a brute-force approach. There could be significant collateral damage. The resulting inquiry—"

"Devil take the resulting inquiry! In thirty hours, it will be of no account, no account whatsoever. Provided we stop them now!"

✦

There was no stopping them now. Even allowing for the inevitable stack-up in Greater New York air space, Air France Flight 011 had landed just after eight in the evening. A short hop to Dulles, and they'd be home free.

As the Airbus taxied toward its gate, Knox suddenly found his arms full of Marianna once again.

She kissed him, taking her time about it. "Last chance for a bit," she said. "We're being met."

Sure enough, two men in plainclothes were outside waiting when the forward pressure door swung open. They stepped into the cabin and nodded to the flight attendant. In response, she squeezed her way upstream around exiting VIPs until she was two rows past where Knox and Marianna were sitting. There she stood her ground. With her holding up the line, the aisle cleared quickly.

The larger of the two newcomers, a big, blocky, dark-haired man, sauntered down the now-empty aisle grinning at Marianna. "Good evening, Deputy Director."

"Hello, Compliance," she said, her voice neutral. "They got you on this babysitting detail?"

"Only as far as your transport. Matt here," — he jerked a thumb at the black man behind him — "got stuck flying you back to D.C." Matt flashed them a quick smile.

Compliance flicked his gaze over to where the flight attendant was still doing her Horatio-at-the-bridge thing. "C'mon, let's get you out of here before the dam busts."

The Compliance guy made something of a production of getting them off the plane — eyes darting side to side, hand poised inside his jacket pocket, looking every inch the armed-and-dangerous escort. Knox suspected it was all an act to get out of helping them lug their carry-ons.

Compliance led them out the emergency door at the elbow of the exit ramp, then down the stairs onto the tarmac. Fifty yards across the apron, gleaming in the last rays of the sun, a Learjet sat waiting.

Knox watched Marianna latch onto their pilot as the group walked toward the little twin-engine jet. What was she up to now?

"Oh, wow — one of the new 33As?" she was saying.

"Yep, nothing but the best when you fly the secret skies."

"Say, Matt," she went on, "if you're going to be all alone up in the cockpit, would you mind if I sat in? Just to observe."

"Depends. Are you rated for jets?"

"I'm instrument-certified for twin-engine props. But I'd love to move up, if I could just find a way to put in the hours. Susan Alloway — you know her? — she's let me second-chair a time or two."

"Okay, provided you look but don't touch."

"Deal!" She paused at the foot of the Lear's retractable stairs. "Coming, Jon?"

While Marianna was busily sweet-talking her way into a ride up front, Knox stopped to look back at the Airbus, now ringed round with catering trucks and luggage trailers. He stood watching the unloading operation with professional interest, having taken part in the postmortem for the botched automated baggage-handling system at Denver International a few years back. One area where humans still beat machines, hands down.

Not these humans, though. Knox winced as one of the jumpsuited baggage crew dropped yet another Samsonite suitcase. To a man, they seemed singularly inept. Maybe if they'd pay more attention to what they were doing, instead of looking around all the time, instead of looking over here, in his direction.

Suddenly Knox experienced that familiar shiver, that hair-standing-on-end feeling of imminent pattern apperception. Not knowing why, only knowing not to question the impulse, he reached out and grabbed Marianna, pushed her to the ground, threw himself down alongside her.

"Stay down!" he hollered in her ear, as the first bullets whistled over their heads and thudded into the bodies of their escorts.

✳

"*Oof!* Jon? What the hell do you think you're —" Marianna cut off in mid-protest as she heard the slugs whine and hit, watched Compliance topple over, his left eye a red ruin. Saw Matt falling from the boarding ramp to land in a crumpled heap.

Christ! They were under attack!

"Jon," she whispered, "don't move, okay? Not till I've got— *Ungh!*" She heaved with all her strength and managed to roll Compliance's body over enough to pull his Glock-17 from its holster. She felt the bulge of a spare clip in his jacket pocket. She grabbed that too.

She did a low-crawl over to the stairs, then risked a look. Five men in gray jumpsuits were advancing cautiously toward the Learjet, the muzzles of their guns weaving back and forth like snake-heads.

"Listen up, Jon. In about ten seconds, those guys are going to start hitting the deck. When they do, you get your ass up the stairs and into the plane, okay?"

"Okay." He sounded as scared as she felt.

"And, Jon?"

"Yeah?"

"Take care. I…" She couldn't bring herself to say it. "Nothing. Just keep your head down."

A thousand one, a thousand two… She braced her elbows and took aim at the guy out front. A thousand four, a thousand five… Funny, the fear she'd felt a moment ago was gone. Like it wasn't her lying there, finger on the trigger. A thousand eight, a thousand nine... Like it was somebody else, somebody she didn't even know.

A thousand *ten!*

She squeezed off a round. Felt the Glock kick in her hands. Saw the hole in the line of attackers where her target had been. Aimed and fired again—damn! Only winged that one.

Then the remaining gray men were scattering for cover. She stood, taking what shelter she could behind the retractable stair, and began laying down a suppressing fire. Off in the distance she could hear sirens wailing. Up close and personal she could smell the sharp bite of cordite mingled with the sourness of her own adrenaline-doped sweat.

She looked over to see Jon still crouching beside the stairway. "Now, Jon! *Go!*"

That got him moving. He pounded up the no-skid treads and dived in the open hatch. She followed him, fully expecting to be hit. But their assailants were falling back in confusion. Maybe they hadn't expected resistance. Or maybe they'd just gone after more firepower. She wasn't waiting around to find out.

"Here, take this!" She shoved the pistol and spare magazine into Jon's hands. "Anything shoots at you, you shoot back, okay?"

"Don't I have to flip the safety off or something?"

"Not on a Glock. It's got three safeties, but they all turn off automatically the instant you squeeze that trigger. Think you can hold the fort, tiger?"

"Uh-huh." He looked pale and sweaty, but—hell, so did she. He was maintaining, that's all that mattered.

"Where are you going?" he asked as she turned away.

"See if I can get us out of here." She yanked open the cockpit door.

The flight deck layout looked pretty much like that of the prop-jobs she'd trained on. She sat down and belted in. Her mind raced as she studied the controls. Like she'd told poor Matt, she'd never actually flown a jet. But second-chairing with Susie Alloway had been the next best thing. Susie had been as good as any flight instructor Marianna'd ever had—patient, friendly, talking through all the moves before committing to them, and sometimes letting Marianna get the feel of the wheel when it was just the two of them aboard, and…what was she forgetting?

Oh, right, there was one extra step to the start sequence for a jet: you had to spin up the compressor first. She flipped what looked like the right switch and was relieved to hear the whine of the electric motor.

"Jon," she shouted through the cockpit door, "what's happening back there?"

"Quiet for the moment," came the reply. "No, wait. A boom truck just pulled out on the field, off our port wing. Maybe the cavalry's arrived."

A momentary pause, just long enough for Marianna to begin to wonder why the airport SWAT team would show up in a boom truck. Then Jon was talking again: "Damn! It's not the cavalry; it's Apache reinforcements. That guy in the cherry-picker's aiming something our way!"

Marianna leaned far enough forward to catch a glimpse of a jump-suited figure with a two-handled tube resting on his shoulder. *Oh, shit!* An RPG-7! A direct hit from that rocket-propelled grenade would peel this little jet like a grape!

Praying the compressor was nearly at operating revs, Marianna opened the fuel valve and lit the igniter. Under her coaxing, the jet whined and began to spin in a ninety degree arc. Give them as small a target as possible.

She could hear Jon firing out the door, hear him holler, "Marianna, this bastard's going to—"

The rest of his words were drowned out in a whoosh and a deafening blast. A yellow-white fireball blossomed in the windshield. The yoke shook violently beneath her hands.

"Jesus *Christ!*" she could hear Jon shouting. But how could she hear anything at all, when she was dead?

"Jesus Christ," he yelled again, "they bagged the *Airbus!*"

Missed us! It happened sometimes with RPGs. Easy enough to flinch at the last instant, even when there wasn't somebody shooting at you. They'd missed and…

My God! The Airbus! Those poor people! Had they all gotten out in time?

No time, no time to think about that. The guy'd be reloading, determined not to screw up this time.

"Jon! Button us up—we're punching out of here!"

Even as she heard him yell "*Clear!*" and felt the thunk of the door-lock mechanism sliding home, she was nosing the jet down the taxi-way.

"Ground," she said into her headset mike, "Lear 4325 alpha requesting permission to taxi." Better late than never.

A momentary pause. "Roger, 25 alpha, taxi runway four left and hold short."

Now what? It would take forever to taxi the Learjet all the way out to the runway, and all of thirty-five seconds for the opposition to lock and load a second RPG.

Well, she *did* have permission to taxi; might as well stretch a point. "Jon? Sit down and buckle in. Evasive maneuvers!"

She didn't have clearance to take to the sky, but even on the ground the Lear was nearly as fast and maneuverable as a Formula One racer. She pushed the throttles forward and careened down the taxiway, sluing the jet from side to side, doing her level best to be an uncooperative target.

She glimpsed flashing lights off to her left. An emergency vehicle, by the look of it. Could be a friendly. Then again, it could be wheels for a more experienced RPG marksman. Having seen what the opposition had done to the horse they rode in on, she was in no mood to take chances. Not to mention the guy was coming in on a collision course!

Screw this! Some of these JFK taxiways were as long as regulation airstrips. She sure hoped this was one of them.

"Jon! Prepare for takeoff!" Marianna prayed this was going to work; no way she'd had time to complete the preflight. *Shit!* Just do it! She leaned into the throttles, shoving them forward all the way to the stops.

The Lear gave a shudder, then lifted just in time for the would-be interceptor to pass harmlessly beneath it.

"Ground?" she said into her headset mike, "got a situation here, under rocket attack—25 alpha taking off!"

"Jesus, 25 alpha! Was that a rocket hit AF 011? We can see the flames from here." A brief pause while Air Traffic Control recovered his composure, then: "Roger, Lear 4325 alpha cleared immediate take-off runway—um, taxiway delta; right turn one eighty-five degrees at five hundred; climb and maintain forty-five hundred, barometer twenty-nine point ninety-four. All traffic be aware: emergency takeoff in progress taxiway delta."

She heard the ATC guy catch his breath, swallow audibly. "Best move your tail, honey—uh, 25 alpha. Looks like they just fired a heat-seeker!"

28 | Flight Plans

MARIANNA STOOD THE little jet on its tail, clawing her way up into the darkening sky.

"Ground?" she gasped when she could breathe again. "That rocket still coming?"

"Right up your ass," the voice said. "Sorry, 25 alpha, it's gaining on you. Looks like you've got maybe thirty seconds till..." Air Traffic Control didn't finish. He didn't have to.

Marianna's eyes darted frantically around the unfamiliar cockpit. CROM usually equipped its custom-order aircraft with—there, thank God!

"Releasing countermeasures," she said, and hit the red button.

Radar-blinding chaff sifted out from a compartment in the jet's underbelly, followed by a "hotspot"—a thermite incendiary that would burn bright enough to divert a heat-seeker, keep it from following the Lear's thousand-degree exhaust straight up a tailpipe. That was the theory anyway.

But she couldn't see if it was working: the fuselage blocked her view of the rocket vectoring in directly behind them. "Ground?" she said, no longer even trying to keep her voice from shaking. "25 alpha here. Want to give me a heads-up?"

"Roger, 25 alpha, still got you on visual." The whole tower must be watching this show, waiting to see the Lear smear out like a Roman candle against the evening sky. "Rocket's still coming. I can see the exhaust plume. It's closing, closing… almost on you… It's—Ow!"

From the sheer volume of that howl in her headphones, Marianna guessed ATC must have been watching through high-powered binoculars when the jettisoned thermite ignited. "Holy shit! 25 alpha, what the hell did you do? It missed! The rocket missed! You, you've got a detonation, immediately to your rear!"

"Tell me about it, Ground!" Marianna fought the bucking control wheel as the concussion threatened to upend the little craft. Rode the Lear like a surfer on the crest of the Ninth Wave. Climb, *climb!*

Suddenly, as if someone had hit the off switch, they were out of the maelstrom, rising through quiet air.

"Nice flying, 25 alpha," the voice of ATC crackled in her headphones. "Um, you could raise your landing gear anytime now."

"Roger that, Ground," she mumbled, embarrassed. She'd had a lot on her mind. Still did.

"25 alpha, you are instructed to land Westchester soonest. Stand by for routing."

That was standard procedure in an incident like this: get the implicated aircraft back on the ground and start the FAA investigation. She had no *time* for this! Fortunately, she knew the magic words.

"Negative. Setting transponder to 7734." She punched in the code.

That got ATC's attention. "Lear 4325 alpha confirm: 7734?"

"You heard right." There were only a vanishingly few situations where a pilot could preempt ground control in assigning the last four digits of the transponder code. Preempt ground control, period. One was a hijacking in progress. This was another. 7734 was CROM's FAA-authorized priority override. As such, it allowed her to commandeer the airspace between here and wherever she wanted to go. So, where did she want to go?

"25 alpha, provide routing please."

"GPS direct DIA." Might as well head toward Dulles, at least till she came up with a better idea.

Marianna switched on the PA and blew into the mike. "Captain has turned off the seat-belt sign. Jon, you want to come forward? We need to talk."

✳

Ship's bells chimed half past midnight. Arkady Grishin sat in his headquarters suite watching the big-screen version of the JFK mopping-up operation now in progress. Millions spent on high-tech surveillance, even a tap into the spy-satellite network, and he had to tune into CNN to find out what was happening!

According to Wolf Blitzer, things weren't going well for the Mafiya. That was acceptable; killed or captured, the mercenaries could betray nothing worth knowing, nothing that might tie the International Arrivals operation back to GEI. CROM would know, but then CROM already knew.

No, that was not the problem. The problem was what he was hearing in Merkulov's droning color-commentary. He swiveled his chair just enough to fix the security chief with a glare. "So, Vadim Vasili-yevich, in non-technical language, you are saying you cannot confirm a kill."

Merkulov seemed to shrink into his chair, as if he could will himself small and unobtrusive enough to escape the director's notice—an effort doomed from the outset by his hundred-twenty-two-kilo bulk.

"Not at this time, Comrade Director. We have reports of a mid-air explosion, but we have also intercepted subsequent cockpit-to-tower communications indicative of survival."

"You have, in other words, failed."

That roused Merkulov from his slouch. "Comrade Director, whether you choose to acknowledge it or not, this was from the outset an action with very little prospect of success. Four hours to plan, to secure the resources, to brief the team, move them into position. *Four hours!* An all but impossible task. Only the dedication of our security cadres brought us as near as we came to achieving our goal."

His outburst over, Merkulov sat back, deflating slowly.

"It may well be as you have said, Vadim Vasiliyevich," Grishin conceded. "In any case, it is of no matter now. Far more important is what we do next. We must assume the targets are still in the air, and heading for home. I trust our own forces are moving into place there?"

"Yes, Comrade Director," Merkulov bobbed his head. "Fully half of them are already deployed just outside the Dulles perimeter, covering all approaches."

"Good." Grishin smiled grimly. "Let us see if our friends can dodge a missile on landing as handily as they did on takeoff."

"Rest assured, Arkady Grigoriyevich, they cannot. But..."

"But *what?*"

"It is our second contingent, Comrade Director—the ones staking out the CROM headquarters facility itself. They are reporting something strange."

✳

With the LearJet still climbing toward its thirty-thousand-foot cruising altitude, it was uphill all the way to the flight deck for Knox, on legs still shaking with reaction. Worth it to see her smile, though. For a while there, he'd thought he never would, ever again.

"Hi, Jon. Sit down and don't touch anything unless I say so, okay?"

"Uh-huh."

He'd barely belted into the copilot's seat when an alarm went off.

"Christ! What now?"

"Cabin pressure," she said, pulling out her oxygen mask from the compartment above her head and motioning him to do the same. "We didn't get away as clean as I thought; the fuselage must've got holed in the firefight."

She broke them out of the climb and leveled off at twenty thousand feet. Knox put on the copilot's headset in time to hear: "Lear 4325 alpha, this is New York Center. Are you experiencing difficulties?"

Are we experiencing difficulties? Does a wild bear shit in the woods?

But Marianna was already responding in that laid-back, no-sweat voice they taught you the first week of flight school. "New York Center,

25 alpha here. Under control now. Request direct DIA, altitude twenty thousand."

"25 alpha, confirm altitude twenty thousand feet."

"Roger that, Center, we have a pressurization, uh, malfunction here."

After a moment, the voice came back. "Roger, 25 alpha. Cleared present position direct DIA, maintain twenty thousand."

She turned to Knox. In a voice muffled by the mask she explained, "Without cabin pressure this is as high as we go: the masks aren't rated above twenty K-feet."

"Is that going to be an issue?"

"The added drag'll slow us down some, not a whole lot. We can still make pretty good time, maybe five hundred miles per hour. Question is, where are we going?"

"Well, the original plan was to fly back to D.C. In this very plane in fact. I guess we could still do that. But are you sure you're okay flying this thing? I mean, I heard what you said before about not being trained on jets. Wouldn't we be better off circling around and landing at JFK? We could both go back to being just passengers." Preferably on a train.

"Not an option. It's a war zone down there right now. Tower's reporting unknown numbers of perps still on the loose, burning hunks of Airbus all over the apron, pitched battles in International Arrivals. Security's called a lockdown; ATC's diverting all inbound flights to Newark and La Guardia. No way they're going to assign us a runway anytime soon."

"Well, what *about* Newark or La Guardia?"

She shook her head. "Even if we got down okay, we couldn't be sure whose people would show up first — ours or theirs."

"So, it's straight through to Dulles? "

"That's our current heading. But there's a problem there, too, Jon. We can't count on CROM extending much of a protective envelope tonight. There's only a skeleton crew on duty, and if Grishin's arranging another reception for us..." She trailed off.

"Skeleton crew? Where is everybody?"

After a long pause she said, "They're out of area, on assignment."

Knox waited, but it was plain she wasn't going to say any more.

"So landing at Dulles could be hazardous to our health?"

"I could always try setting her down on Route 50. Hardly any traffic this time of night. We could taxi right up to the front door."

He shot her a sharp look. She was kidding, right?

"Maybe we're looking at this destination thing all wrong," he said after a moment. "The real question is why Grishin's trying to kill us in the first place."

She shrugged. "Keep us from telling what we know."

"And here's my problem with that: it's been a good twenty-four hours since we left *Rusalka*. Who'd believe we hadn't found a way to report in before now? Grishin's no fool."

"If he's not trying to silence us, what then? Revenge?"

"I don't think so. Old Arkady Grigoriyevich didn't strike me as the type. Swat you like a fly if you got in his way, but nothing personal in it. Anyway, no vendetta could justify the cost of the operation they mounted back there—or the hell it's going to raise. No, I don't think Grishin's out to get us because of anything we've done."

Knox shifted to look out the side window. Though the last rays of sunset still burnished the Learjet's wings, the suburban New Jersey landscape sliding by beneath them had already fallen deep within the Earth's shadow. Houselights and streetlamps were coming on. But he wasn't watching them, he was watching an answer take shape. If not because of anything they'd done, then perhaps because of something they might still do.

He turned back to her. "The only way that industrial-strength reception makes sense is if Grishin thinks we're still in a position to stop him."

"But we don't even know what he's up to."

"Somehow the key must be in us making it back to CROM headquarters. That's what Grishin's trying to prevent, anyway. So what's there? What's Chantilly got that we don't?"

She shrugged again. "Very little that we can't access from out here in the field, one way or another. Really good comm security, of course, the best. Oh, and a world-class Russian-area research library, in case you had it in mind to finish your doctoral dissertation."

A research library? To do what—follow up on that stray thought he'd had back on the transatlantic flight? Well, if world-class research was the key, they didn't need CROM for it. On the contrary.

"Can we make it as far as North Carolina? Out to the west of the state, I mean, toward the Blue Ridge?"

Marianna glanced at the fuel gauge and nodded.

"And can I send an email from here? Encrypted?"

"There's a built-in console back in the main cabin," she motioned with one shoulder. "Just be sure and put on one of the passenger oxygen masks. Why, what've you got, Jon?"

"Don't take this the wrong way, but how's CROM's consulting budget holding up?"

"Based on performance to date, I'd say you've pretty much got carte-blanche. Why?"

"We're going to need it," he said. "Marianna, I think it's time you met Mycroft."

29 | Discovery

ARKADY GRISHIN WATCHED the timestamp floating in the Residence's datawall roll over to 2:30:00 A.M. local and move on. He heaved a great sigh. The flickering digits, the sole light source in the room, continued counting down the hours and minutes toward total disaster. In their pallid glow the portrait of General Secretary Yuri Vladimirovich Andropov over on the far wall regarded his protégé mournfully, reproachfully.

What good, Andropov seemed to be asking, was foresight without follow-through?

Grishin tightened a fist and slammed it down on the desktop; the bang echoed like a pistol shot in the hushed chamber. Foresight without follow-through: the latest timeprobe had told him exactly when and where to intercept the two CROM agents. Perfect information, flawed execution.

Meanwhile, his agents in Washington were reporting no contact with the targets. And that was not the most disturbing thing they were reporting.

The CROM headquarters building in Chantilly was staffed twenty-

four/seven. Usually. Tonight it loomed over Route 50 an all but deserted derelict, two-thirds of its offices dark, an equal proportion of
empty spaces in its parking lot.

Grishin prided himself on being a realist; still, he shrank from pon-
dering the implications of *that* development.

He cursed himself for not having sent Yuri to tend to matters personally. Even with one arm in a cast, he would have gotten the job
done. Especially with one arm in a cast, seeing who put it there. But no,
the timing was all wrong; there was no way the Georgian mercenary
could have arrived in New York in advance of the Air France flight.
Time, again, devil take it!

"If only, if only—" He barked a bitter laugh. "If only mushrooms
grew in your mouth, it wouldn't be a mouth, but a whole garden." The
old nonsense rhyme reminded him just how nonsensically he was be-
having. Such speculation on alternative outcomes was pointless. At
least in the present case.

He returned to the problem at hand. His two fugitives should have
been easy to intercept on the approach to Dulles. A plane in a landing
pattern has few options, and his people had all the approaches covered.
Stingers, too, this time, not those antiquated SA-7s.

He sighed. All to no avail; the quarry was already an hour over-
due at Dulles. Wherever they were bound, it evidently wasn't back to
CROM headquarters. Starting from their last known heading, the
LearJet's fifteen-hundred-mile flying range described a cone encom-
passing most of the southeastern United States. They could be anywhere within that volume.

Where could they be *going*?

So close, he had been so close.

Grishin cradled his head in his arms, in a despondency so deep that
he almost failed to notice his wristtop was chiming.

✳

Mid-morning sun filtered through the stand of birch beyond the
fretted triple windows and into the upstairs den where Jack Adler sat
hunched over a keyboard, putting the finishing touches on his paper.
A bar of vibrant green-gold sunlight had been creeping down along

the tapestry-hung wall since he'd begun work at daybreak, until now it rested on his right shoulder. The warmth felt good, especially on muscles still aching from his encounter with the wolf. Jack made a final edit, then leaned back in his chair and stretched.

One more read-through and his findings should be ready to post to the *arXiv.org* online physics site. Easy enough to do from here: among its other amenities, the *dacha* had its own fiber-optic link to the Tomsk University Internet node. Nineteenth-century charm side by side with twenty-first century gear, as though the lamentable Russian twentieth century had never happened at all.

Medvedev had been far too modest in calling this place a *dacha*. It was a former tsarist hunting lodge, a veritable hobbit-house embellished with the fanciful towers and ornate wooden friezes typical of the pre-revolutionary homes still scattered here and there throughout the Tomsk region.

Officially, the lodge was a national landmark administered by the university. Unofficially, Medvedev had the use of it as a personal retreat. Nothing was too good for the esteemed Academician.

Who was even now tramping up the stairs, his good hand clutching two steaming glasses of amber liquid in chased silver holders. "Tea, Dzhek!" Medvedev boomed. "To keep you on the road to recovery."

"Thanks, Dmitri." Jack accepted a glass. "Actually, I feel pretty recovered already." He did, too, despite the occasional throb at the base of his skull and the twinges from his right arm if he moved it too suddenly.

It felt good just to be back at work again. He'd lost most of a day and a half, drowsing in the peaceful, shuttered dark of the lodge's guest bedroom following his release from the hospital. But today he'd risen with the dawn chorus. The melodic birdsong wafting in through the open bedroom window had reminded him how good it was to be alive…and had reawakened his sense of purpose. Maybe there wasn't anything he could do to stop his mysterious adversaries, but *dammit* he was going to try!

What had that old shaman said about confronting the Wolf with knowledge, not might? Well, here was the means. He glanced over at the last few paragraphs of the electronic submission glowing on the display.

"Do I interrupt your work, Dzhek?" Medvedev asked, settling into an overstuffed armchair.

"No, no, I was just finishing up, in fact." Jack took a sip of the tea. It was hot and sweet, and had a hell of a kick to it. He raised an eyebrow at Medvedev.

"There was no sugar," the Russian said with a grin. "Until I can go into town for provisions, it is necessary to sweeten the tea with rum."

"Breakfast of champions." Jack grinned back, and took another swig. "Gives shy people the strength to get up and do what needs to be done."

Medvedev doubtless didn't recognize the *Prairie Home Companion* tagline, but it elicited a chuckle nonetheless. "And just what is it, if I may ask, that needs to be done? And in such urgency that you must monopolize the Tomsk astrophysics department's computer, rather than wait until you are back at your desk in Teksas?"

"Had to write up my findings from the expedition," Jack said, adding, "Actually, I wanted to ask you about that: is it okay if I post to the physics archive from your email account? I've made it clear in the abstract and the body that you and the University aren't involved in any way."

"Neither involved, nor convinced this is wise, Dzhek." The chair creaked as the big man shrugged. "You are, of course, free to do as you will, but I fear you are making a mistake — one that could have disastrous consequences for you."

Jack swung around to face Medvedev, squinting into the sunlight. "I've been as careful as I could. I couched the whole thing in language only another astrophysicist could love. No one outside the field will pick up on it till it's way too late."

"Dzhek, I must confess I have not the slightest idea what you are talking about."

Medvedev's previous remark had resonated so well with his own forebodings of a shadowy conspiracy that Jack forgot he hadn't broached that topic yet. For good reason.

"Well, uh, that is…" he backpedaled. "What *did* you mean by dangerous consequences, then?"

"Not dangerous, Dzhek—disastrous. Professionally disastrous. You are talking about publishing unsubstantiated opinion as though it were fact. And that to the international physics community."

Jack's sigh set dust motes dancing in the sunbeam that now fell across his chest. Medvedev was right. "Archive" was a misnomer. In actuality, *arXiv.org* was a physics hotline. Between its new-arrivals listing and the associated email-alert service, every astrophysicist in the Western world would be reading the abstract of Jack's paper with their second cup of coffee.

But that was exactly the point.

"I appreciate your concern, Dmitri, but this is something I've got to do."

"But why, Dzhek? Why in such haste? If your micro-hole is real, it will still be there next year."

"*If* it's real? We went all over this last night. My discovery—"

"I know, Dzhek, I know. You saw what you saw. But I did not, nor did anyone else. You must face facts: with no hard evidence, with your equipment and records destroyed, you *have* no discovery. What you do have is no different, scientifically speaking, from a UFO sighting."

Ouch! A week ago it'd been Jack lumping Medvedev in with the flying-saucer fanatics. If the Russian was conscious of the irony, it didn't show in his face.

"But you believe me, don't you, Dmitri?"

"I believe you to be a man of integrity, a serious scientist. Few have dared confront me as you have done." A small smile played for a moment about the bearded lips. "But, *as* a scientist, you must know that it matters not what I believe, only what I can prove."

"That's what I've been trying to tell you: the proof is out there, waiting for us!"

"And, as I have been trying to tell you, there is always tomorrow. Speaking for myself and my colleagues, we would welcome your participation in next year's Tunguska Expedition."

We may not *have* until next year! But Jack couldn't say that—coming on top of his wolf-man "delusion," running off at the mouth about shadow conspiracies was sure to land him back in Ward Seven. For his own good, of course.

Instead, with as much calm as he could muster, he said, "I appreciate your invitation very much, Dmitri, but I've got to get back there *now*. Summer's almost over. When does the snow start to fall in Tunguska, anyway?"

Medvedev thought a moment. "First or second week of September, at the latest."

"You see? I've got to start right now, or there's going to be zero chance of a return expedition before spring. I've got to start building support in the astrophysics community, pulling together equipment and funding. And all of that means publishing my results." He wrenched his chair around till he was facing the keyboard again.

"Dzhek," Medvedev was rising even as Jack's fingers flew over the keys. "I beg you to reconsider, to entertain the possibility that you might be wro—"

"Too late," Jack declared, and clicked the *Send* button that would dispatch his paper to *arXiv.org*, and the world.

✳

Grishin regarded the newly-arrived cylinder where it lay on his otherwise bare desktop, sparkling in the light from the single overhead spot. This one was the least distorted yet, its inscription legible almost without straining—a sign they must be close, very close. Five words this time, one of the longer messages. It varied between three and five. Seven once, but those were all short words. One thing didn't change. Regardless of the length of the message, it had about it an air of the cryptic, of the confounding convolutions of prescience.

The first three message-units were clear enough: a word, *Weathertop*, followed by latitude and longitude for a location in the northwestern corner of North Carolina. So far, so good: not only the name of the fugitives' destination, but precise coordinates for finding it. It was the last two words that had Grishin puzzled: *Return Them*.

No matter—that's what Sasha was for. The telltales from the younger man's badge were already tracking his progress along the main corridor of accommodations deck in the direction of the Residence. His agonizingly slow progress: Sasha was taking his time, giving himself a chance to come fully awake before he got here. It *was* three in the morning, after all.

Sasha wasn't alone. No one would be getting much sleep tonight. The whole vessel was stirring to life as the strikeforce assembled for departure still within the hour. Grishin himself should be up on the bridge by now, supervising the operation.

One thing to do first, though.

The steel portal slid back soundlessly and admitted Sasha. He stood a moment framed in the doorway, peering into the gloom, hands hanging at his sides. "Good evening again, Arkasha. Or perhaps I should say 'Good morning.' Is something happening?" Then his gaze fell upon the desktop. "Another probe?"

"Sit down, Sasha. I have something to tell you."

Disbelief alternated with consternation on Sasha's guileless face as Grishin sketched out the duplicity of his "friends."

"So, Yuri's presence onboard the helicopter *was* intended—"

"Yes, an attempt to dispose of the problem once and for all time. It failed."

"But, but why was I not informed?"

"I told you plainly enough the evening of their departure. It was you who refused to hear. I saw no reason to involve you further. It could only prove a distraction, just when you most needed to focus on your tasks."

"In that case, why are you telling me now?"

Grishin sighed. "Things are evolving rapidly, Sasha. We can afford no more mistakes. I thought it best to consult with you as to the meaning of this latest message before giving the final go-ahead."

Sasha reached out and plucked the cylinder off the desk. He sat peering at it, twirling it in his hands. "Well," he said finally, "map coordinates, of course. Where Dzhon and Marianna might be found? And instructions to bring them back here. Yes, that all seems to fit."

He laid the probe back in the center of the table. "Arkasha, with your permission, I should like to accompany the strikeforce."

Grishin looked up in surprise. "You, Sasha?"

"Yes, of course, me. Coordinates can err. It might become necessary to ask the local inhabitants for directions to this Weathertop. Who did you imagine would do that? Yuri?"

Grishin chuckled at the mental image of Geladze trying to understand, or make himself understood by, the hillfolk of rural North Carolina. Perhaps he could explain that he was from neighboring Georgia?

"It is merely that—forgive me, but I hadn't pictured you taking part in a termination action. Not your line of work at all, even if the targets were not formerly your friends."

"Termination?" It was Sasha's turn to show surprise. Astonishment, really. "But I thought—"

"Termination," Grishin repeated evenly, careful not to let his tones betray the flash of anger he felt toward this indispensable, yet hopelessly naïve and criminally negligent subordinate. Not for the first time in their long association, Grishin had to fight down a sudden urge to personally snap his young colleague's spine for him.

"Why, Sasha?" he said. "What did you think was going to happen?"

"Well, that is, the message itself seems clear enough."

"Yes, 'Return them.' This is precisely the riddle I called you here to unravel. On the one hand, the probe tells me how to find your friends. On the other, it tells me to bring them back here to *Rusalka,* alive. But why? Why spare them?"

"Let me reverse the question, Arkasha: why go to so much trouble to kill them now?"

Was that sweat sheening Sasha's forehead in the dim light? Could it be that the sentimental fool still harbored some sympathy for these enemy agents?

"Mounting a raid at so great a distance, on the adversary's home ground, is hardly without risk," Sasha went on quickly. "And I see no gain to offset it. If Dzhon and Marianna are truly spies, they have doubtless already told what they know."

"I expected as much from Merkulov, Sasha, not from you. Surely you can see that what they now know and what they might still discover are two different things."

"But how can you be sure they have not discovered the truth already?"

"Sure? How can I be *sure?*" Grishin paused to lower his voice again before continuing. "Because we have yet to see the first flight of cruise missiles come sailing in over the horizon! That is how I can be sure. For that will in all likelihood be our first and only indication that CROM appreciates the Project's true potential. Not that things are not bad enough already."

"What do you mean, bad enough?"

Grishin suddenly felt very tired. His fingers mussed his graying, carefully combed hair. "CROM, it seems, already feels it has enough to move against us. Virtually the entire Chantilly operations staff has departed on an unscheduled exercise. An exercise coinciding with an unannounced redeployment of American naval assets stationed in the Western Mediterranean. They are still moving cautiously. Cautiously enough to show they have yet to put all the pieces together. But time grows short, my friend, very short indeed. Are you certain we cannot pull up our own timetable?"

"The probes say no, Arkasha. But we are halfway through the acceleration phase even now. Only some twenty-six hours remain on the clock. Add perhaps another three or four hours for calibration, and to sequence the probes properly. We could be ready for the omega sequence by, say, eight A.M. on Friday."

"Even that may be too late. And we are so *close*!" Grishin pounded his fist on the desktop, causing the distorted metal cylinder before him to bounce and sing.

He fixed Sasha with a baleful glare. "I need the answer to my riddle now: What is so essential about bringing these spies back to *Rusalka*?"

✴

Sasha sat there immobile, his mind racing furiously. He did not believe for a minute that his friends were spies. That was, had to be, just Grishin's occupational paranoia talking. Still, delusional or not, it marked Dzhon and Marianna for death.

Unless the paranoia itself, the obsessive secrecy that had shrouded their every move, might contain the seeds of its own solution.

"Arkasha," he said softly, "I believe I may understand your riddle."

Grishin said nothing, but the glint of menace faded from his eyes, to be replaced by a scintilla of hope.

Sasha took this as license to go on. "I cannot help but think that the probe's command bears on the larger problem. Properly interpreted, it will lead us to the success that its own arrival portends."

Grishin frowned. Sasha knew his master detested the counterintuitive logic needed to divine the probes' meanings. He hastened to the point. "What if our adversaries knew of the danger a precipitous strike might bear with it?"

"Danger? I do not understand."

"What if they *knew about Vurdalak?* Knew an attack would set the world-eater free once more?"

"They, they would have to stand down!" Grishin's eyes were shining now. "Sasha, this is brilliance. Sheer brilliance! I have lived so long with the necessity of concealing this secret that I have never even considered what impact its disclosure at the proper moment might have."

Then, quickly as it had appeared, the gleam winked out. "It will not work."

"Because?" Lead him, lead him.

"Because no one would believe it. At most, CROM has only some videos of untended laboratory workstations and a recording of a single seismic event. Will they make the logical leap from those few observations to the conclusion that we now hold the power to end the world in our hands? I think not. You might, or your Mr. Knox, perhaps. But it is extremely unlikely that I would arrive at such a conclusion—plodding, unimaginative functionary that I am. And, I can assure you, my counterparts in CROM are far closer in spirit to me than to you."

"I will not have you comparing yourself to those gray bureaucrats, Arkasha. You, who have brought us to the very brink of this glorious victory!" Perhaps one more hint. "And yet, perhaps they are not all so close-minded. The woman, for instance. For all that circumstances make her an adversary, still she seemed bright, and open to the possibilities. What might happen if she were to see Antipode itself?"

Sasha stopped. Grishin was still looking at him, no longer seeing him. "Yes-s-s. She knows the half of it already. She, if anyone, might be made to believe, and believing, might convince her superiors. Enough to give them pause, to stay their hand for the few hours more we need."

"And do not forget Dzhon," Sasha added, "I sense that he may understand this better than anyone on the other side. We could need *him* to convince *her*."

"Is there a possibility he might penetrate the ultimate purpose behind Antipode as well?"

"I think not, Arkasha. No, surely not. But he *will* accept the reality of Vurdalak, of that you may be certain."

"Very well. Both of them. The message does say 'them,' does it not?"

Yes! Thank you, Arkasha! Aloud he said, "It does. And may I suggest again that I accompany the team to ensure that—how shall I put it?—that your instructions are followed to the letter?"

They looked at one another, sharing a single, unspoken thought: Yuri was useful, but sometimes suffered from poor impulse control.

"I see your point," Grishin said. "Yes, yes, of course you must go along."

Then, to himself: "'Return Them'—I see it now! It was staring us in the face all along. To think, I was trying to stop them from uncovering the truth, and now that is our only hope!"

The despair was gone. Grishin seemed to loom larger, to fill the room with newfound energy and ebullience. One final time, his gaze, no longer cold now, came to rest on Sasha.

"Aleksandr Andreyevich Bondarenko," Grishin spoke at last, his broad grin belying the formality of his words, "I order you, I command you: *Return Them!*"

✳

"You will also need a helicopter, Dzhek." Medvedev thumped a thick index finger on the project plan's *Arrange Transport* task-box. "A Mikoyan-2 or -3 should do for so small a team; no need to go to the expense of chartering one of the big 8s. What do you think?"

Jack Adler looked down at the diagram and nodded cautiously. He was having a hard time adjusting to the transformation that had come over Medvedev once Jack's paper had been posted. Russians had a long tradition of yielding to the inevitable, but this was ridiculous.

Grumbling that if Jack were going to insist on returning to Tunguska this summer, he might as well do it properly, Medvedev had hauled out the charts and checklists for the expedition just completed and spread them all over the desk. Then, over the past two hours, he'd cobbled together a strawman budget and schedule that, to Jack's unpracticed eye, looked eminently doable. He'd even volunteered to come along himself. "To see this marvel with my own eyes," as he put it.

Medvedev brushed a couple of stray worksheets aside and unearthed the desk clock. "Time for lunch, Dzhek!" He slapped his ample belly. Then, with a nod toward his handiwork, "We have made a good beginning in any case, eh?"

Left to himself, Jack surveyed the snowdrifts of grid paper and ledger sheets that had all but buried the pristine desk surface he'd worked on this morning. Amazing that Medvedev could organize anything, much less an entire expedition, in this mess. What was the kitchen going to look like when he got done making lunch? From the clatter of pots and pans downstairs, it didn't sound good.

The epicenter of chaos having shifted elsewhere, Jack seized the opportunity to reimpose order. It was a good five minutes of sticking stray documents back in their folders before he'd exhumed Medvedev's PC from its burial mound of prior-year Tunguska reports. As luck would have it, that was when it happened.

The computer, which had hitherto been silent, cleared its throat and said, "Aha!"

30 | Midnight to Dawn

THE HUMID EXHALATIONS of the earth enveloped the little landing strip in a fine, ground-hugging night mist. The Wilkes County airport tower poked up through it like the last spire of a drowned city. Overhead, though, the sky was clear and filled with stars. From the foot of the Lear's boarding ramp, Marianna watched Jon roll up in the rental car he'd reserved via the Wilkesboro Avis website—a late-model white Corvette.

"This was all they had left on the lot," he said.

"Uh-huh." She flashed a grin to show he wasn't fooling anybody: boys and their toys.

She stowed the carry-on she'd somehow hung onto ever since JFK, then settled into the passenger seat. "How long a drive is it to this Weathertop place?"

"Couple hours. But there's no point going there tonight; we can't get in. Mycroft won't lower the drawbridge again till ten-thirty tomorrow morning. End of civilization notwithstanding."

That's right. He'd warned her about his friend's weird work habits. At least Jon had managed to email this Mycroft person enough material to get him started before Weathertop's self-imposed communications lockdown went into effect at ten p.m. The night shouldn't be a total waste.

"The rent-a-car website had hotlinks to local restaurants and hotels," Jon was saying. "I found us an overnight a few miles up the road. A little B&B, looked nice."

Maybe the night wouldn't be a waste at all.

It was midnight by the time they rolled into the sleepy North Carolina hamlet of Millers Creek. The live-oaks lining the town's main street breathed a night breeze cool and heavy with the promise of rain. Across a rivulet barely visible in the starlight, the village clocktower tolled the hour.

The Catawba Inn was easy to find—the only building in town with its porchlight still on and its sidewalk not yet rolled up for the night.

The desk clerk, whom they'd evidently kept up hours past his bedtime, yawned and asked "One room or two?"

"One," Marianna put in quickly, rather than give Jon a chance to say the wrong thing.

✳

They lay nestled together like spoons in a drawer.

"Mmmm, that was nice," Marianna said. "A whole 'nother side of consulting practice I'd never realized existed."

"Archon is, after all, a full-service agency," Knox murmured in her ear, regretting the facile comeback even as he said it.

I don't know how to deal with this, he realized. For me, there may *be* no way to deal with this.

He ran his fingers through her hair. We are the same breed of cat, you and I. We live by our words, build worlds out of our words, distance and defend ourselves with our words, until our words are all there is to us.

How good it would be, for once, to let go of all the words—the insulating, isolating words—and just *be*.

His right hand cupped one small, perfect breast, its nipple still erect from her orgasm. She snuggled back against him, turning her face for a kiss. With the fingers of his left hand, he sought the core of her.

"Jon," she whispered as he entered her again, "I won't talk any more if you don't."

✴

In her line of work, Marianna only ever seemed to meet two types of men — two types of prospective bedmates, anyway. Type One felt intimidated by her. Sometimes they tried to hide it, sometimes not; it was worse when they tried. Type Two fancied themselves to be in some kind of macho competition with her. That, at least, had its amusing side. A relationship with either type was a recipe for disaster, pure and simple. She knew. She'd tried.

Jon didn't seem to fit into either category. He wasn't afraid of her, and he didn't try to dominate her. Much. He just had his own thing going.

Maybe all consultants were like this? But, no, she suspected that, even in his chosen profession, Jon broke the mold.

She looked down to where he was nuzzling her breast, his head cradled in her arms. He didn't mind that she was so small on top. On the contrary, he seemed enchanted by what he'd called her "bite-sized" breasts.

Enchanted, she thought dreamily, by all of her.

Oh, Jon, I don't care if I ever sleep again — let's just play all night long, okay?

She moaned as he teased her nipple with his teeth and tongue. She stroked his hair. Could it be that she was falling in...

Oops! Let's not go there. Don't even *think* the 'L' word, Marianna!

✴

Jonathan Knox drifted in a mixed state between sleep and wakefulness. It was here, on the borderlands of oblivion, that his old demons, puissant and menacing, were wont to prowl, ever ready to transform dream into nightmare.

Not tonight.

Tonight he felt utterly at peace. Suffused with peace. Adrift, floating on the gentle tides of night.

He envisioned the little town out beyond the open window, its houses dark, their roofs rimed with starlight, outlined against the dark backdrop of the sheltering hills. He smelled the freshness of the air, pregnant with rain, laden with ozone from the coming storm. The Perseids weren't due till next week, but he imagined he saw twin meteors inscribe lines of fire across the starry summer sky.

Without perceptible transition, his perspective altered. Now he was looking down as from a great height on the villages and isolated farms dotting the hills hereabouts, scattered lights of human habitation glowing like candles in the dark. Off to the east, the luminous spiderweb of the Raleigh-Durham-Chapel Hill metroplex glimmered on the horizon.

Then it was as if the Earth plummeted away beneath him. Vertiginous as it was, he felt no fear, only exhilaration. Far, far below now, the eastern seaboard was embroidered with dim radiance where its coastal cities met the night sea in a weave of lights emblematic of the interconnectedness of all things.

And now he could see the arc of the world itself, the curve of the world, the whole of the world, infinitely beautiful, infinitely precious.

Infinitely fragile, if what he suspected were in the least way true.

The sun was just peeking around the eastern rim of the dark planet.

He watched as sunrise sped across the breadth of the Atlantic, igniting the vast, slow pinwheels of summer storm systems in transient blazes of glory. Watched as the sun emerged full and warm from behind the limb of the Earth…

…And shone its beams through the window of an inn in Millers Creek, North Carolina.

Knox opened one eye. The clock on the nightstand read 6:13. Marianna was awake and sitting up, though he wasn't sure why. Their audience with Mycroft wasn't on for hours yet. Maybe she's a morning person. *That* was going to take some getting used to.

A single shaft of sunlight angled across the bed, traveled up the taut planes of Marianna's naked back, and turned the fine, downy hairs on one superbly toned shoulder all to gold. It's good to be a mammal, Knox thought in drowsy appreciation. Then she turned and reminded him how *really* good it could be to be a mammal.

Marianna stood and stretched unselfconsciously. Knox watched through half-closed eyelids as she began an aerobic routine. She made it look like a form of erotic ballet. By morning light her areolae were the pale, velvety auburn of young rose petals, the 'V' of her pubic tuft shone jet black against her tawny, tight-muscled abdomen. A sheen of sweat bathed her torso.

A man could get used to this. Just then she segued into a lethal-looking kickboxing sequence.

Well, most of it, anyway.

✳

Marianna was midway through her cool-down series when a voice from behind her said, "Good morning."

She lowered her arms and turned to see Jon still lying in bed, propped up on one elbow.

How does he manage to get better-looking every time I look at him?

"Good morning, yourself. If I'd known you were awake I'd have made you join me." Considering how little she'd seen him exercise, he looked to be in pretty good shape. He'd certainly managed to keep up with her last night.

"Actually, I had something like that in mind," he said, smiling. The tented topography of the bedsheet draping his torso left little doubt as to what that "something" was.

Marianna glanced at the clock; the meeting with Mycroft was hours away. Plenty of time. She walked slowly, very slowly back over to where he lay. She was still hot and slick with sweat from her workout. This might be *very* nice.

"It's exercise too," he said, reaching up for her.

31 | The Way to Weathertop

By half past eight Marianna and Jon were checked out of the inn and back on the main road, headed west toward a line of low mountains on the horizon.

A front had come through after midnight, sweeping the sky clean and leaving the day bright and clear. The trees bent low over the road, their leaves still heavy with the overnight rain. Jon had put the Corvette's semi-rigid top down, so they drove drinking in the lush scents and melodious bird-calls of a hill-country summer morning.

Marianna stretched sensually. On a day like this, all things seemed possible. Mycroft would furnish whatever key Jon needed to solve the mystery of Antipode. CROM would crush Grishin's nefarious schemes. She and Jon would...

God, she felt good! Jetlag, Jon, and a not exactly restful night had left Marianna in a fey and frisky mood. She stroked the back of Jon's neck, ran a finger along the line of his jaw. All the while Route 421's two-lane blacktop was winding through somnolent Piedmont forest on its way into the foothills of the Blue Ridge.

She leaned over to run the tip of her tongue around the rim of his ear.

"Now," she breathed, "tell me what you've got this Mycroft guy working on."

＊

Yuri Vissarionovich Geladze was not a happy camper this fine midsummer morning. Not happy with having spent the night in transit. Nor with the mission objective: return them. *Both* of them.

Together with the rest of his striketeam, Yuri had been left to cool his heels in the lobby of the main GEI Systems Research building. He looked out on the green, sun-streaked lawns of Grishin International's Raleigh-Durham campus, and subjected them to a withering glower.

His yawn spoiled the effect.

Yuri stood and stretched, still stiff from over eleven hours in transit. Departure at three-thirty in the morning, Azores time. Nearly three hours on the helicopter just to get to Horta. Then another eight-hour flight on the GEI corporate jet. Shouldn't have taken more than six, six and a half hours to cross the Atlantic, but the pilot'd had to deviate far to the south, into the Gulf of Mexico, there to enter the old "Calle Corridor"—the air-route long favored by Colombian cocaine runners for its spotty radar coverage and corruptible Floridian officialdom. Finally touching down on the private airstrip at ten A.M. local. He'd managed to snatch no more than two, three hours sleep in all that time.

And his cast was itching again, devil take it!

Yuri glared at the timestamp over the reception desk. Half past ten already. What the devil was keeping Bondarenko? He had disappeared shortly after they'd arrived—off seeing about something he called a "Denial of Service" attack. Something to do with technology.

How was it possible even to speak of technology in the same breath as attack? Technology was for men who kept their consciences as clean as their fingernails. When technology reached the point where men ceased to die from a bullet through the brain, then it might be time to take notice.

Attack, on the other hand—now that was something Yuri knew something about.

Yuri did not much care for abstractions. He thought not about attacks in general, but about one attack in particular. The attack they would be launching within the hour.

And, even thinking about that attack, he did not picture the overall evolution of action and counteraction. Instead, he focused on one moment in the ebb and flow of the battle to come.

The cast was driving him mad! If he only had something, some sort of implement that he could slip beneath its polyurethaned fiberglass to scratch this ferocious itch. Even a pencil might do. He scanned the empty, antiseptic lobby again. Nothing!

Yuri grimaced and returned to his contemplation of that single, anticipated instant—the moment he and Marianna "Peterson" met once again.

There was an itch he *could* scratch.

He frowned. That was the problem with the mission parameters. What would happen once he had that bitch in his crosshairs was not covered by his instructions. Not at all.

Quite the contrary, Grishin had expressly ordered him to return the woman to *Rusalka* alive and unharmed. There had followed a long-winded explanation from Bondarenko as to why they needed her and her companion back aboard before the final phase could begin. Yuri had only half listened. Much too complicated. He preferred things simple.

This was going to be simple. In the confusion of the action, an opportunity would no doubt present itself. If not, Yuri would create one. Either way, the bitch would die, and by his hand.

This would make trouble, Yuri foresaw. But perhaps not *so* much trouble. Bondarenko would still have the other one, the man, for whatever scheme the devious little weasel was concocting. And, once Peterson was dead, Grishin would put it behind him. Too much else going on to waste time crying over one dead woman, and a spy at that.

For the first time that sunny August morning, Yuri smiled. No, this would not make much trouble at all.

✴

The scrub woods of the Piedmont lay behind them now. The air had turned cooler as the 'vette climbed through transition forest toward the higher elevations. Still plenty of oak and hickory and tulip trees, but increasingly interspersed with groves of northern hardwoods and the occasional stand of spruce or fir.

Knox was beginning to regret having shared his hunch with Marianna.

"That's *it?*" she was saying. "I flew us all the way out here for this, this Tunguska thingee?"

He downshifted as the Corvette hairpinned into yet another of the Blue Ridge Highway's countless switchbacks. "I warned you it was a crazy idea."

"There's crazy and there's crazy, Jon. This is just plain bonkers! Why would Grishin give a damn about a hundred-year-old meteor strike? Why would anyone?"

Knox sighed. "You're not listening. It wasn't a meteor. It was … something else."

"I *am* listening. I'm not hearing anything worth listening *to*. If it wasn't a meteor, what was it?"

"Well, there's no dearth of theories: a comet, a hunk of antimatter, reactor meltdown in a nuclear-powered starship, the list goes on and on."

"Starship? As in, like, extraterrestrials?"

Knox nodded. "Would've had to have been. Humanity barely had heavier-than-air flight back in 1908, much less space travel."

"CROM doesn't do aliens; you want the FBI. And I wasn't asking what everybody else thought it was. You tell me what *you* think it was."

"Let's save that till we're there. Not much further now." The dashboard GPS showed they were approaching the turnoff.

He slowed and eased them in through the break in the guardrail, past the *Keep Out* sign, down a brief stretch of blacktop so overgrown that branches screeched against the car's sides. Then they were bumping along on dirt track, paralleling a deep gorge being cut ever deeper by a tumultuous mountain stream. Their way led through sunlight and shadow cast by tattered wisps of cloud grazing the mountaintop, at times almost whiting out the blue of the sky. Flowing in around the windshield, the misty air was redolent of bee balm and the summer's last Catawba rhododendrons.

Marianna broke the silence. "So he's really got a photographic memory?"

"Mycroft? You bet. Why else do you think he moved way the hell out here?" He pointed across the gorge and up. Through intermittent gaps in the leaf cover, the dark shape of Mycroft's demesne could be glimpsed, wreathed in pale tendrils of fog.

"It's very beautiful, Jon."

"I suppose. But it's not the scenery that does it for Mycroft. It's, well…things change slowly up here on the Blue Ridge. Some of these little off-road towns aren't much different from the way they were back before the turn of the last century."

"So, less change, less stimulation, means less new stuff to remember?"

"Basically. He's afraid too much trivia and he'll overload his indexing capacity. When he worked out of the head office, people were always giving him stuff to read just so they could call it up later. He was getting to be sort of this informational dumping ground. Nowadays he only gets assigned to special projects."

"Like this wild goose chase?"

"Uh-huh," he said, not really listening. He was looking up again.

Weathertop was built on what the locals called a "bald," one of those grassy summits peculiar to the Southern Blue Ridge. Balds are so named because, to the bafflement of botanists, no trees will grow on them. In result, Weathertop enjoyed an unobstructed three hundred sixty degree panorama. Maybe Mycroft was a closet scenery buff after all.

Almost there, just around one last bend.

Knox had only visited here once before in the five years of Mycroft's self-imposed exile, but it was all coming back. Now, roll to a halt in front of the crossing gate.

Marianna laughed. "You've *got* to be kidding me. I thought that business about not lowering the drawbridge till ten in the morning was just a figure of speech."

"Ten-thirty," Knox corrected, peering through the haze to where the steel-framed drawbridge stood, still raised, on the other side of the gorge. "And, no, metaphors are risky business where Mycroft is concerned—too many of them turn out to be true. Hop out of the car now, and stand still for the scan."

✳

The mists that gave the Blue Ridge mountains their pastel hues, and their name, seemed to cling especially close around Weathertop's carriage entrance. Knox watched a shadow separate itself from swirling billows of particulate fog and move toward the car.

"Jonathan, welcome." Mycroft's voice echoed off walls faced with dripping cedar shakes. "And this must be the special client who summons us to duty at the crack of dawn." Little more than a shape in the mist, but it sounded like Mycroft.

Knox looked closer. Uh-huh, he could just make out the pattern of the ornately carved front doors showing through the silhouette's chest.

He raised his voice. "Cut the crap, Mycroft. Turn off the doorman and let us in."

The figure abruptly vanished.

"Real-time, full-motion hologram," he explained to a startled Marianna. "He's got a fog-generator built into the entryway, see? That's for times like now, when the real thing isn't thick enough to sustain a solid-looking projection."

"Too *weird!*" She was still staring at the spot where the image had been. "What's it for?"

"Oh, stray backwoodsmen, lost hunters, other folks he'd rather not deal with in person. Shouldn't include us. Not today." He pounded on the heavy door. "Hey, Mycroft, open up!"

With a muted hum, the door swung open to reveal Weathertop's post-and-beam greatroom.

Oaken timbers, reclaimed from the ruins of some antebellum mill, played counterpoint to a late-model plasma-screen monitor occupying half of one wall. The whole front of the room was window doors giving out on a broad expanse of cedar deck. Beyond its parapets, range after range of hazy blue-green mountains gradually blended into the azure of the sky. The vista was dominated by the six-thousand-foot crags of Grandfather Mountain twelve miles away to the southwest.

Their host—the flesh-and-blood person this time, not a holographic image—was still seated at his console, resetting the wards he'd lifted long enough to allow them entry. That done, he rose and walked towards them.

Knox noted with relief that Mycroft had dressed for the occasion. Which is to say he had dressed, period. In place of the usual ratty old bathrobe, his gaunt frame was decked out in jeans and a threadbare LL Bean workshirt. The gleam of a smile flickered in Mycroft's dark face, but couldn't dispel the impression of fatigue. And of something else.

Mycroft got to within maybe ten feet of his guests and ground to a halt. His eyes darted around the room, looking everywhere except at Marianna, finally coming to rest on Knox's face. That tentative smile again, followed by a release of breath shaped into a greeting: "Jonathan. Hello."

Knox closed the distance remaining between them and clasped his friend's hand. He was surprised to feel it trembling. "Mycroft? You okay?"

Mycroft swallowed. "I must apologize, Jonathan. I don't entertain many visitors these days. I had no idea it would induce such a reaction. Please bear with me, I'll be all right in a moment."

"Sure, sure you will. Just take it easy, okay?"

Knox felt a tug on his arm. Oh, right—the formalities. "Marianna, I'd like you to meet—"

"No, no, not now," she whispered. "We've got to move outside his critical radius first."

Knox stared at her a moment; then he placed it. "Critical radius" was a measure of how close one wild animal could approach another without triggering a fight-or-flight reaction. It varied from species to species. By the way she was eyeing the couch on the other side of the greatroom, Marianna had pegged the safe distance for *Homo sapiens Mycrofti* at six or seven yards out.

"Whoa!" he said. Trust Marianna to conceptualize every situation in terms of attack and defense. But she didn't know Mycroft. "Hold on a minute."

For Mycroft had adopted a familiar stance: head inclined, eyes closed, a thumb and forefinger pinching the bridge of his nose.

After a few moments Knox asked, "Better?"

Mycroft opened his eyes, expelled a breath, and nodded. More or less back to normal... or what passed for normal, given an IQ in the one-eighties.

"Marianna," Knox picked up where he'd left off, "I'd like to have you meet Finley Laurence, Archon's Senior Vice President for Intractables," adding, "Don't ask" under his breath.

He turned to Mycroft. "Finley, this is Marianna Bonaventure, Deputy Director of CROM Reacquisition." He didn't bother expanding acronyms or organizational affiliations: that had all been in last night's encrypted email.

"Pleasure to meet you, Dr. Laurence," Marianna said, her voice low and soft, her eyes directed downward at the wide-plank flooring. Very nonthreatening.

She needn't have bothered. Mycroft shook himself, walked up to her and held out his hand. "Call me Mycroft, please, my dear. Everyone does."

"Marianna," she said, taking the hand gingerly, as though mistrustful of this sudden transformation.

"I never forget a face, Marianna," Mycroft said, releasing her with what looked like reluctance, "but I will take special pleasure in remembering yours."

Knox choked on a laugh. He'd never seen Mycroft's courtly side before.

"Thank you, uh, Mycroft," Marianna said. "Are you sure you're all right now?"

"Much better, thank you. A little concentration works wonders to lower the pulse rate. If the mind is calm, the body must follow. Enough so, at least, that I can properly welcome you to Weathertop." A sweep of Mycroft's arm took in the house and the panorama beyond. "A name perhaps more than usually appropriate, under the circumstances."

"*Lord of the Rings*," Marianna picked up without missing a beat. "The mountain where battle was first joined against the forces of darkness. Though this feels more like the refuge at Rivendell."

Two Tolkien references were about Knox's limit. "Speaking of the forces of darkness, Mycroft, were you able to confirm..."

"Yes, yes, Jonathan." Mycroft sounded peeved at the interruption. "You'll be pleased to know that your 'guess' was dead on. As usual."

"So, there *is* a connection? Between Galina's Tunguska toast and Sasha's old obsession?"

"It took some digging, but yes—a connection called the Jackson-Ryan hypothesis. Fallen into disrepute these past thirty-odd years. No one ever followed up on it. Almost no one, I should say."

"What's the Jackson-Ryan hypothesis?" Marianna wanted to know.

"It's this, Marianna, right here." Mycroft crossed to his console and spoke a command. "Unless I very much miss my guess, there's your—how do you pronounce it, Jonathan?"

"Vurdalak."

The wall-filling plasma screen now held a close-up of a single page from the British journal *Nature*, dated September 14, 1973. A headline had been circled in red: *Was the Tungus Event due to a Black Hole?*

"Oh, now, wait a minute." Marianna shot Knox a hard look. "A black hole?"

"I wish for all our sakes that it were not," Mycroft said. "As it happens, there is proof. Of a sort."

"Proof?"

"All in good time. There's someone you need to meet first." Mycroft turned to his console again, spoke into its mike. "Lestrade, link Tomsk-1."

A videoconference window popped open on the screen. In it there appeared a man's face. A homely, smiling face. The man smiled and tipped what looked like a cowboy hat.

"Mr. Knox, Ms. Bonaventure, pleasure to meet you. My name's Jack Adler."

32 | Doomsday Scenario

JACK SPENT THE next fifteen minutes giving his audience of three the short course in primordial black hole physics, with emphasis on the Tunguska event. Just like around the Siberian campfire a week ago. Except here, thanks to the one called Mycroft, he could call on the 3-D simulations from his home lab as a visual aid. Those vivid sims of the first moments of creation were great for snapping undergrad classes out of the afternoon doldrums. Today, though, Jack suspected he could've got by with bright lights and bird shadows; his audience was hanging on his every word, focusing with an almost eerie intensity.

Question was, were they buying it?

The two guys, Knox and Mycroft, were at least nodding in the right places. The woman, Bonaventure, was going to be to be a harder sell. He'd seen that skeptical look before, though seldom in eyes so beautiful. Beautiful eyes that had just now begun to widen. She was staring, not at Jack, but at the simulation.

"*That!* I've seen that before. What *is* that?"

Jack paused in mid-sentence to check where the sim had got to.

"That's the PBH — Vurdalak, you call it? — orbiting inside the Earth. Uh, where'd you say you'd seen it?"

"I'm sorry, but that information's only available on a need-to-know basis."

Mycroft hadn't told Jack much about this "client," this Marianna Bonaventure. Not as much as she'd just told him with that one rapid-fire disclaimer: government, for sure. And not the National Park Service, either. Maybe some agency with enough in the way of discretionary funding to bankroll a Tunguska-II expedition?

"And you're saying you can prove all this, Professor Adler?" Did she sound marginally more concerned?

"Call me Jack," he said. "And, yes, I did prove it. It's just the proof got itself smashed into a million pieces and scattered all over the taiga." He went on to tell them about the wreck of his experiment, the murder of his friend, his own brush with death.

"This man, the one you say killed Igor — could you describe him?" For a skeptic, she seemed to be having no problem at all swallowing what was, to Jack, far and away the most fantastical part of his tale.

"I didn't get a real good look, you understand. Too far away. If I'd been much closer, I expect I'd be dead now too." He paused, tried to reconstruct horrific memories. "A, a big guy. Dressed all in black. Dark hair, moustache. ...This isn't helping, is it?"

"Fits too many people." But she was listening even more intently now.

What else was there? "Oh! The guy smiled at the end there. A real evil grin. And there was something funny about it. Almost as if a couple of his side teeth were made of metal."

"Yuri," the woman whispered. It wasn't a question.

✳

Marianna's head was spinning.

She hadn't believed it. Didn't really believe it even now. But when Jack Adler's animated slideshow had all of a sudden morphed into a much more elaborately rendered twin to the wire-frame diagram she'd seen in *Rusalka*'s secret lab, Jon's hunch had taken one giant step from fever dream to barely tenable hypothesis.

And now this. She wished she could shrug it off as a coincidence, or a trick of the light, or even a false, trauma-induced memory. But it sure sounded like it had been Yuri there in that remote corner of Siberia. And why else would he have traveled literally halfway around the world to obliterate some obscure researcher and his even more obscure experiment?

She stole a glance at Jon. He'd tried to tell her, and she'd snapped at him. If it had been left up to her, they'd have never uncovered this, this—call it a lead, for now. A lead linking the globe-spanning Grishin Enterprises corporation to an event long, long ago and far, far away.

Jon turned and met her gaze. "I think it's time we pooled information here. Tell Jack what we know. About Antipode and the rest of it, I mean."

She wished he hadn't gone and blurted that word out, before she'd had time to think it through. "That's all need-to-know, Jon. I've been stretching a point even divulging it to Dr. Laurence. I'm for sure not comfortable sharing it with an uncleared individual over a non-secure link." She waved a hand in the general direction of Mycroft's console.

And saw that Mycroft was staring at her, with an unfamiliar expression on his face. He cleared his throat and said in a slightly strained voice, "I think you'll find my communications security more than adequate to the circumstances."

That was the strange expression—she'd offended him. "I'm sure that's so…on this end. But how can you vouch for the other side of the videoconference?"

"Set your mind at ease, ma'am," Jack said. "The first thing we did after Dr. Laurence found me was download his communications-encryption software. Sets up something called a 'VPN with IP tunneling.'" A whimsical smile. "Too deep for me. But it's running on my end, too."

"And just where is your end?"

"A hunting lodge outside Tomsk. Belongs to a colleague, a friend in need: Academician Dmitri Pavlovich Medvedev."

"A Russian?" Marianna let that sink in. "Christ! He's not on line too, is he?"

"No, he's in town for the evening. But it wouldn't matter if he was. I'd trust that man with my life—have done, in fact."

"You said he's a colleague, right? An astrophysicist?"

"Planetologist, actually. But, yeah, close enough."

"Well, where does *he* stand on this, this micro-hole impact theory of yours?"

Jack gave a rueful laugh. "He thinks I've been smoking my socks. Says I've got no evidence, now my experiment's been trashed. He's right, too…unless you folks have dug up something new?" His mild blue eyes looked at her expectantly.

Jon didn't say anything, but he too was looking at her, waiting.

"Oh, go ahead," she told Jon. "If there ever was a need-to-know situation, this is it."

✳

And here Jack had thought *he'd* had a wild story to tell! It took a conscious effort to keep his mouth from hanging open as Jon Knox filled him in on missing magnetohydrodynamicists, on a defrocked cosmologist commanding the resources of Russia's third-largest con-glomerate, on a banquet featuring room-temperature superconductivity and a strange toast, on a nuclear-powered installation with the curi-ous name of Antipode at the bottom of the Atlantic Ocean, on a man named Arkady Grishin sitting in the middle of the web spun from all these separate strands.

The man who, more than likely, had ordered Jack killed.

Jack sat there integrating what he'd just learned with what he al-ready knew.

"Well," he said, "they could've found one of the hole's other apogees. Calling the place Antipode kind of hints at that. Not that the Azores are opposite Tunguska on the globe. But they *are* where the thing was supposed to come out the other side. Other side of the Earth, get it?"

By the look on her face, the "client" still didn't want to believe it.

"How could Grishin and company have found it, though?" Jon Knox said. "That's a big ocean out there. Marianna and I can personally vouch for that."

Jack thought a moment. "Let's see. Given unrestricted access to the impact site, their best bet would've been analyzing the throw-down pattern of the trees. With a good enough fix on the entrance angle, they could've ballparked the Azores apogee to within, oh, I'd guesstimate twenty miles or so. What I'm having a hard time with is how they narrowed it down from there."

The Bonaventure woman spoke up. "Would a detailed seismographic survey of the North Atlantic have helped?"

"Helped? Pinpointed it, more like."

"Well, Grishin's done one. The *Rusalka* oceanographic team published it five-six years ago."

Jack mulled it over. "And from there they could've run confirmation sweeps with a SQUID. This boat of Grishin's, did she ever spend a lot of time steaming in circles?"

"A year after that survey came out, come to think," Bonaventure said. "Her single longest summer voyage: twelve weeks, all told. She spent almost half that time sailing round and round a stretch of ocean northwest of—oh, shit!—northwest of the Azores!"

"What I don't get," Knox was saying, "is why they wouldn't just set up shop in Siberia, on the impact site itself. It has to have been simpler than building on the seabed."

"That's an easy one," Jack said. "Sounds like this Grishin fellah likes his privacy. Tunguska's no place for that; you'd have researchers crawling all over you every year or so. Besides, have you ever tried building anything on permafrost? Most treacherous stuff in the world. stress it wrong and it goes from concrete to putty faster than you can blink. No, I'd bet real money Grishin's found another semi-stable apogee and built this Antipode Station on top of it. Question is, what's he planning on doing with it?"

"We were kind of hoping you'd tell us," Knox said.

"Well, I saw what looked like signs they've been trying to true up the orbit. A pretty hairy proposition in its own right, but it can't be the whole story."

Knox shook his head. "It's not. Our best information comes down to a single word: 'capture.'"

This time Jack didn't even try to keep his jaw from dropping, "Sweet Jesus! I was afraid you were going to say that."

✳

Knox didn't understand. "Isn't it better to catch the damned thing and have done with it?"

"I guess so." Jack sounded dubious.

"Anyway, it's probably academic by now: The capture was slated for 10:47 p.m. on the third of August—two nights ago."

Knox stopped talking then and looked over at Marianna. He recognized that look she was giving the floorboards: something had just clicked for her. For some reason—the mention of the date just now?—the whole thing had right this instant stopped being an intellectual exercise. She *believed*.

When she looked up again, her face was several shades paler. "Would it even be *possible* to catch such an object?"

"Possible, sure," Adler said. "And, with those room-temperature superconductors, Grishin's got the right butterfly net. That's why he needed your missing magnetohydrodynamics experts, by the way: to build an electromagnetic cage."

He sketched out how the primordial black hole's magnetic charge offered a hook to grapple it by. "So, yeah, it's possible. But you'd have to be damn sure you weren't going to drop the ball, so to speak."

Marianna's "Why, what happens then?" was barely on the edge of audibility.

"Wouldn't it just go back into 'orbit' again?" Knox asked, somewhat louder.

"No, no, no! Catching the thing means stopping it in its tracks. If you lose hold of it after that, it for damn sure won't fall back into its old trajectory. Best case, it'd pass close enough to the Earth's core to slingshot into a whole new orbit, and then good luck ever finding it again."

"If that's the best case, what's the worst?"

"Doomsday scenario. Major deceleration as it hits the high-conductivity zone at the core. The object comes to rest at the center of the Earth, not in centuries, but in decades or less. Here, watch."

Adler keyed in a command and his sim resumed running in its separate window. The little computer-generated Vurdalak paused and held at the top of its arc, then it was back in motion again. But this time it wasn't tracing out any delicate Spirographic rosette. Its new path through the Earth resembled more the dynamics of another childhood plaything.

A yo-yo.

A yo-yo on an ever-shortening string.

As they watched, the orbit degenerated further and further, the micro-hole finally coming to rest at the center of the simulated Earth.

"And that's the beginning of the end." Adler said. "From there it starts gulping down core material like there's no tomorrow. And there won't be."

"But only if they screwed up the capture." Knox gave Marianna what he hoped was a reassuring smile. She nodded and tried to smile back, but her eyes still held that haunted look. As if she needed to say something but couldn't decide how to say it.

"Just hypothetically, Dr. Adler—Jack," she began finally, "let's assume Grishin's succeeded in caging this thing. What would happen if, if the cage were, um, jostled?"

"Jostled?" Knox's eyes narrowed. "Jostled, how?"

"Let's say, by a—" Marianna took a deep breath. Her next words came fast and low. "—a low-yield tactical nuclear device."

"Jesus H. Christ, Marianna!" Knox exploded. "Is Pete out of his fucking mind? Are you *all*?"

"But it's an unmanned target—," Marianna started to reply, thought better of it, tried again.

"Sorry, Jon. I wanted to tell you all along, honest. It's all this damned need-to-know bullshit—" she flared briefly, then broke off. When she resumed, her voice was shaking. "Oh, God, Jon. What else can we do if Grishin really has got hold of that—that *thing*?"

She looked sorry and angry and scared as hell. Knox's own anger drained out of him. It was all he could do not to take her in his arms and hold her.

Contraindicated. Once she'd mastered her immediate reaction, she'd like as not go back to stonewalling on them.

He settled for saying, "Okay, it's okay. We'll work through this somehow. You'd better give us the whole story, though." He tried giving her a hard look, failed utterly.

She drew a shuddering breath. "All right. Can I make a call first?"

✴

Marianna inserted a one-time encryption tab into her handheld, and keyed in Pete's reach number.

"Aristos," said the familiar voice, backed by an unfamiliar rumble of powerful engines. Pete must be en route to the taskforce already. She knew better than to ask.

"Pete? Marianna."

"Marianna? Where in hell are you? The New York office was supposed to pick you up and escort you out to Tsunami."

"The escort didn't—they didn't make it, Pete. And it's Tsunami I'm calling about. We—Listen, Pete, I think we've got to put it on hold, at least until—"

"*What?* We bail now, we're fucked. Not just you and me. It's CROM's ass on the line, too!"

"I know, Pete—believe me, I know. But we've got no choice. Grishin's got hold of a—" How did she put this across to Pete when she wasn't sure she believed it herself? "—call it a doomsday device. You hit Antipode now, you'll trigger it!"

"Doomsday device?" Pete was nearly shouting now. "Like in *Dr. Strangelove*?"

"Pete, you don't— Okay, it's not really a doomsday device. If anything it's worse."

"*Worse?* How in hell could it be worse?"

Oh, Lord, here goes. "It's—it's a black hole, Pete. A real little one. That hydrophone alert Tuesday night? That was Grishin catching it. I'm in videoconference right now with an astrophysicist who's been tracking the thing, and—"

"Black hole? It's that Knox guy, isn't it? He put you up to this. Christ on a crutch, Marianna, I had you figured for more sense."

Stay calm, stay calm. "You're not listening, Pete. I know it sounds crazy, but there are ways to check it out. Have Research verify an explosion in the middle of Siberia ninety-some-odd years ago. Check with the airlines: Grishin flew that hired gun of his, Yuri, out to the same impact site last week to whack the scientist who discovered the thing, the one who's conferenced in with us right now. It's why Grishin needed the MHD proles, Pete, to build a magnetic cage for the hole. And now that they've caught it, we can't—" She stopped. "Pete, you there?"

"I've heard just about enough of this. Think what you're saying for godsake, then answer me one thing: why? Research pegged the price tag on this Antipode Station at two to five billion—that's dollars, not rubles. And you tell me it's all about catching a *hole*? What for?"

"Believe me, Pete, if I knew what Grishin's doing it for—"

"I don't have time for this. You don't either. You're going to hustle your butt out to the taskforce, now. Give me your GPS coords and I'll set up transport. Where in hell are you anyway?"

"Sorry, Pete," she said, "that information is only available on a need-to-know basis." And she hit the *Exit* key.

✳

Her handheld beeped immediately. Pete, trying to home in on her. Marianna opened the back of the unit and yanked the battery.

She couldn't talk to him again just yet. Not when the only thing he'd listen to was hard facts, whys and wherefores. She didn't have any. And she wasn't going to get them onboard a C-141 bound for the Azores. In fact, the only place she stood a chance of getting the answers she needed was right here at Weathertop. And to get, she'd have to give, need-to-know be damned!

She walked back to where Jon and Mycroft were talking quietly with Jack. Her own little think-tank—could they do it? Tell her what she needed to know? Had to: they were all she had.

Time to spill the rest of the beans. She sat down, cleared her throat. "You were right, Jon. They've got it, Grishin's definitely got it. Like I tried to tell Pete: it's the only explanation that fits the facts." Quickly, then, she filled them in on the hydrophone event at 2347 Zulu Tuesday night.

"And SOSUS ruled out an undersea volcano?" Jack asked when she'd finished.

"That's just what Sasha said it was. But, no, this was no natural eruption. No preambles, no aftershocks. Just one god-awful crunch, total duration maybe forty-five seconds. Then all quiet again. I'm sorry, Jack, I'd love to be wrong on this, but it was the capture, all right."

"Let's just pray they can hold onto it," he whispered.

"The hydrophone reading was enough to triangulate in on Antipode, I suppose?" Jon said.

She nodded. "The epicenter was on top of a mile-high mountain out in the Newfoundland Basin. The same place *Rusalka* was cutting donuts six summers back."

"Now," Jon said quietly, "the rest of it."

"Right," she went on unhappily. "Well, between that and our own intel on Antipode, Pete got the Energy Secretary to recommend a go on Operation Tsunami—that's the codename for an all-out air-and-sea assault on *Rusalka*—"

"But now with a little something extra thrown in for good measure?" Jon prodded.

Marianna nodded again. "Tsunami has been reconfigured as a two-pronged attack, coordinated to take out both the surface *and* undersea elements in one shot. Given a choice, we'll capture *Rusalka* rather than sink her."

"And Antipode?"

"Well, it's not as if there'd be people there, not two miles down. And the best guesses on what *could* be down there have got the National Security Council climbing the walls. Not that it's anybody's preferred outcome, you understand, but if need be CROM's ready to nuke it first, and ask questions later.

"The whole thing's good to go for first light tomorrow," she finished bleakly.

"Jesus H. Christ!" Jack echoed Jon's earlier sentiments. "You've *got* to find a way to call it off!"

"But wouldn't a nuclear explosion destroy this Vurdalak?" she asked.

"Not hardly. It took the biggest explosion of all time to *create* it—the Big Bang." Jack shook his head. "No, as far as Vurdalak is concerned, all your piddling little low-yield device will do is momentarily increase its food supply. But the impact on Antipode itself is a different story: the blastwave from a nuclear explosion at that depth is going to crack your mountaintop wide open."

"And then?"

"And then it's doomsday all over again, except we do it to ourselves this time. As to what happens—hell's bells, what doesn't?" Jack waved an arm distractedly. "Tectonic upheavals, the mantle buckling, ultimately, collapse of the Earth itself. Maybe I should've taken the sim all the way through to the finale. If you could see—"

"That's okay," Knox said. "We get the picture—giant sucking sound, end of story."

That tore it for her. "Jon, please don't. That's ghastly."

Try as she might, Marianna couldn't seem to get her hands around this situation. Something that a nuke couldn't put a dent in, something that could eat the world. No wonder Pete didn't believe it. What could Grishin—what could anyone—possibly want with such a monstrosity? When she'd called it a doomsday device, had she hit on the literal truth?

Marianna shivered. Five years with CROM had pretty much desensitized her to the prospect of thermonuclear and biochemical terrorism. This was a whole different threat-level. Black holes and global annihilation could *not* be happening, not on her watch.

She rose and walked to the wall of glass fronting the greatroom, arms hugged tight against her body as if huddling against a freezing wind. She gazed outward, seeking to purge nightmare images with vistas of the gentle, eternal mountains. But the Blue Ridge brought her no peace. The ancient range looked fragile somehow—as though it, and the whole Earth with it, might be swept away, swallowed up in an instant. As though the ground might suddenly open up beneath her feet to reveal the yawning void.

She pressed her forehead against the cool glass, tried to calm down.

Grishin *can't* be planning to use the thing as a doomsday weapon. That scenario only made sense, if it ever did, when your back was against the wall. His wasn't, not yet. What did that leave? What else was there?

She turned back to the group. "Okay." She let out a breath. "I'll go to the mat with Pete one more time for you. But first there's something *you've* got to give *me*."

Three faces—two in the flesh, one in videoconference—turned to look at her expectantly.

Her gaze came to rest on Jon.

"A reason," she said. "There's no way in hell Pete'll pull the plug on Tsunami if I can't even tell him what they want this Vurdalak thing for in the first place."

She nearly succeeded at keeping the shudder out of her voice as she added, "End of the world aside, what's the worst Grishin could do with it?"

33 | Hackers

WHAT'S THE WORST Grishin could do with it?

Jack put his hands behind his head and tipped his chair back while he considered Marianna's question. The only answer that came to him was another question. "Why're we assuming the worst from the get-go here?" he said, half to himself. "Isn't saving the world enough of a reason?"

"You've seen Yuri in action," Marianna said, "you tell me."

Jack fell silent, remembering. When he did speak it was to say, "Right. Scratch that theory, then. It's just you're talking like they're going to make some sort of weapon out of it, and I just can't for the life of me see how."

"Something so powerful, so destructive," she prompted him, "there just *has* to be a way."

"Don't get me wrong, it's plenty dangerous."

"Dangerous how?"

Jack scratched his head. He wasn't used to thinking in these terms. "Well, the Hawking radiation alone'd crisp you to a cinder if you got close enough. Closer in still, and the tidal distortion'd pull you apart like saltwater taffy. But it's all real short-range effects. The thing's not about to reach out and grab you from miles away. You'd have to move it pretty close to a target to do much damage...and there's no practical way to move it at all."

Marianna buried her face in her hands. "All that does is rule things out. I've got to know what Grishin *is* planning to do, not what he isn't."

Jack shrugged. "Sorry, ma'am, with no hard data to go on, your guess is good as mine. Maybe if I could get a look at what's going on down in that station—"

"Now there," said Jon, "I think we may be able to help you."

✴

Sasha jumped at the slam of the lab's heavy firedoor. He called out, "Quiet, please!" without looking up, then went back to his consultation with Irina Konstantinovna Kuznetsova, head of GEI's Raleigh-Durham telecommunications laboratory.

He sensed a presence behind him, and turned to see Yuri standing there in black body armor, glaring down at him.

"Ah, good morning, Yuri. Are we almost ready to go?" Sasha forced a smile. Truth be told, the hulking Georgian made him nervous. Especially out here in the field, with his blood up and no Grishin around to restrain him.

"*We* have been ready for half an hour. The delay is *you*."

"Yes, well, some things cannot be rushed, as you will appreciate."

If Yuri did appreciate it, said appreciation failed to register on his implacable features. He stood there like an obsidian statue, motionless, waiting.

"We are very nearly done, Irina Konstantinovna and I," Sasha said. "Already we have programmed the voice-line overloads for the 5E switch and cell-phone base station serving northern Watauga County. It only remains now to hack Weathertop's high-speed dataline."

"How long?"

Sasha's eyes flitted to the display's menubar clock: five after eleven. "Perhaps another fifteen minutes. We have determined that Weathertop is connected via a so-called digital subscriber line. Because DSL is essentially independent of the public switched telephone network, our standard denial of service strategies are useless. Instead, we must—I beg your pardon?"

"I said, five minutes," Yuri repeated.

"You must have patience, Yuri Vissarionovich. It is essential to cut Weathertop's links to the outside before we close in. It will be difficult enough to spirit our captives out of the country under the noses of the authorities. It becomes impossible if CROM has been forewarned."

"Five minutes!"

"You do not understand, Yuri Vissarionovich. Such 'hacking,' as the Americans call it, is a delicate operation. And it is essential that the outage appear accidental. If we are not careful, we could—"

"It is you who do not understand, Bondarenko. I am in operational command of this mission, and I give you five minutes. If you are not ready by then, we leave without you."

✳

Knox shifted around to face Adler. "Jack, what if we could tap into the telemetry bitstream from Antipode to *Rusalka*? Would that do it for you? Give you enough to figure out what Grishin's up to?"

The talking head in the videoconferencing window nodded warily. "Sounds like."

Knox turned to Marianna again. "Didn't you tell me you'd patched a surveillance device into the secret lab's local area network? A device with remote-access capability?"

"Uh-huh, my LAN-bug. Pete could read it from his desktop in Chantilly, if it came to that."

"If Pete can, how about us?"

She shook her head. "Nice try, Jon. But it won't work."

"Why not?"

"Look around—do you see any satellite tracking facilities? NSA's birds aren't geosynchronous like the one that little dish out there is pointed at." She waved a hand at the commercial satellite receiver off to one side of the deck. "They're in near-Earth orbit, constantly moving across the sky—the hand-off's nontrivial. Besides, like I told you, the data stream's spread-spectrum encrypted. Even if you could intercept the signal, it'd read like random noise."

"But Aristos could access your bug from the machine in his office? And read the data in the clear?"

"Sure, he could link in over dedicated landlines to the NSA ground station in Bethesda, for all the good that does us—Pete and I aren't exactly on speaking terms at the moment, remember? And no way he'd do it now anyhow. Not with Tsunami going on radio silence in three hours."

"Sounds like we're going to have to hack our way back in, then."

"That's just not possible. I know, I know—" She held up a hand. "Your friend here broke in once. But he needed you on the inside to run that scam. Here he'd be up against the frontline defenses. And, like I was saying before," looking directly at Mycroft now, "CROM's got the best communications security in the world."

Mycroft snorted. She ignored it. "I guess I could try talking Pete around."

"That's okay. I think we can leave your boss out of this. That is, if…" Knox turned to Mycroft. "Please tell me you didn't pick the day of your recent CROM infiltration to go straight."

"Jonathan—" Mycroft began, his complexion darkening a shade further.

"It's okay, we're all friends here. Isn't that right, Marianna?"

She said nothing, just gave a suspicious nod of her head.

"Well, then," Mycroft said, "what Jonathan is referring to is my penchant for leaving behind a backdoor module on any of the sites I, um, visit."

"Back door?"

"Technically," Knox said, "it's called a Trojan Horse, or just plain Trojan for short. It's software that hides away inside a machine till it's time to come out and boogey."

"No way." Marianna sounded indignant now. "Pete had his machine purged down to the bare silicon after you pulled that little stunt. If this Trojan of yours was ever there, it's long gone."

"I seriously doubt that," Mycroft said. "Most antivirals look for malicious activity: file deletions, disk erasures, what have you. My Trojan Horses would never give themselves away like that; they burrow deep and lie quiet. And open a channel to the outside world once every ten minutes, of course, to see if I want to come back in."

He glanced at the timestamp in the upper right corner of the screen. "We're coming up on a check-in window in, um, three minutes forty-five seconds. Jonathan?"

"Go ahead. You never needed my permission before."

With Marianna peering over his shoulder, Mycroft busied himself at his console. The seconds ticked by. Stretched into a minute. Then two. Three.

A final clatter of keys and, somewhere in the depths of CROM headquarters, in the darkened lair of the Director, Reacquisition Working Group, a monitor sprang to life.

"We're in," Mycroft breathed.

✳

Marianna watched with mixed feelings as a new window popped open on the screen. On one level, she knew they really, really needed this to work. On another, well, who on earth would want to see their organization's best defenses fall to some...some hacker?

She was concentrating so intently on what the hacker in question was doing that she didn't notice Jon standing behind her until he spoke.

"If this is the Trojan I think it is," he said, "then once it wakes up, it deploys as a telnet server."

"Meaning?"

"Meaning Mycroft can slave the Chantilly machine to this one here. As if he were sitting at Pete's desk, typing in commands on his keyboard." Sure enough, the new window was displaying her boss's favorite screensaver.

She got a sinking feeling in the pit of her stomach. *Twice!* That made twice this odd little man had simply thumbed his nose at the best comm security in the world.

As if reading her thoughts, Mycroft muttered, "If this is CROM's idea of world-class communications security, no wonder they're losing magnetohydrodynamicists right and left!"

"*What* did you say?"

"Um, I apologize, Marianna." Mycroft looked flustered. "It's not your fault, really—CROM's, that is. It's just that government bureaucracies are no different from any other large organization: it's not in their best interest to nurture excellence of any stripe."

"And what's *that* supposed to mean—," she began.

"Whoa, *whoa!*" Jon held up his hands. "He's on our side, remember? Come on, let's leave the man to do his work." He took her by the arm and steered her off toward the kitchen alcove.

He looked back over his shoulder: "Mycroft, we're going to make coffee. You want some?"

✳

Knox scanned a kitchen sparsely furnished even by Mycroft's spartan standards. Refrigerator-freezer, yes. Convection/microwave oven and electric range, yes. A pantry stocked with spices and coffees and other comestibles, of course. But no pans or dishes; nothing to prepare food in, or eat it on. The L-shaped butcherblock countertop that divided the alcove from the greatroom proper sported only an inset stainless steel sink and a rather elaborate console. Nor was there any of the usual cabinetry beneath the counter, mostly just blank black panels.

"Hey, Mycroft! Where's the coffee maker?"

"Gone," Mycroft's voice came from the far end of the greatroom. "Gone along with the rest of the kitchen paraphernalia. Nowadays I make my cookware on the spot, with a Replicator solids-prototyper."

"I know those," Marianna said. "3-D copy machines, right? That's it down there, Jon. And the computer up topside must run the CAD software and the template database."

"Replicator, huh?" Knox bent to inspect the unit he'd mistaken for a dishwasher, set flush with the paneling in the space directly below the countertop console. "Like in *Star Trek*?"

"Not really." Mycroft had risen by now, and stuck his head around the corner. "Brand name aside, solids prototyping is old technology; the early experimental models go back to the mid-nineties. This production version is nothing more than a computer-assisted design system, as Marianna said, married up to a polymer-extrusion device. The end-result is a three-dimensional casting of whatever is imaged on the screen. Simple."

"Still, it's kind of cutting-edge for a kitchen appliance, wouldn't you say?"

"As to that, cutting edges are one of the things it *can't* do. Bread knives, carving knives, blades of any kind are still beyond reach of the current top-of-the-line. This model can manage pots and pans and dishes, but nothing that has to slice or dice."

"Kind of limited, then."

"You're missing the point, Jonathan: when you're done cooking and eating there's no clean-up. Just throw the dirty dishes in the intake hopper, and they're rendered back to raw material for whatever you want to fabricate next time."

"Wow! Just what every bachelor pad needs," Knox said. He spied Marianna's frown out of the corner of his eye and switched tacks. "I'm holding off getting one till they can do lawnmowers."

"You might as well get onboard now, Jonathan; this is where we're all headed. Buy the pattern and you own the thing. In the long run, intellectual property will be the *only* property. Bits over atoms." Mycroft shrugged and turned back to his work.

After several false starts, Knox and Marianna persuaded the modeler to fabricate three mugs and a coffee pot with a heating element. The actual replication process went quickly enough—perhaps forty-five seconds all told—once they'd gotten past finding the right design-templates. Even with its limitations, the unit's repertoire of possible objects was enormous.

Marianna really got into it, perusing the catalog of CAD patterns as if off on some virtual shopping spree. Women! They're all alike.

Or not. Glancing over her shoulder, Knox could see she'd hacked her way past the childproof lockouts and into the armaments templates. The Replicator could no more do swords than it could carving knives, but wireframe schematics for a surprisingly wide variety of bludgeons, garrotes, and other non-edged lethalities scrolled across its display.

Knox shook his head and went back to making the coffee.

"Um, Jonathan?" Knox looked up to see Mycroft standing just outside the kitchen alcove. "I'm about ready to try accessing the datastream from *Rusalka*," he said. "I've located the satellite-communications facility via Pete's machine. It's tracking over a hundred devices worldwide, including one out in the mid-Atlantic that I take to be our LAN-bug. Their activation routines are all passworded, though. Uh, Marianna, I don't suppose you—"

"Why, Dr. Laurence, I would have thought a hacker of *your* world-class abilities would have punched through our flimsy password protections without even pausing for breath."

"Now, Marianna, I never meant to imply—"

"Evil bitch queen!"

Mycroft blinked at her. "I beg your pardon?"

Marianna sighed and repeated it. "Evilbitchqueen. I thought you wanted my password. That's it. Do I have to spell it out? Capital E, lower case v-i-l-b-i-t-c-h-q-u-e-e-n. No spaces."

Knox coughed in an effort to cover his laugh.

"It wasn't my idea," she said, glaring at him. "Pete's the one who assigns them."

＊

Sasha let out his harness and wriggled around trying to get comfortable, only to discover his seat did not recline. He was sweating buckets in the body armor Yuri had made him wear, and the EH101 Merlin wasn't even air-conditioned. The big helicopter was roomy enough—especially with only the seven-member strikeforce occupying a cabin intended for thirty—but otherwise its amenities left much to be desired. Well, and what did one expect of a troop transport?

Think about something else. Sasha glanced down at the mission chronometer integrated into his Kevlar sleeve. Quarter to noon. Twenty-five minutes out from the target. And in just fifteen of those minutes, his own virtual attack would begin, a precursor to the physical one.

He tried to get his mind off the raid. Why had he volunteered for this? He possessed no expertise applicable to what was about to happen. He doubted if any such expertise existed, or if combat wasn't simply a chaos phenomenon, its outcome uncertain until the event itself.

And his friend's life hinged on that indeterminate outcome. He had done all he could do to ensure Dzhon, and Marianna too, would come out of this alive. But persuading Arkasha was one thing; forcing the random evolution of events themselves into a desired course, quite another.

Especially with that wild card, Yuri, in charge of the operation. Sasha glanced across the cabin to where the big Georgian sat hunched over opposite the hatch, caressing his Glock-18 machine pistol. What thoughts were going through *his* mind in these last moments before the action?

With an effort, Sasha refocused on the denial of service attack, trying to contemplate it as an exercise in abstract design. Though Yuri had managed to intrude even on this, Sasha's own domain, hustling him off before the arrangements could be completed.

It shouldn't really matter; Irina Konstantinovna had seemed perfectly competent once she understood what was needed. He pulled out his handheld. It never hurt to check.

It took him three tries before he got a ring and an answer.

"Telecommunications, Kuznetsova."

"Irina Konstantinovna? Bondarenko. How are things progressing?"

"Ah, Aleksandr Andreyevich. Things go well. Five minutes ago we set the demon-dialers to begin building traffic on the wireline and wireless switches. Gradually, of course, in order not to arouse suspicion. Even so, you may already have noticed an effect."

"Yes, I had to redial several times. I kept getting fast-busy."

"Ten minutes more and the trunks will be so overloaded you will not be able to get through at all."

By Russian standards, the American telephone system was a miracle of reliability. That did not make it invulnerable. Cost-effectiveness dictated that the networks be engineered to deal with ordinary peak loads, not extraordinary ones. A presidential assassination or a local team's upset victory or a snowstorm in the Sun Belt—any freak occurrence that prompted everyone to pick up the phone and try calling everyone else—could so swamp the switches that no one could place an outbound call.

As could enough automatic dialers deliberately tying up all the lines in a given area.

"And what of the target's DSL service?" This was to be the *pièce de résistance*: leeching away the bandwidth from Weathertop's digital subscriber line.

"I have hacked into the DSL Access Multiplexer colocated in the Boone Central Office. I have granted myself supervisor status; their DSLAM now belongs to us."

"Excellent, excellent."

DSL was an access technology that transformed the twisted-pair copper wire of an ordinary analog telephone line into a high-speed multi-megabyte digital conduit, turning a soda straw into a fire hose, so to speak. All that extra bandwidth made possible real-time Internet access, two-way videoconferencing, low-cost virtual private networks, a host of other marvels.

All that extra bandwidth was the challenge. To seal Weathertop off from the rest of the world, they'd had to find a way to shut down its DSL line.

The access multiplexer was the key. With DSLAM supervisor privileges, Irina Konstantinovna could run resource-consuming line tests against all subscribers to the service. The more capacity devoted to the spurious tests, the less left over for Weathertop. Yet there would be nothing overt to give the game away at the target site itself, just a gradual attenuating of bandwidth.

With any luck, it would have the appearance of normal service degradation, ending in total outage.

"Is there anything else, Aleksandr Andreyevich?"

"No, Irina. You have authorization to go for totality. Prepare to initiate full Denial of Service in twelve minutes."

Sasha smiled as he hung up. Such an elegant plan. Its elegance totally lost on that thug, Yuri. Ironically, the one best able to understand Sasha's accomplishment here today was the one who would shortly fall victim to it. Dzhon, with all his years of consulting to the telecommunications industry, would surely appreciate how cunningly he had been trapped.

Sasha made a mental note to tell his friend all about it once this was all over.

Provided Dzhon survived.

34 | Spin Doctor

Jack Adler leaned back in his chair and studied the image filling his computer screen. "Well, that puts a different spin on things," he said, then chuckled at his own small joke.

When no one joined him, he explained, "They're rotating it, see?" He moved the cursor to the readout showing Vurdalak's rate of spin. Its ever-increasing rate of spin.

It had taken Mycroft another quarter hour to reverse-engineer the telemetry signals coming in from Antipode Station by way of the bugged LAN in *Rusalka*'s secret lab, but it was well worth the wait. Somewhere in the images now flowing in lay the answer to their mystery.

They had already downloaded a time-compressed recording of the capture and watched as Armageddon Phases One, Two, and Three played out in edge-of-the-seat half-second increments. The last vestiges of doubt were gone now: Grishin had Vurdalak. And the containment configuration looked stable, thank God! More than stable; its simple, elegant metastability was a work of art. Jack would have liked to shake the designer by his hand.

Her hand, rather—a Dr. Galina Postrel'nikova.

But that was old news. What they were watching now was the late-breaking story: a real-time schematic showing Vurdalak being spun ever faster, as part of something called Phase Four.

"What's speeding it up, Jack?" Jon asked.

"Good question." Jack peered again at the cutaway diagram of Antipode's containment chamber being transshipped to him from Weathertop.

"There," he said, "see the particle beams? With room-temperature superconductivity, you could build a linear accelerator to put Brookhaven's Heavy Ion Collider to shame. Not just protons, but whole atomic nuclei, boosted close as you like to lightspeed. And the closer you get to c, the more the mass increases. Think of a continuous beam of particles, each with an energy hundreds or thousands of times its rest mass. Individually, their momentum is tiny compared to Vurdalak's inertia, but collectively they pack one hell of a punch."

"But why? Why run the risk of destabilizing it like that?"

Why indeed? Jack leaned back in his chair, folded his arms behind his head, and gazed off into the middle distance. He passed perhaps thirty seconds that way, sifting through the possibilities. Then he sat bolt upright. "Oh, now, wait a minute."

"What is it, Jack?" Marianna said. "What've you got?"

"The difference in scales had me going there for a minute, but this is one of those times size doesn't matter. The spin's the giveaway: they're trying to turn your Vurdalak into a SEKO."

"Lot of trouble to go to for a Japanese watch," Jon said.

"Huh? Oh, no, not a Seiko—an S-E-K-O: a Super-Extreme Kerr Object. Kerr-Newman Object, to be precise."

"You've lost me." It was Jon doing the talking, but he wasn't alone; all their faces wore some variant of that puzzled look. Well, maybe not Mycroft's.

Jack thought a moment, then said "Okay, let's step back and start over. Do any of you know what a singularity is?"

✳

"It comes in sight now, Dr. Postrel'nikova," the pilot said as *Navtilus* began to level off.

Galina walked to the bathyscaphe's forward viewport. Strange, she had anticipated this descent into the abyss with utmost trepidation, yet now there was only room in her for awe.

At first she could make out nothing but darkness through the centimeters-thick Plexiglas. Then *Navtilus*'s floods were playing over the upper slopes of Mount Nadyezhda. Ellipses of wan light illuminated acres of surrealism: a ring of colossal trapezoids jutted upright out of the flattened summit like bony plates on the back of a stegosaurus designed by Salvador Dali — Antipode's radiator fins.

The pilot swung the bathyscaphe hard a-port, steering clear of the turbulent updrafts spawned by the release of so much waste heat into the near-freezing water. Steering clear, too, of the shoals of bathypelagic monstrosities attracted by the warmth of the convection currents. Galina craned for a glimpse of the weird sealife, caught only dimly limned amorphousness.

She refocused her attention on the radiator array as the 'scaphe skirted its base. Now she could see where the great fins tapered into the heat pipes that formed the heart of Antipode Station's cooling system.

Those heat pipes…a stroke of genius, really: maintenance-free, quadruply redundant, no moving parts to break or wear. All that from a simple double tube filled with a liquid-metal eutectic. The refrigeration cycle started hundreds of meters below in Antipode's containment chamber, where liquid metal circulated between the inner and outer walls of the spherical heat shield surrounding Vurdalak. The PBH's radiation heated the coolant to its high-temperature boiling point, and the resulting pressure gradient forced the vapor all the way up the heat pipes to the fins, where it cooled and condensed back into liquid form for the return trip to the evaporator. Not only did the eutectic fluid dump Vurdalak's excess thermal output into the enormous heat sink of the North Atlantic, it was an efficient absorber of gamma rays, too, lessening the need for radiation shielding in the human-occupied areas of Antipode Station.

A real *Russian* solution, Galina thought with quiet pride. Simple, robust, one more example of her countrymen's unparalleled talent for making do. The old adage said it all: "if you've no plow, you'd best furrow with a stick."

Of course, the Americans, in their high-tech arrogance, would have derided such an approach as "brute force and awkwardness." Worse, a *roobgoldberg*. So little they understood the satisfaction that came from solving a problem, not by simply throwing microchips at it, but by creatively exploiting circumstance, scarce resources, and available technology.

Navtilus continued her slow descent down the rugged north face of the seamount. The ovoids of light from her spots were now rippling across a myriad of bulbous lava pillows marring Nadyezhda's complexion and betraying its ancient origins. Born on the active volcanic axis of the North Atlantic Ridge, the mountain had crept many kilometers to the west over the course of millennia, as tectonics gradually ratcheted the seabed apart. And that was a good thing; engineering Antipode Station had been challenge enough as it was without the additional complication of having to buttress the facility against the eruptions that periodically shook the rift proper.

But even if Nadyezhda had been closer to the midocean rift valley, its unique topography would have made it hard to pass up. The sheer drop-off on its southeastern side in particular had afforded an ideal site for the braking train: it had been possible to install the last kilometer and a half of the train's superconductor deceleration rings with no excavation whatsoever.

Navtilus's spotlights were already picking up all that remained of the last few links in that chain: a wrack of shattered, contorted toroids littering the cliffside below. Rest in peace, Galina bade these warped and silent sentinels. You have done your work. Now I go to do mine.

Yet the nature of that work was shifting under her. She had seen the Antipode Project as her gift to the world, harnessing a dread threat in the service of all humankind. It was only in the early morning hours following Vurdalak's capture that Arkady Grigoriyevich had explained—had argued, had cajoled, in their marathon *tête-à-tête*—that Russia's own needs must come first.

For, known only to Grishin's inner circle until a scant forty hours ago, there was a secret within the secret: *Vurdalak could alter Russia's destiny!* Its spin-up to relativistic speeds would open a doorway to some as-yet undisclosed turning point from which their suffering mother-land might take a new and different path into the future.

Well, and what of it? Why should Russia not reassume her former greatness, reclaim her rightful place in the council of nations? It was high time she ceased being the lapdog of the Americans, as Arkady Grigoriyevich had said. — As *Arkasha* had said, Galina corrected herself, reliving that surge of pride she had felt when he'd first asked her, in view of their new and closer working relationship, to address him with the familiarity, the collegiality connoted by the diminutive.

And hadn't the main thing already been accomplished, after all? Vurdalak's fangs had been drawn. It hung caged and confined within her electromagnetic web, never again to break free. The world would go on, the planet would continue to bear its precious freight of humanity through the starry night, forward into the far future.

She, Galina Mikhailovna Postrel'nikova, had saved it for — had bequeathed it to — the children.

The silence of the deep was broken by the variable rumble and whine of *Navtilus*'s engines and the metronomic pinging of sonar sweeps as the pilot maneuvered in toward the main airlock. A few more minute adjustments, then he cut power and let the bathyscaphe drift the final few centimeters into its socketed berth. A muted clunk re-sounded throughout the cabin. They had arrived at Antipode Station. Galina was home!

✳

"A singularity?" Though the quasi-mysticism of quantum mechanics had always held first claim on Knox's imagination, the pseudo-paradoxes of relativistic physics ran a close second.

And he was pretty sure "singularity" rang a bell. "It's this thing at the center of a black hole, isn't it? The rabbit hole all the mass disappears down. A point of infinite density and infinite gravity, a place where the laws of physics break down."

"Close enough for government work," Jack said. "And, yeah, those infinities are a bitch. All kinds of strange things happen in an infinite gravity field, things us physicists would as soon not deal with.

Fortunately, we don't have to; black holes just naturally wall themselves off from the rest of the universe. It's called an event horizon."

"That's like the cosmic point of no return, right?"

"Uh-huh. Once you're in past the horizon, the hole's pull gets so strong not even light can escape. That means nothing can—no material body and no coherent information, either. And that's a *good* thing. It means no matter how weird things get down at the singularity, none of that weirdness can ever reach out and pollute the universe at large."

Another time, Knox could've talked about this stuff all day. But the clock was ticking on Operation Tsunami. "Uh, Jack? We're still waiting to hear how all this ties in with what Grishin's up to."

"Getting there. See, the thing about event horizons is, they're not some sort of physical barrier. All they really are is a fancy piece of spacetime geometry. That suggest anything to you?"

Mycroft jumped in before Knox could open his mouth to say no. "You imply there might be other geometries where an event horizon never forms. Or forms, but does not persist."

"Uh-huh. Resulting in what we call a naked singularity—a singularity without an event horizon to hide behind, accessible from anywhere in the universe."

Jack frowned. "Now, a lot of physicists don't believe that could ever happen. Steve Hawking has declared naked singularities to be anathema. Roger Penrose goes one him better with his "Cosmic Censorship Conjecture"—claims nature herself forbids a singularity from exposing itself in public."

"Why worry about it, if it's impossible?" Knox asked.

"Who says it's impossible? Conjecture's just a fancy word for guess. And Roger's guess hasn't been doing too well lately. Matt Choptuik found the first stellar-collapse configuration leading to full-frontal singularity way back in '96. Since then seems like somebody comes up with a new one every year or so. It's looking like the cosmic censors are whistling in the dark."

Jack made a sound somewhere between a snort and a sigh. "Still, I know where they're coming from. As a group, us physicists've got a lot riding on the proposition that the cosmos is mostly a nice, dull, predictable place. So this is pretty scary stuff. Because if naked singularities *are* possible, there's no way to quarantine the madness."

"And yet you think Grishin is trying to create one of these...things?" Marianna asked.

"Sure looks it. Leastways it's the only reason I can figure to boost the hole's spin."

Knox was almost afraid to ask. "How's that, Jack?"

"Here. let me show you. Mycroft, could you load my SEKO-1 simulation? Thanks."

The window that had held Jack's lecture animations blanked briefly, then filled with an image of a matte-black spheroid. Longitudinal reference lines superimposed on its surface showed it was spinning at a furious pace.

"A Kerr Object is just a rotating black hole, like you see here. Spin her up to the speed of light and you get an Extreme Kerr Object."

As Jack spoke, the spin increased to where the white reference lines and the black of the simulated hole itself merged into a uniform gray.

"Now, if we could give her one more nudge, so she's rotating faster than the speed of light, we'd get a Super Extreme Kerr Object—a SEKO. At that point, the event horizon just plain evaporates and leaves the singularity behind." Jack flashed a quick grin. "That's a big *if*, though. In the real world nothing beats lightspeed. 299,792 kilometers per second—it's not just a good idea, it's the law."

"Sounds like this is a dead end too, then." Marianna put in.

"Hold your horses; we're not done yet. Not if we can magically reduce the mass just a tad."

A small twinkling object spiraled into the wildly gyrating hole. As it hit, the horizon shimmered and froze. Then it was gone. Knox strained to see what was left behind, but a blinking question mark interposed itself, blocking off whatever the horizon's annihilation had revealed.

Jack grinned. "Naked singularity city! And we didn't have to break the lightspeed barrier to do it."

The question mark was still blinking.

"That pretty much concludes the science portion of our program," Jack said. "You're all probably wondering what's behind the question mark. Me, too. Unfortunately, the simulator halts as soon as the infinities start cropping up. Anything beyond this point would be wild-eyed speculation. I've got a canned lecture on that, too, if you're interested."

"What was that thing at the end there?" Knox asked. "The magic part, I mean."

"Exotic matter, maybe. Something with an average negative energy density, anyway."

"Exotic? And you think Grishin's got hold of some?"

"Okay, okay, you got me—I don't really know how they plan to do it. But the thing you've got to understand about black holes is, they're really simple objects: there just isn't that much you can do with them. And given what Grishin *is* doing, a naked singularity's just about the only thing he could be shooting for."

"I'm sorry, Jack," Marianna said, "but I'm still not clear on the 'why.' Say Grishin actually could create this, this abomination. What's in it for him?"

Jack leaned forward and began to talk again. At least it looked like he was talking—the sound had suddenly cut out.

"Mycroft, what's happening?"

Mycroft bent over the console. Diagnostic mini-windows sprang into existence in response to his spoken and keyed-in commands. "We're losing DSL bandwidth, Jonathan," he reported. "It happens, especially after a storm like the one last night. Let me see what I can do."

Mycroft tapped at the keyboard again. "There, that should be better: I've lowered the video frame rate to free up more room for the voice-band."

With its refresh rate cut in half, Jack's image was now perceptibly stuttering, looking more like a series of still photographs than realtime video. But the sound was back. Sort of. "So, what I think Grishin—with Vurdalak—closed timelike curve—"

"Can't you do something? We're missing every other word, or worse."

"Working, Jonathan."

"What's going on?" Marianna was staring at a blank window where the Antipode telemetry had been.

"Jack, can you repeat? You're breaking up here."

Jack's mouth was no longer even close to synching with his words, what there were of them: "—way too dangerous—grandfather paradox—"

"Mycroft, we're losing him!"

Jack's face assumed a haunted look, a look that froze there as one last burst of speech came through: "—global causality violation—"

And with that, the videoconferencing window filled with snow.

35 | Closed Timelike Curve

"**N**OTHING?" KNOX GLARED at the dead videoconference window. "Archon's shelling out five hundred a month for that VDSL hook-up of yours. How in hell can the bandwidth go to *zip?*"

"The automated diagnostics are checking it right now, Jonathan. If you'd like me to see to it personally, I will. I suspect, though, that Marianna would rather have the answer to her question first." Mycroft looked to her for confirmation.

She nodded a response, but Knox wasn't having any. "Same thing, no? We need the connection back up for Jack to tell us what Grishin's planning with his singularity."

"I believe Jack already *has* told us that, in a manner of speaking."

Knox hated it when Mycroft went all delphic on him. "Well, aren't you going to share?"

"It was the last thing he said. But perhaps it would be better if he tells us in his own words." Mycroft leaned forward to the console mike. "Lestrade, search directory 'Adler libe' for 'naked singularity,' 'closed timelike curve,' and, uh, 'wild-eyed speculation.'"

Best match: 'Beyond the Black Horizon,' QuickTime file containing three out of three subject terms. Duration: four minutes seventeen seconds. Play it?

"Go ahead, please."

A new window appeared on screen. It held a freeze-frame image of Jack Adler's head and shoulders, cowboy hat and all. Alongside Jack, an intaglio displayed the same blinking question mark that the SEKO-1 sim had ended with. Lou Christie's rendition of "Beyond the Blue Horizon" lilted softly in the background.

As the song drew to a close, Jack's image came to life and said, "Hi there. Ready for some wild-eyed speculation?"

"Where's this coming from?" Marianna asked, "I thought we were off line."

Mycroft paused the video. "We are. This is running locally." He smiled at her, all innocence. "In light of your expressed concerns about Weathertop's communications security, I deemed it unwise to stay logged on to Austin any longer than necessary. So I downloaded the contents of the physics simulations library as soon as Jack gave me entrée, then closed the link. Everything we were watching, from the Big Bang to the SEKO, was resident on Lestrade here. As is the—mmph!"

The rest of his words were muffled by the headlock Knox had him in, the better to administer a vigorous Dutch rub. "Yes! My man, Mycroft! Do we love this guy, or what?"

"I—*ow!* Jonathan, please, try to restrain yourself!"

But Knox was already past his momentary breach of decorum and back to business. He released Mycroft and asked, "What was that search-term again? 'Closed timelike curve'? Jack said that too, at the end. Something about Grishin and Vurdalak and closed timelike curves."

The curious phrase sounded familiar somehow, and not just from the aborted videoconference. Then it clicked. Oh-oh!

"Guys!" Marianna was getting impatient. "Would someone please tell me what's going on? What's a closed timelike curve?"

"It's, it's a euphemism. Kip Thorne at Caltech came up with it, to put the media off the scent when they started sensationalizing his research. I'm still not sure how or why, but Jack seems to think Grishin's planning on using Vurdalak to create one—a closed timelike curve, that is."

Knox glanced over at Mycroft, saw him nodding agreement. Right track, then, more's the pity.

Marianna didn't look nearly as pleased as Mycroft with Knox's performance. From the frown on her face to her folded arms to the way she was tapping her foot, her body language was silently screaming at him *Answer the damn question!*

She'll have to know sooner or later. He took a deep breath and said, "A closed timelike curve is a physicist's way of talking about time travel."

✳

"Time travel?" As she was speaking the words—shouting them, more like—Marianna flashed on a curious, half-forgotten image, of a sealed wall-safe in a secret lab, with something visible through its glass door that hadn't been there a moment before. She brushed the stray thought aside in order to concentrate on glaring at Jon. "*Time travel?*"

"Look, Marianna," Jon began. "Try to keep an open mind on this. I agree, it's kind of far out."

"Far *out?*" She became aware she was yelling again and dialed the decibels back down into the merely strident range. "Look, Jon, I cannot go back to Pete with this. Hell, he couldn't even get past miniature black holes. How do I tell him it's all about some mystical closed timewise—"

"Timelike," he said. "Closed timelike curves. And there's nothing mystical about them. 'Timelike,' for instance, just means... Uh, what *does* timelike mean, Mycroft?"

At moments like this, an eidetic memory helped. Mycroft looked inward momentarily, then said, "'Timelike' refers to any mode of motion that takes more time to cover a given distance than a photon would. In other words, that does not require equaling or exceeding lightspeed—which is, of course, prohibited for material bodies by special relativity. In our current context, a closed timelike curve refers to a path that would allow anyone who traversed it to travel backward in time without going faster than light."

"Thanks," she said, "that makes it *so* much clearer. Where's Jack when we need him?"

Mycroft sounded crestfallen as he said, "Jack's right here. Lestrade, continue."

"If you linked in from the SEKO simulator," Jack's recorded introduction resumed, "then you saw how it runs out of gas right where Einstein's tensor calculus breaks down. Once the equations that embody our best understanding of macroscopic physical law start churning out nonsense, it's time for science to pack it in. That doesn't stop us from speculating, though. So, for the next couple minutes we'll try taking a peek under the hem of Mother Nature's gown."

Marianna breathed a sigh of relief. No offense, but for unscrewing the inscrutable a canned Jack Adler beat a live Mycroft any day.

"The bad news is," Jack was saying, "we're going to have to do without the pretty pictures this time around. This stuff goes way beyond the limits of our visualization technology, beyond our own human visualization faculties too, maybe. So, if you don't mind, I'll just talk you through it." The image gave an apologetic shrug.

"Now, let's imagine we've stripped the event horizon off of our singularity, and it's standing there in what my granddaddy used to call its bare nekkids. What's it like? Going out on a limb here, but I suspect the first thing we'd notice is, no more Hawking radiation. It's an artifact of the event horizon, after all, and when that goes away, it should too. That wouldn't matter much one way or the other for the stellar-sized holes, since their radiation output is so low to begin with. But it'd mean you could even cozy up to a primordial-sized singularity without getting fricasseed.

"So, say you could get in close, what would you see? Wish I had a nickel for every time somebody's asked me *that* one. But try thinking about it like this: the singularity itself's just a point source. So you wouldn't be able to see *it* at all—too infinitesimally tiny. What you *might* see is instantaneous cross-sections of all the worldlines caught up in its vortex. Sort of a smorgasbord of local history, only with everything all happening at once."

"Like 'The Aleph.'" Marianna whispered.

"Like which Aleph?" Mycroft had overheard her and paused the video again. "Aleph as in the first letter of the Hebrew alphabet? Or as in Cantor's symbol for the cardinality of transfinite numbers?"

"Neither," she said. "As in the short story by Jorge Luis Borges. Haven't you read it?"

"Not that I can recall," Mycroft said. In his case, that must simply mean no.

"Well," she went on, "Borges' Aleph is this thing in the basement of a Buenos Aires apartment. It looks like a one-inch sphere, but somehow it contains everything there is—lions and tigers and bears and such. Gaze into it and you see all the objects, all the actions, all the times and places in the universe from every angle all at once."

"Perhaps it's in the Library." Mycroft turned to his console mike. "Lestrade: Borges, 'The Aleph.'"

A text window appeared on screen and began scrolling, the original Spanish side-by-side with Andrew Hurley's English translation. Lestrade's synthesized voice began to recite, not without feeling, the opening lines about the death of the narrator's unrequited love, Beatriz Viterbo.

"Lestrade: Stop," Mycroft said. "Search 'lions and tigers and bears.'"

No match, Lestrade reported. *Going to closest near-miss.* Marianna looked. There were no lions or bears in the lines Lestrade had matched, but there were the tigers she'd remembered all right, part of a catalog of phantasmagoria that went on to list pistons and Persian astrolabes and armies, not to mention all the ants on the planet.

"Lestrade: Pause," Mycroft turned to Marianna: "Is that the passage you meant?"

She set down her coffee mug and walked over to the console for a closer look.

"Lestrade: Back up a bit," she said into the microphone. "Pretty good speaker-independent recognition," she added to Mycroft as, after a momentary pause, the text began to scroll back.

"Speaker adaptive, actually," Mycroft said. "Lestrade has been listening to you the whole time you've been here."

"There! I mean, Lestrade: Stop!" she said, and then she began to read aloud herself, about all the actions of human history, all squeezed into the same infinitesimal point, all rolled up into one single gigantic instant. "'...and I felt dizzy, and I wept,'" she finished, "'because my eyes had seen that secret, hypothetical object whose name has been usurped by men but which no man has ever truly looked upon: the inconceivable universe.'"

Marianna fell silent then, confronted by her own visions, not of the inconceivable universe, but of its fiery, inconceivable destruction. It took her a moment before she realized that Mycroft had started the video again.

"Whatever it looks like," Jack's image was saying, "the key point is, you'd get to see it up close and personal. With no Hawking radiation to fry you, and no event horizon to trap you, there'd be nothing to stop you from skirting the singularity and coming back on out again. And that's where the real trouble starts. Because the singularity puts out a gravitational field of, far as we know, infinite power. Enough power to do really weird things to space and time.

"How weird? Well, what if I told you there are orbits around a singularity—closed timelike curves, we call them—that could let you arrive before you left? Meet yourself coming and going. Or your older self would meet your younger self, whatever. Weird enough for you?

"Okay, you say, that's pretty weird all right, but where's the problem? You give yourself a wave and wish yourself a nice life. End of story, right? Wrong. Because what if your future self somehow prevents your past self from entering that orbit in the first place? Then how'd that future self get back there to do that? What you wind up with is an effect that can negate its own cause, because the effect can *precede* its cause chronologically.

"Now, we expect this sort of thing goes on all the time inside black holes, and it just doesn't matter. Normal cause-and-effect can go to hell in a handbasket, so long as it stays under wraps, behind the event horizon. What's different here is there *is* no event horizon. Turn this kind of craziness loose on the outside universe, and you've got yourself global causality violations, grandfather paradoxes galore. Worst case, you could wind up punching holes in the fabric of spacetime—and you don't want that, believe me. So let me wind up our magical mystery tour here with an important safety tip..."

The blinking question mark in the small corner frame was now surrounded by a red circle with a diagonal line through it. Jack's image grinned and snapped the brim of its cowboy hat. "Just say 'no' to naked singularities!"

A fade to black and then Lou Christie was singing a reprise over closing credits.

Jon turned to her. "Remember the 'scary stuff' that the real-live Jack was talking about before? Well, this is it. Do you know about grandfather paradoxes?"

"Isn't that where you go back in time and kill your own grandmother before your mother is born?"

"Well, yeah. Only without the gender-bending."

"I prefer my version. With grand*fathers*, how can you ever be sure? Grandma might have been entertaining the gardener on the side." Marianna stopped then. Could Jon's flippancy in the face of the monstrous possibly be catching? He certainly didn't seem so blasé about *this*.

"This is what Jack was trying to warn us about, right at the end there, before the link went dead," he said. "What Grishin could do with Vurdalak."

Rips in spacetime? Global causality violation? Scary stuff, for sure. But it didn't seem right somehow—didn't seem to fit. She gazed into the depths of her cooling coffee.

"We've been asking the wrong question," she heard herself say. "We've been trying to figure out what Arkady Grishin would want with a singularity, when what we should have been asking is...

"What could the KGB do with a time machine?"

36 | Big Bang

WHAT *COULD* THE KGB do with a time machine?

Marianna's question hung in the air. For long moments the only sound to be heard in Weathertop's greatroom was the anachronistic ticking of an antique brass clock.

Knox's mind kept edging in toward the topic, only to skitter away again. That hollow feeling in the pit of his stomach was back. Closed timelike curves, time machines—it was all a little too close to his own quantum-inspired nightmare.

Meanwhile, Marianna was waiting for an answer.

"Too many possibilities," he said at last, after it became clear no one else was going to speak. "Too many hinge-points where things could have turned out differently." Too many knots and elbow joints of sheer potentiality, too many snags where the veneer of everyday reality might wear thin, allowing what lay beneath to gleam through...

"Different how?" Marianna broke in on his thoughts. "Better or worse?"

"Hmm? Oh, better for Grishin, worse for us."

"Give me a for instance."

Knox sighed. "Well, how about the 1991 putsch? The KGB's Alpha Group commandos were supposed to detain Yeltsin at his villa the morning of the coup. Never happened somehow, but it wouldn't take much tweaking to make sure it did. And, say what you will about old Boris, with him out of the picture that takeover could have worked."

"Way too late in the game," she said. "By the beginning of the nineties, the Soviet Union was already dead and just looking for a place to fall."

"A lot of people weren't so sure back in August of '91," Knox reminded her, warming to the debate and grateful for the distraction. "In D.C. they were bracing for another half-century of Cold War, I seem to recall."

"How about Lavrentii Beriya?" Marianna said.

"The old NKVD chief? Possible. He looked like a shoo-in for the Premiership after Stalin died in 1953. Didn't happen, thank God. It took another three decades for the secret police to maneuver one of their own into the top slot, and even then Andropov didn't last long enough to make much of a difference. But, say they could fix it so Beriya *did* come to power in the early fifties. Give the KGB a free hand and thirty years' head start, and I don't like to think about the consequences."

"Jon? Remind me again why I'm supposed to want to *stop* Tsunami from happening?"

"It's damned if we do, damned if we don't, for sure." Literally, in his case at least. "But at least holding off on the strike keeps some options open. Speaking of which, could we make that call now?" He glanced at his wristtop; there were, believe it or not, more pressing pretexts for an anxiety attack. "We can play guess-the-master-plan some more afterwards. Right now we're running up against your communications-blackout deadline."

"You're right," Marianna said. "We'll have to go with whatever we've got."

She reinstalled her handheld's battery, then looked up at him again. "Keep thinking about those what-ifs anyway. You never know."

Knox nodded. "You never know" about summed it up. On those

occasions when inspiration did strike, it wasn't because he'd consciously set out to find it — if anything, *it* found *him*.

"Jon?" A touch of Marianna's hand on his arm. "I'm getting a busy signal on Pete's reach number. That can't be right; this is a priority patch-through."

"Let me listen," he said. She handed him the handset and he put it to his ear. "That's a fast busy. Means there's a trunk overload. Pete's line isn't tied up. The problem's local — whatever cellular switch serves this area is getting hit by more traffic than it can handle."

He glanced at his watch: shortly after noon. It was the lunch-hour spike, when everybody returned the morning's calls in hopes the other party will be out and they can just leave voicemail.

But that was in Manhattan, not the backwoods of North Carolina. The cell-phone density wasn't high enough around here to tie up the lines like this. And there was that DSL outage just a few minutes ago.

Oh, shit.

"Mycroft," he said slowly, "I don't think this is just a normal trunk overload —"

"Denial of Service?" Mycroft looked blank for a moment, his typical reaction to one of Knox's sudden context-shifts. Then his train of thought started to roll down the new track. "It would be easy enough to do."

"Jon, I'm sorry," Marianna said. "What is it you're saying?"

He turned to her and smiled grimly. "It's beginning to look like we're under attack."

✳

"Attack?" Marianna wondered if she'd heard right. "Just because the phone's busy?"

"Not just the cell phone, the high-speed data line too. The two systems are entirely separate — what are the odds against them both being out?

"It's called a 'Denial of Service' attack," Jon went on. "Hackers do this sort of thing all the time, against switches and Internet sites. Normally, it doesn't buy the attacker anything but bragging rights on the outlaw bulletin boards. Here, though…"

"Here, it cuts us off from the outside world," she finished for him. "And from *Pete!*"

"You see the problem."

"What can we do? Get in the car and drive out from under?"

"That could be a long drive," Jon said. "No telling how wide an area they'd have blanketed if they're really serious. And all the time, the clock keeps ticking. But there may be another way."

He turned to Mycroft. "Does that satellite receiver of yours have enough juice to transmit?"

"More than adequate for what you're thinking, Jonathan."

Jon looked at Marianna again. "That's it, then. We'll bypass the local switch entirely, hack the satellite uplink and establish our own call direct from here to the COMSAT transponder."

"You can do that?"

"Well, Mycroft can. It's really just coding up the SS7 call-setup header and wrapping it in a COMSAT message envelope. Dead simple." He smiled reassuringly.

Not reassuringly enough for her taste. "Once more, only in English this time."

"Trust me," he said, "it shouldn't take Mycroft more than five or ten minutes to hack. Then we'll establish your call to Pete and you can take it from there. Uh, it's going to involve Weathertop setting up shop as an unauthorized COMSAT ground station, though. I assume CROM will square things with the FCC if it comes to that?"

Marianna nodded numbly. Mycroft knows everything and Jon can figure out the rest. So what did that leave for her to do?

Find a way to get this across to Pete, that's what. She shook her head, imagining his reaction. He hadn't even wanted to hear about mini black holes, so now she was going to call him back with time machines? Phrased in standard bureaucratese it all sounded just plain *wacky*. There was no way she could hope to explain it in terms Pete would understand. Would he just take her word for it for? Hold off the attack at least until…

Attack—there was that word again. Jon had used it just a moment ago to describe the problem they'd experienced getting through to

Pete. She blinked. If Weathertop was under some sort of virtual assault, could a real one be far behind?

She looked over to where Jon was sitting halfway across the room, waiting for Mycroft to finish his hack. She rose, just in time to hear a muffled roar echoing off the surrounding hills, rattling the glass of the window doors.

She opened her mouth to speak.

❋

Having framed out the functionality, Knox went and sat on the sidelines while Mycroft coded it up. He tried to relax, make his mind a blank, but to no avail; now that there was nothing to talk about, there was nothing to hold the thoughts back. Leitmotifs of relativistic physics, Siberian ethnology, and Soviet political economy glided unbidden across the retina of his mind's eye. And behind them all, the void.

He took a deep breath and slowly released it. Now that he *wanted* to turn it off, his subconscious had gone into overdrive, churning up grandfather paradoxes, pivot-points in time, half-forgotten rumors, George Orwell…and where had that one come from?

He looked up. Marianna was rising, turning to look out.

She had just begun to say "Jon?" when something went *Whump!* and the glass doors lining the front wall of Mycroft's greatroom imploded.

Knox felt the flash and the blast, but what imprinted itself on his memory was the warm breeze suddenly stirring his hair, and the hundreds of tiny tempered-glass cubes now covering his lap—as if a rock had hit the windshield of a BMW doing one-ninety.

Ears ringing, flare afterimages dancing before his eyes, Knox shook his head and looked around. Smoke from the rocket's near miss was pouring into Weathertop's breached greatroom. The black blot of a helicopter gunship hung against the noonday sky. How in *hell* had Grishin found them? They'd been so careful. Marianna had even filed a bogus flight-plan—

Marianna! Where was she?

Okay. She was crouching, gun drawn, behind an upended marble coffee table, looking shaken, disheveled, and almost…elated, as if she'd finally found a problem she could sink her teeth into. She motioned Knox and Mycroft down, then opened fire at the body-armored invaders now rappelling out of the hovering gunship and into the smoke.

Knox needed no invitation to take cover; he was already hunkered down behind the couch. Mycroft was another story. He had risen from his seat and was standing there paralyzed, eyes darting, like a deer caught in the headlights.

"Mycroft! *Get down!*"

Shit! He wasn't listening. The men outside had begun returning Marianna's fire with a fusillade of outsized, slowly tumbling canisters. Mycroft, still a perfect target, was a good fifteen feet away.

Knox took a deep breath. Keeping low as he could, he sprinted across the open space and dived.

"*Jon!*"

Knox heard Marianna's warning shout just as he slammed into the still-frozen Mycroft—and something slammed into him. He felt a sudden stab of pain in his thigh. He tried to ignore it long enough to shove Mycroft into the well of the workstation desk, then looked down. No blood, thank God! Instead, there on the floor lay the olive-drab canister that had hit him. About the size of a beer can, and pouring out clouds of bilious yellow-gray smoke.

"Tear-gas!" Marianna coughed, but Knox had already caught a whiff. He fought the reflexive gasp for breath, forced himself to exhale instead. Beside him, Mycroft was wheezing and gibbering in fear and fumbling with some sort of catch recessed into the wall behind the desk.

Knox's lungs were screaming for air. He obliged them, only to gag on the acrid smoke. Stimulating the tear ducts was the least of the gas's effects: with his second breath, Knox was violently sick to his stomach. Heaving and retching, he raised his head in time to see a gasmasked figure marching toward him through the choking fumes, pointing an evil-looking gun-muzzle at his heart.

In the instant before the gun fired, before the void could finally claim him for its own, it came to Knox at last: what the shadow KGB would do with a time machine.

✳

Jon was down. Marianna couldn't tell how bad. Too much smoke.

Too much *gas!* Her eyes were stinging fiercely now, sinuses on fire. She tried to make out the forms of Jon and his attacker, but they were lost in a blur of tears.

She fought down an urge to cough lest she give away her position behind the coffee-table barricade. Tear gas went straight for the mucus membranes; the only variation in physiological response was due to attitude and motivation. Marianna had plenty of both. Breathe shallow, hang on, tough it out.

Maybe not for too much longer. Weathertop's climate control was smart enough to respond to the influx of noxious fumes. High-speed ventilators kicked in, sucking clean, cool, humid air in through the gaping hole in the deckside wall.

Marianna watched six gasmasked raiders, wraithlike in the smoke, take up position just outside, establishing a free-fire zone covering every inch of the room. Saw the textbook perfection of their formation disarrayed as a seventh figure barged through.

On he strode, a black, body-armored form gaining solidity as he emerged into the clearing air of the greatroom. He stood there at the threshold, one arm in an off-white cast held stiff across his chest, the other hand clutching a machine pistol. Behind tinted assault goggles, cold black eyes tracked across the room, the pistol muzzle tracking with them. Searching for something, searching for—

"Where is she?" Yuri's shout echoed off the beams. Marianna's rudimentary Russian sufficed for most of it. "Where is the little *shlyukha*? She's *mine!*"

✳

Marianna gauged the distance to where Yuri stood amid the flinders of Weathertop's window-doors. A good twenty feet away. Too far for a take-down. Yuri would be ready this time anyway. She'd make a perfect target flying through the air at him.

She took quick inventory: nothing in the way of protective gear; her blouse barely stopped light, much less lead. Weaponry? Only the Glock she'd taken off Compliance's lifeless body last night, and no more spare magazines, dammit! One bullet left, then, if she hadn't miscounted. And judging by how ineffectual the others had been against the invaders, she'd need a lucky shot to do Yuri any damage at all.

Think, Marianna! What can take down a heavy-armed man in full body armor?

Out of the corner of her eye she caught a glimpse of a lighted screen down at the other end of the greatroom. The kitchen! Mycroft's words came back to her: no blades, no machines, certainly—but, still, a slim chance. If only Jon hadn't hit the reset.

One way to find out.

She tucked the Glock in the belt of her jeans, sprang up and sprinted the length of the room. At the last instant she vaulted over the butcherblock and into a tuck-and-roll that fetched her up against the kitchen range. She scrambled back onto hands and knees and peeked up over the countertop, half expecting to see Yuri grinning down at her. But he was still halfway across the room, arguing with one of his black-suited friends. Looked like—could that be Sasha?

If Sasha could slow him down enough, this might have a chance of working yet.

She looked up at the Replicator's catalog screen. Still on the same page she'd left it, thank God! She exposed a hand just long enough to tap her selection and hit enter. The prototyper acknowledged her order. She heard a liquid hiss that she hoped was the extrusion process kicking off. The console displayed a countdown: thirty seconds.

Thirty? She had maybe five at most.

She had to buy more time somehow. She flung her body flat out on the countertop, arms extended, the pistol in a two handed grip. Saw Sasha moaning on the floor, and Yuri advancing confidently toward her, not even troubling to use the cover afforded by Weathertop's freestanding oak pillars. *Aim for the cast, the cast!* He couldn't be bulletproofed there.

She pulled the trigger. And heard the click of an empty chamber.

She straightened and hurled the pistol directly at Yuri's head, then hugged the floor behind the counter again as a hail of fire tore through the space she'd just vacated. She could hear shouts coming from the other end of the room, could hear Yuri's footsteps quicken. The Georgian was pursuing his own unsanctioned agenda, and his compatriots were taking exception. But not in time to save her.

She looked pleadingly at the Replicator's countdown display. Come on, come *on!* 3, 2, 1, *Yes!*

The unit dinged. Heedless of the residual heat inside, she yanked the door open to see her only hope.

It didn't look like much: just three small heavy spheres connected to a common center by thongs of pliable plastic. In particular, it didn't look much like the *bolas* she'd trained with in her six-week Indigenous Weaponry course, but it'd have to do.

She grabbed the makeshift weapon, then ducked aside just as a second volley tore into the Replicator's innards.

Got to remember how this works. It can't be all that hard if *gauchos* do it from horseback. Let's see: right hand grasps the centerpoint where the three thongs come together, left hand holds one of the balls. Deep breath, then — *quick!* — stand. And — *quick!* — one horizontal whirl of the two free weights, then — *hunh!* — expel the breath and *throw!* Now hit the deck as the shots bored into the butcherblock.

Yuri must have guessed something was amiss: he hastened to close the remaining distance to his quarry. As he did, the *bolas*, spinning like a three-bladed helicopter rotor, flew straight to meet him. And if she'd done it right...

Yes! The whirling weights caught Yuri in mid-stride, wrapping their trailing cords around and around both legs. With his knees lashed together and no way to kill his forward momentum, the Georgian went down as if poleaxed, crashing to the floor not ten feet from where she huddled. Jarred loose by the impact, his machine pistol skittered to a halt up against the ruined Replicator.

Extra added bonus: all of Yuri's weight had landed on his already injured arm. He howled in agony. One fewer black hat to worry about for the moment.

Plenty more on the way, though. Marianna was just reaching for Yuri's machine pistol when the nets got her.

✳

Through a miasma of pain and nausea, Knox realized he was still alive. His long-term memory was missing several key minutes in there, though, and was frantically trying to spackle over the gaps with a montage of freeze-frames: The blacksuited invader pulling the trigger. The strangely-flared gun-muzzle ejecting some sort of sticky netting, ensnaring him. A bumpy view of a burning Weathertop, shot as he was carried on his captor's shoulder out to the waiting Merlin and dumped unceremoniously on the copter's floor. A wave of relief as another black-clad figure deposited Marianna — cursing, kicking, wrapped in not one but two coats of adhesive webbing — alongside him. That wave of relief being followed by another wave of nausea. And then...

He remembered the rest of it now. Remembered wrenching his head around to peer out the open hatch as the gunship lifted off, hovered fifty feet off the deck and fired salvo after salvo of incendiaries. Remembered Weathertop's autonomic systems countering with fire-suppressant foam. Mycroft, looking hazy as the smoke somehow, stumbling out of the wreckage, clambering over — or through? — the fallen timbers of the erstwhile greatroom.

A figure in black body armor, its darkness contrasting with the off-white of a badly-damaged cast on one arm, standing in the hatchway. Raising an automatic pistol, aiming it one-handed, firing at point blank range.

The mountains echoing the staccato gunfire. Mycroft's limp body falling backward into the rubble. Someone — Sasha? — shouting in protest from the cockpit. Yuri's voice making laconic reply, "Grishin gave no instructions regarding that one."

Oh, God, Mycroft! I'm sorry, so sorry.

"Is the woman secure?" Sasha's shout could barely be heard above the roar of the engine. "Arkady Grigoriyevich *did* give you instructions regarding *her*, I believe?"

Yuri scowled. "The medic sees to her now, the bitch!"

"And Dzhon?"

Yuri reached down with his good hand and rolled Knox onto his back. "Your friend has puked all over himself," he said, grinning unpleasantly. "Otherwise, he is unharmed."

"See that he remains so."

A stranger in a white coat knelt by Knox's side, rubbing at his neck with a cotton swab. The reek of alcohol, a sharp jab in the carotid, and oblivion claimed him again.

37 | Dry Run

GALINA GLANCED THROUGH the control room window at the time display suspended above the darkened observation gallery. 4:15 A.M. Up above on the surface, it was the cold, gray hour before dawn. Here in Antipode Station, in the heart of a mountain three kilometers beneath the sea, all times were the same.

She checked the confinement-field readouts for what must be the hundredth time since arriving twelve hours ago. All nominal: the forces pinning Vurdalak to the center of its spherical prison were holding, holding as they would tomorrow, and next year, and forever. Straight ahead through the gloom, she could make out the curve of the ten-meter containment sphere itself, or at least the section of it intersecting the forward wall. The section containing the Portal.

And, off to the left, filling one-third of the hall, an enormous crane-like mechanism crouched in the shadows, silent and immobile for now. But soon, very soon, its spidery robot arm would reach out bearing a gleaming message-probe, and, as it did, the Portal would crack open…

What could be keeping Sasha? He wasn't going to leave her to do this, this impossible thing all by herself, was he? He had promised.

"Galya?" Sasha's videoconference window popped open on her workstation's display.

"Sasha! Glory to God! It was growing so late. I was becoming afraid."

"No need, no need. I told you I would be back in time, yes?" Sasha smiled, but it was a tired smile, worn thin with care and exhaustion. "Now, have you reviewed the insertion procedures?"

"Yes, yes, I have been over and over the materials ever since arriving. The designs, the documentation, the simulations, I know them all by heart now. But..."

"But what, Galya?"

"But this has never been tried, none of it. There is no way to test any of it short of actually *doing* it. How can we possibly be sure it will work?"

"We have the best possible assurance: the probes themselves. Our correct choices here in the present are the enabling conditions for their return to us from the future." Sasha chuckled. "I thought you said you had read the materials."

"Read? Yes. Understood? Perhaps. Believed? Sashenka, I confess I do not know what to believe."

"Well, for instance, did you follow the part describing how we designed the insertion process? How we used the probes themselves to verify the plan for the system that would send them?"

"I think so."

"Take, for example, your calibrator headset." Once Sasha was in lecture mode, one could forget about getting a word in. "Its proper design is key to the entire program, since without it we could not aim the probes. How did we design it? Simple: we tried multiple promising alternatives. At the point where we had found the correct one, a probe returned, confirming the choice."

Galina nodded doubtfully.

"All right, then," Sasha went on. "The procedure is the same at every branch-point: we make a commitment to ourselves that 'if such-and-such is the correct way to proceed, then I will send a probe back to, say, tomorrow confirming that fact.' If the choice is not correct, the plan as a whole will fail, and no confirming probe will or can be sent back.

Only correct decisions create the necessary preconditions for a future with probes in it—that is, the necessary preconditions for confirming the decision itself."

"So," she said slowly, "the probe will not come until the plan is correct. Because, until the plan is correct, the future from which the probe comes does not exist."

"Bravo! You have it exactly. Except, of course, that, as of today, that future is the future no longer—it is here and now!"

Galina's head was spinning. Sasha's "explanation" seemed no explanation at all, smacking more of black magic than of science. There had to be some fundamental flaw in the logic.

"But does this not mean that we would possess more information than we have expended effort to gather? And does this not, in turn, violate the Second Law of Thermodynamics, or perhaps even Conservation of Energy?"

"It only seems that way. Entropy, after all, is not a principle, merely a statistical phenomenon—a general tendency toward increasing disorder, and one, moreover, that admits of localized exceptions. As for Energy Conservation, it is well known that this may be violated on quantum scales: energy and time are as complementary as position and momentum. Think of what we undertake here as the intrusion into the macrocosm of a microcosmic uncertainty. Just as your headset itself is a marvelous example of a scaled-up quantum effect."

"The headset, ah, yes! Is it not time to use it, to launch the first timeprobe?" Anything to stop *thinking* about this.

Sasha stopped talking so suddenly that for a moment she thought his end of the videoconference had crashed and left her staring at a freeze-frame.

He blinked. "The probe. Yes, of course, you are right. I will talk you through the first two or three insertions. Thereafter you must manage by yourself, as I will be en route to Antipode for the omega sequence."

"Understood." It felt as if a cold, indigestible lump had congealed in her stomach.

Sasha's eyes shifted to one side for a moment, as though checking something on an out-of-frame display. "Very well then, if you are ready, let us begin." He was typing as he spoke. "Enter the combination now appearing on your screen into the keypad of the lockbox."

"Lockbox? Ah, yes!" She had been wondering about the buffed steel panel set into the surface of her control console. As she tapped in the last digit, that panel slid back to reveal a rack holding eighteen stubby metallic cylinders, each with a date stamped on its top.

"Select the earliest probe—the one dated 05/III/92—and have one of the techs load it into the launcher. Advisse me when this has been done."

At the press of a call-button, a tech came over and picked up the cylinder. He walked back to the launcher. She couldn't help noticing how cautious he became where his path skirted the red line marking off the higher-gravity zones.

Galina watched as he laid the probe gently in the open launch-chamber and locked it down, then gave her a thumbs-up.

"Done," she reported.

"Next, put on the calibrator and activate the MRI."

She lifted the strange-looking headpiece off its stand. It was cool to the touch, of beige plastic molded into an outsized skullcap. Its padded interior fit snugly onto the back of her head, with only a braid of cabling hanging down behind. She reached up gingerly and depressed the button located at the front of the device, imagining she could feel the flux as the magnetic resonance imager began scanning her visual cortex.

"Done," she said. Her heart had begun to pound. Frightened as she'd been on the night they'd captured Vurdalak, it was as nothing to this sudden dread in the face of the unknown, the unknowable. In a few moments more, the worldline calibrator would begin capturing what her eyes witnessed, as the Portal opened and revealed…what?

"We are almost there now, Galya," Sasha said. "The launch computer will take over as soon as you have fired the Casimir capacitor."

The Casimir capacitor was a small device made up of two concentric superconducting spheres nested excruciatingly close together. Like all capacitors, it was made to store energy, but that's where the resemblance ended. The Casimir capacitor stored *negative* energy. To do so, it employed a quantum effect discovered in 1948 by the Dutch physicist H. B. G. Casimir. Galina wasn't too clear on the details. Something about suppressing some of the electromagnetic vacuum fluctuations in the gap between the spheres. But the end-result was straightforward enough: inject a jolt of negative energy into a charged black hole already rotating at nearly the speed of light, and its event horizon would be annihilated.

What would happen then, no one, perhaps not even God himself, knew.

"Galya? Can you hear me? You must fire the capacitor now."

Galina took a deep breath and spoke the command. From the apex of the containment sphere, an injector tube took aim and spat the capacitor directly downward, into the black hole. The reduction in mass was miniscule, but Vurdalak was already poised on the knife-edge of extremality. Its whirling horizon blurred, melted. Then it was gone.

To Galina's right, the workstation beeped a brief alarm, then recovered and set to work modeling a wholly new, hopefully still stable field configuration.

The subliminal hum of the generators changed pitch. With its event horizon gone, Vurdalak had stopped emitting radiation. Now only an accretion disk was left to generate power, at an ever-diminishing rate.

A countdown was added to the overhead time display: fifteen minutes until the cryostats red-lined and Vurdalak fell. Galina must complete the launch before then, and still have time to inject a Casimir "rectifier" that would close the event horizon and restore full power again.

"Singularity exposed," the launch-control computer said. "All readings nominal. Commencing worldline calibration."

Sasha's voice, sounding only marginally more human, spoke in her ear, "Now, Galya, you must concentrate."

Her eyes widened in awe as, directly before her, a strange light began to spill from the gradually widening Portal.

38 | Welcome Back

AGAIN, THAT STINGING in his neck. Knox swallowed, tasting the sourness of stale vomit in the back of his throat. He pried open eyes still smarting from the tear-gas's aftereffects and looked around. Same white-coated stranger, same hypodermic maybe. Everything else was different. He was lying on a bed, a familiar bed with a matte-gold coverlet. The clock on the wall read 4:45 — he'd lost four and a half hours somewhere.

No, wait. That was a twenty-four hour display — 4:45 meant quarter of five in the morning. And, sure enough, the rounded window in the far wall gave out on blackness just beginning to pale with false dawn.

The *rounded* window? Realization hit him an instant before he felt the residual pitch and roll beneath him. He was back on *Rusalka*!

But why? Why not just shoot him where he stood — where he lay, rather — like poor Mycroft?

Mycroft! It was all coming back. Didn't want it to. Not right now. Thank God, Marianna was okay. Last he'd seen, anyway. No, don't go there either. Think about something else.

The hand shaking his shoulder saved him the trouble. The medic, if that's what he was, was saying something in Russian. "*Gospodin* Knox, please, we must hurry. Are you able to sit up?"

With the medic supporting him, Knox tried to rise, and was immediately rewarded with a vision of encroaching darkness and the onset of a splitting headache. His stomach, which had been clamoring for attention for some time, now seemed on the verge of open revolt.

He fell back on the bed, panting and shivering. "Go 'way."

Through slitted eyes, Knox watched the medic hold a whispered consultation with someone standing at the door. Two blurry presences entered the room and approached the bed.

"Dzhon," said a familiar voice, "it is good to see you still alive. I cannot tell you how good."

"Wish I could say the same, Sasha."

"Enough of this!" Yuri shouldered Sasha aside, glowered down at Knox. "Stand!"

Head reeling, Knox did his best to comply. After two abortive attempts, he was more or less upright, hanging onto the night table for dear life, gasping for breath, his heartbeat thundering in his ears. The medic helped matters no end by shining a blinding light in his eyes.

"Listen, Dzhon," Sasha said, "we get you cleaned up now. But we must hurry." He glanced at his wristtop. "We have not much time."

Sasha's voice seemed to be coming from the bottom of a rain barrel. That couldn't be right, could it? Knox raised his head and squinted. Sure enough, Sasha's face was framed in a swirling tunnel of fuzzy black nothingness, was receding even as he watched into a pinpoint of light, like the image on a monitor after the power's been cut.

"Devil take it! Get up!" The Georgian-accented bellow brought the world back, in patches anyway. Knox tried again to bestir himself. Time to be up and about...though actually it was kind of restful just lying there with Yuri kicking him in the ribs.

✳

The world snapped back into focus once again, along with his headache. Arms draped around the shoulders of his two boon companions Sasha and Yuri, Knox was being half frogmarched, half carried down the exterior companionway to lab deck. The fresh breeze wafting into the open stairwell was doing more to revive him than the antidote had. The golden light from the sliver of sun just peeking over the horizon was helping too. The start of yet another beautiful day aboard *Rusalka*.

Not that he'd be spending much of it outdoors. Their trail led into the interior, along the familiar passageway to *Rusalka*'s "public" lab.

Where there had been some changes made. The firewalls were gone, and with them the jellyfish camouflage that had kept the secret lab secret. The partitioned compartment had become a single open space centered on the banks of workstations monitoring Antipode. They'd needed the room: the facility was now cluttered with equipment and jammed full of people. And, over in a corner, there was one person in particular…

Looking somewhat the worse for wear: bruised, smudged, thoroughly disarrayed, wearing makeshift manacles of adhesive mesh, and sporting more of the sticky stuff—emblematic of the ferocity of her resistance—in the most unlikely places. And, despite it all, utterly beautiful in his eyes. Marianna stood flanked by a brace of security guards, one of whom was holding a gun on her while the other wielded a sponge and a small bottle of solvent in an effort to scour residual patches of webbing from her arms.

Knox's escort hustled him past newly-installed workstations and around rat's nests of exposed cabling. Given they were headed for Marianna, he did his best to help out. He was surprised to find that his legs, though still wobbly, would now support his weight. Even so, he felt in far worse shape than she looked; they must have revived her first for whatever reason.

That she was fully recovered from the knock-out shot there could be no doubt: Marianna was glaring fiercely around the room, ready to take on Grishin's minions one at a time or all together, looking for something to kill. The intensity of her gaze softened several orders of candlepower when she saw Knox.

"Jon! Thank God! I got worried when they didn't bring you down. It's seemed like hours."

He was close enough to touch her, if only Yuri weren't keeping him on so short a leash.

"My friends here insisted I get properly attired first." Knox was wearing shirt and slacks on loan from Sasha. "I see *your* handlers didn't enforce the same dress-code."

Marianna was in the same sleeveless blouse and black jeans she'd been wearing at Weathertop. The only new additions to her wardrobe were the strips of sticky-web fastened tightly around her wrists.

"Oh, they tried," she told him. Then she turned to the guard doing the scrubbing. "Didn't you, you—you *svoloch'! Yob tvoyu mat'!*"

Hunh! CROM's survival-Russian instructors must have a whole different take on core vocabulary. Strictly speaking, though, the act Marianna claimed to have performed on the guard's mother wasn't anatomically feasible. The guard got the message regardless. Abandoning his clean-up-Marianna campaign, he set sponge and solvent on a nearby table and sucker-punched her in the kidney.

Knox strained against Yuri's grip. No luck. He could only watch as Marianna doubled over from the surprise blow. She gripped the edge of the table for support and came back swinging. If she was hampered at all by the fact that her wrists were glued together, you couldn't tell it from the pounding she began giving her luckless assailant.

Knox's view of the fracas was cut off abruptly. Yuri's injured arm, cast and all, had wrapped itself around his neck in a grip so tight it forced his head back. He struggled to draw breath through his constricted windpipe, then froze as he felt the cool kiss of a gun muzzle against his temple.

"Stop. Now." Yuri's voice was conversational in tone. Marianna knew enough Russian to understand—or maybe not: what counted was that she looked in his direction. *Then* she stopped. With Yuri, actions spoke louder than words, especially since his next action might be to pull the trigger.

Once he was sure the dust had settled, Yuri released Knox to rub his bruised larynx and think dark thoughts.

His client, his woman, his lover, on so many levels he ought to be doing something to help her. Instead he was being used against her—a hostage to her good behavior. That must be all they thought he was good for. They hadn't even bothered reviving him until they'd found out what a handful she was.

Hunched over, still wheezing, it hit him with the force of a revelation: he was tired of it. Sick and tired of being a pawn in somebody else's game.

For most of his professional life, Jonathan Knox had worked at solving other people's problems. In all that time, he'd never lost sight of the essential distinction between the client's best interests and his own. On balance, that was a good thing. A modicum of distance, of professional detachment, was key to maintaining his objectivity, to offering the best advice he could no matter the consequences.

Where was that distance now? It had gotten lost somewhere, squeezed down and collapsed into nothingness by Mycroft's death, by his...his relationship with Marianna, by the sheer, globally catastrophic price of failure. Detachment be damned.

Knox straightened up slowly. Even a pawn had the power to change his lot in life, his status in the game—if only he could go the distance, make it into the last row.

One way or another, Knox vowed, he was going to make it into the last row on the chessboard and promote himself—from incidental nuisance to Arkady Grishin's worst nightmare.

39 | Descent

Knox worked his way down the stairs. Carefully, so as not to trip and stumble into Yuri again and earn himself another fist to the gut. It wasn't all that easy to negotiate a spiral staircase wearing handcuffs, but GEI Security had insisted no outsider be admitted into the presence of the "Comrade Director," save under restraint.

Nearly there now, just a few more steps. What had Marianna said was down here? A bathyscaphe? He stepped off the last riser onto the deck and looked up. And up.

The mother of all bathyscaphes!

Every time Knox thought he finally had a handle on how *big* *Rusalka* was, she'd throw him a curve like this. Floating in a moon pool, the bright yellow submersible took up less than a third of the vast hold, yet seen from the foot of the stair she loomed out of the floodlit darkness like a zeppelin. Cyrillic script emblazoned across the bow proclaimed her the good ship *Navtilus*. The Russians always had been big Jules Verne fans.

No time to see the sights. Yuri was already marching him up the gangplank toward *Navtilus*'s airlock. Knox paused in the entrance to look around, seeing nothing that would've been out of place in the cabin of a corporate jet—outsized desk-cum-console with a fifty-inch flatscreen on the wall behind it, several rows of armchairs maglocked to the floor plates, a mini-galley off to one side. No door through to a cockpit, though; the 'scaphe was piloted via sonar displays, so the navigational station could be set far to the rear, reserving the view out the forward ports for the paying customers.

Knox's survey of his new surroundings was forcibly interrupted as Yuri tired of waiting on the ramp and hustled him into the cabin.

Marianna entered behind them, still glaring defiance at her minders, still worrying away at her bonds. Why, Knox wondered, would Grishin leave her wearing the same sticky-mesh they'd been captured in at Weathertop? Why not steel shackles like his? Not that the webbing wasn't up to the job. Pliant enough to permit some freedom of movement, the adhesive manacles were resisting her every effort to twist or tear loose.

Captors and captives were still settling in when more footsteps sounded on the gangplank. Knox craned around curiously. One by one, seven refugees from the geriatrics ward filed through the airlock and took seats to the left of the big desk. All in their late sixties to mid seventies, all looking like well-cared-for wax effigies of themselves. Even their eyes looked dead. Knox hadn't seen so many bleak, wintry faces all in a row since Boris Yeltsin had made the old Politburo stop holding its annual November get-togethers atop Lenin's Mausoleum. Come to think, one or two of them looked vaguely familiar...

Finally Arkady Grigoriyevich deigned to grace *Navtilus* with his presence. He strode through the hatch, issuing instructions to a hastily-scribing Sasha. Grishin was in a good mood, to judge by the way he gladhanded the seven gaffers on the way over to the big desk. Once there, he rubbed his hands briskly and bestowed a winning smile on one and all. Motioning Sasha to a chair at his right hand, Grishin took his own seat and gave a nod.

The pilot moved to the navigation console and busied himself with pre-launch checks. A uniformed crewmember swung the hatch to and initiated its locking sequence. Outside, his compatriots could be heard retracting the gangplank.

Forty-five seconds went by before the pilot spoke the launch command into his console mike. Nothing happened for a moment, then a low rumble, more feeling than sound, vibrated through the cabin. The scene out the viewport grew brighter as green-gold light began to filter up through the moon pool. *Rusalka*'s underwater hatch yawned wide to release *Navtilus* into the open sea.

The submersible dropped like a stone. Knox watched the sunlit water swirl past the portholes. That sparkling green was already faintly tinged with blue. Soon it would turn to black.

Navtilus was on her way to the depths.

✶

The USN *Piccard* fell through the empty dark. The view out her forward port showed only the milky cones cast by her exterior spots and, occasionally, a blurred vertical streak of light that meant they'd just plummeted past another drifting bioluminescent lifeform.

It wasn't much brighter inside, where *Piccard*'s crew compartment was lit all in red. The effect was like riding to the bottom of the sea in a photographer's darkroom.

A crowded photographer's darkroom. Euripedes Aristos found himself crammed together with ten fully armed and armored Ops Team six-footers, not to mention one civilian. All of them in a space designed to seat seven, uncomfortably.

Pete Aristos was not a nervous man. Still, these accommodations were enough to give a sardine claustrophobia. The creaking of the pressure hull's ceramic-metal composite wasn't helping either. Add to that the fact that he was sitting on top of a low-yield nuclear device and, well, anybody could get a little edgy.

Anybody but *Piccard*'s civilian passenger, that is. He looked sound asleep, dead to the world and good to stay that way the whole trip. Pete would've given anything to kick back and catch some z's like *that* guy. Burdens of command.

Speaking of which. "Sir? Mr. Aristos?" What with the whir of the engines, the bleeps of the acoustic tracking pulses, and the background hum of the CO_2 scrubbers, the pilot's soft drawl was barely audible.

Still, Pete thought he made out the words, "Could you step forward a minute?"

By the time he'd reached the pilot's station, he was hoping he'd heard right. The cramped quarters had made stepping forward a semi-major operation.

"What've you got, Harry?" Pete hunched down and looked over the pilot's shoulder.

Lieutenant JG Cindy Lee Harris, "Harry" to her friends, turned her round, freckled face toward him. "Not out there, sir—here, on the scope." She tapped a green-lit screen to her left.

They were not alone in their hurtling dive toward the mysterious installation called Antipode. Sonar had picked up another vessel. Still maybe five hundred meters above *Piccard*, but descending fast.

"Casualty?" Tsunami wasn't scheduled to kick off for a couple hours yet, but some sonofabitch might have jumped the gun and got sunk for his trouble.

"Huh? Oh, no, sir. She's in a controlled dive, just like us."

"Jesus! Kind of big for a 'scaphe, isn't she?"

"Sir, yes, sir. A Cadillac to our Volkswagen."

"Shit!" Their best intel was that Antipode was unoccupied. That had made things real simple. But if there was a submersible heading for it, well, it might not stay unoccupied for long. Which could change things.

"Harry, how maneuverable is this tin can of yours? Can you hold us in place a couple minutes?"

"Let her catch up with us? Yessir. Sucks juice like Times Square at New Year's, though."

Normally, *Piccard* just filled her negative-buoyancy tanks with enough seawater to fall to her target depth. Stopping anywhere short of that took extra power. Power they'd be needing for, among other things, life support.

"I hear you. Do it anyway. And, Harry?"

"Yessir?"

"Rig for silent running and plot me an intercept course. Let's go have a look at that Caddy of yours."

*

Grishin sat gazing out the bathyscaphe's forward port into the silence of the deep ocean, and silently gathered his thoughts. There had been so many obstacles blocking his path, so many adversaries ringed around him, and yet he had overcome them all. Nothing could stop the Antipode Project now.

A small smile played over his features; he clapped his hands once and swiveled to face his fellow Council members. Time to begin.

"Comrades, permit me to welcome you aboard *Navtilus*. The pilot informs me that we have now reached our terminal free-fall velocity of thirty meters a minute. And since our destination is some three kilometers down…"

A groan of tortured metal issued from *Navtilus's* walls. Several members of the Council looked about them nervously.

"Pay that no mind," Grishin said with studied nonchalance. "A certain amount of structural stress is the price we pay for maintaining a sea-level cabin pressure. But it is no cause for alarm. Three kilometers is nothing to *Navtilus;* she is rated for four times that depth. Now, as I was saying, between our rate of descent and the distance to be traversed, we have another hour and a half before we arrive at Antipode Station. At the same time, circumstances have compelled us to curtail our original agenda somewhat, so… Yes, you have a question, Pyotr Fillipovich?"

The sharp-featured little man with the intent, glittering eyes lowered his hand and said "As to these 'circumstances,' Comrade Director—I am sure I speak for the Council as a whole when I insist on knowing their nature and origin. We had been told we would have the entire morning to review and approve your final report on the Antipode Project. Yet no sooner did we arrive on *Rusalka* than we were escorted to this vehicle and launched on our voyage."

"Yes, yes, I was on the point of explaining this."

"Permit me to finish, Comrade. This was not the only curious circumstance. As the helicopter was ferrying us in from Horta, we overflew an aircraft carrier group steaming in the direction of *Rusalka* under blackout conditions. I demand to know what is going on!"

"There is no cause for alarm, Pyotr Fillipovich. If you had troubled to read your Project briefing book, you would have noted that the probability of American detection of, and response to, the capture event has been assessed at greater than seventy percent. Accordingly, this contingency has been planned for. It is, in fact, the reason for the presence onboard *Navtilus* of our guests."

At a nod from Grishin, Yuri prodded the spies to a standing position.

"Members of the Council for National Resurrection," Grishin said with a small flourish, "Permit me to introduce Ms. Marianna Bonaventure and Mr. Dzhonathan Knox, representatives of the American Critical Resources Oversight Mandate."

Karpinskii shot to his feet. "Have you gone mad, Grishin, to bring two CROM agents aboard? Comrade Council Members, I appeal to you—"

"Sit *down!*" Grishin said. "I warn you, Karpinskii: another such outburst will not be tolerated." He leveled a finger at his opponent as if aiming a pistol.

The little man took his seat again, slowly, his features contorted with now-silent rage.

"To resume then. It is precisely because Ms. Bonaventure and Mr. Knox represent the adversary that they are being brought along. They are here in the capacity of an insurance policy, to attest to the innocuousness of our intentions—and the credibility of our threat—should need arise."

As if on cue, *Navtilus*'s hull rang with the echo of a single active-sonar ping. The passengers had only an instant to look around in bewilderment. Then a videoconferencing window popped open on the flatscreen display behind Grishin's desk. The image that formed in it left much to be desired: low-rez, black and white, five-frame-a-second refresh rate, tops. Still it was the best that very-low-bitrate underwater video transmission had to offer, and it was enough to depict recognizably the face of a nearly bald, scowling man.

"Attention, unidentified craft," the man said in English. "Drop ballast and surface immediately. Or the next sound you hear will be a torpedo in the water."

✳

Marianna barely had time to see Grishin gesture over her shoulder, to Yuri. Then she was being jerked forward, into the line of sight of *Navtilus*'s own VLB videocam. She recovered her balance — less easy than it looked with her hands tied — then raised her head and looked at the man in the conferencing window.

"Hi, Pete," was all she could think to say.

"Marianna? What the f-—what are you doing there?"

"If you will permit me, Ms. Bonaventure," Grishin cut in, in passable English, "Mr. . . . Aristos, is it not? My name is Grishin, Arkady Grigoriyevich Grishin. I am responsible for the presence of your associate and Mr. Knox aboard *Navtilus*. I ordered it done against the chance that CROM might put in an appearance. And here you are."

"Here we are," Pete echoed. "And if you think for one damn minute I'm going to hold fire just because you've got a gun to Bonaventure's head—"

"Please, Mr. Aristos." Grishin held up a hand. "Nothing of the sort is intended, I assure you. Your colleagues are here as witnesses, not hostages."

"Witnesses? To what?"

"Why, to the undesirable — extremely undesirable, I might say — consequences of any attempt to interfere with my plans. I intend to show Mr. Knox and Ms. Bonaventure what we have been laboring on these past twelve years and let them judge for themselves."

Pete just said, "Huh?"

"Think of it as one of CROM's famous on-site inspections, if you like," Grishin said smugly. "Your representatives can serve as your eyes and ears within Antipode Station. I am confident that, once you hear what they have to say, you will see the wisdom of pursuing a strict non-interference policy as far as Grishin Enterprises is concerned. Pending their report, I would appreciate it if you would have your surface forces hold at their current ten-mile perimeter, and if you yourself would withdraw your little submersible an equivalent distance from Antipode."

"Marianna?" Pete said. "Help me out here. What's this guy talking about?"

Would the fact that Grishin had gone to the trouble of kidnapping them make the story any more plausible than last time? "Pete," she began, "it's complicated."

"Skip the complications. What the fuck is he up to?"

"At last," came a voice from behind her, "I was beginning to think nobody would ever ask."

Marianna spun around. She had nearly forgotten who was still standing back there all by himself.

"It's simple, really," Jon said. "Arkady Grigoriyevich here is going to undo the assassination of Yuri Andropov in 1984. And resurrect the Soviet Union."

40 | Project Report

Yes, Jonathan Knox had worked it out, all right. What would the shadow KGB do with a time machine? The key lay buried in a rumor about murder and mayhem at a very exclusive Moscow hospital two decades ago, a rumor Knox had first heard from a Russian gypsy cab driver.

Despite its lowly origins, the insight was having a gratifyingly major effect. The scene in *Navtilus*'s passenger cabin took on the aspect of a single moment frozen in time. No one moved, no one spoke. Still-life with mouths agape.

Then everybody began shouting at once.

Pete bellowed, "What the fuck is that supposed to mean?"

He was all but drowned out by Grishin. "This is an *internal* matter, of interest solely to the peoples of the Russian Republic, and of no concern to the international community what-so-*ever!*"

That foxy-faced midget who'd locked horns with Grishin earlier on—Karpinskii or something—was back on his feet, spewing out recriminations. The rest of the Comrade Director's kangaroo Council contented themselves with muttering incoherently, like an aphasic Greek Chorus.

Knox paid no heed to the hubbub he'd raised; time enough for that in a bit. For the moment he just basked in the warmth of Marianna's astonished smile.

"*Silence!*" Grishin fairly shrieked. He whirled to face Aristos in his videoconf window.

"This. Changes. *Nothing!* Your sole duty here, Mr. Aristos, is to verify the terrible power that my associates and I now wield. To that end, you will receive Ms. Bonaventure's report no later than one hour after our arrival. I recommend you consider it carefully. Until then, I insist that you hold at your ten-mile perimeter, and—to use an Americanism—that you *get out of my face!*"

✳

Speaking of faces, Marianna wished she had an eight-by-ten glossy of the look on Grishin's when Jon had pulled that latest rabbit out of his hat. You just had to love the guy.

Pete was talking to her. "Marianna?"

"Um, sorry, Pete." She turned back to her boss's grainy image.

"Listen, I've got to make a judgment call here. You're the AIC of record. Like it or not, I've got to factor in your input."

She looked over to where Grishin and his minions were staring at her, waiting. Was she really supposed to discuss the disposition of a case in the presence of the perpetrator? Didn't seem like she had a whole lot of choice.

"Okay, sure. Just bear in mind we've got an audience."

"Makes no never-mind. I've only got the one question."

"Go ahead."

"Is this stuff for real?"

"Real as it gets, I guess. It's what I was trying to tell you yesterday." Seeing his frown she hastily added, "Look, Pete, it'll only cost you an extra hour to find out for sure. There's no way Grishin can get out from under the hammer in that amount of time. It's not a whole lot to ask, if you think about the downside."

She held her breath. Pete hadn't wanted to think about the down-side before. And who could blame him? End of the freaking *world?*

Please, let him think about it now.

The silence stretched on. Marianna looked away from the flatscreen display, looked out one of the forward viewports. There was nothing to be seen, though. The two vessels hung suspended in deepest indigo, bordering on utter black. Falling together through limbo.

"Okay," Pete said finally.

His gaze shifted then, and locked on Grishin. "You've got your hour. The clock starts ticking soon as you dock. And one more thing…"

"Yes, Mr. Aristos?"

"When this is all over, I get my people back, good as new. You fuck with them, I will personally carve you a new asshole. That understood?"

"I believe we understand one another perfectly."

Pete cut the transmission without another word.

✳

That went about as well as might be expected, Grishin thought to himself.

"Well, Comrades," he said aloud, reseating himself behind the big desk, "we have the better part of an hour remaining before our arrival at Antipode. And, as Pyotr Fillipovich reminded us earlier, our departure from *Rusalka* was too, ah, hectic to allow for the Council's scheduled consideration of our final Project report. I move we take up this agenda item now."

"You cannot be serious, Grishin!" Karpinskii had remained standing. "Surely you do not propose to discuss affairs of such sensitivity in *their* presence?" He waved a hand at the two Americans.

"Permit me to point out, Pyotr Fillipovich," Grishin said, "that Mr. Knox has just now demonstrated he knows most of these affairs already." Which reminded him. "Mr. Knox? I confess to being curious myself as to how you learned of our ultimate intentions."

"Not as curious as I am about how you've been tracking us ever since we left *Rusalka.*"

"Ah, as to that, once Yuri had alerted me to the likelihood of CROM's involvement, we employed—or, more properly, will have employed—some rather extraordinary means at our disposal to establish your whereabouts. Now, as to how you penetrated our security..."

"I'd say 'extraordinary means' about covers that one, too."

The woman smiled at this last remark.

"No matter." Grishin dropped the subject and turned to face the Council again. "As regards Pyotr Fillipovich's objection, the terms of our, ah, arrangement with Mr. Aristos dictate that we conceal nothing. The plain and simple truth is our best ally."

He could hardly believe he'd said that. He had detested Gorbachev's disastrous policy of *glasnost,* of openness, and history had borne him out. Yet Sasha had been right about the effect of a full disclosure regarding Vurdalak. Very well, then, for as long as it served his purposes, he would play at being this curious creature, this new, open Arkady Grishin.

"And in that spirit," —he turned to the Americans— "it is time I properly introduced myself." He couldn't very well bow sitting down, but he straightened in his chair and inclined his head, "Mstislav Platonovich Gromov, Colonel KGB, at your service."

The woman, Bonaventure, knit her brows in concentration. Then she gasped. "Of course! You were Shebarshin's protégé; he made you deputy director of Foreign Intelligence when he moved into the top slot in 1988. No wonder we couldn't match you back to the old KGB—that's one amazing job of plastic surgery."

"Thank you. I am quite pleased with it myself." Grishin stroked his cheeks and chin. "Some of my colleagues here did not fare nearly so well under the knife, in my opinion."

Bonaventure's eyes grew wide. "Wait a minute. You're dead. Shot during the '91 coup."

"Not quite dead, though I still carry a fragment of that bullet lodged in my skull. The surgery in question was reconstructive in intent. But it seemed a shame to waste the opportunity to, ah, put a new face on things, so to speak."

"Mstislav Platonovich, huh?" Knox said. "Listen, I'm just going to stick with 'Arkady Grigoriyevich,' if you don't mind. One first-name-plus-patronymic per person is about my limit."

"As you wish, Mr. Knox," Grishin nodded agreeably. Truth be told, he'd grown used to the pseudonym himself, to living within the legend, like any good undercover operative. "And, while we are all being so convivial, we may as well see to your comfort. I think you'll find these chairs will afford you a better view. Yuri?"

His face an expressionless mask, the Georgian installed first the man, then the woman, in two of the armchairs adjoining Grishin's desk.

Grishin glanced down and frowned. "Yuri, please be so kind as to remove Mr. Knox's handcuffs." Turning to the woman, he said, "I regret, Ms. Bonaventure, that you are a bit too, ah, formidable to extend you a similar courtesy."

He smiled at her apologetically. She grimaced in return.

"However," he went on, "I can offer you one small amenity, in view of the fact that our discussion will be in Russian. Sasha, would you mind serving as interpreter for Ms. Bonaventure?"

Grishin waited while Sasha changed places. Then he placed his hands together, in an attitude resembling prayer, and said, "Let us begin."

✳

Knox watched the wall-mounted display behind Grishin's desk come to life. A single image filled the fifty-inch screen: the wizened corpse of an elderly man lying in state, coffin all trimmed in red, an enormous hammer and sickle as a backdrop, honor guard to left and right.

"We start," Grishin said, "by returning to that pivotal moment in Soviet history which Mr. Knox alluded to earlier. To February 9th, 1984, the sad day when Soviet Premier and former Chairman of the Committee on State Security, our Yuri Vladimirovich Andropov, died. Of renal collapse, according to our official pronouncements. Though, as always in such cases, it proved impossible to prevent rumors from circulating."

Knox nodded. "I remember those rumors. They must have peaked just around the time I got to Moscow. I was barely off the plane before I started hearing all about how Andropov had been murdered." Those same half-remembered rumors had helped weave the pattern he'd first glimpsed back at Weathertop.

"A lot of it was just plain weird, though," Knox went on. "Death by knitting needle or some such. Heard that one from the cab driver on the way in from Sheremetevo airport. And that wasn't even the strangest part."

It was Grishin's turn to nod. "The self-immolating assassin."

"I guess you must have taken that same cab ride sometime."

A melancholy smile flitted across Grishin's face. "No, Mr. Knox. I did not need to hear this tale second hand. I was there."

The display now held an image of a lavish hospital suite with a clunky-looking dialysis unit against one wall and a still figure, recognizably the man from the funeral scene, lying on a cot. A banner at the bottom of the frame proclaimed Совершенно Секретно—Top Secret—all in red.

Grishin leaned back in his chair and contemplated the image in silence. The Council seemed equally rapt. The only sound in the cabin was the occasional groan of metal as *Navtilus* shouldered the Atlantic's ever-increasing weight.

When Grishin resumed speaking, addressing the Council now, his voice was slow and solemn. "I stood in Yuri Vladimirovich's hospital room that dreary February morning. Saw with my own eyes what Mr. Knox has called a 'knitting needle.' Stood at the foot of Yuri Vladimirovich's deathbed and beheld the smoldering corpse of his murderer there on the floor beside him." The camera now panned down alongside the bed to reveal...

"I say 'corpse,'" Grishin's voice dropped to a whisper, "but in truth what remained of the assassin's body bore no resemblance to a human being, living *or* dead. It was merely a single long, fine strand of protoplasm, burnt to a crisp. It took an electron microscope to confirm its human origin. To the unaided eye, it looked more like a heap of charred spaghetti, of the very thinnest kind."

"A self-destruct that turns a person into angel hair pasta?" Knox said. This was *grotesque!* But then, he'd expected no less of Arkady Grigoriyevich. "How?"

"Ah, if we only knew that, Mr. Knox." Grishin sighed and shook his head. "I will not deny it: long after we had abandoned the goal of unmasking the assassin's co-conspirators, we continued our investigation solely in hope of recovering that miraculous device. Then, as now, we could have put it to good use."

I'll bet! Knox could picture KGB hit squads roving the back streets of the world's capitals, transforming enemies of the people into *primo piatto* at a blast from Grishin's magic vermicelli gun.

But Grishin was rattling on. "Rivals in the apparatus," — here he paused to look meaningfully at the little guy he'd called Karpinskii — "had engineered my appointment as chief investigator, trusting I would fail. In that they were not disappointed, not for the longest time.

"It seemed hopeless, after all. KGB Ninth Directorate had followed prophylaxis SOPs to the letter: no human soul could have entered that facility undetected. And, press them as we might, none of the guards would confess to having seen a thing. All we had to go on was the murder weapon itself — this."

He punched a combination into a keypad and pulled open a drawer. He reached in and withdrew a long, twisted metallic shape, set it down carefully on the surface of the desk.

"This is the actual implement that pierced our Yuri Vladimirovich's heart that winter day in 1984. On it are inscribed what appeared to be words. Don't trouble to strain your eyes, Comrades, the writing is warped beyond all recognition. As if this object had been through the fires of hell." Grishin quivered minutely, momentarily caught in the grip of some disquieting inner vision. "Only much later would we come to realize how close that metaphor was to the literal truth.

"Even so, with the aid of ultraviolet illumination, x-ray microscopy, various other techniques..." A dismissive shrug; Grishin was not a technology guy. "Suffice it to say we managed to decipher the inscription. It read: *Tunguska Cosmologist VII-1989 Support.*"

Grishin held up his right hand, four fingers raised. "Four words. Only four. Rather cryptic for a claim of responsibility, if that was the intent. Doubtless there had been no room for more on the object's surface. Still, four clues.

"Tunguska?" Grishin ticked off the first of the four fingers. A tired smile tugged the corner of his mouth. "We knew where that was well enough. We instituted the appropriate inquiries in that hell-hole, searching for any trace of an aboriginal nationalist movement with the wherewithal to have perpetrated this outrage. We found nothing—nothing smelling of an assassination plot against the premier, in any case."

Counting off the second finger now. "That left 'Cosmologist' as the only other substantive clue. Over the next eighteen months, until that ingrate Gorbachev shut down the investigation, we interviewed any number of researchers, eventually getting around to our young friend Sasha here.

"You know, Comrades," Grishin mused, "in some ways that aspect of the investigation was even more bizarre than tracking down leads through the wastes of Siberia had been. Quasars, Big Bangs, heat-death of the universe..." That slight quiver again. "But in any case, it, too, only led to a dead end.

"As to 'Support'—not to mention VII-1989, which we took to be a calendar notation—well, where could we turn?" Grishin appealed to his audience. "'Support' for what? And when? In July of '89? A date five years in the future? It plagued me, this four-part riddle. My, shall we say, precarious situation in the wake of the debacle forced my attention away, onto more pressing concerns. Nonetheless, I never forgot the mystery of those four words.

"So, you can imagine my surprise when, in mid-summer of 1989, who should turn up again but our young astrophysicist." Grishin gave a nod in Sasha's direction. "Best of all, *he* came to *us*. Arrived on our doorstep, so to speak, petitioning for access to the secret archives of Kulik's second Tunguska expedition.

"Our interviews with Sasha during the assassination inquiry must have started something stirring in him. He had already been working on black hole formation in the very early universe, you see." Grishin smiled indulgently, as if no more ridiculous waste of time could possibly be imagined. "And, with the clue of the inscription to go on, had become increasingly convinced of something called the Dzhakson-Ryan hypothesis."

"Jackson-Ryan, sure." Knox was getting tired of listening. "But with the added twist that the thing's still down there."

"Precisely." Grishin didn't bat an eye at Knox's recognition of the two astrophysicists' names. "Sasha thought he saw a way to investigate one of his precious primordial objects at first hand. But he needed our authorization to view Kulik's sequestered archives."

Grishin chuckled. "Suddenly, after a lapse of five years, all the pieces of the puzzle had fallen into my hand: here was a *cosmologist* asking our *support* for research into *Tunguska*—all of this in *July of 1989!*"

"What did you do?" Knox asked.

"Do?" Grishin laughed outright. "What do you think I did? I had him arrested, of course."

Then he turned to Sasha and, as if to say it was all in fun, gave him a big grin.

✳

It was all Sasha could do to smile in return. The images now chasing one another across the datawall weren't making it any easier: a montage of his younger self, mere hapless junior astrophysics professor that he'd been, traversing the stations of KGB in-processing: handcuffed, strip-searched, peering out at the camera through a tiny grate in a massive ocher door…

"Regrettably," Grishin was saying, "we could turn up nothing to tie our young friend to the Andropov affair. Still, just to be on the safe side, we held onto him."

Sasha wiped suddenly sweaty palms against his trouser legs. If Grishin was aware of the effect these reminiscences were having, he gave no sign.

"Then one day," he went on, "perhaps three or four months after we had first detained him, I received word that Sasha wished to confess—but only to the officer in charge of the investigation. Nominally, that was still myself. Though I had since moved on to other responsibilities, I arranged to have him brought in on the chance that I might, after five long years, wipe the stain of that one egregious failure from my record.

"But Sasha surprised me." Grishin winked at him—winked! "He had not come to confess to anything, you see, but rather to tell me— Actually, Sasha, you tell it better than I."

Sasha swallowed the lump in his throat and dutifully picked up his cue. "Well, yes, what else had I to do for all those months, after all, but think. And my interrogators' questions told me more, I fear, than my answers told them. In my cell at night, long after lights-out, I would puzzle over what I knew of the affair: over why, in particular, an assassin would think to write an endorsement of cosmological research on his murder weapon. Until finally there came a day when I had it all worked out—"

"Most of it, anyway," Grishin reminded him. "We *still* do not know all of it."

"True. But, in any case, near enough for me to ask to talk with Arkasha again."

"To talk with me," Grishin said. "Indeed to spin out for me what was perhaps the most fantastic tale ever told in the cellars of the Lyubyanka." He gave a brief chuckle. "As you will appreciate, Comrades, that took some doing; there has been stiff competition for that particular honor, over the years."

"Fantastic? No, Arkasha," Sasha protested, "once all the facts were taken into account, it—"

"It still remained science fiction of the rankest sort," Grishin cut him off. Then he turned to address the Council once again. "Yet, Comrades, I must confess it: that curious interview remained in my mind long after I'd had Sasha thrown back in his cell. In the darkening days that followed, as the strength of will that alone had made Russia great crumbled all around us, I found my thoughts turning to it again and again. How differently things might have been made to turn out if what Sasha claimed were true…

"And then I thought: why not make him prove it?"

✳

A wry smile on his face, Knox listened to the tale of how, six months later, Grishin had had Sasha transferred to a minimum-security facility attached to Foreign Intelligence headquarters in the Yasenevo suburb of Moscow.

"Out there in 'The Woods,' as we called it," Grishin was saying, "I could keep a closer eye on our young friend. For his part, Sasha found his new situation far more conducive to research—not to mention, more congenial—than his accommodations as a mere detainee had been."

Knox shook his head in wonderment. Against all odds, Sasha had once again managed to ingratiate himself with the powers-that-be. Dale Carnegie's disciple rides again!—this time winning friends and influencing people in that selfsame state security R&D establishment made infamous by Solzhenitsyn's *First Circle*.

"Our working relationship, too," Grishin went on, "was evolving in those final months of Soviet power. From jailer and prisoner, we were becoming something more like co-workers—even colleagues, if you will."

"That's just hostage syndrome," Marianna cut in. "Long-term captivity creates a dependence on the captor that's easy to mistake for friendship, even love." She caught Grishin's mocking smile, and glared back. "Don't look for it to happen *here* anytime soon, Grishin!"

"You may call it what you will, Ms. Bonaventure. The fact remains, Sasha and I became indispensable to each other: he designing each new experiment; I overcoming all obstacles standing in its way, making it happen. And always our young friend would urge me on to yet greater efforts with the words: 'It *must* be true, Comrade Director, *for it has already happened!*'"

His voice dropped a register or two, "And Sasha was right. Thanks to him, when the end came in 1991 we had a plan in place. A plan to literally turn back the clock!"

Knox was obscurely pleased to see Grishin pull a handkerchief from his jacket pocket and mop his brow. Thank goodness *some*one else found this whole business as unsettling as he did.

"To turn back the clock," Grishin repeated. "Yes, but how far? To when? Even as we were assembling the wherewithal to realize the 'time warp' capability itself, a separate study group was already poring over the turning points of recent history, searching for a fulcrum—a single event which, had it gone another way, would yield an outcome out of all proportion to the effort required to alter it."

"The biggest bang for the buck," Knox volunteered.

Grishin ignored him. "We examined many such scenarios, weighing each carefully, since it is in the nature of the case that one only gets one chance at changing one's own past. Still, even the most drastic proposals were given their fair hearing." He stared at Karpinskii, as if challenging the little man to deny it.

"At one point, we went so far as to consider canceling out Stalin's murder of Kirov back in 1934, in hopes of averting the lamentable episode of the cult of personality altogether." Grishin sighed. "Alas, uncertainty effects are said to make the consequences of intervention more indeterminate the further back one goes. The alternative futures begin to multiply beyond the possibility of prediction or control."

That was too much for Knox. "Translation: you would have liked to undo the horrors of Stalinism, but you couldn't be sure what that drastic a change might have done to your own cushy lifestyles."

"That is the trouble with you, Mr. Knox. You cast everything in the worst possible light. Try to see things from our perspective. In retrieving the Tunguska Cosmic Object, my associates and I have saved the world itself from the ultimate catastrophe. Are we not then entitled to promote our own best interests as well—interests virtually synonymous, I remind you, with the welfare of our nation as a whole?"

"Why do I get the feeling that, for you, saving the world is just a means to an end?"

Grishin shook his head in irritation. Still, he seemed determined to finish his rambling project report. "In the end—and I will not pretend this decision was a matter of indifference to me personally—we elected to negate the assassination of the one man who, had he but lived, could have averted our national tragedy. A man who had the wisdom and the will to guide Russia through her difficult transition to a new, information-based Communist society. The man who died that February morning twenty years ago, with a fragment of the future piercing his heart: Yuri Vladimirovich Andropov."

Naturally. Who better than the patron saint of state security to ensure the KGB's continued dominance on into the Newly-revised World Order? There was a problem, though…

Knox felt compelled to talk out of turn again. "My own memories of Andropov aren't anywhere near as fond as yours, Grishin. I seem to recall that, between the two of them, he and Ronald Reagan nearly started World War III."

Andropov had only held the post of General Secretary of the Soviet Communist Party for fifteen months before death deposed him. But in his brief hour of strutting and fretting on the international stage, tensions between the superpowers had escalated to the point of spawning a whole grass-roots Nuclear Freeze movement. Those were the days when Soviet MIGs were downing Korean jetliners, when a made-for-TV movie called *The Day After* could touch off a national epidemic of weeping, wailing, and gnashing of teeth. Long-nurtured arms-control negotiations were crashing and burning right and left while facile sound-bytes like "evil empire" and "fascism, American style" winged their way back and forth between the hemispheres, catch-phrases taking the place of diplomacy — taking the place, indeed, of rational thought of any kind.

Grishin seemed to have forgotten all that. He merely smiled patiently at Knox and said, "I weary of your cynicism, my friend. You are the sort of fellow who sits on the sidelines and carps, while others must act to bring about what they believe in."

Oof, low blow! Knox was about to respond in kind when Yuri placed a heavy, admonitory hand on his shoulder. Rule Number One of debating the KGB: always let the KGB win.

"Even as we must act now," Grishin went on. "We go to set matters right at long last. We go to Antipode Station to ensure the future — our future."

He rummaged in his desk drawer. Withdrew a gleaming object, balanced it on his palm.

"Sasha tells me the simultaneous existence of these two manifestations violates the Conservation of Energy principle, or something of that nature." That offhanded shrug again.

Knox felt chill: ripping holes in the fabric of spacetime was all in a day's work for the new, improved KGB.

Grishin looked up. "First, we shall expunge from history the senseless atrocity that put an end to the life of our Yuri Vladimirovich on the morning of February 9th 1984. And, then, having done so, we will lock in the new timeline — by sending back this."

A metallic ring resounded through *Navtilus*'s cabin as Grishin dropped a short stubby cylinder onto the desktop. It rolled to a stop in front of Knox, the inscription facing up.

Knowing what it had to say, Knox read it anyway. The Cyrillic letters were crisply, cleanly incised, with no trace of heat-warp: Тунгуска Космолог VII-1989 Поддержать.

Tunguska Cosmologist VII–1989 Support.

41 | The Singularity

"**M**ETAL OBJECTS? ANY metal objects? Very dangerous to enter Antipode Station bearing things of metal." This high-pitched singsong, in alternating Russian and English, greeted them as they filed out of *Navtilus* and into Antipode's cramped antechamber.

Once through the airlock, Knox could see the source of the incantation: a stocky middle-aged woman in a white lab coat and radiation badge was working her way down the line of new arrivals. She waved a magic wand over each in turn, and, when it buzzed, collected watches, key chains, and other shiny trinkets for deposit in individually-labeled envelopes.

Not his gold-nibbed Waterman, too? That was a bit of an overkill. Only ferromagnetic materials should be susceptible to Vurdalak's monopolar field—metals like iron, nickel, cobalt. Come to think, that explained why Grishin had ordered his handcuffs removed. And why Marianna, the more "formidable" threat in their eyes, had been trussed in non-metallic webbing from the get-go.

For his part, Yuri had to part with his blued-steel machine pistol. He hefted one of the short-stock laser rifles the rest of the six-man guard detail had been issued, but rejected it in favor of a lethal-looking ceramic revolver. Just not the slice-and-dice type, our Yuri. Likes to blow holes in things.

By now the last of *Navtilus*'s passengers had been processed, but still they all stood there waiting in front of the heavy inner door. A door carved from the same basalt as the walls of the antechamber itself and emblazoned with a trisected magenta circle on a field of yellow—a warning of radiation hazards beyond.

Even Grishin and his cronies, from their privileged position at the head of the line, were bearing the delay with stoic equanimity, patiently waiting for that door to swing back and admit them. What was it about Russians and lines? Something about queuing up that seemed to strike a responsive chord in the national character.

Knox stood there watching the frosty clouds of his own breath, watching rivulets of moisture trickle down the rock walls in defiance of Antipode's climate control. The chill, damp air of the antechamber was an unwelcome reminder that the primeval cold of the deep sea was encamped just beyond the airlock, seeking the least fissure through which it might breach the station's defenses and pour in.

Finally the line began moving, the inexplicable logjam inexplicably broken at last. As Yuri propelled Marianna forward, she cast a fleeting glance back at Knox, whether to seek reassurance or to offer it, he couldn't tell.

Then Knox was through the doorway himself and into a darkness relieved only by glowworms and fireflies. The glowworms were workstation displays in a glass-walled booth immediately to the right of the entrance, and the fireflies, the flashing of jib lights on a huge crane-like structure positioned somewhat left of center. Overhead, the disembodied red digits of a time-display plaque showed local and GMT time, plus a countdown with ten minutes and change to go till some unnamed event.

As his eyes grew accustomed to the gloom, Knox could see that they were standing at the lip of a small amphitheater. Nine wide concentric tiers led downward into the dark, bottoming out in a narrow proscenium. The wall at the rear of that sunken platform bulged into the room, as if it were one section of a larger sphere. The only flat space on that wall was dead ahead, where an intricate-looking aperture sported its own circle of warning lights.

Yep, this layout pretty much matched the schematics Marianna'd brought back from her foray into the then-secret lab. That meant the control room should be located against the wall to his right. There it was, the booth he'd noticed a moment ago, separated from the main chamber by walls of thick, green-tinted glass. And the operator sitting at the console wearing the funny hat. Hard to make out with only the light from the displays to go by, but — could that be Galina? Yes, it could, if her wave to Sasha was any indication.

Was Galina in on this mad scheme to restore the *ancien regime*, too? Didn't seem like her.

No time to pause and reflect. They were on the move again, as Grishin led his entourage down to a seating gallery on the fifth level.

It felt as if the whole chamber were tipping forward more and more the further down they went. Knox tightened his grip on the handrail as the floor seemed to slope away, an incline on its way to becoming a drop-off. Or was it all just imagination? Judging from the curvature of the wall-section ahead of—below?—him, and allowing for the thicknesses of heat- and radiation-shielding he hoped they'd thought to install...he had to be a good twenty-five or thirty feet out from the primordial black hole at Antipode's heart. Could Vurdalak possibly exert its influence from that far away? It didn't even mass as much as, say, Mount Everest. Then again, it *was* a point-source.

He was trying to do the math, hampered by a blank spot in his memory where he thought he'd left the gravitational constant, when he chanced to look down. There, inset into the obsidian surface of the tier they'd halted at, glowing yellow characters read 9м — 0.46 тяг.

Let's see, *9m* just meant the nine-meter mark. And *tyag.* was most likely an abbreviation for *tyagoteniye*, gravity. So that meant...

Christ! Knox felt tiny droplets of perspiration dot his brow. Vurdalak was exerting nearly half a gee of pull on him, right where he stood!

He groped his way to a seat, bringing up the rear behind Sasha, Yuri, and Marianna. He was moving with elaborate caution now, bracing himself against a strategically-placed guardrail to keep from falling forwards — or was it downwards? Half a gee at nine meters out was no joke; at his weight, he was resisting a ninety-pound pull toward the front of the room. He studied the tiers below the seating level: two steps down, at the seven-meter mark, the micro-hole's tug was over three-quarters of a gravity. The proscenium floor, where it abutted the outer hull of the containment sphere, sported a large, Day-Glo red 5м — 1.5 тяг.

One and a half gravities down there! That was half the acceleration you'd feel blasting off in the Space Shuttle, and it was being generated by an object the size of an atom from five meters away. Knox was still trying to get his mind around that when he heard someone coming down the aisle.

Grishin spoke, "Ms. Bonaventure, Mr. Knox, welcome to Antipode Station. You have arrived just in time for the penultimate act in our drama." He nodded toward the countdown display. Less than seven minutes left.

Grishin reached inside his jacket pocket and withdrew a handheld. "Ms. Bonaventure, we have reconfigured your communicator to route through Antipode's local transponder, so that you may report to Mr. Aristos when the time comes. Yuri will hold onto it for you until then."

He handed the unit to the Georgian, then straightened. "As you can see, we conceal nothing. You will have every opportunity to judge the extent of our power, of our victory—in the few moments you will have to appreciate it."

A few moments? That didn't sound good.

"Ah, Arkasha?" Sasha raised his hand. "Perhaps if I were to explain what is about to happen?"

"Do as you will, Sasha. I must see to our guests." Grishin turned and crabwalked down the row of seats behind them, toward where his Council was settling in for the show.

Sasha eased himself out of his seat and stood facing his impromptu audience, bracing himself on the handrail against Vurdalak's insistent tug. The perch looked so precarious Knox was getting queasy just watching. But, then, Sasha had always been oblivious to external stimuli once in lecture mode.

"As is well known," he said, in English for Marianna's benefit, "for complex undertakings, the most important thing is control and verification at every step along the critical path. Our Antipode Project is perhaps more complex than most." He grinned. "On the other hand, it enjoys much greater possibilities for self-verification." Sasha was taunting Knox—figure it out for yourself.

Knox had, though only just this instant: "You mean you've been keeping your project on track using messages from the future?" The ultimate project-management utility! What Archon wouldn't give for that.

Sasha grinned again, as if at an apt pupil. *"Molodyets!"*—Attaboy!—"Yes, Dzhon, at each of eighteen key decision points over the lifetime of the project, we have received guidance from a timeprobe cylinder not unlike the 'needle' Arkady Grigoriyevich showed to you. The very first message, regarding selection of the Antipode site, was sent back to twelve years ago. The message arrived extremely distorted, almost as difficult to read as in 1984. But, of course, we were ready for this one, knew what it might say."

"Of course." Knox was thinking ahead: they would have identified, twelve years in the past, what range of alternatives their future selves might pick among, and to where and when they'd send the message-probe announcing the correct choice. Then, once they'd received the probe, it was just a question of remembering to actually *send* it.

"The rest of our probes did not go nearly so far back," Sasha was saying. "Less distortion, easier to read. The writing on the one giving the go-ahead for capturing Vurdalak was quite clear. As Marianna, I believe, had the possibility to observe?"

Marianna looked away. Doubtless would have crossed to the other side of the room if she could. That option was denied her: Yuri had spray-glued her makeshift manacles to the arm of her chair.

Sasha affected not to notice the snub. "In any case, it is necessary now to provide causes for all those effects, returning each probe to the space-time coordinates where it first appeared."

"By all means. One Global Causality Violation could ruin your whole day."

Sasha grinned again. "Ah, you understand."

Knox could read Sasha's mind: this convivial give-and-take was just like the old days in Moscow. No, Sasha, even the old days won't be like the old days anymore, if Grishin gets his way.

"Yes, it is necessary to keep temporal paradoxes to an absolute minimum," Sasha said. "Over the past four hours, we have returned seventeen message probes to the times and places where they belong. So it is that we balance accounts with the universe, paying back now the loan of information previously borrowed from the future." He winked. "And you did not believe me, Dzhon, when I told you cosmology was just like high finance."

Knox forced a half-hearted chuckle in return.

"In any case, what you will witness in—" Sasha glanced over his shoulder at the countdown. "—one minute thirty-five seconds is the launching of our eighteenth and most recent timeprobe, for arrival less than thirty hours in the past. But enough talk, watch now."

As Sasha groped his way back to his seat, Knox sensed movement in the darkened hall. The crane arm to his left was beginning to shift position, stretching out toward the curved wall that formed the outermost shell of Vurdalak's containment chamber.

For long moments the only sound was the protesting of metal as the weight of the arm grew with its increasing proximity to Vurdalak. By the time the mechanism came to rest again, it was almost touching the still-closed Portal. Six lateral braces mounted evenly around the business end of the mechanical arm found corresponding sockets on the Portal's rim and locked in place. The crane needed all the support it could get: the primordial black hole was only five meters away on the other side of the Portal.

"Here. Put this on." Sasha was holding out a small plastic rectangle with a blank gray window taking up half its surface: a radiation badge.

"What's the story, Sasha? You're not seriously going to crack the seal on the containment chamber, are you? That thing in there puts out enough hard radiation to cook us in a microsecond!"

"Not to worry, Dzhon. Badges are a precaution only," Sasha said as he velcroed one on Marianna's blouse as well.

"Good news is, there is no radiation danger," Sasha went on. "In, uh, forty-seven seconds we inject a Casimir capacitor into the chamber.

Vurdalak's event horizon goes away. And when it does, the radiation goes away with it."

Oh, right. No horizon, no radiation. Jack Adler had mentioned that. As rank speculation, though, not as something to bet your life on.

"If that's your idea of the good news, Sasha, I'm not sure I want to hear the bad."

"Bad news is: when radiation goes away, our power output drops. Bottom line: we must act quickly."

Of course. They'd be using Vurdalak's radiation as a power source. With it cut off, there was a limit to how long the cryostats could stay at full strength. But if they browned out, the magnetic arrays would stop superconducting. The confinement field would fail, and it was all that was holding the black hole in place.

Ulp! "Define 'quickly': how long have we got?"

"To the cusp of destabilization? At least one thousand seconds."

"Please tell me those aren't Chernobyl seconds, Sasha, old friend." Russian engineers had a bad habit of slicing their safety margins to the bone, and this one was only fifteen minutes long to begin with.

"Dzhon, relax. Computer alignment takes the longest, maximum two hundred seconds—for recent timeframes at least. Then we quick launch the probe, close the door, release the Casimir rectifier. Vurdalak reestablishes its event horizon. Radiation returns. We power up again. Simple."

Knox's expression must have betrayed just how un-simple that sounded to him, because Sasha added quickly, "Galina has done this seventeen times already without mishap. In a certain sense, there can *be* no mishap—everything we do now has already happened."

He raised a hand as Knox opened his mouth to protest. "Stop talking, now, and watch. See our gateway into the past."

Knox looked up just as the countdown overhead went to zero. A synthesized female voice, vaguely reminiscent of Galina's, said in Russian: "Singularity exposed. All readings nominal. Commencing world-line calibration."

Directly ahead, directly below, the iris began to dilate.

And then...

An eldritch light came seeping out through the widening Portal and around the eclipsing crane-arm, bathing the room in a nacreous glow.

Adler and Sasha both had claimed a naked singularity wouldn't give off any hard radiation. Knox hoped to hell they were right. He could almost feel the gamma rays sleeting through his unprotected body. Sometimes an overactive imagination was just no fun at all.

And then...

He was lost in wonder, fears forgotten, gazing on what Vurdalak had become. Gazing on the Singularity.

He had been here before: that single hallucinogenic rollercoaster ride that had brought an end to his grad school career, and, very nearly, him with it. He shuddered, remembering again that endless night two decades back. That experience, too, had begun with the world and everything in it splintering into delicate pointillistic patterns.

He remembered how it had ended, too, with him spiraling down into the nothingness that waited in between the dots... Take it easy, Knox. The difference is, this time you can turn the whole thing off just by closing your eyes.

Or could he? There was something odd about that light. He could see the whole of the circular aperture through which it poured, as if the spidery crane-arm which should have blocked his view wasn't there at all. He held a hand in front of his face, lost sight of it in the gentle, insistent glow. Turned his head away, and found he was still looking at the light-show dead-on. It was as if the Singularity's radiance weren't entirely an objective, external phenomenon, as if it were something his consciousness was collaborating on—a joint effort between a self-aware observer and the universe at large.

Experimentally, Knox squeezed his eyes shut. The effulgences shone bright as ever. What changed was he could no longer see his surroundings. The chair in which he sat, Marianna, Sasha, the whole room had gone away, leaving him floating disembodied and alone in the eerie lambency.

And now the visions came.

They had been there all along perhaps, the worldlines of every place and thing on Earth all tangled together by the Singularity into a tumult of white light. But with his eyes closed Knox found he could sort individual strands out of the flood. At first all he caught were random, dissociated glimpses of things—the tigers and pistons, astrolabes and armies of Borges' Aleph flashing by him in dizzying succession: a small boy in homespun asleep beneath a tree of unfamiliar species; a bald, bespectacled man in formal attire sipping from a glass of water at a rostrum; a hydroelectric dam towering amid granite monoliths, water coursing down its spillway; a lone pine on a windswept hillside; a sundrenched bed nestling two lovers *in flagrante delicto*, both of them female; a latticework of underground conduits, vast mechanisms performing incomprehensible tasks off in the middle distance...

Was everyone seeing the same thing he was, or was each individual consciousness following its own path through the hyperspatial maze? If the latter, that would make the Singularity the first-ever quantum wave function that didn't collapse to a determinate *eigenvalue* under observation. No wonder Sasha was going along with this: there had to be a Nobel Prize, or three, in it for him!

Knox was discovering he could influence the flow of impressions, or attune his awareness to specific sequences within the jumble. Concentrating, he could see...*Rusalka*, her deck lights ablaze under the stars of a summer night. A stray impulse, a flicker, and he was playing voyeur in his own stateroom, watching himself and Marianna in their first brief, disastrous tryst. Another random thought, and he stood looking over Marianna's shoulder as she paced through the secret lab five nights ago.

So that's how Grishin had tracked them down so effortlessly. "Extraordinary means," indeed! It worked both ways, though: another instantaneous transition and he hovered unseen in a dimly-lit chamber where Grishin conferred with Sasha, their lips moving soundlessly.

Forget about changing the past! Just being able to *view* it made the Singularity an espionage device of unparalleled power and scope. No secret in the world, past or present, could be hidden from its all-seeing eye. The ultimate destabilizer. If such a thing ever fell into the wrong hands—

No, he kept forgetting: it already had.

There were other temptations as well. To lose oneself in memory, in regret. Weathertop's greatroom, whole and inviolate, swam into view. For a moment Knox stood once more peering into a plasma screen filled with snow as Mycroft, alive again, called up canned speculations about what one might see if one gazed into a naked singularity.

With a flash, the peaceful scene dissolved in flames. Again he watched his friend stagger out of the smoke and into a hail of bullets. There was something wrong with the images the Singularity was conjuring up. Images of Mycroft wandering lost midst the wreckage, his body seeming almost to pass through the now-canted beams of the greatroom.

No more! Knox forced his eyelids open and found himself staring again into the Singularity's undifferentiated opalescence. It felt as if he'd been gone for hours. The countdown display, its digits nearly lost in the uniform, ubiquitous glow, showed twelve minutes twenty seconds still on the clock. Less than three minutes had passed since the Portal first opened.

"Lock on target spacetime confirmed," the synthesized voice proclaimed. "Commencing insertion sequence."

A plasma screen, lost till now in the gloom, came alight with an image of a microwave oven. A digital display above the glass door gave the date and time as 2:00 A.M. August 5th. The picture was fuzzy, warped by the screen's proximity to Vurdalak's magnetic field. Even so, Knox could recognize the probe receptacle Marianna had videoed in the secret lab.

He heard the computer-controlled crane arm screech as it reconfigured itself, inching a slender extension down into the heart of Vurdalak's containment chamber. A digital readout mounted on the body of the crane tracked how the force was rising on the arm as it drew ever closer to the Singularity:

5.0 meters: 1.50 gravities

4.5 meters: 1.85 gravities

4.0 meters: 2.35 gravities

3.5 meters: 3.00 gravities ...

By the time the mechanism whirred to a halt, its business end was two and a half meters from the pulsating vortex and straining under six times its normal weight!

Then a whine, the abrupt click of a release mechanism, and a fleeting glimpse of something arcing into the radiance: a metallic cylinder, a twin to the one Grishin had been waving around at his show-and-tell. Except this one was shrieking at the edge of human hearing and beyond as it warped and twisted in the grip of Vurdalak's gravity.

It was falling far too fast to follow now, but the display on the crane posted the numbers in quick succession: forty gravities, a hundred fifty gravities, six hundred, more zeroes than the display could hold.

A final burst of light and the probe was gone, gone off in a direction the eye could not follow, leaving the chamber reverberating with the thunderclap of its passage.

42 | A Stitch in Time

MARIANNA BARELY NOTICED when the synthetic voice announced, "Insertion complete at three minutes seven seconds. Reestablishing event horizon," and the Portal began to close, blocking off the Singularity's luminescence.

She sat there in the sudden dark, trembling, tears streaming down her face and no way to wipe them away with her fettered hands. She'd seen—she'd seen her Mom and Dad, alive again. And so young. Young as when the world was new, a full moon rising out of the Aegean as they wandered up into the hills.

She choked back a sob and looked around in the gloom. Grishin and company had risen from their gallery seats and were standing at the far end of the aisle congratulating one another. Even Yuri was down there getting instructions of some sort. That left only Sasha and Jon.

"Sasha?" she whispered. It probably came under the heading of consorting with the enemy, but she had to know. "What was it I saw when the Portal opened? Was it, was it just a dream?"

Sasha shook himself, summoned back from some transport of his own. "Each person sees something different in the timefield," he said slowly. "Still, it is not a dream. The search through the maze is guided by each individual mind and heart, but all of the worldlines are real."

"Worldlines? The automated announcement said something about worldlines, too. What *is* a worldline?"

"A worldline is—Humpf! How to explain?" Sasha frowned, and ran his fingers through his frizz of hair.

Finally, he said, "Think of the path of an object through time and space, as if you could see it from outside. Everything and everyone traces out such a path, including you and me. From hyperspace, every moment in your life appears all merged together into a continuous 'tube.' It splits off from your mother at the moment of birth, and terminates, or perhaps not, at the hour of your death. Slice through this four-dimensional tube anywhere along its length, and the resulting three-dimensional cross-section is you, at the corresponding point in time."

"Like a motion picture, maybe?" Jon spoke for the first time. "If every instant of my life, every 'now,' were a single frame in the film, then the worldline would be the whole reel, considered as a single thing?"

"Yes, Dzhon, excellent analogy."

"And these worldlines, they still exist?" Marianna asked. "Even the ones from the past? They don't just…go away?"

"They still exist, Marianna, as you saw." Sasha paused a moment, then added quietly, "The worldlines are real. Some believe it is the flow of time itself that is the illusion."

"Sasha?" Galina's voice emerged from a loudspeaker positioned overhead.

"Excuse me, please," Sasha said, rising. "I must go to confer with Galya on the final shot."

Marianna barely noticed him leaving. Her tears had begun to flow again. She let them.

Alive! They were still alive. Still in love, somehow, somewhere in time.

Perhaps they always would be.

✳

"Marianna? You okay?" Knox slid into the seat Sasha had just vacated and held her to him. It was an awkward embrace with her hands still stickywebbed to the arm of her chair, but it seemed to help. Her trembling went away bit by bit. He felt her take a deep breath, then release it slowly, relaxing in his arms.

"Better now," she sighed against his chest. "Better with you here." She leaned back just far enough to lift her face for a kiss.

A kiss she broke off after only a few moments, as if suddenly remembering where they were, and why. She pressed herself tightly against him again. "Jon, what are we going to do?"

"I'm working on it."

"Maybe…maybe we should just let it go. Maybe it *is* all just an internal Russian affair, like Grishin said."

He pulled back and looked at her. Was this the woman warrior he'd spent the past week with? Where was the edge, the attitude? She was the last person he'd have thought would go all warm and fuzzy on him. What had the Singularity *showed* her?

"Dammit, Marianna, that's wrong and you know it! The world may not be perfect the way it is, but it's a damn sight better than it'd be if the KGB had been left in charge of the only other superpower for the last twenty years."

"You're right. Of course, you're right." She was looking down, biting her lip. When she met his gaze again, she had her game face back on. "Sorry. I let myself get a little…" She took one shuddering breath. "I'm okay now."

He said nothing, just reached out and gently wiped a last tear from her cheek.

"So," she said, "what *are* we going to do about it?"

He looked around. No one within earshot.

"I'm going to try turning Sasha."

✳

Knox only wished he felt as confident as he sounded. Still, turning Sasha was their best shot. If anyone was in a position to pull the plug, it was GEI's second-in-command. Galina would listen to Sasha. And, from what Knox had seen, Galina was the one running the show.

So, the why worked; the question was, how? A lot hinged on just how committed to Grishin and his revanchist fever-dreams Sasha really was. GEI was his meal-ticket, sure, but that didn't necessarily buy a man's soul. And it sounded like Sasha'd been through hell at the hands of the old KGB. Had he caved at the end, succumbed to hostage syndrome like Marianna'd said? Or was the old Sasha still buried deep down inside, waiting on the right word to draw him out?

And, if so, what *was* the right word, *le mot juste*? Knox tried to focus, but nothing came.

Marianna whispered, "Here he comes."

Knox released her and turned to watch Sasha feeling his way down the aisle through half-light and variable gravity.

Reaching their row, Sasha leaned over and slapped Knox on the back. "You see, Dzhon, no need to worry. Galina reports all parameters well within safety tolerances. In thirty seconds more, power generation will be back at self-sustaining levels."

Sasha settled into the aisle seat. Good: the glow from the lighted handrail made it easier to read his face.

Oh, well, got to start somewhere. "So, Sasha, you said that last probe was being sent back only thirty-something hours? That's way too early—too late?—to have been the same one Marianna saw arrive in the lab five days ago."

"You mean the probe with the go-code for capture? No, that was not it."

"What *was* on this one, then?"

"You disappoint me, Dzhon. I was certain you would have figured it out before now."

"Well, if I had to guess, it'd be something to do with how you managed to pick up our trail again."

"Bravo! Yes, the message giving the name and location of Weathertop. And one thing more, two words I personally added: 'Return Them.'"

"Didn't trust your boss to bring us back alive, huh?"

"Not that I didn't trust. But Arkasha is more inclined to do the right thing when the timeprobes tell him to." Sasha almost smiled, then became utterly serious. "I did not want you and Marianna killed, Dzhon.

Alas, I could not do as much for your friend, Dr. Finley Laurence. I am sorry."

Knox let that last remark slide; he wasn't ready to go there just yet. Instead he said, "So, what comes next here?"

"Next comes what we have called the 'omega sequence.' First we rebuild our power reserves to maximum levels; for omega, we must go into the far past—two decades back. So far, in fact, that we cannot trust the computer to manage the energy expenditure—too delicate, too much variability. Instead, Galya must control the process manually."

Sasha glanced back smiling in the direction of the operator's station. "She is a true magician at the weaving of fields."

"I'm sure she is. You must be really proud of yourself for having dragged her into this nightmare."

That got a reaction! Sasha turned beet-red and began mouthing protestations of innocence.

"Skip it." Too much, too soon. Just keep him talking for now. "What's this about an omega sequence?"

"Yes, well…" Sasha seemed relieved to return to a less sensitive topic. "The point is to sift through the worldlines and lock onto the time and place where Andropov was killed: 7:35 A.M. February 9, 1984, Moscow, Special Polyclinic #17, Suite 12. All under computer control, of course."

"Hold on. I thought it took a conscious observer to isolate any particular strand in the timefield."

"This is so. However, the computer qualifies as an observer for purposes of this interaction. We have a DSP-7 parallel processor running a neural net over there." Sasha pointed toward a matte-black cube about a meter on a side; it was cabled into the crane installation.

"You've got a computer capable of simulating consciousness crammed into a box that size?"

"Not consciousness, Dzhon—vision. Much simpler. Fortunately, as regards observation, the universe appears not to distinguish between a simulation and the real thing. Once Galina finds the desired worldline, the DSP can match input from her visual cortex well enough to lock on."

"So that's what the helmet is for. There's a SQUID in there reading her brain's bioelectric field."

"An MRI," Sasha corrected, "to read the chemical state of the striate cortex. Room-temperature superconductivity makes possible very precise magnetic resonance imaging in a very small package."

Small indeed! Most MRIs were big enough to swallow you whole. This one could've come straight out of a millinery catalog. Just another everyday miracle from GEI's Materials Sciences Division.

"Once the pseudo-visual lock-on-target is confirmed," Sasha was saying, "the computer aligns the launcher accordingly. The entire apparatus enters a discrete quantum state entangled with the target spacetime. Much more reliable than human guidance: the neural net is not prone to distractions; it remains focused on the target until probe launch and beyond, until a human operator intervenes to reset or adjust it. Simple."

"Uh, simple's not the word I would have chosen, Sasha. How about 'unbelievably complicated'?" Knox wouldn't have believed it could work at all if he hadn't seen it in action a moment ago. "And you've only had the past day or so to experiment. How'd you know it would…oh!"

"Yes, Dzhon: time travel again. Probes twelve and thirteen: the first to explain the basic principle twenty four months ago; the second to confirm our final design seven months later."

"Whatever." Knox gave up. Thinking about this business of magicking up information via messages from the future was making his head hurt. There just had to be a paradox in there somewhere.

Side issue. Knox didn't need to buy into Sasha's bizarre reasoning. All he needed to do was find, somewhere amid the technobabble, the hook that would land his fish.

Till then, keep the conversation going. "So, okay—you stake out the crime scene. Andropov's assassin shows up on schedule, somehow evading an entire platoon of Ninth Directorate guards in the process. What then?"

"Then comes the omega sequence itself: two separate insertions, one after another. First, the extensor arm launches one single bullet along a trajectory that intersects with the assassin's worldline all those years ago. Intersects, more precisely, with the back of his head. In result, the threat to Andropov is eliminated. With luck, even the marvelous self-destruct device may be recovered intact."

"If that's phase one, then the second phase must be your Ourobouros patch, right? Where the snake eats its own tail?"

"Ah, you have deciphered our GEI corporate crest, Dzhon. Very good! But, yes, you are right: having shifted the timeline by this little bit, we must ensure that the new course taken by history also includes a research program leading to our present timewarping capability."

Sasha sobered suddenly, his voice dropping almost to a whisper. "Without that, our intervention to save Andropov could create a true temporal paradox: an effect without a cause."

"And what would happen then?"

"Nobody knows." Sasha's eyes held a haunted look. "Worst case, a rip in space-time continuum leading to collapse of the so-called false vacuum, and the end of all existence. Or an infinite temporal cycle, like a forever loop in a computer program. Nothing good, this much is certain."

He took a breath before going on. "But this will *not* happen, because in the second, final phase we launch one more probe back to the same point in space and time. Investigating the *un*successful assassination attempt in the revised timeline, Arkasha will still find the same cylinder with its message about Tunguska and cosmology... only this time on the floor beside Andropov's bed, not sticking through his chest as in our own history. This should ensure essentially the same subsequent progression of events as brought us to here. Novikov's Conservation of Reality principle will work to preclude any causality violation."

"One question, Sasha: you don't really believe all of this is going to work, do you?"

"It has been working up to now," Sasha reminded him.

"But up to now you've just been recapitulating events you know have already taken place. Sending your 'timeprobes' back to when and where you first received them, that sort of thing. You have no idea what'll happen when you actually try to change something, do you?" This was it, the hook he'd been looking for. "Well, *do* you?"

Sasha glanced around before replying. When his answer came it was pitched so low that even sitting next to him, Knox had to strain to make it out.

"No result in science is ever assured until the experiment has been conducted, Dzhon. Our best mathematical models imply support for the Novikov principle. Still, it is impossible to altogether exclude the possibility of a less desirable result."

"That's about as coolly as I've ever heard someone talk about the end of everything!" If they managed to rip a gash in the fabric of space-time, the whole universe could collapse to a lower energy state like a punctured beachball. Couldn't Sasha see how *crazy* this all was?

Or maybe Sasha saw, but didn't believe he could change what was going to happen? "I get the feeling you haven't shared these misgivings with your beloved leader."

"And would he hear them, if I did?" Sasha smiled ruefully. "It makes no difference in any case: to yield to such concerns would be to abandon the very process by which science advances the progress of humanity."

"Or puts an end to it, once and for all."

"As Arkasha said, in a very short while now, you will have the possibility to judge which it is we have accomplished here today."

"Thanks for reminding me. I'd been meaning to ask what that was all about—why Grishin said we'd only have a few moments to marvel at his triumph. Is he planning on deep-sixing us after all?"

"Not at all, my friend. Nothing of the sort will be necessary."

"Sure sounded like *some*thing's going to happen to us."

"Not to you only—to all of us. The consensus among our chrono-physicists is that the new reality will propagate forward in time from the event epicenter, like a wave through water—like a temporal tsunami. It will hit us here, transforming all our circumstances to what they would be on the adjusted timeline."

Knox shuddered. "Sounds like a kind of death to me. Those people on your new timeline, they're not you and me. They're doppelgangers: same names, same faces, whole different set of memories. To all intents and purposes, you and I and Marianna, Grishin—*hell!*—everybody on the planet, will cease to exist the instant your omega sequence goes through."

"I subscribe to a different interpretation. Different circumstances, but the same consciousness. How did Saint Paul say it? 'In an instant we shall all be changed.'"

"Saint Paul? The KGB has changed for sure. Since when did you guys get religion?"

Sasha's face wore a pained expression. "Please, Dzhon, I am not part of the so-called shadow KGB. I am..." He brightened suddenly. "Yes, am merely a consultant, like yourself."

"In that case, there's a little matter of professional ethics we need to talk about. Seriously, Sasha, how can you countenance this as a scientist? I mean, warping the continuum out of shape just so 'Comrade Director' gets to collect on his state-security retirement benefits?"

Sasha's hurt look deepened into one of wounded dignity. "Even trivial motives may serve great scientific ends, Dzhon," he said solemnly. "Galileo himself perfected his first telescope merely for the purpose of persuading the Senate of Venice to increase his yearly stipend."

"Take a look around before you go citing Galileo. In case you hadn't noticed, you're working for the Inquisition!"

Knox knew that he shouldn't let himself get worked up like this, that his only chance was to stay cool, stay rational. Good advice. Too bad he couldn't take it. Sometimes anger is the only rational response. "Think about it, Sasha. Think about your KGB towering over a resurrected Soviet Union like a colossus. Think about a tyranny that will never end, because the tyrants have got a surveillance device of inconceivable power. Desktop omniscience. No more missteps, no more unintended consequences, no more chance of toppling *that* regime — not when they can *see the fucking future!* They'll rule forever, a rule that will spread to engulf the globe. And you gave it to them, Sasha — *you!*"

Sasha held up his hands as if to ward off any further blows. "Dzhon," he said, "even if I believed this, what would you have me do?"

At last! A chink in the armor, maybe. Now, if he could just pry it open.

"Places, please," Galina's voice boomed out of the overheads. "Final insertion is about to begin."

Grishin and the rest of the Council for National Resurrection were already taking their seats at the far end of the row. Yuri had returned and was taking up position on Marianna's right again.

A buzzer began to ring.

No! Not now. He was almost there, he was sure of it. He *knew* that the right word could still turn this around, if only he could find it in time.

Too late. The clock had run out on him. The main event, the omega sequence, was about to begin.

Knox turned away from Sasha, turned to Marianna. She was still glued to her seat, literally. Tears of frustration filled her eyes.

"I'm sorry," Knox said, stroking her hair. "No more time. I tried."

"I know. It's all right. I just wish... Jon, if this all happens like Sasha says, do you think we'll even... even know one another in that other timeline?"

"I think, I think maybe we were meant to be together, you and me," he whispered, holding her close. "Together no matter what."

The synthesized announcement cut off Marianna's reply: "Singularity exposed. All readings nominal. Commencing worldline calibration."

The Portal cracked open again, the light of the Singularity once more leaking around the launcher arm to flood the chamber beyond.

Knox averted his gaze from the growing radiance. Found himself staring into Marianna's impossibly widening eyes, saw her lips peel back from her teeth, heard the beginnings of her scream, even as he realized it himself.

Something was very *wrong!*

43 | Le Mot Juste

MORE THAN WRONG — *horrific.*

It began with Grishin. Lit by the unearthly glow from the reopened Portal, a dour, seamed visage, bearded and scarred, superimposed itself over his genial features, the sky-blue epaulets of a KGB Colonel flickering into quasi-existence on his shoulders. Scar tissue crinkled one cheek as he turned to grin at Knox.

The grin grew wider. The light shifted again to reveal a skull, gobbets of rotting flesh framing empty eye sockets.

Now the faces of all the onlookers were melting and flowing in the Singularity's ghastly coruscations. As the change-winds blew through them, the occupants of the observation gallery flickered out like guttering candles; in their place oozed the festering ruin of long-dead corpses. Shrieks were torn from decaying throats, putrefied limbs writhed in torment. Only the baleful digits of the time display seemed unaffected; barely visible in the hideous radiance, they continued counting down toward the moment of target lock and insertion.

Knox had been here before. If, indeed, he had ever really left. This was it, his own personal hell, the gaping maw that had swallowed him whole and vomited him back out on that one bad trip two decades ago, only to lurk ever after out at the nightmare edges of his dreams.

Welcome home, smiled the void.

He held up his own hand, a hand now become a skein of rotting sinew and cartilage binding knobs of dactyloid bone. The pain! As if he were being flayed alive. Yet the aching fingers could still move. This was illusion, appearance somehow — or was it premonition?

He tore his gaze away from the corruption his own flesh had become. It wasn't real, wasn't happening. Get a grip, Knox, you've lived through flashbacks before. Except this was more of a flash-forward, wasn't it? — the leading edge of a phantasmagoric change-wave propagating outward from some past event that had yet to transpire, some sort of quantum nonlocality simultaneously skewing probabilities all along the timeline. Sasha had spoken truer than he knew. *In an instant we shall all be changed.*

But into what? And why?

Knox forced his eyes closed — did he even have eyelids to close any more? — and peered once again with his mind's eye into the maelstrom of light.

And *saw* why.

The pain went away, along with everything else. There was nothing there. Rock, clay, sand, yes, stretching endlessly beneath a sky of swirling soot. But nothing living, nothing green. The whole Earth a charnel house, darkness moving on the face of the inky waters.

Judging by last time, the most recent, most accessible moments would surface first. Left to its own devices, unguided by any act of will, the Singularity was showing him the present, or near enough.

Why, then, was it so dead, and so dark, everywhere?

Show me life, show me a friend!

The Singularity strove to comply. Succeeded, almost. Knox found himself looking into Galina's face, a much younger Galina, looking much older. Her eyes were filmed over with agony, staring into nothing. Or staring, somehow, at him? Bloody phlegm bubbled on her lips as she tried to speak. With her last breath, she mouthed a word; could it be... *Spasibo*?

Behind a jam of crumpled bodies, a near-spent kerosene lamp

picked out a sign on the rough-hewn wall. The Cyrillic lettering read бомбоубежище. A fallout shelter.

A horrible foreboding gripped him. Let me out! Show me the sky! A timeless transition and he stood amid wrack and ruination under churning black thunderheads. Intermittent lightning glinted on blackened skeletons, the ravaged remains of buildings and men.

The Day After, years after.

Present day, he willed. And found himself in graveyard gloom as before. He looked back across the snake's nest of worldlines, found the one where uniformed men sat two by two in hardened silos, tore open red envelopes, inserted keys in practiced syncopation, shot their ballistic wads.

The final piece fell into place. Talk about the biggest bang for the buck. They'd gotten it, in spades! Thwart one assassination and reap the whirlwind.

Back in 1984, the Reagan administration's unremitting hostility toward the "Evil Empire" had been enough to provoke even an enfeebled successor regime into baring its teeth. It was anybody's guess what would have happened had Reagan faced, not the sclerotic Konstantin Chernenko, but a Yuri Andropov at the height of his powers.

Knox didn't have to guess; he was looking at it. Only…

Only who could have guessed that nuclear winter would last two whole decades?

Knox opened his eyes. Bad move! His body was aflame again with the agony of anticipatory transformation. Even so, he was faring better than the others. He seemed to be the only one who could still move, the only one not paralyzed with horror and dismay. Even Yuri, author of so much death and destruction, seemed utterly debilitated by this vision of his own mortality. None of them had ever experienced the incapacitating despair of a really, really bad trip before. Perils of a too-sheltered upbringing.

What was it Nietzsche said? Whatever doesn't kill you makes you stronger? The abyss had barely missed killing him on that long-ago night. Time to see about the rest of it.

Knox willed his muscles to move, muscles that his eyes told him had long since decayed into dust. He moved notwithstanding, struggled out of his seat past a moaning Sasha, began the long climb out of Vurdalak's gravity well, toward the control booth. Dead man walking.

On his right the great crane was even now swinging into position, extending its arm, readying itself to make the till-now merely potential an irrevocable actuality. Knox pushed himself to hurry, though the pain of the added exertion nearly doubled him over. But he was almost there now, just a little further.

His stomach churned as he hobbled the last few steps to the door of the glass-walled booth, as he saw what Galina had become…

It's not real!

The blackened tongue protruding… the skin of her face, what there was left of it, blistered with pustulating radiation burns…

It *can't* be real!

…her cratered ruin of a mouth open wide as if to scream, only a hoarse rattle coming out…

Please, God, don't let it be real!

"Galina! Close your eyes!" Knox tried the door to the booth. Locked, from the inside. He slammed his fist, not daring to look at it, against the glass wall. "Close your eyes, and let me in!"

She turned fevered eyes toward him, and gasped. What must *she* be seeing?

"Never mind me! Close your eyes and *look!*"

She shut her eyes. Her breathing steadied, but not for long. Her sunken chest heaved. She cried out in anguish, as she beheld utter desolation.

"Galina, let me in!" He pounded on the door again. "It's not too late—we can *change* this!"

Tears ran down her ravaged cheeks as her consciousness frantically winnowed the worldlines. Searching somewhere—anywhere—for life, for hope. Finding none. Finding only…

"Lock on target spacetime confirmed. Reconfiguring launcher for first insertion." The computer's synthesized voice sounded impatient almost, eager to bring the Jubilee. The crane arm began to swing on its gimbals.

Squinting into the Singularity's dreadful glare, Knox watched an image form in the forward display: a hospital room in early morning, the winter sun just beginning to tint the curtains with pale rose, an old man lying abed in fitful sleep.

So this is the way the world ends. It all looked so normal—anything would, after the post-apocalyptic abattoir the Singularity had conjured up for him. The system was running on automatic now, scanning for the mythical assassin. What would it do when he failed to appear? Would it time out, abort the bullet launch, and insert the message probe instead? Whatever it would do, had done, it had led to Andropov's survival. And Armageddon.

Only seconds left till the omega sequence kicked in. He had to stop it!

Knox pounded on the door again. Galina was not responding, she was lost among worldlines portending holocaust, gigadeath, the end of days.

Got to get through to her. If only he didn't hurt so much. If only he could *think!*

"For God's sake, Galina, open the door!"

Somewhere, somehow there was a right word to say, if only he could find it. A word that held the key to the pattern of her life...

"Galina, *please! For the love of God!*"

A word, all he needed was the right word...

"Galya! We've got to save the *children!*"

44 | Last Row on the Chessboard

"**W**E'VE GOT TO save the children!"

Was it only Knox's imagination, or did the horrorshow abate slightly as he spoke the words?

Galina opened her eyes. And screamed. "Aaiiiieee! Help me, Dzhon. Please! My hands! Everything hurts. Cannot bear to look!"

"It's all right, Galina. None of this is real. Yet. And it won't be, if you do exactly as I say."

"Wh-what must I do?" she choked out, between racking sobs.

"Start by letting me in."

Galina took a shuddering breath and spoke an open sesame into her console mike. Nothing happened: her voice was too hoarse from screaming for the speaker-verification routines to confirm her identity. In desperation, she keyed in the command sequence, touch-typing, her gaze averted from her dissolving fingers.

The door swung open. Knox groped his way to the console. Had the pain in his limbs subsided just a bit? He stood there, eyes darting across control panels and workscreens, trying to sort out the interface. No time! He'd have to talk her through it.

"Galina?" It hurt to draw breath enough to talk. "We've got to cancel the bullet launch."

"The bullet? But the assassin! Arkasha said—"

"Forget about what Grishin said! There is no assassin!" Not yet, anyway. "Trust me, Galya, just do it!"

He watched as, operating by keyboard feel and voice command, Galina canceled the first launch of the omega sequence. The computerized voice murmured its disappointment. The crane arm seemed to ripple in response, as if gaining solidity. Or was that another trick of the unearthly light?

"Done," Galina said. "And now?"

"This is the tricky part. The second insertion, for the message cylinder, can you reorient it?"

"Reorient? Yes, but to when and where? Dzhon, we have all space and time to reorient in. Except..." Was that a hint of hysteria in her sudden, incongruous giggle? "Except our own time runs out." She pointed up at the time display.

Knox looked. He couldn't believe it: less than five minutes left on the countdown! Sasha had said the further back you went, the longer it took the computer to lock in on the right worldline segment. He'd neglected to mention that zeroing in on the February 9, 1984 calibration would chew through two thirds of their safety margin. Chernobyl engineering again.

Stay calm. "Can you lock down the time coordinate and put the spatial settings into a slow scan, three meter radius?"

"Yes, but... scan for what?"

"You'll know it when you hit it." He hoped. Who was he to bad-mouth Chernobyl? The containment field's backup power was red-lining, and what was he doing? Playing dice with the space-time continuum, is all—and that on a hunch.

But, then, Jonathan Knox trusted his hunches. "Just do it!"

A few more keystrokes entered by aching, decomposing fingers, then: "Is done. Now, what—" Galina stopped.

She looked in wonder at her hand. Flexed fingers suddenly made whole again. Touched her face, feeling tears on cheeks miraculously restored to smoothness. "But how?"

"That'll have to be close enough. Lock it there, and prepare for launch," Knox said. He shut his eyes again just to be sure. Images of a living past, his past, flowed out of the Singularity to greet him.

Intention is the key! A conscious choice by a conscious mind. The working out of the event itself was almost an afterthought by comparison; it was the human will that warped the worldlines. Talk about Nietzsche!

"Will take some seconds to realign crane arm for new target." Below them the mechanism shuddered, awaiting the command to reconfigure itself. Still focused on her console's readouts, Galina asked, "Where we are aiming at now?"

Moment of truth. Knox had hoped it wouldn't come to this, hoped he could leave Galina in the dark, an accessory after the fact—*twenty years* after the fact. No good, any moment now she'd look up and see the new target centered in the forward monitor.

"Andropov," he said.

He heard a sharp intake of breath. Her hand hovered indecisively over the keyboard.

"Galina, we've got to do it. Otherwise there *is* no future. Think of the children, all the children." Knox burned with shame at manipulating her like this. Just this once he almost wished he hadn't intuited exactly the right word. No matter if it was true.

But it worked. *Le mot juste* always works. With a sob, Galina hit *Enter*, initiated the retargeting procedure. Gears shrilled as the arm began shifting into the new position. At the same instant, a shout went up from the viewing gallery three tiers below them.

Too soon! Knox had been expecting Grishin and company to come around once the hellish hallucinations let up. That wasn't the same as knowing what to do about it.

✴

Marianna shook off the remnants of the nightmare. Turned to where Jon had been sitting. He was gone. She scanned the hall for him, finally spotted him in the control booth with Galina. What was he doing up there?

A shout to her right. Grishin was rising from his chair, pointing at the main display screen. She took a look herself. And stared in disbelief at the target in the crosshairs.

Andropov!

She looked down the row of seats. Nobody else in the VIP section was stirring yet: the geriatric Council members still looked pretty dazed. But Grishin was making up for the rest of them. He was on his feet, waving his arms, shouting out commands.

"Sasha, stay here and keep watch on Bonaventure! Yuri, see to *them!*" His finger stabbed in the direction of the control booth, even as he himself began moving toward the crane-arm. "I will manually abort the insertion!"

Yuri heaved himself to his feet and lumbered to the aisle. Then he turned and stood there, not moving. His grin widened as he drew his ceramic pistol and aimed it at Marianna's forehead.

Oh, shit!

Suddenly, something blocked her view of the gun muzzle.

Sasha! Sasha was rising from his seat to stand between her and the Georgian hitman.

She heard Yuri say, "Move aside!" Heard the pistol being cocked.

Sasha flinched but did not budge. The moment stretched out. Two seconds. Three.

"Yuri!" Grishin's shout echoed through the bay. "Forget the woman! Stop *them!*"

Yuri scowled, but he turned away and began hauling himself up the stairs toward the control room.

Sasha turned to her, pale as death, breath coming fast. He licked his lips. "Marianna, I—"

"Sasha, thanks. I...I owe you one."

"Was nothing." He looked like he was about to faint. Then he was too busy watching what she was doing.

Twisting round in her chair till she'd bent over the arm, Marianna brought her hands close enough to the waistband of her jeans to reach in and extract a small bottle from its hiding place in the utility pocket. Unscrewing the lid, she poured its contents over the adhesive webbing that bound her wrists to the chair frame.

Sasha looked at her quizzically. "How did you get that past the strip-search?"

"Shhh!" she explained.

✦

"Galina? Lock the door again, please," Knox said. "And get down."

He waited while she keyed in the command, then hustled her to shelter behind the heavy desk.

Yuri, at the control room door now, was aiming the muzzle of his ceramic pistol in their direction. Sure hope this glass is bulletproof! The first shots stitched a row of little starred holes into the glass of the door; a mated set of pockmarks appeared in the wall opposite. Guess not!

"Careful, Yuri!" Grishin could be heard shouting from below, "You'll hit the controls! Key in the combination—it's 314159! And *hurry!*"

Yuri reluctantly transferred the pistol to his other hand and turned to study the keypad set into the adjacent wall. He punched in the combination, then cursed. Not good with numbers, evidently.

Knox and Galina looked out from behind the desk. "How long to launch?" he asked her.

"Arm is repositioning now. Maybe five seconds more." She cast a fearful glance over to where Yuri was pounding at the keypad, swept her gaze down into the observation bay, to the—

"*Look!*" she cried.

They had bigger problems. A hush fell over the room. Even Yuri stopped hammering away and turned to watch.

Grishin had reached the probe-launcher and climbed out onto one of the struts of its arm. Clinging to the rungs running down it, he began descending hand over hand toward the launch tube containing the last message probe.

Why was he doing this, when he'd seen what would come of it? Or had he? Had he ever managed to close his eyes long enough to look?

Knox turned to Galina. "Is the added weight going to knock the arm out of alignment?"

"Should not do, Dzhon. Launcher must endure far greater stresses."

Sure enough, the crane-arm was holding rock-steady. Overengineered, no doubt. After all, the business end of the launcher had to come within two or three meters of Vurdalak's singularity, with gravity increasing by leaps and bounds as the distance diminished.

Grishin was hanging on to a rung and kicking at one of the struts, trying to dislodge the timeprobe. No go — that arm had to be built to withstand maybe fifty or a hundred gravities. He'd have to go down and physically pull the probe out of the insertion tube if he wanted to abort the launch.

He didn't just want to; he had to. If there was even a trace of residual radiation on the containment chamber's interior walls, Grishin had already taken a lethal dose. He was a dead man now, unless he could climb down and change the past.

And that was proving not so easy. Along about now Grishin was probably wishing he'd paid more attention at Sasha's physics briefings. Especially the one about how drastically your weight would increase the closer you got to a gravitational point-source.

Already he'd been forced to swing his body around and work his way down the crane-arm feet first. His eyes sank deep in their sockets, runnels of sweat coursing down cheeks distended like those of a jet pilot in a power dive. His knuckles whitened with the effort needed to hang onto each next rung against his body's increasing weight. His labored breathing echoed loud in the silent chamber. He was almost at the launch tube.

"Why isn't it firing?" Knox whispered.

Galina frowned. "Launcher must be reading movement on crane arm and thinking reconfiguration is still in progress. It will not launch probe until alignment completes."

"Is there an override? Tell me how."

"No, Dzhon. Command sequence is too complex, would take too long to tell."

She looked into his eyes. Her face took on an almost ethereal tranquility. "I go. Like you say, is for the children."

Before he could respond, she was out from behind the desk and into the operator's chair. Her fingers danced frantically across the workstation's keyboard. All the while her lips were moving, silently forming words. To Knox, it looked as if she were saying *"Gospodi, pomilui"* — Lord, have mercy upon us.

The glass door exploded.

Yuri dropped the fire axe with a thud and strode into the control room, transferring the ceramic pistol to his good hand again as he came on.

Galina lifted her face to look him in the eye…and hit the *Enter* key.

The launch tube coughed, hurling the stubby message cylinder on its predestined trajectory into the Singularity's timefield. The tough metal keened as tidal forces stretched the probe near its breaking point. The sound cut off abruptly as it vanished in a silent starburst.

A single shot rang out. Grishin had told Yuri to be careful. The soft-nosed slugs inflicted minimal collateral damage, all their insult being absorbed by the target, and Yuri had only used one of them.

Galina expelled a breath and slumped sideways, a red stain spreading across her blouse. Her chair tipped over and dumped her sprawling into Knox's arms. He cradled her head, barely noticing as Yuri's shadow fell across them where they huddled on the floor.

A scream echoed through the bay. Grishin! *Vurdalak had him!*

Grishin scrabbled for purchase as the vortex left by the probe's passage reached for him. His shriek rose in pitch and volume, then suddenly cut short. It was all over in an instant as he sailed in past the Singularity and vanished down the same rabbit hole as the message cylinder before him.

Knox averted his face and reflexively squeezed his eyes shut. Bad move, as it turned out, since Singularity-light showed him what he had sought to avoid seeing and could not otherwise have seen.

All over in an instant, perhaps. But Grishin was under constant acceleration throughout his headlong plunge into the Singularity's gravity well, and general relativity dictates that a distant observer would see something quite different. As the Comrade Director approached light-speed, his metabolism, his awareness—indeed, time itself—ran slower and slower. Though the gruesome sight grew dim and dimmer, faded to black, still, from the perspective of the outside world, Grishin's final moments stretched out into an excruciating eternity.

Even as he himself was stretching. As he neared the Singularity, Grishin's six-foot height was enough to put his head and his feet in entirely different gravitational regimes. It was the same force-differential as powered the tides of Earth's oceans, played out on a scale of millimeters. And human tissue could not withstand Vurdalak's tides the way the tungsten steel of the timeprobe cylinders could. Muscle and bone and nerve fiber gave way in a series of bloody discharges as Grishin's body elongated far beyond what flesh was meant to endure.

A long, thin filament charred black by friction was all that was left of him by the time Arkady Grigoriyevich departed the present for the morning of February 9, 1984.

"Insertion complete at thirteen minutes twenty-two seconds," the synthesized announcement heralded the closing of the Portal.

Just before it went dark, the forward display showed an old man, thrashing feebly in pain and clutching at the long thin metal needle which had suddenly materialized deep within his chest. And, on the floor beside his bed, a mound of scorched, braided flesh, ground exceeding fine.

The mission-control computer began speaking again. *"Warning: one minute thirty seconds to cryostat shutdown. Awaiting command to reestablish event horizon."*

Knox barely heard. He held Galina's head in his lap and stroked her forehead. *Two* friends this damned assignment had cost him now. It hadn't been enough to reach the last row; he'd had to go upend the chessboard and scatter the pieces all over the floor.

"Warning: sixty seconds to cryostat shutdown. Awaiting command to reestablish event horizon." There it was again. Would somebody shut that damned thing off?

Galina looked up into Knox's face. Her eyes misted over with pain, then widened. He turned to see what she was looking at.

The countdown stood at 00:48, still running.

She struggled to rise, fell back. "Please, Dzhon, event horizon must be closed, and power restored, or cryostats stop running…"

"It's okay, Galina," Knox soothed. "The computer will do all that; the whole sequence is automated."

"No…not automated… For so far into past, had to disengage safeties, go to manual…"

"*Warning: thirty seconds to cryostat shutdown*," launch control informed them.

Knox swallowed. He remembered now; Sasha had said something about the omega sequence requiring a human operator. "Quick! What do I have to do?"

Galina's voice was fading. He had to lower his ear almost to her lips to hear. "Casimir rectifier queued up, ready to go, but could not release before probe launch... Just... hit *Enter*."

Knox looked up. Out in the bay, the overhead display was reading 00:24, 00:23, 00:22... He turned toward the console.

And saw Yuri standing there, his face swollen with fury, his pistol aimed between Knox's eyes.

Galina seized his arm with desperate strength. "Please, Dzhon, hurry... In fifteen seconds, containment fails... Vurdalak... falls through to center of Earth... Will be... end... of everything..."

Knox gauged the distance. Could he make it before Yuri gunned him down? Yuri was looking him straight in the eye, smiling. He *wanted* Knox to try it.

"*Warning: ten seconds to cryostat shutdown.*

Yuri's finger tightened on the trigger, his eyes not moving from Knox's face ...

Nine

... the second time he will have made that mistake.

Eight

A flash of ruby light from behind him. A sizzle and a sudden puff of steam. The pistol falling from his hand, the hand falling from his arm. Yuri stood there in shock, staring at a blood-gouting stump where his gunhand used to be.

Seven

He whirled in time to see Marianna re-aim her commandeered laser rifle a notch higher. "*You!*" he began.

Six

That's all he had time for. Her second blast took off his head.

Five

Knox vaulted over the decapitated corpse...

Four

...and stabbed a finger at the *Enter* key.

Three

Two

"Command acknowledged. Reestablishing event horizon."

Knox looked out into the bay, where the countdown had halted at 00:02.

He turned and knelt again beside Galina. Her eyes burned fiercely for a moment. "Did you...did you..."

"Not me," Knox told her, as the bright eyes slowly dimmed. "You did. You saved the children."

✳

"Jon?" Someone was trying to get his attention.

Marianna. She was crouching at the door, aiming the laser rifle out into the bay. "Check if Yuri's still got my handheld on him."

For a moment, Knox wondered why. The little battery-powered unit wasn't going to transmit through the two miles of seawater that separated them from the surface. Then he remembered: Grishin said he'd had it rigged to piggyback off Antipode's own communications link.

He rolled the headless body over. Averting his eyes, going mostly on feel, he found the communicator in an inside jacket pocket. He yanked it out and handed it to Marianna.

"Thanks." She glanced down just long enough to enter a key sequence. "I'd have done it myself, but I've kind of got my hands full right now."

As if to underscore that, she raised the rifle and pulled the trigger, then ducked as return fire gouged the wall behind her.

"How many?" Knox asked.

"I count five. The guard detail, minus the one I took out to get this." She hefted her weapon again and fired back.

"This help?" Knox scooped up Yuri's discarded pistol and aimed it awkwardly.

"Careful where you point that thing! Yeah, get over here!"

He joined her at the door. Now he could see the ring of guards advancing cautiously, using the auditorium seats for cover, slowly tightening the noose. He stole a glance at Marianna, seeing again the naked ferocity, the wildness in her. Seeing something else, as well. "Marianna, you've got less than half the charges left on that rifle!"

"Tell me something I *don't* know. We'll just have to make them last till Pete gets here!"

If he gets here, Knox thought. If he even gets the signal.

Marianna fired again, then said, "One less." Knox wasn't sure if she was referring to the remaining charges or the remaining guards.

It didn't matter. Best case, it was going to take Aristos and company an hour to cover the ten miles between the perimeter of Grishin's exclusion zone and Antipode Station, and they had minutes at most before their ammo ran out and the guards rushed in.

Worth it, though, he thought as he raised his gun to fire. Definitely worth it.

There came one final, blinding pulse of light, and, on its heels, an ear-splitting crash.

45 | Mopping Up

"ONATHAN? CAN YOU hear me?" The familiar voice seemed to be coming from the same direction as the glaring green afterimages.

"Mycroft?" Knox could barely hear his own words over the ringing in his ears.

"Yes, Jonathan, it's me."

Knox shook his head. That didn't seem right somehow, unless... "If you're supposed to be guiding me toward the light, you're going to have to talk me through it. I can't see a damned thing."

"Yes, I am sorry about our *son et lumière* entrance. I managed to convince Euripedes that barging into this facility with conventional guns blazing would have been ill-advised. The effects of the flash-bang grenades should begin wearing off in a minute or two."

"Mycroft, if I'm not dead, what are *you* doing here?"

"The people that CROM sent to pick up Marianna, ah, persuaded me to accompany the Antipode Expeditionary Force. It meant doing my biofeedback exercises six hours running just to survive the trip, but when Euripedes explained—rather forcefully, I might add—that the alternative was indictment for violations of the Homeland Security Acts, well, I —"

"Wait a minute — Euripedes? You mean Pete? Pete Aristos?"

Knox's vision had cleared to the point where he could make out a fuzzy gray outline: Mycroft's head nodding a yes. "He'll want to talk to you himself, I'm sure, but he's rather busy just now with the mopping-up operations."

Knox blinked again. He could see now, sort of. Well enough to tell he was still in the control room of Antipode Station. Well enough to watch as several black-garbed SWAT-team types rounded up Grishin's stunned guards and Council-critters, while others fanned out to take up positions along the rim of the observation gallery.

"Pete'll keep," Knox said, struggling to his feet. "Give me a hand here."

Mycroft helped him up. Knox turned to look back down at the control-room floor. Galina's body was nowhere to be seen. He hoped that she wasn't being treated as just another detail to be mopped up. That, wherever she was, they were taking good care of her.

He turned back to his friend. "Jesus, Mycroft! It *is* you!" Knox was about to grab him and give him a hug, when he remembered whom he was dealing with. He settled for saying, "When I asked what you were doing here, I didn't mean *here* specifically, I meant anywhere."

"Why am I still alive, in other words?" Mycroft hung his head sheepishly. "Jonathan, I must apologize for taking leave so abruptly. Even without the guns, crowds make me nervous. Exiting down the ventilator shaft behind my desk seemed the better part of valor."

"But I saw you almost cut in two! I saw…" Knox paused, considering exactly what it was he *had* seen. Then, "Oh."

"Yes, Jonathan, you saw my holographic doorman, running in real time courtesy of an auxiliary projector in the subbasement. I had little choice, you know: your assailants seemed the sort to burn Weathertop to the ground rather than leave witnesses behind. It was either provide them with a reasonable facsimile of a corpse or risk having them do the job in actuality. Fortunately, all that smoke was just the thing for projecting a nice, solid image."

"Except when you walked through those oak beams. Try stepping around them next time. Incorporeality kind of spoils the effect."

"I sincerely hope there is not going to *be* a next time, Jonathan. I'm not sure I'd enjoy working for these CROM people on a long-term basis. To say nothing of the places they transact business in." His eyes nervously scanned the arched ceiling above their heads, as if expecting it to collapse at any moment under the hundreds of atmospheres of water pressure just outside.

"A client is a client, after all, Mycroft."

Mycroft inclined his head, not so much in acknowledgement of this time-hallowed truth as to practice that biofeedback thing he did. When he looked up, the twitchiness was back in its box again. "Well, on the bright side, they do seem to get things done, in their way."

"Uh-huh. Like showing up here in time to save our butts. How'd they manage that, incidentally?"

"Oh, readily enough, given that Euripedes had convinced the Office of Naval Research to loan him an experimental stealth submersible. The *Piccard* is quiet enough in silent-running mode that we were able to lurk right outside Antipode's auxiliary airlock until we received Marianna's *All Clear*. After that we just fitted the universal docking collar and cut our way in."

One of CROM's body-armored 'borgs walked up to them. A voice issued from behind the Vectran visor: "Dr. Laurence? Mr. Aristos would appreciate a word with you, sir." A nod over to the guardrail ringing the gallery, where Pete was haranguing a dejected-looking Sasha.

"Yes, of course."

The 'borg moved off, to Mycroft's evident relief. Well, guns and crowds did make him nervous, and here he had to contend with both.

Mycroft sighed. "An analyst's work is never done. Will you be all right, Jonathan?"

Funny to hear Mycroft asking *him* that.

"Yeah, sure; you go ahead." Knox walked with his friend to the shattered control-room door and out into the bay. "And tell Pete to go easy on Sasha; he may be the only one left that can tell us how to keep this place running. Until you've done your own analysis, that is."

"To be sure." Mycroft smiled and made as if to leave, then paused. "Speaking of analysis, you seem to have done a fair job of it here your-self, in that idiosyncratic way of yours. You must tell me all about it when you get the chance."

"Long as you're buying the beer."

"Oh, I suspect it will be Pete Aristos buying the beer for some time, Jonathan. Quite some time to come." Mycroft turned and walked off in the direction of Archon's new meal-ticket.

Two arms encircled his waist from behind. A new voice, decidedly female and very welcome, breathed a "Hi!" in his ear.

Knox worked his way around till he was facing Marianna, still locked in her embrace. She had thrown a lab coat over her torn blouse, but was otherwise just as disheveled, and just as magnificent-looking, as before.

"You've got to stop sneaking up on people like that!" he said, and kissed her.

"—Not that I minded you sneaking up on the late Mr. Geladze, of course," he added when an opportune moment arrived. "Were you go-ing to tell me how you got loose, or must I guess?"

"Guess away," she said, her lips brushing his cheek.

"The way you staged that scuffle with the guard just before we left *Rusalka*? Great verisimilitude! Still and all, it did not entirely escape notice that the bottle of sticky-web solvent was gone from the desktop when the dust had cleared."

"Wow." Her breath tickled his ear again. "You must be a trained analyst."

After another long moment, Marianna pulled away and glanced over to where Pete Aristos was eyeing them curiously.

"You know how this works by now, Jon." She disengaged herself, gently. "Debriefing first, displays of affection later. Well worth the wait, I can assure you. Now talk: how did you do…whatever it was you did?"

So he did what he always did. He talked.

Epilogue
The Bridge

Like ships at sunset in a reverie,
We are shadows of what we are.
— F.D. REEVE, "COASTING"

JONATHAN KNOX STOOD on *Rusalka*'s flying bridge under the dim, frozen pyrotechnics of a North Atlantic midnight.

Piccard's strike against Antipode Station had coincided with an assault on *Rusalka* herself. But, where improvisation had been the order of the day in the Antipode raid, the opposite was the case for Operation Tsunami proper.

In preparation for months, the game plan for invading the megayacht had gone off pretty much without a hitch. A low-level EM pulse had disabled the bulk of *Rusalka*'s electronics-based security countermeasures and disrupted its telecommunications. As an added bonus, keypads intended to limit access to restricted areas had ceased to function entirely, effectively segmenting the vessel into multiple sealed-off zones ready to be neutralized one at a time.

Trained to deal with attempted piracy and to repel other *personae non grata* boarders, the megayacht's security forces proved no match for the SEAL teams that came grappling over the gunwales and dropping out of the sky in two-seater Flying Inflatable Boats. A hard core of ex-Alpha Group commandos had battled on, acquitting themselves well until a couple of dummy air-to-sea torpedoes slammed against *Rusalka*'s hull. Then, to a man, they chose surrender over treading water.

As the mercifully brief firefight wound down, a dozen or so GEI executives barricaded themselves in the megayacht's panic room. Designed as an impregnable stronghold from which the owners could steer a hijacked vessel to safety via an auxiliary bridge, it became a holding pen for the shadow KGB's remaining brass, once its control lines to the engine room had been severed.

By sundown, the short-lived skirmish was fading into history. When an exhausted Knox, debriefed to within an inch of his life, accompanied Marianna and an assortment of Aristos's cyber-ninjas upstairs aboard a commandeered *Navtilus*, he found the giant vessel already well along in her transformation into a base of operations for CROM's hastily-organized interagency Singularity Control Initiative.

The ripples continued to spread. Already there was talk of creating an international authority to oversee CROM's operational administration of Antipode Station and its uniquely dangerous, uniquely valuable captive. Shoo-in Nobel laureate Dr. John C. "Jack" Adler had already been named the embryonic agency's chief technical advisor.

Sasha was still down at Antipode Station showing the new proprietors how to work the cigarette lighter and sunroof, get the best gas mileage, that sort of thing. Cooperating fully, in other words—as why would he not? Together with Adler, he was still going to wind up one of the world's two premiere black hole experimentalists. Had he known the likely outcome from the first? Had he just been manipulating Grishin, and everyone else, toward the most spectacular revenge ever visited upon the KGB by one of its erstwhile detainees?

Is that what Sasha had meant by "*It has happened already*"? Knox wasn't sure he'd ever know.

But maybe there was a hint in what Sasha'd said when he'd seen Knox off: "Through everything, Dzhon, I always kept my faith in Novikov and his Conservation of Reality principle. But, please believe, I never thought that the price of conserving reality would be Galya's life."

The Kremlin, leavening its public outrage at CROM's piratical intervention with backstairs winks and nudges, had already launched a far-reaching investigation of Grishin Enterprises. At the same time, in a move calculated to play up the positive aspects of the *Rusalka* affair, the Duma posthumously awarded the Cross of Saint Vladimir to Galina Mikhailovna Postrel'nikova, savior of the Earth, defender of its future and all its children.

Knox didn't know whether to laugh or cry—at Galya's sudden secular sainthood, at Sasha's ability once again to emerge from a pile of horseshit riding a pony. Time enough to think about all that later.

Time now, for remembrance. And for other thoughts.

"There you are." Marianna had stolen up behind him. "I've been looking all over for you."

"Just saying goodbye to a friend."

"She was a wonderful person, Jon. She came through, saved us all."

"Maybe more than you know," he said. He took Marianna in his arms and kissed her.

"Jon, what's wrong? You're shaking."

"Just a momentary glimpse of the abyss, is all. It comes and it goes. Worse since this all started."

"Do you need to talk about it?"

He sighed. "We've been given a peek at the foundations of the Earth. The universe isn't all these surface manifestations—" The arc of his hand took in the whole of the sky. "That's just for show. Quantum reality is the only real reality, the ground of our being, the bedrock. And on that fundamental level…"

He trailed off, then exhaled a shuddering breath and finished, "…I think maybe we exist only provisionally, if at all."

✳

Marianna knew better than to laugh. There'd been one incident back in college where a freshman had telephoned his Philosophy 101 instructor late one night, after too much Descartes: *Professor, I'm afraid I don't exist.* To her credit, the instructor had recognized the seriousness of the situation, had spent the next hour and a half on the phone talking the student down. The following morning he appeared in class and handed her, "for safekeeping," the revolver he'd been holding to his temple throughout their midnight colloquy.

She wasn't going to lose Jon to this. Not now. Not after what they'd been through.

Aloud, she said, "I'm not sure I understand."

"Well, think about it: what sets this whole train of events in motion? That first damned timeprobe, is what. It's that message from the future, the whole *Tunguska Cosmologist Support* thing, that gets Sasha seriously considering the possibility of a black hole impact, and eventually brings him—how did Grishin put it?—right to the KGB's doorstep. And it's Sasha who then convinces Grishin. Convinces him to bankroll a harebrained scheme, the ultimate outcome of which is to send back the message-needle that started it all, not incidentally using Yuri Andropov as a pin cushion. It's a causal loop: Ourobouros eating its own tail. We are where we are right now only because we altered the past enough to put us here."

"But the KGB had all the files from the original Tunguska expeditions." Keep him talking! "Somebody would've pieced the picture together even without the probe."

"Convincingly enough for Grishin and company to bet billions on a longshot of cosmic proportions? I don't think so. I think what got the shadow KGB behind this project was Sasha's mantra: *It has already happened.*

"It gets worse," he continued bleakly. "Take all that away: no project, which means no probe, which in turn means no assassination. Now, what was the likelier outcome back then, in the mid-eighties? A world like ours, imperfect as it is? Or that nuclear-winter nightmare? I think the effect produced the cause. Without the timewarp, Andropov never would have been...never would have died. Not soon enough, anyway. And then what?"

He shook his head. "No, that nightmare was the odds-on reality. It's all this that's the dream."

Marianna blinked back a tear. This *was* serious. Some sort of metaphysical cul-de-sac, a pitfall dug by a connoisseur of abstraction—for himself. Was he succumbing to this weird existential despair as a way of punishing himself? Out of some misplaced remorse over having caused the death of another human being? Couldn't he see that killing Andropov had prevented World War III, had almost certainly saved the world? She gripped him tightly, willing him to come back, to believe. In her. In anything.

Just talk him through it. "If what you say is so, then why are we here at all?"

"Choices," he said, so low she could barely hear the words. "Choices and dreams. Quantum theory's riddled through with indeterminacies, loopholes where the individual conscious mind gets to call the shots. So many branching paths for the awareness to pick and choose among. Maybe Novikov's Conservation of Reality principle only works when there are enough minds around to form a consensus about what's real. Who knows whether the constraints would still hold if you were the last man left alive…or the last woman…"

He seemed to lose focus for a moment. Then, "I keep remembering something the Singularity showed me, just before I…just before things changed back. And I keep thinking: what if Galina—years ago on an alternate timeline, dying in a fallout shelter somewhere in a dying Russia, on a dying Earth—what if Galina dreamed us all? Dreamed the whole world back into existence? Out of compassion, out of love for the children…"

"But then we *are* real," Marianna insisted, "as real as any other possible outcome. More real: we're *here*!"

"It doesn't alter the fact that reality has been shown up for the fraud it is, exposed as radically contingent, fundamentally undermined." His voice had strengthened though. He was past the worst of it now, or resigned to it again. Maybe they were the same thing.

He paused to gaze up at the stars. Or down into the well of the night. It all depended on how you looked at it. "Like the man said, 'If you choke on water, what can you wash it down with?' If you can't trust in reality to be real, what's left?" He turned to her and tried to smile.

He seemed to be coming out of it. As if he'd made a conscious choice, choosing to turn away from that bottomless pit, to turn back toward the only world there was.

Choosing to turn back to her, to reach out for her.

She came into his arms. In the last few moments, she'd made a conscious choice too.

"Love is real," Marianna kissed him and held him close, the ancient light of faraway suns glistening in her tears. "Trust in that."

Further Reading

you might be surprised
at just how much of this stuff
I didn't make up.
— PETER WATTS, *STARFISH*

I
T TOOK A lot of books to make this one. But this one started with a
TV program. Perils of couch-potatohood, I guess.

WISH I DIDN'T KNOW NOW...
It was years back, a rainy Saturday afternoon in mid-summer. I was
sitting around watching a rerun of *Cosmos*, Episode IV: "Heaven and
Hell"—the episode that deals with meteor and cometary impacts.

So, about midway through, Carl gets around to the Tunguska
Event. And from there to the Jackson-Ryan hypothesis: that the event
was a collision between the Earth and an atom-sized black hole. And
then he's refuting J&R, citing the standard missing exit-event objection—namely, that the black hole should have cut through the Earth
like a knife through morning mist, and come exploding up out of the
North Atlantic about an hour later, wreaking all manner of havoc.
Never happened. QED. And, next thing you know Carl's gone on to
Meteor Crater in Arizona or some such.

Meanwhile, I'm sitting there, staring at the TV. "But, Carl," I say
slowly, "what if the damn thing never came out?"

Wish I didn't know now what I didn't know then. The idea wouldn't leave me in peace. It kept rattling around in my hindbrain, gradually accreting mass as more and more pieces from my personal history fell into place: my background in Sovietology, my career as a consultant, just enough physics to glimpse what the KGB might want to do with a captive black hole... Over the next couple years, that one minuscule germ of an idea grew into a plotline.

Finally, on an equally rainy Saturday over a lost Memorial Day weekend, I sat down at the word processor, and *Singularity* began to write itself!

...What I didn't know then.

It was at that point that all those other books came in. It didn't hurt that I'd always read a lot of popular science: cosmology, relativity, quantum mechanics, all in the "physics for poets" vein. *Singularity*, though, called for more breadth and more depth, beginning with...

The Tunguska Event

A good friend once remarked that more trees have been destroyed in publishing books and articles about Tunguska than in the event itself. I don't know about that, but there have been a bunch over the years. Even an unambitious bibliography can easily run to a couple hundred titles. My publisher's frowning, though, so here I'll stick to some of the more readily available book-length ones, in English.

Roy A. Gallant's *The Day The Sky Split Apart: Investigating a Cosmic Mystery* (Atheneum, 1995) is both history, science, and travelogue, Roy having been one of the first Western astronomers to visit the impact site after the fall of Communism and live to write about it. *TDTSSA* is aimed at younger readers, but Roy's recently come out with a version for grownups, too: *Meteorite Hunter: The Search for Siberian Meteorite Craters* (McGraw-Hill, 2002). Its chapter-length discussion of Tunguska cribs a lot from the kiddies' book, while omitting a good deal of (mostly inessential) detail. A summation generously declares the question of what caused the Tunguska Event to be "still open." Privately, though,

Roy's own assessment of the Jackson-Ryan hypothesis remains a resounding "Ugh!"

That about wraps it up for serious, book-length treatments of late. Most of the debate action has shifted to the pages of scholarly journals, or to that same arxiv.org Internet site where Jack Adler broke the news of his earthshattering (literally!) discovery. Among the most recent articles are: Luigi Foschini, "A Solution for the Tunguska Event," (www. arxive.org/astro-ph/9808312v2, 2001), which backtracks the cosmic object's trajectory in an attempt to prove it had to be a meteorite; V. Bronshten, "On the nature of the Tunguska meteorite," (*Astronomy and Astrophysics*, No. 359, 2000), which uses the lack of physical evidence on the ground to prove it couldn't possibly have been a meteorite; and back again to Zdenek Sekanina's "Evidence for Asteroidal Origin of the Tunguska Object," (*Planetary and Space Science*, vol. 46, No. 2/3, 1998). It gets so it's like watching a tennis match.

Moving further off in time, there seems to have been something going on in the 1970s. Not only did that decade kick off with the Jackson-Ryan hypothesis itself (Albert A. Jackson IV and Michael P. Ryan, Jr., "Was the Tungus Event due to a Black Hole?" *Nature*, vol. 245, 1973), but it wound up with the publication of not one but three books on the topic, all in a two-year timespan. First out of the gate was John Baxter and Thomas Atkins, *The Fire Came By: The Riddle of the Great Siberian Explosion* (Doubleday, 1976), sporting an introduction by none other than Issac Asimov; this one wholeheartedly embraces Kazantsev's UFO-crash theory, as do Jack Stoneley's *Cauldron of Hell: Tunguska* (Simon & Schuster, 1977) and Rupert Furneaux's *The Tungus Event: the unsolved mystery of the world's greatest explosion* (Panther Books, 1977) to varying degrees.

But if it's real science you're after, you'll have to dig a bit deeper down through the decades—to E. L. Krinov's *Giant Meteorites* (Pergamnon, 1966). This tome, by a veteran of Leonid Kulik's first Tunguska expeditions, contains a 140-page chapter on "The Tunguska Meteorite," replete with historical data, eyewitness accounts, and the then-latest research. The aspiring student of the Tunguska Event could do a lot worse than to start with Krinov, then jump into the recent journal articles.

BLACK HOLES

Nowadays black-hole books are thick as flies on an accretion disk, but I still remember when the idea was fresh-minted and new (to the general public, at least), and John Taylor's *Black Holes: The End of the Universe?* (Avon, 1973) was about the only thing an interested layman could find on the subject. Then a dry spell of five years before Issac Asimov came along with his *The Collapsing Universe: The Story of Black Holes* (Pocket, 1978). Another five for George Greenstein's *Frozen Star* (Freudlich, 1983). It wasn't till the 1990s that the dam burst.

There's no way my publisher'll sit still for a recitation of every black-hole monograph in print, with or without the occasional side comment. So, instead, I'll just give you some of the ones that I kept coming back to over the course of writing *Singularity*.

Gravity's Fatal Attraction: Black Holes in the Universe by Mitchell Begelman and Martin Rees (Scientific American, 1996) holds a special place in my affections. I picked it up one afternoon in the late nineties in the bookshop of the Monterey Aquarium, back when I still thought I might be able to evade the compulsion to art that resulted in *Singularity*, but was no longer so sure that I was about to pass up a likely sourcebook. In *Gravity's Fatal Attraction*, Britain's Astronomer Royal (and Stephen Hawking's old classmate) Martin Rees, weighs in (no pun intended) on the topic. This one won the American Institute of Physics' 1996 Science Writing Award.

Then there's the man himself, Stephen W. Hawking's *Hawking on The Big Bang and Black Holes* (World Scientific, 1993) — the first book I got after I'd begun writing the novel in earnest. This one's the real deal: Stephen Hawking's original papers on primordial black holes, black hole radiation, et cetera ad infinitum. Not for the innumerate, or the faint of heart.

If you'd prefer Hawking-lite, then Stephen W. Hawking, *The Illustrated Theory of Everything: the Origin and Fate of the Universe* (New Millennium, 2003) is your ticket. Chapter 4, "Black Holes Ain't So Black" offers a nice, accessible introduction to Hawking radiation, as well as some background on Hawking's vexed and vexing relationship with Jacob D. Bekenstein, the young Princeton post-doc who first started him thinking along those lines.

No black-hole bibliography, however brief, would be complete without a nod to the man who named the things: John Archibald Wheeler. Check out his *A Journey into Gravity and Spacetime* (Scientific American, 1990) or his autobiography (with Kenneth Ford) *Geons, Black Holes & Quantum Foam: A Life in Physics* (Norton, 1998).

COSMOLOGY

Where would primordial black holes be without the Big Bang? For that matter, where would *we* be?

Not to worry, Timothy Ferris has got it covered in *The Whole She-bang: A State-of-the-Universe(s) Report* (Simon & Schuster, 1997). Or, if you'd like to step back a little further, there's always Martin Rees's *Before the Beginning: Our Universe and Others* (Addison-Wesley, 1997).

Pride of place, though, goes to Alan H. Guth's *The Inflationary Universe: the Quest for a New Theory of Cosmic Origins* (Perseus, 1997). It was this one that got me started on the quest for magnetic monopoles. And it was Tom Banks and W. Fischler's article "An Holographic Cosmology" (www.arxiv.org/abs/hep-th/0111142) that brought me home. This is the one that predicts an era during which all the primordial black holes formed would have been magnetic monopoles as well — "black monopoles" as Banks and Fischler call them. Vurdalak, in other words. And here you thought I was making this stuff up!

CLOSED TIME-LIKE CURVES

It's really a toss-up as to whether Kip Thorne's *Black Holes and Time Warps: Einstein's Outrageous Legacy* (Norton, 1994) belongs here or back up under Black Holes. I vote for here (and I'm the only one voting). After all, there are shelves full of black-hole books, but until Kip came along, there weren't many serious scientists willing to seriously entertain the notions of faster-than-light travel or time machines — not in print, anyway.

In *Black Holes and Time Warps*, Kip recounts the by-now familiar story of how Carl Sagan asked him to come up with a scientifically-credible means of faster-than-light travel for his novel *Contact*. And of how Kip solved Carl's problem using wormholes, only to realize he'd also invented a time machine into the bargain.

If you're looking for a survey of the whole time-travel landscape, you couldn't do better than Paul J. Nahin's *Time Machines: Time Travel in Physics, Metaphysics, and Science Fiction* (Springer, 1993, 1999)

Paul Davies' *The Edge of Infinity: Where the Universe Came From and How It Will End* (Simon & Schuster, 1981) is getting a bit long in the tooth, but it still offers an excellent introduction to naked singularities, which Davies' 1995 *About Time: Einstein's Unfinished Revolution* (also Simon & Schuster) updates as regards the possibility of using these bizarre objects as time machines. Even more to the point is Davies' recent *How to Build a Time Machine* (Viking, 2002), a slim volume, made slimmer by the inclusion of many illustrations—but it *does* have blueprints for the machine itself (p. 70), if there are any gazillionaires out there willing to ante up. J. Richard Gott III's *Time Travel in Einstein's Universe: the Physical Possibilities of Travel through Time* (Houghton-Miflin, 2001) takes an equally down-to-earth approach and covers much the same ground, before veering off into the *terra incognita* of the so-called "Carter Conjecture" (don't ask).

Even assuming time machines are possible, though, could we use them to change the past? The "Conservation of Reality" principle which Sasha Bondarenko, rightly or wrongly, sets so much store by is propounded in Chapter 15 of Igor Novikov's *The River of Time* (Cambridge, 1998). (Novikov called the inability to change the past the "self-consistency principle." I took the liberty of renaming it—"conservation of reality" sounded a lot sexier to me.) You'll also find the same issue covered from a more philosophical perspective in chapter 6 of Richard Hanley's *The Metaphysics of Star Trek* (Basic Books, 1997).

Both Novikov and Hanley proceed from Sasha's premise that if time travel is possible, then "it has already happened." More generally, that *everything* that can happen has already happened—i.e., that the present state of the universe is the sum total of everything that ever took place, *including* any actions ever undertaken by any eventual time travelers. In other words, any closed timelike curves, and any purposes good or ill to which they might be put, have already been factored into the equation that gets us to where we are at this present moment. You can't go back and change the past, because the past already includes the fact that you went back and tried to change it.

It's a neat argument, but it's always seemed like begging the question to me.

Finally, you'll find much of the science behind Singularity presented in loving and lucid detail, in a series of "soapbox seminars" hosted by none other than John C. ("Doctor Jack") Adler at the website devoted to his "Vurdalak Conjecture," www.vurdalak.com.

—Bill DeSmedt
Milford PA, 2004

Acknowledgements

To the many friends and total strangers I armtwisted into reading part or all of *Singularity* in manuscript — thanks. Without your generous advice, encouragement, and, above all, criticism, *Singularity* might never have seen the light of day.

Among your number, special thanks are due to:

–Paul Blass, architect and general contractor for Antipode Station;

–Norma Cernadas and Steve Kocan, consultant-warriors;

–Elizabeth Cochrane, who believed;

–Jeff DeSmedt, who critiqued it first of all, and gentler than most;

–Nancy Holland DeSmedt, for Marianna;

–Jake Elwell of Wieser & Elwell, friend and agent;

–Larry Finch (or is that Finley Laurence?), who piloted our heroes safely out of JFK;

–Roy A. Gallant, for tales from around the Tunguskan campfire;

–Georg Gerber, for lighting a fire under me over dinner at Green's, by rubbing a pencil and a napkin together;

–Dick Guare, who knew just how different female action heroes can be;

–Scott Hughes, for patching a theoretical hole in my extremal black hole;

–Albert A. Jackson, IV and Michael P. Ryan, Jr., for Vurdalak;

–Mark Joseph, taskmaster;

–Joanne Kalish and Joe DiMaggio, who kept Knox and Marianna afloat in their darkest hour;

–Jak Koke, freelance editor extraordinaire;

–Alan Leventen, for ultralights and RPGs;

–Marilyn Mower, who laid *Rusalka's* keel;

–Catherine Nye, for telling me to quit stalling and write it;

–Tony Olcott, who fixed *Singularity* once, and kept on fixing it;

–Bruce Sterling, who really, really tried, all for the loan of a laptop powerpack.

Finally, to my wonderful wife Kathrin, who tended the hearth and fanned the flames, and whose desire to "finally read the whole thing all the way through for once" I hope I have now fulfilled.

About the Author

Bill DeSmedt has spent his life living by his wits and his words. In his time, and as the spirit has moved him, he's been: a Soviet Area expert and Soviet exchange student, a computer programmer and system designer, a consultant to startups and the Fortune 500, an Artificial Intelligence researcher, a son, a husband and lover, a father and grandfather, an omnivorous reader with a soft spot for science fiction and science non-fiction, and now, Lord help us, a novelist. He's tried to pack as much of that checkered history as he could into *Singularity*. Bill lives with his wife of 37 years in Milford, Pennsylvania, a town whose long tradition in speculative literature serves as a constant source of inspiration. He is currently hard at work on a sequel to *Singularity* entitled *Dualism*.

Colophon

The body of *Singularity* is set in Adobe Caslon, with Minion Cyrillic for the Russian. The display font is Gill Sans.

Singularity is printed on 55# Tradebook, with endpapers of 80# Rainbow Eclipse. The cover materials are Pearl Linen Deep Scarlet and 80# Rainbow Red. Jacket is 100# stock, matte laminated with a UV spot gloss.